Carole Mortimer

Rumors on the Red Carpet

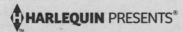

HARLEQUIN PRESENTS®

Recycling programs
for this product may
not exist in your area.

ISBN-13: 978-0-373-13201-0

First North American Publication 2013

RUMORS ON THE RED CARPET
Copyright © 2013 by Carole Mortimer

THE TALK OF HOLLYWOOD
Copyright © 2012 by Carole Mortimer

Printed in U.S.A.

CONTENTS

RUMORS ON THE RED CARPET   7

THE TALK OF HOLLYWOOD   195

All about the author...
Carole Mortimer

CAROLE MORTIMER is one of Harlequin's® most popular and prolific authors. Since her first novel, published in 1979, this British writer has shown no signs of slowing her pace. In fact, she has published more than 135 novels!

Her strong, traditional romances, with their distinct style, brilliantly developed characters and romantic plot twists, have earned her an enthusiastic audience worldwide.

Carole's early ambition to become a nurse came to an abrupt end after only one year of training due to a weakness in her back, suffered in the aftermath of a fall. Instead, she went on to work in the computer department of a well-known stationery company.

During her time there, Carole made her first attempt at writing a novel for Harlequin®. "The manuscript was far too short and the plotline not up to standard, so I naturally received a rejection slip," she says. "Not taking rejection well, I went off in a sulk for two years before deciding to 'have another go.'" Her second manuscript was accepted, beginning a long and fruitful career. She says she has "enjoyed every moment of it!"

Carole lives "in a most beautiful part of Britain" with her husband and children.

Other titles by Carole Mortimer available in ebook:

A TOUCH OF NOTORIETY *(Buenos Aires Nights)*
HIS CHRISTMAS VIRGIN
A TASTE OF THE FORBIDDEN *(Buenos Aires Nights)*
HIS REPUTATION PRECEDES HIM *(The Lyonedes Legacy)*

Rumors on the Red Carpet

Peter, as always.

CHAPTER ONE

'ENJOYING THE VIEW...?'

Thia tensed, a shiver of awareness quivering down the length of her spine at the sound of that deep voice coming out of the darkness behind her, before turning quickly to search those shadows for the man who had just spoken to her.

She was able to make out a tall figure in the moonlight just feet away from where she stood, alone on the balcony that surrounded the whole of this luxurious penthouse apartment on the fortieth floor of one of the impressive buildings lighting up the New York skyline. Only dim light spilled from the open French doors of the apartment further down the balcony—along with the sound of tinkling laughter and the chatter of the fifty or so party guests still inside—making it impossible for Thia to see any more than that the man was very tall, dark and broad-shouldered. Imposingly so.

Dangerously so...?

The wariness still humming through her body just at the sound of the deep and seductive timbre of his voice said a definite *yes!*

Thia's fingers tightened about the breast-high balustrade in front of her. 'I was, yes...' she answered pointedly.

'You're a Brit,' he observed deeply.

'From London,' Thia confirmed shortly, really hoping that he would take note of that terseness and leave her to her solitude.

The New York night skyline, amazing as it was, hadn't been Thia's main reason for coming outside into the balmy evening air fifteen minutes ago, when the other guests had all been preoccupied with their excitement at the late arrival of Lucien Steele, American zillionaire businessman, and the party's guest of honour. That so many high-profile actors, actresses and politicians had turned out for the event was indicative of the amount of power the man wielded.

After all Jonathan's hype about him Thia had to admit that she hadn't found him so prepossessing—a man of middle age and average height, slightly stocky and balding. But maybe all that money and power made him more attractive? In any event, Thia had just been grateful that he had arrived at last—if only because it had allowed her to slip outside and *be* alone—instead of just *feeling* alone.

Thia certainly hadn't intended to find herself alone on the balcony with a man who exuded such an intensity of power and sexual attraction she could almost taste it...

'A Brit, from London, who's avoiding the party inside...?' that deep voice guessed with dry amusement.

Having been to three other parties just like this one in the four days since her arrival in New York, Thia had to admit to having become slightly bored—jaded?— by them. The first one had been fun—exciting, even— meeting people she had only ever seen on the big or little screen before, world-famous actors and actresses and high-profile politicians. But the artificiality of it was all becoming a bit samey now. The conversations were repetitive and too loud, the laughter even more so, with everyone seemingly out to impress or better everyone else, their excessive wealth literally worn on their sleeves.

This constant round of parties also meant that she'd had very little opportunity for any time or private conversation with Jonathan, the man she had come to New York to visit…

Jonathan Miller, the English star of *Network,* a new American thriller television series set in New York, directed by this evening's host, Felix Carew, and co-starring his young and sexy wife Simone as the love-interest.

The show had been an instant hit, and Jonathan was currently the darling of New York's beautiful people—and, as Thia had discovered these past four days, there were a *lot* of beautiful people in New York!

And not a single one of them had felt any qualms about ignoring the woman who had been seen at Jonathan's side on those evenings once they'd learnt that Thia was of no social or political value to them whatsoever.

Not that Thia minded being ignored. She had very quickly discovered she had no more in common with New York's elite than they had with her.

She was pleased for Jonathan's success, of course. The two of them had known each other for a couple of years now, after meeting at the London restaurant where Thia always worked the late shift, leaving her free to attend her university course in the day.

She and Jonathan had met quite by chance, when he had been appearing in a play at the theatre across the street from the restaurant and had started calling in late in the evening a couple of times a week for something to eat, once the theatre had closed for the night.

They had chatted on those evenings, then dated casually for a few weeks. But there had been no spark between them and the relationship had quickly fallen into the 'just friends' category. Then, four months ago, Jonathan had landed the lead role in the television series over here, and Thia had accepted that even that friendship would be over once Jonathan moved to New York.

He had telephoned a couple of times in the months that followed, just light and friendly conversations, when they had caught up on each other's lives, and then a month ago Jonathan had flown back to England for the weekend, insisting he had missed her and wanted to spend all his time back home with her. And it had been fun. Thia had arranged to have the weekend off so that they could have dinner together in the evening, visits to museums and walks in the parks during the day, before Jonathan had to fly back to New York to start filming again on the Monday.

But no one had been more surprised than Thia when a first-class plane ticket for a week-long stay in New York had been delivered to her by messenger just two days later!

She had telephoned Jonathan immediately, of course, to tell him she couldn't possibly accept such generosity from him. But he had insisted, saying he could well afford it and, more to the point, he wanted to see her again. He wanted to show her New York, and for New York to see her.

Thia's pride had told her she should continue to refuse, but Jonathan had been very persuasive, and as she hadn't been able to afford a holiday for years the temptation had just been too much. So she had accepted, with the proviso that he cancelled the first class ticket and changed it to a standard fare. Spending that amount of money on an airfare seemed obscene to her, in view of her own financial difficulties.

Jonathan had assured her that she would have her own bedroom in his apartment, and that he just wanted her to come and enjoy New York with him. She had even gone out and spent some of her hard-earned savings on buying some new clothes for the trip!

Except Jonathan's idea of her enjoying New York with him was vastly different from Thia's own. They had attended parties like this one every night, and Jonathan would sleep off the effects the following morning. Meanwhile his late afternoons and early evenings were usually spent secluded somewhere with Simone Carew, going over the script together.

Seeing so little of Jonathan during the day, and attending parties in the evenings, Thia had started to wonder why he had bothered to invite her here at all.

And she now found herself irritated that, once again, Jonathan had disappeared with Simone shortly after they had arrived at this party he had claimed was so important to him on account of the presence of Lucien Steele, the American billionaire owner of the television station responsible for *Network*. That desertion had left Thia being considered fair game by men like the one standing in the shadows behind her...

Well...perhaps not *exactly* like this man. The way he seemed to possess even the air about him told her that she had never met a man quite like this one before...

'Beautiful...' the man murmured huskily as he stepped forward to stand at the railing beside her.

Thia's heart skipped a beat, her nerve-endings going on high alert as her senses were instantly filled with the light smell of lemons—his cologne?—accompanied by an insidious maleness that she guessed was all him.

She turned to look at him, tilting her head back as she realised how much taller he was than her, even in her four-inch-heeled take-me-to-bed shoes. Taller, and so broad across the shoulders, with dark hair that rested low on the collar of his white shirt and black evening jacket. His face appeared to be all hard angles in the moonlight: strong jaw, chiselled lips, long aquiline nose, high cheekbones. And those pale and glittering eyes—

Piercing eyes, that she now realised were looking at *her* in admiration rather than at the New York skyline!

Thia repressed another quiver of awareness at having this man look at her so intently, realising that she was completely alone out here with a man she didn't know from—well, from Adam.

'Have they all stopped licking Lucien Steele's highly polished handmade Italian leather shoes yet, do you think?' she prompted in her nervousness, only to give a pained grimace at her uncharacteristic sharpness. 'I'm sorry—that was incredibly rude of me.' She winced, knowing how important Lucien Steele's goodwill was to Jonathan's success in the US. He had certainly emphasised it often enough on the drive over here!

'But true?' the man drawled dryly.

'Perhaps.' She nodded. 'But I'm sure that Mr Steele has more than earned the adoration being showered upon him so effusively.'

Teeth gleamed whitely in the darkness as the man gave a hard and humourless smile. 'Or maybe he's just so rich and powerful no one has ever dared to tell him otherwise?'

'Maybe,' she conceded ruefully. 'Cynthia Hammond.' She thrust out her hand in an effort to bring some normality to this conversation. 'But everyone calls me Thia.'

He took possession of her hand—there was no other way to describe the way the paleness of her hand just disappeared inside the long bronzed strength of his. And Thia could not ignore the jolt of electricity zinging along her fingers and arm at contact with the warmth of his skin...

'I've never been particularly fond of being a part of what everyone else does,' he murmured throatily. 'So I think I'll call you Cyn...'

Just the way he said that word, in that deliciously deep and sexy voice, was enough to send yet more shivers of awareness down Thia's spine. Her breasts tingled with that awareness, the nipples puckering to tight and sensitive berries as they pressed against the sheer material of the clinging blue ankle-length gown she wore.

And it was a totally inappropriate reaction to a complete stranger!

Jonathan might have done yet another disappearing act with Simone forty minutes ago, but that certainly didn't mean Thia was going to stand here and allow herself to be seduced by some dark-haired hunk, who looked sinfully delicious in his obviously expensive evening suit but so far hadn't even been polite enough to introduce himself!

'And you are...?'

Those teeth gleamed even whiter in the darkness as he gave a wolfish smile. 'Lucien Steele.'

Thia gave a snort. 'I don't think so!' she scoffed.

'No?' He sounded amused by her scepticism.

'No,' she repeated decisively.

He raised one dark brow. 'Why not?'

She breathed her impatience. 'Well, for one thing you aren't nearly old enough to be the self-made zillionaire Lucien Steele.' She estimated this man was aged somewhere in his early to mid-thirties, ten or twelve years older than her own twenty-three, and she knew from the things Jonathan had told her about this evening's guest of honour that Lucien Steele had not only been the richest man in New York for the last ten years, but was also the most powerful.

He gave an unconcerned shrug of those impossibly wide shoulders. 'What can I say? My parents were wealthy to begin with, and I'd made my own first million by the time I was twenty-one.'

'Also,' Thia continued, determined, 'I saw Mr Steele when he arrived.'

It had been impossible to miss the awed reaction of the other guests. Those incredibly rich and beautiful people had all, without exception, fallen absolutely silent the moment Lucien Steele had appeared in the doorway. And Felix Carew, a powerful man in his own right, had become almost unctuous as he moved swiftly across the room to greet his guest.

Thia gave a rueful shake of her head. 'Lucien Steele is in his early forties, several inches shorter than you are, and stocky, with a shaved head.' In fact on first glance she had thought the man more resembled a thug rather than the richest and most powerful man in New York!

'That would be Dex.'

'Dex...?' she echoed doubtfully.

'Mmm.' The man beside her nodded unconcernedly.

'He takes his duties as my bodyguard very seriously—to the point that he always insists upon entering a room before I do. I'm not sure why,' he mused. 'Perhaps he expects there to be an assassin on the other side of every door...'

Thia felt a sinking sensation in the pit of her stomach as she heard the amused dismissal in this man's—in Lucien Steele's?—voice. Moistening her lips with the tip of tongue before speaking, she said, 'And where is Dex now...?'

'Probably standing guard on the other side of those French doors.' He nodded down the balcony to the same doorway Thia had escaped through minutes ago.

And was Dex making sure that no one came outside, or was he ensuring that Thia couldn't return inside until this man wished her to...?

She gave another frown as she looked up searchingly at the man now standing so near to her she could feel the heat emanating from his body on the bareness of her shoulders and arms. Once again she took note of that inborn air of power, arrogance, she had sensed in him from the first.

For all the world as if he was *used* to people licking his highly polished handmade Italian leather shoes...

Lucien continued to hold Cyn's now trembling hand and waited in silence for her to gather her breath as she looked up at him between long and silky lashes with eyes a dark and mysterious cobalt blue.

Those eyes became shadowed with apprehension as she gave another nervous flick of her little pink tongue over the moist fullness of her perfectly shaped lips. 'The same Lucien Steele who owns Steele Technology, Steele

Media, Steele Atlantic Airline *and* Steele Industries, as well as all those other Steele Something-or-Others?' she murmured faintly.

He shrugged. 'It seemed like a good idea to diversify.'

She determinedly pulled her hand from his grasp before tightly gripping the top of the balustrade. 'The same Lucien Steele who's a zillionaire?'

'I believe you said that already…' Lucien nodded.

She drew in a deep breath, obviously completely unaware of how it tightened the material of her dress across her breasts and succeeded in outlining the fullness of those—aroused?—nipples. Nipples that were a delicate pink or a succulent rose? Whatever their colour, he was sure they would taste delicious. Sweet and juicy, and oh so ripe and responsive as he licked and suckled them.

He had noticed the woman he now knew to be Cynthia Hammond the moment he'd entered Felix and Simone Carew's penthouse apartment a short time ago. It had been impossible not to as she'd stood alone at the back of the opulent room, her hair a sleek and glossy unadorned black as it fell silkily to just below her shoulders, her eyes that deep cobalt blue in the beautiful pale delicacy of her face.

She wore a strapless ankle-length gown of that same deep blue, leaving the tops of her breasts, shoulders and arms completely bare. The smoothness of her skin was a beautiful pearly white unlike any other Lucien had ever seen: a pale ivory tinted lightly pink, luminescent. Smoothly delicate and pearly skin his fingers itched to touch and caress.

The simple style of that silky blue gown allowed it to cling to every curvaceous inch of her full breasts, slender waist and gently flaring hips, so much so that Lucien had questioned whether or not she wore anything beneath it.

He still questioned it…

But what had really made him take notice of her, even more than her natural beauty or the pearly perfection of her skin, was the fact that instead of moving towards him, as every other person in the room had done, this pale and delicately beautiful woman had instead taken advantage of his arrival to slip quietly from the room and go outside onto the balcony.

Nor had she returned by the time Lucien had finally managed to extract himself from the—what had she called it a few moments ago? The licking of his 'highly polished handmade Italian leather shoes'. His curiosity piqued—and very little piqued his jaded palate nowadays!—Lucien hadn't been able to resist coming out onto the balcony to look for her the moment he had managed to escape all that cloying attention.

She drew in another deep breath now before speaking, causing the fullness of her breasts to once again swell deliciously over the bodice of that clinging blue gown.

'I really do apologise for my rudeness, Mr Steele. It's no excuse, but I'm really not having a good evening—and my rudeness to you means that it has just got so much worse!' she conceded with another pained wince. 'But that is really no reason for me to have been rude about you—or to you.'

He quirked one dark brow. 'I don't think you know me well enough *as yet* to speak with any authority on whether or not I *deserve* for you to be rude to me or about me,' he drawled mockingly.

'Well…no…' She was obviously slightly unnerved by his emphasis on the words 'as yet'… 'But—' She gave a shake of her head, causing that silky and completely straight black hair to glide across the bareness of her shoulders and caress tantalisingly across the tops of her breasts. 'I still shouldn't have been so outspoken about someone I only know about from the media.'

'Especially when we all know how inaccurate the media can be?' he drawled wryly.

'Exactly!' She nodded enthusiastically before just as quickly pausing to eye him uncertainly. 'Don't you own something like ninety per cent of the worldwide media?'

'That would be contrary to monopoly regulations,' he drawled dismissively.

'Do zillionaires bother with little things like regulations?' she teased.

He chuckled huskily. 'They do if they don't want their zillionaire butts to end up in court!'

Thia felt what was becoming a familiar quiver down the length of her spine at the sound of this man's throaty laughter. As she also acknowledged that, for all this man unnerved her, she was actually enjoying herself—possibly for the first time since arriving in New York.

'Are you cold?'

Thia had no chance to confirm or deny that she was before Lucien Steele removed his evening jacket and placed it about the bareness of her shoulders. It reached almost down to her knees and smelt of the freshness of those lemons as his warmth surrounded her, and of the more insidious and earthy smell of the man himself.

'No, really—'

'Leave it.' Both his hands came down onto the shoulders of the jacket as she would have reached up and removed it.

Thia shivered anew as she felt the warmth of those long and elegant hands even through the material of his jacket. A shiver entirely due to the presence of this overwhelming man—also the reason for her earlier shiver—rather than any chill in the warm evening air...

His hands left her shoulders reluctantly as he moved to stand beside her once again, that pale gaze—silver?—once again intent on her face. The snug fit of his evening shirt revealed that his shoulders really were that wide, his chest muscled, his waist slender above lean hips and long legs; obviously Lucien Steele didn't spend *all* of his days sitting in boardrooms and adding to his billions.

'Why aren't you having a good evening?' he prompted softly.

Why? Because this visit to New York hadn't turned out to be anything like Thia had imagined it would be. Because she had once again been brought to a party and then quickly abandoned by—well, Jonathan certainly wasn't her boyfriend, but she had certainly thought of him as a friend. A friend who had disappeared with their hostess within minutes of their arrival, leaving her to the untender mercies of New York's finest.

Latterly she wasn't having a good evening because she was far too aware of the man standing beside her—of the way the warmth and seductive smell of Lucien Steele's tailored jacket made her feel as if she was surrounded by the man himself.

And lastly because Thia had no idea how to deal with the unprecedented arousal now coursing through her body!

She gave a shrug. 'I don't enjoy parties like this one.'

'Why not?'

She grimaced, taking care not to insult this man for a second time this evening. 'It's just a personal choice.'

He nodded. 'And where do you fit in with this crowd? Are you an actress?'

'Heavens, no!'

'A wannabe?'

'I beg your pardon…?'

He shrugged those impossibly wide shoulders. 'Do you wannabe an actress?'

'Oh, I see.' Thia gave a rueful smile. 'No, I have no interest in becoming an actress, either.'

'A model?'

She snorted. 'Hardly, when I'm only five feet two inches in my bare feet!'

'You aren't being very helpful, Cyn.' There was an underlying impatience in that amused tone. Thia had seen far too much of the reaction of New York's elite these past four days not to know they had absolutely no interest in cultivating the company of a student and a waitress. Lucien Steele would have no further interest in her, either, once he knew. Which might not be a bad thing…

Her chin rose determinedly. 'I'm just a nobody on a visit to New York.'

Lucien totally disagreed with at least part of that statement. Cynthia Hammond was certainly somebody. Somebody—a woman—whose beauty and conversation he found just as intriguing as he had hoped he might…

She quirked dark brows. 'I believe that's your cue to politely excuse yourself?'

His eyes narrowed. 'And why would I wish to do that?'

She shrugged her shoulders beneath his jacket. 'It's

what everyone else I've met in New York has done once they realise I'm of use to them.'

Yes, Lucien could imagine, knowing New York society as well as he did, that its members would have felt no hesitation whatsoever in making their lack of interest known. 'I believe I've already stated that I prefer not to be like everyone else.'

'Ain't that the truth? I mean—' A delicious blush now coloured those pale ivory cheeks as she briefly closed her eyes before looking up at him apologetically. 'I apologise once again. I'm really *not* having a good evening!' She sighed.

He nodded. 'Would you like to leave? We could go somewhere quiet and have a drink together?'

Cyn blinked those long lashes. 'I beg your pardon...?'

Lucien gave a hard, humourless smile. 'I hate parties like this one too.'

'But you're the guest of honour!'

He grimaced. 'I especially hate parties where I'm the guest of honour.'

Thia looked up at him searchingly, not sure whether or not Lucien Steele was playing with her. Not sure why he was bothering, if that should be the case!

The steady regard of those pale eyes and the grimness of his expression told her that this was a man who rarely, if ever, played.

He was seriously asking her to leave the Carews' party with him...

CHAPTER TWO

THIA GAVE A rueful shake of her head as she smiled. 'That really wouldn't be a good idea.'

'Why not?'

'Are you always this persistent?' She frowned.

He seemed to give the idea some thought before answering. 'When I want something badly enough, yes,' he finally murmured, without apology.

The intensity in that silver gaze as he looked down at Thia told her all too clearly that right now Lucien Steele wanted *her*.

Badly.

Wickedly!

She repressed another shiver of awareness just at the thought of how those chiselled lips and strong hands might feel as they sought out all the secret dips and hollows of her body.

'I really think it's time I went back inside.' She was slightly flustered as she slipped his jacket from about her shoulders and held it out to him. 'Please take it,' she urged when he made no effort to do so.

He looked down at her searchingly for several seconds before slowly taking the jacket and placing it dismissively over the balustrade in front of him—as if it *hadn't* cost as much as Thia might earn in a year as a waitress including tips!

'Cyn…'

He wasn't even touching her, and yet he managed to hold her mesmerised just by the way he murmured his own unique name for her in that deeply seductive voice, sending more rivulets of awareness down Thia's spine and causing a return of that tingling sensation in her breasts, accompanied by an unaccustomed warmth between her thighs.

'Yes…?' she answered breathlessly.

'I *really* want you to leave with me.'

'I can't.' She groaned in protest at the compulsion in the huskiness of his voice, sure that this man—a man who was not only sinfully handsome but rich as Creosus—rarely, if ever, asked for anything from anyone. He just took.

'Why not?'

'I just— What colour are your eyes, exactly…?' Whatever colour they were, they held Thia captive by their sheer intensity!

He blinked at the unexpectedness of the question. 'My eyes…?'

'Yes.'

His mouth twisted in a rueful smile. 'I believe it says grey on my passport.'

Thia gave a shake of her head. 'They're silver,' she corrected, barely able to breathe now, even knowing this was madness—that she was so totally aware of Lucien Steele, her skin so sensitised by the intensity of that glittering silver gaze fixed on her so intently, that she could feel the brush of each individual strand of her hair as it caressed lightly, silkily, across her shoulders and the tops of her breasts.

A totally unexpected and unprecedented reaction. To any man. Goodness knew Jonathan was handsome enough, with his overlong blond hair, laughing blue eyes and lean masculinity, but for some reason she had just never found him attractive in *that* way. Just looking at Lucien Steele, knowing she was aware of everything about him, of all that underlying and leashed power, she knew that she never would be attracted to Jonathan—that Lucien Steele was so overpowering he ruined a woman's appreciation for any other man.

'Grey…silver…they can be whatever the hell colour you want them to be if you'll only leave with me now,' Lucien Steele urged again, with that same intensity.

She was tempted—Lord, was Thia tempted!—but it wouldn't do. No matter how distracted and inattentive Jonathan might choose to be, she couldn't arrive at a party with him and then leave with another man. Especially a man she found as disturbing as she did Lucien Steele!

A man who was over six feet of lean and compelling muscle. A man who was too handsome for his own good. A man who was just too…too intense—too much of everything—and whom she had discovered she found so mouthwateringly tempting.

Thia straightened her spine determinedly. 'I came here with someone.'

Those silver eyes narrowed with displeasure. 'A male someone?'

'Yes.'

His gaze moved to her left hand. 'You aren't wearing any rings.'

Thia gave a shake of her head. 'He isn't that sort of friend.'

'Then who is he?'

'I don't think that's any of your business—'

'And if I choose to make it so?'

'He's just a friend,' she dismissed impatiently, not sure even that was true any longer. Jonathan had made it obvious he inhabited a different world from her now—a world she had no inclination or desire ever to become a part of.

Lucien Steele's expression was grim as he shook his head. 'He can't be that much of a friend if he brought you here and then just left you to your own devices.'

This was the same conclusion Thia had come to over the past four days! 'I'm an adult and perfectly capable of looking after myself, thank you very much,' she assured him tartly.

Lucien Steele raised dark brows. 'So much so that you came out here alone rather than remain at the party?'

She felt stung by the mockery in his tone. 'Maybe I just wanted to get away from all that boot-licking?' she challenged.

'Handmade Italian leather shoes,' he corrected dryly.

'Whatever,' Thia dismissed impatiently. 'I'm sure you didn't come here alone tonight, either...' She vaguely recalled Jonathan mentioning something about Lucien Steele currently being involved with the supermodel Lyndsay Turner. A woman who, six feet tall and blond, couldn't be any more Thia's opposite!

Lucien's mouth thinned as he recalled the scene that had taken place with Lyndsay a week ago. A scene in which the supermodel had seriously overestimated his feelings for her and that had resulted in the end of their

month-long relationship. Hell, he didn't *do* promises—
let alone engagement and wedding rings.

He grimaced. 'As it happens, I did. And I want to
leave with *you,*' he added determinedly, knowing it had
been a long time since he had wanted anything as much
as he now wanted to spend time alone with Cynthia
Hammond.

'You don't know the first thing about me,' she dismissed exasperatedly.

'Which is precisely the reason I want the two of us to
go somewhere quiet and talk—so that I can get to know
you better,' he pushed insistently. The more this woman
resisted him the more determined he became to leave the
party with her this evening. At which time he intended
to find out exactly which of Felix Carew's male guests
was the friend Cyn had mentioned…

She attempted to tease. 'Has no one ever told you that
it isn't possible to have *everything* you want?'

'No.' A nerve pulsed in Lucien's tightly clenched jaw.

'Because you're so rich and powerful no one would
ever dare to tell you otherwise?' she asked softly, reminding him of his earlier comment.

'No doubt.' Again he answered unapologetically.

Thia gave an exasperated laugh at this man's unre-
lenting arrogance; she really had never met a man quite
like him before! 'Then I shall have the distinction of
being the first to do so! It's been…*interesting* meeting
you, Mr Steele, but I really should go back inside and—
What are you doing…?' She gasped softly as his gaze
continued to hold hers captive even as his head slowly
descended towards her, the warmth of his breath as light
as a caress against her cheeks and lips.

'I want—I'd *like* to kiss you,' he corrected huskily,

his lips just centimetres away from her own. 'Are you going to let me?'

'No…' Thia was aware her protest sounded half-hearted and she found herself unable to look away from those mesmerising silver eyes.

'Say yes, Cyn.' He moved slightly, his lips a hot and brief caress against the heat of her cheek before he raised his head and looked at her once again, not touching her with anything but the intensity of that glittering gaze.

She couldn't breathe, couldn't move so much as a muscle, as she continued to be held captive by the intensity of those eyes. Much like a deer caught in the headlights of an oncoming car. Or a freight train. Either of which was capable of flattening whatever stood in their way. As Lucien Steele's brand of seduction was capable of crushing both Thia and her resistance…

She drew in a shaky breath before stepping back and away from him. 'Thank you for the invitation, Mr Steele, but no.'

'Lucien.'

She shook her head. 'I believe I would prefer to continue calling you Mr Steele. Not that we'll ever meet again after this evening. But even so—'

'Why not?'

Thia gave a lightly dismissive laugh at the sharpness of his tone. 'Because you inhabit this world and I—I inhabit another one.'

'And yet here you are…?'

'Yes, here I am.' And she wouldn't be coming back again if she could help it! 'I really do have to go back inside now—'

'And look for your *friend*?' he prompted harshly.

'Yes.' Thia grimaced, very much afraid that she and

that 'friend' were going to have words before the evening was over. Certainly she had no intention of letting Jonathan get away with bringing her to another party like this one and then leaving her to go off somewhere with the beautiful Simone. Jonathan's habit of just forgetting Thia's existence the moment they arrived at one of these parties was becoming tedious as well as a complete waste of her time, when she really didn't enjoy being here.

'Who is he?'

'It's really none of your business,' Thia snapped in irritation at Lucien Steele's persistence.

Those silver eyes narrowed, his jaw tightening. 'At least tell me where you're staying in New York.'

She gave an exasperated grimace. 'That's even less your business! Now, if you'll excuse me…' Thia didn't wait for him to reply before turning on her four-inch-heeled shoes and walking away, her head held determinedly high as she forced herself not to hurry, not to reveal how desperately she needed to get away from Lucien Steele's disturbingly compelling presence.

Even if she *was* completely aware of that silver gaze as a sensual caress across the bareness of her shoulders and down the length of her spine and the slender curve of her hips!

Lucien Steele was without doubt the most disturbingly sexual man she had ever—

'Where the *hell* have you been?' Jonathan demanded the moment she stepped back into the Carews' huge sitting room. The expression on his boyishly handsome face was accusing as he took a rough hold of her arm.

An entirely unfair accusation, in Thia's estimation, considering *he* was the one who had gone missing with their hostess for almost an hour, leaving her to be approached by Lucien Steele!

'Can we talk about this somewhere less…public, Jonathan?' She glared at him, very aware of the silent—listening?—presence of Lucien Steele's bodyguard, Dex, just feet away from the two of them. 'Preferably in the privacy of your car, once we've *left,*' she added pointedly.

Jonathan looked less than pleased by her last comment. 'You know damned well I can't leave yet,' he dismissed impatiently, even as he physically dragged her over to a quieter corner of the room.

'Could that possibly be because you haven't yet had a chance to say hello to Lucien Steele?' Thia felt stung into taunting him as she rubbed the top of her arm where Jonathan's fingers had dug so painfully into her flesh that she would probably have bruises to show for it tomorrow. 'I noticed you and our beautiful hostess were noticeably absent when he arrived.'

'What does *that* mean?' he glowered darkly. 'And what the hell's got into you, talking to me like that?'

'Nothing's got into me.' She gave a weary sigh, knowing that not all of her frustration with this evening was Jonathan's fault. Her nerves were still rattled from that encounter with Lucien Steele on the balcony—to a degree that she could still feel the seductive brush of those chiselled lips against her cheek and the warmth of his breath brushing against her skin… 'I just want to leave, that's all.' She grimaced.

'I've told you that I can't go just yet.' Jonathan scowled down at her.

'Then I'll just have to go downstairs and get a taxi—'

'It's a cab,' he corrected impatiently. 'And you aren't

going anywhere until I say you can,' he added determinedly.

Thia looked at him searchingly, noting the reckless
brightness of his eyes and the unaccustomed flush to his
cheeks. 'Have you been drinking...?'

'It's a party. Of course I've been drinking!' Jonathan
eyed her impatiently.

'In that case I'm definitely taking a cab back to your
apartment,' Thia stated firmly.

'I said you'll leave when I *say* you can!' His eyes
glittered.

Thia's cheeks warmed as she stared at him incredulously. 'Who do you think you are to talk to me like
that?' she gasped.

Jonathan's expression darkened. 'I think I'm the man
who paid for you to come to New York!'

Her eyes widened incredulously. 'And you believe that
gives you the right to tell me what I can and can't do?'

'I think it gives me the right to do with you whatever
the hell I feel like doing!' he sneered.

Thia felt the colour drain from her cheeks at the unmistakable threat in his voice. 'I don't know what's got
into you, Jonathan.' Her voice shook as she tried to hold
back tears of hurt. 'But I do know I don't like you like
this. You're obviously drunk. Or something.' She wasn't
a hundred per cent certain that reckless brightness in
his eyes and the flush to his cheeks had been caused by
alcohol alone...

Jonathan certainly wasn't behaving this evening—
hadn't been for the past four days, if she was completely
honest—like the charming and uncomplicated friend she
had known in England...

She drew in a deep breath. 'I think it's best if I leave now, Jonathan. We can talk later. Or tomorrow—'

'You're staying put, damn it.' He reached out and grasped the top of her arm once again, the fingers of his other hand like a vice about her wrist as he twisted painfully.

Thia gave a gasp at the pain he was deliberately—viciously—inflicting on both her arm and her wrist. 'You're hurting me, Jonathan,' she breathed, very much aware of the other guests in the room and the curious sideways glances that were now being sent their way.

'Then stop being so damned difficult! I've said you aren't going anywhere and that's an end to it—' Jonathan broke off abruptly, his gaze moving past Thia and over her left shoulder and his eyes widening before he abruptly released her arm and wrist and forced a charmingly boyish smile to his lips.

Thia's spine stiffened as she guessed from the sudden pause in the conversation around them, the expectant stillness in the air and the way her skin tingled in awareness, exactly who was standing behind her.

Only one man had the power to cause such awe in New York's elite and the ability to possess the very air about him…

The same man who exuded such sexual attraction that it caused every nerve-ending in Thia's body to react and strain towards the pull of that raw sensuality!

Lucien Steele…

Lucien had remained out on the balcony for several more minutes after Cynthia Hammond had walked away from him, giving the hardness of his arousal time to subside even as he pondered the unexpected fierceness of his physical reaction to her.

Her skin—that pearly, luminescent skin—had been as soft and perfect to the light caress of his lips against her cheek as he had imagined it would be, and he could still smell her perfume…something lightly floral along with underlying warmly desirable woman. The same warmth that had surrounded him, enveloped him, as he'd shrugged back into his evening jacket ready for returning to the Carews' party as if the woman herself were wrapped around him.

Lucien couldn't remember the last time he'd had such a visceral reaction to a woman that he wanted to take her right here and right now. If he ever had…

All the more surprising because Cynthia Hammond, at little over five feet tall, ebony-haired and probably only twenty or so, wasn't the type of woman he usually found himself attracted to. He had always preferred tall, leggy blondes, and women nearer to his own age of thirty-five. Women who knew and accepted that his interest in them was purely physical, and that it would be fleeting.

Cynthia Hammond looked too young, too inexperienced to accept the intensity of passion Lucien would demand from her even for the brief time that his interest lasted. And it would be brief—a week or two, a month at the most—before Lucien once again found himself feeling restless, bored with having the same woman in his bed.

No, better by far, he had decided, that he stay well away from the too-young and too-inexperienced Cynthia Hammond.

And he would have done so if, when he had finally

stepped back into the Carews' apartment, Dex hadn't felt it necessary to take him to one side and inform him of the way Jonathan Miller had verbally berated Cynthia Hammond the moment she'd returned to the party, before physically dragging her away.

Did that mean that Jonathan Miller, the star of one of the television series currently airing on Lucien's own network, was the friend Cyn had come to the party with?

Watching the couple as they'd stood together on the opposite side of the room, talking softly but obviously heatedly, Lucien had been unable to stop the narrowing of his eyes when he saw the way Cyn suddenly paled. His fists had clenched at his sides as he'd realised that Miller had a painful grip on her arm and his other hand was twisting her wrist, despite Cyn's obvious efforts to free herself. The thought of a single bruise marring the pearly perfection of her skin had been enough to send Lucien striding forcefully across the room.

Jonathan Miller was one of the reasons Lucien was back in New York at the moment. The actor's behaviour this past few months had become a definite cause for concern and required that Lucien intervene personally after receiving information that the verbal warning he had given Miller six weeks ago, about his drug habit and the affair he was having with his married co-star—the wife of the show's director—had made little difference to the other man's behaviour.

Another private meeting with Jonathan Miller would have to wait until tomorrow. At the moment Lucien was more concerned with the aggressive way the younger man was currently behaving towards Cyn. No matter how intense or demanding Lucien's own physical needs might be, he would never deliberately hurt a woman—he much preferred to give pleasure rather than pain—and he wouldn't tolerate another man behaving in that way in his presence, either.

His gaze settled on Cyn as she stood with her bared shoulders turned towards him. 'Are you ready to leave now…?' he prompted huskily.

Thia's heart leapt into her throat as Lucien Steele re-iterated his invitation to leave the party with him, as he offered to take her away from this nightmare. Away from Jonathan. A Jonathan who was becoming unrecognisable as the charming man she had met two years ago—a man she had thought was her friend.

But friends didn't deliberately hurt each other, and the top of her arm still ached from where Jonathan's fingers had dug so painfully into her flesh just seconds ago, and her wrist was sore from where he had twisted it so viciously. Not only had he hurt her, but he had frightened her too when he had spoken to her so threateningly. And it shamed her, embarrassed her, to think that Lucien Steele might have witnessed that physical and verbal attack.

'Cyn…?'

She could see the confusion in Jonathan's eyes and he was the one to answer the other man lightly. 'I think you've made a mistake, Mr Steele. This is Thia Hammond, my—'

'Cyn…?'

Long, elegant fingers slipped possessively, gently beneath her elbow and Lucien Steele continued to ignore the other man as he came to stand beside her. Thia felt that now familiar shiver down the length of her spine just at the touch of those possessive fingers against her skin, accompanied by the compulsion in Lucien Steele's husky voice. She could actually *feel* that compulsion as that voice willed her to look up at him.

She turned slowly, much like a marionette whose strings were being pulled, her lids widening, pupils expanding, and all the air suddenly sucked from her lungs as she took her first clear look at Lucien Steele in the glare of light from the chandeliers above them.

Oh. My. God.

She had thought him mesmerising, compelling, as they had stood outside together in the moonlight, but that was as nothing compared to the intensity of the magnetism he exuded in the brightly lit sitting room of the Carews' apartment. So much so that even this huge room, the size of a tennis court, seemed too small to hold all that raw and savage power.

His hair was so deep a black it appeared almost blue beneath the lights of the chandelier, and his bronzed face was beautifully sculptured. His high, intelligent brow, the sharp blade of a nose between high cheekbones, and his mouth—oh, God, his mouth!—were sinfully, decadently chiseled. His top lip was slightly fuller than the bottom—an indication of the sensuality he had exuded when they were outside together on the balcony?—and his jaw was square and determined, darkened by the shadow of a dark stubble.

It was the face of a warrior, a marauder, a man who took what he wanted and to hell with whoever or whatever stood in his way.

As if that savagely beautiful face wasn't enough, his perfectly tailored evening suit—had Thia *really* had that gorgeous jacket wrapped about her just minutes ago?—and white silk shirt showed the perfection of his widely muscled shoulders and chest, his tapered waist, powerful thighs and long, lean legs encased in matching black trousers above those soft Italian leather shoes she had referred to so scathingly such a short time ago.

All the trappings of urbanity, in fact—an urbanity that was dispelled the moment she looked at that handsomely savage face!

A face that was dominated by those amazing and compelling silver eyes surrounded by long and silky dark lashes.

Those same compelling silver eyes now held Thia's own gaze captive, hostage, and refused to release her until she acquiesced, surrendered to that raw and demanding power…

CHAPTER THREE

'CYN...?' LUCIEN QUESTIONED for the third and last time—
and that was twice more than he would have allowed
any other woman.

If Cyn Hammond ignored him for a third time then
he would take it that she was a willing participant in
Miller's abusive treatment. It wasn't to Lucien's personal
taste, but that was Cyn's business—not his. No matter
how much he might desire her himself...

'Thia?' Jonathan Miller looked totally confused by
this whole encounter.

Lucien's eyes moved past Cyn to the other man, hardening to steel as he pinned Miller with his razor-sharp
gaze. Bruises were already forming on Cyn's arm where
Miller had held her too tightly just minutes ago, and her
wrist looked red and sore. An unforgivable assault, as
far as Lucien was concerned, on the perfection of that
pearly unblemished skin.

'You hurt her, Miller,' he rasped harshly, his own fingers curling reassuringly about Cyn's elbow as he felt
the way she still trembled. An indication that she really
wasn't happy about Miller's rough treatment of her...

The other man's face flushed with anger—an emotion
he quickly masked behind the boyishly charming smile

that was currently holding American television audiences so enrapt, but succeeded only in leaving Lucien cold.

'Thia and I have had a slight misunderstanding, that's all—'

'It was *your* misunderstanding, Jonathan, not mine.' Cyn was the one to answer coldly and Lucien felt her straighten determinedly. 'Mr Steele has very kindly offered to drive me home, and I've decided to accept his offer.'

There were two things wrong with that statement as far as Lucien was concerned. One, he knew he was far from kind. Two, he had offered to take Cyn for a drink somewhere quieter than the Carews' apartment—not to drive her home. Especially if that 'home' should also happen to be Miller's apartment...

But the details could be sorted out later. For the moment Lucien just wanted to get Cyn away from here. He could still feel the slight trembling of her slender but curvaceous body. Those cobalt blue eyes were dark, there was an enticing flush to her cheeks, her pouting lips were moist and parted, and those deliciously full breasts were once again swelling temptingly against the bodice of her gown as she breathed.

And Lucien could think of a much better use for all that pent up emotion than anger...

'How do the two of you even know each other?' Jonathan Miller scowled darkly.

'If you'll excuse us, Miller?' Lucien didn't spare the other man so much as a glance, let alone answer him, as he turned to give Dex a slight nod of his head. He held Cyn to his side by a light but firm grasp of her elbow as he walked away, the other guests immediately clearing a pathway for them to cross the room to the Carews' private elevator in the hallway.

'What the hell is going on—?'

Lucien gave a cold smile of satisfaction as he heard Miller's protest cut short, knowing that Dex would have responded to his silent instruction and, in his own inimitable and deadly style, prevented the actor from attempting to follow the two of them. Lucien's smile hardened, his eyes chilling to ice as he thought of the conversation he was going to have with Jonathan Miller tomorrow. A conversation that would now include a discussion on the other man's treatment of the delicately lovely woman at his side...

Thia had no idea what she was doing, agreeing to leave the Carews' party with the dangerously compelling Lucien Steele, of all people. Especially when he had made his physical interest in her so obvious during the time the two of them had been outside on the balcony together!

She just wanted to get away from here. From a Jonathan she no longer recognised. And from the curious glances of all the other guests as they observed the tension between the three of them—some surreptitiously, some blatantly.

But was leaving with the dangerously attractive Lucien Steele, a man who was so arrogant she wasn't sure she even liked him, really the answer...?

'Shouldn't we say goodbye to the Carews before we leave?' she prompted hesitantly as Lucien Steele pressed a button and the lift doors opened.

'Dex will deal with it,' he dismissed unconcernedly.

'I—then shouldn't we at least wait for him...?' Thia

made no move to enter the lift, her nervousness increasing the longer she spent in this man's compelling company.

'He'll make his own way down.' Lucien Steele released her elbow as he indicated she should enter the lift ahead of him.

Thia still hesitated. She wanted to get away from Jonathan, yes, but she now realised she felt no safer with Lucien Steele—if for a totally different reason!

'Changed your mind…?' he drawled mockingly.

Her chin rose at the taunt. 'No.' She stepped determinedly into the lift, her gaze averted as Lucien Steele stepped in beside her and pressed the button for the mirror-walled lift to descend.

Thia shot him several nervous glances from beneath her lashes as he stood broodingly on the other side of the lift, feeling that now familiar quiver trembling down her spine as she found herself surrounded by numerous mirrored images of him. This man was impressive under any circumstances, but she stood no chance of remaining immune to him in the confines of a lift.

Lucien Steele was sin incarnate, right from the top of his glossy hair—so much blacker than Thia's own, like shiny blue-black silk, the sort of tousled, overlong hair that made Thia's fingers itch to thread their way through it—to the soles of those Italian leather shoes.

He was a man so totally out of Thia's league that she had no business being there with him at all, let alone imagining threading her fingers through that delicious blue-black hair.

'Ask.'

Thia's startled gaze moved from that silky dark hair to the sculptured perfection of his face. Once again she felt that jolt of physical awareness as she found herself ensnared by the piercing intensity of those silver eyes. 'Um—sorry?'

He shrugged. 'You have a question you want to ask me.'

'I do…?'

His mouth twisted ruefully. 'You do.'

She chewed briefly on her bottom lip. 'Your hair—it's beautiful. I—I've never seen hair quite that blue-black colour before…?'

He raised a brow equally as dark. 'Are you sure you want *that* to be your one question?'

Thia blinked. 'My one question?'

He gave an abrupt inclination of his head. 'Yes.'

She frowned slightly. Surely he wasn't serious…? 'I've just never seen hair that colour before…' she repeated nervously. 'It's the colour of a starless night sky.'

His mouth twisted derisively. 'That was a statement, not a question.'

Yes, it was. But this man unnerved Thia to such a degree she couldn't think straight.

Lucien Steele sighed. 'Somewhere way back in my ancestry—a couple of hundred years or so ago—my great-great-grandfather is reputed to have been an Apache Indian who carried off a rancher's wife before impregnating her,' he dismissed derisively. 'The black hair has appeared in several generations since.'

Dear Lord, this man really was a warrior! Not an axe-wielding, fur-covered Viking, or a kilt-wearing, claymore-brandishing Celt, but a clout-covered, bow-and-arrow-carrying, bareback horse-riding Native American Indian!

It was far too easy for Thia to picture him as such—with that inky-black hair a long waterfall down his back, his muscled and gleaming chest and shoulders bare, just that clout-cloth between him and the horse he rode, the bareness of his long muscled legs gripping—

'Surely I haven't shocked you into silence?' he taunted.

Thia knew by his mocking expression that he wanted her to be shocked, that Lucien Steele was deliberately trying to unnerve her with tales of Apache warriors carrying off innocent women for the sole purpose of ravishing them.

In the same way he was doing the modern equivalent of carrying her off? Also for ravishment…?

Her chin rose. 'Not in the least.'

Those silver eyes continued to mock her. 'My father is a native New Yorker, but my mother is French—hence I was given the name Lucien. My turn now,' he added softly.

She gave a wary start. 'Your turn to do what…?' she prompted huskily.

Those chiselled lips curled into a derisive smile as he obviously heard the tremble in her voice. 'Ask you a question.'

She moistened dry lips. 'Which is…?'

'Cyn, if you don't stop looking at me like that then I'm going to have to stop the elevator and take you right now.'

As if to back up his statement he pressed a button and halted the lift's descent, before crossing the floor with all the grace of the predator he undoubtedly was and standing just inches in front of her.

Thia's eyes had widened, both at his actions and at the raw desire she could hear beneath the harshness of his tone. 'I—you can't just stop the lift like that…!'

'I believe I already did,' he dismissed arrogantly.

Thia found herself totally unable to look away from

the intensity of that glittering silver gaze as Lucien looked down at her from between narrowed lids, her cheeks flushed, her heart beating wildly—apprehensively?—in her chest. 'I—that wasn't a question, either.'

'No.'

She winced. 'How was I looking at you…?'

'As if you'd like to rip my clothes from my body before wrapping your legs about my waist as I push you up against the wall and take you!' His voice was a low and urgent rasp.

Thia's breath caught in her throat as she imagined herself doing any or all of those things, her cheeks flushing, burning. 'I don't think—'

'It's probably better if you don't.'

Lucien Steele's gaze continued to hold hers captive.

She stepped away instinctively, only to feel her back pressing up against the mirrored wall. Lucien Steele dogged her steps until he again stood mere inches away from her and slowly raised his hands to place them on the mirror either side of her head. Lowering his head, he stared down at her with those compelling silver eyes, causing Thia to once again moisten her lips with the tip of her tongue.

'I advise you not to do that again unless you're willing to take the consequences!' he rasped harshly.

Thia's tongue froze on her parted lips as she was once again beset by the feeling of being trapped in the headlights of a car—or, more accurately, the glittering compulsion of Lucien Steele's gaze.

Her throat moved as she swallowed before speaking. 'Consequences?'

He nodded abruptly. 'I'd be more than willing to participate in your fantasy.' His jaw was tight, and desire gleamed in his eyes.

It was a depth of desire Thia had never encountered before, and one that caused her breath to hitch in her throat and her skin to flush with heat: a single-minded depth of desire that made her feel like running for the hills!

'What's Miller to you?' Lucien Steele prompted abruptly.

She blinked long dark lashes. 'Is that your question?'

He bared his teeth in a parody of a smile as he nodded. 'Contrary to my Apache ancestor, I make it a rule never to take another man's woman.'

"Take another man's'—!' She frowned. 'You really *are* something of a barbarian, aren't you?'

Rather than feeling insulted at the accusation, as she had intended, Lucien Steele instead bared his teeth in a wolfish smile. 'You have no idea.'

Oh, yes, Thia definitely had an idea. More than an idea. And her response to this man's raw sexuality terrified the life out of her. Almost as much as it aroused her...

'Cyn?' Lucien pressed forcefully.

She shrugged bare shoulders, those ivory breasts swelling invitingly against her gown. 'I already told you—Jonathan is just a friend—'

'A friend who had no hesitation in hurting you?' Lucien glared his displeasure as he looked down to where dark smudges were already appearing on the smooth paleness of her arm. Her wrist was still slightly red too. 'Who left his mark on you?' he added harshly as he gave in to the temptation to brush his fingertips gently over those darkening smudges.

'Yes...' Her bottom lip trembled, as if she were on the

verge of crying. 'I've never seen him behave like that before. He was out of control…' She gave a dazed shake of her head. 'He's never behaved aggressively with me before,' she insisted dully.

'That's something, I suppose.' Lucien nodded abruptly.

'I—would you please restart the lift now…?' Those tears were trembling on the tips of her long dark lashes, threatening to overflow.

He was *scaring* her, damn it!

Because this—his coming on to her so strongly— was too much, too soon after Miller's earlier aggression.

Or just maybe, despite what she might claim to the contrary, her relationship with Miller wasn't as innocent as she claimed it to be…?

In Lucien's experience no woman was as ingenuous as Cyn Hammond appeared to be. Her ingenuousness had encouraged him to reveal more about himself and his family in the last five minutes than he had told anyone for a very long time. Not that Lucien was ashamed of his heritage—it was what it was. It was his private life in general that he preferred to keep exactly that—private.

He straightened abruptly before stepping back. 'A word of advice, Cyn—you should stay well away from Miller in future. He's bad news.'

Her expression sharpened. 'What do you mean?'

'I believe you've more than used up your quota of questions for one evening.' His expression was grim.

'But you seem to know something I don't—'

'I'm sure I know a lot of things you don't, Cyn,' he rasped with finality, before turning to press the button to restart the elevator.

'Thank you,' Cyn breathed softly as it resumed its soundless descent.

'I didn't do it for you.' Lucien gave a hard, dismissive smile. 'The elevator has been stopped between floors for so long now Dex is probably imagining you've assassinated me.'

Thia frowned. 'Is it a defence mechanism, or are you really this arrogant and rude?'

His gaze was hooded as he answered her. 'Quite a bit of the latter and a whole lot of the former.'

'That's what I thought.' She nodded, able to breathe a little easier now that he wasn't standing quite so close to her. Well…perhaps not easier. Lucien Steele's presence was still so overpowering that Thia challenged anyone, man or woman, to be completely relaxed in his company.

He put his hand beneath her elbow again as the lift came to a stop, the doors opening and allowing the two of them to step out into the marble foyer of the luxurious Manhattan apartment building.

Thia's eyes widened as she saw Dex was already there, waiting for them. 'How did you…?'

'Service elevator,' the man supplied tersely, dismissively, his censorious glance fixed on his employer.

'Stop looking so disapproving, Dex,' Lucien Steele drawled. 'I checked before getting in the elevator: there's absolutely nowhere that Miss Hammond could hide a knife or a gun beneath that figure-hugging gown.'

Thia felt the colour warm her cheeks. 'Definitely a *lot* of the latter,' she muttered, in reference to their previous conversation and heard Lucien Steele chuckle huskily beside her even as she turned to give the still frowning Dex a smile. 'Mr Steele does like to have his little joke.'

There was no answering smile from the bodyguard as he opened the door for them to leave. 'I've had the car brought round to the front entrance.'

'Good,' Lucien Steele bit out shortly, his hand still beneath Thia's elbow as he strode towards the black limousine parked beside the pavement, its engine purring softly into life even as Dex moved forward to open the back door for them to get inside.

'I can get a taxi—a cab—from here,' Thia assured Lucien Steele quickly. His behaviour in the lift wasn't conducive to her wanting to get into the back of a limousine with him.

'Get in.'

That compelling expression was back on Lucien Steele's face as he raised one black brow, standing to one side as he waited for her to get into the back of the limousine ahead of him.

Thia gave a pained frown. 'I appreciate your help earlier, but I'd really rather just get a cab from here...'

He didn't speak again, just continued to look down at her compellingly. Because he was so used to everyone doing exactly as he wished them to, whenever he wished it, he had no doubt Thia was going to get into the limousine.

'I could always just pick you up and put you inside...?' Lucien Steele raised dark brows.

'And I could always scream if you tried to do that.'

'You could, yes.' He smiled confidently.

'Or not,' Thia muttered as she saw the inflexibility in his challenging gaze.

Sighing, she finally climbed awkwardly into the back of the limousine. She barely had enough time to slide across the other side of the seat before Lucien Steele got in beside her. Dex closed the door behind them before getting into the front of the car beside the driver and the car moved off smoothly into the steady flow of evening traffic.

'I don't like being ordered about,' Thia informed Lucien tightly.

'No?'

'No!' She glared her irritation across the dim interior of the car. The windows were of smoked glass, as was the partition between the front and back of the car. 'Any more than I suspect you do.' Once again he was intimidating in the close confines of the car, so big and dark, and she could smell his lemon scent again, the insidious musk of the man himself, all mixed together with the expensive smell of the leather interior of the car.

'That would depend on the circumstances and on what I was being ordered to do,' he drawled.

Her irritation deepened along with the blush in her cheeks. 'Do you think you could get your mind out of the bedroom for two minutes?'

He turned, his thigh pressing against hers as he draped his arm along the back of the seat behind her. 'There's no need for a bedroom when this part of the car is completely private and soundproofed.'

'How convenient for you.'

'For *us,*' he corrected huskily.

Thia's throat moved as she swallowed nervously. 'Unless it's escaped your notice, I'm really not in the mood to play sexual cat-and-mouse games.' She moved her thigh from the warmth of his and edged further along the seat towards the door. 'You offered to drive me home—not seduce me in the back of your car.'

'I believe my original offer was to take you for a quiet drink somewhere,' he reminded her softly.

She gave a shake of her head. 'I'm not in the mood for a drink, either,' she added determinedly.

He smiled slightly in the darkness. 'Then what *are* you in the mood for?'

Thia ignored the innuendo in his voice and instead thought of Jonathan's brutish and insulting behaviour this evening—that reckless glitter in his eyes—all of which told her that it wouldn't be a good idea for her to go back to his apartment tonight. In fact after tonight she believed it would better for both of them if she moved out of Jonathan's apartment altogether and into a hotel, until she flew back to London in a couple of days' time.

Not that she could really afford to do that, but the thought of being any more beholden to Jonathan was no longer an option after the way he had spoken to her earlier. She was also going to repay the cost of the airfare to him as soon as she was able. She was definitely going to have bruises on the top of her arm from where he had gripped her so tightly. It was—

'Cyn?'

She turned sharply to look at Lucien Steele, flicking her tongue out to moisten the dryness of her lips—only to freeze in the action as that glittering silver gaze followed the movement, reminding her all too forcefully of his earlier threat. 'I—could you drop me off at a hotel? An inexpensive one,' she added, very aware of the small amount of money left in her bank account.

This situation would have been funny if Thia hadn't felt quite so much like crying. Here she was, seated in the back of a chauffeur-driven limousine, with reputedly the richest and most powerful man in New York, and she barely had enough money in her bank account to cover next month's rent on her bedsit, let alone an 'inexpensive' hotel!

Lucien Steele pressed the intercom button on the door beside him. 'Steele Heights, please, Paul,' he instructed the driver.

'Will do, Mr Steele,' the disembodied voice came back immediately.

'I totally forgot about the worldwide Steele Hotels earlier in my list of Steele Something-or-Others…' Thia frowned. 'But I'm guessing that none of your hotels are inexpensive…?'

The man beside her gave a tight smile. 'You'll be staying as my guest, obviously.'

'*No!* No…' she repeated, more calmly. 'Thank you. I always make a point of paying my own way.'

Her cheeks paled as she recalled that the one time she hadn't it had been thrown back in her face. She certainly had no intention of being beholden to a man as dangerous as Lucien Steele.

Unfortunately she was barely keeping her head above water now on the money she earned working evening shifts at the restaurant. That would change, she hoped, once she had finished her dissertation in a few months' time and hopefully acquired her Masters degree a couple of months after that. She could then at last go out and get a full-time job relevant to her qualifications. But for the moment she had to watch every penny in order to be able to pay her tuition fees and bills, let alone eat.

A concept she realised the man at her side, with all his millions, couldn't even begin to comprehend…

'Why the smile…?' Lucien prompted curiously.

Cyn gave a shake of her head, that silky dark hair cascading over her shoulders. 'You wouldn't understand.'

'Try me,' he invited harshly, having guessed from her request to go to a hotel that she had indeed been staying at Miller's apartment with him. Lucien had meant it when he'd said he didn't poach another man's woman. *Ever.*

His own parents' marriage had been ripped apart under just those circumstances, with his mother having been seduced away from her husband and son by a much older and even wealthier man than his father. They were divorced now, and had been for almost twenty years, but the acrimony of their separation had taken its toll on Lucien. To a degree that he had complete contempt for any man or woman who intruded on an existing relationship.

The fact that Cyn Hammond claimed she and Jonathan Miller were only friends didn't change the fact that she was obviously staying at the other man's apartment with him. Or at least had been until his aggression this evening...

She gave a grimace as she answered his question. 'I'm a student working as a waitress to support myself through uni. *Now* do you believe you inhabit a different world from me? One where you would think nothing of staying at a prestigious hotel like Steele Heights. I've seen the Steele Hotel in London, and I don't think I could afford to pay the rent on a broom cupboard!'

'I've already stated you will be staying as my guest.'

'And I've refused the offer! Sorry.' She grimaced at her sharpness. 'It's very kind of you, Lucien, but no. Thank you,' she added less caustically. 'As I said, I pay my own way.'

He looked at her through narrowed lids. 'How old are you?'

'Why do you want to know?' She looked puzzled by the question.

'Humour me.'

She shrugged. 'I'm twenty-three—nearly twenty-four.'

'And your parents aren't helping you through university?'

'I'm sure they would have if they were still alive.' She smiled sadly. 'They were both killed in a car crash when I was seventeen, almost eighteen,' she explained at his questioning look. 'I've been on my own ever since,' she dismissed lightly.

The lightness didn't fool Lucien for a single moment; his own parents had divorced when he was sixteen, so he knew exactly how it felt, how gut-wrenching it was to have the foundations of your life ripped apart at such a sensitive age. And Cyn's loss had been so much more severe than his own. At least his parents were both still alive, even if they were now married to other people.

The things Cyn had told him went a long way to explaining the reason for her earlier smile, though; Lucien had more money than he knew what to do with and Cyn obviously had none at all.

'I can relate to that,' he murmured huskily.

'Sorry?'

'My own parents parted and divorced when I was sixteen. Obviously it isn't quite the same, but the result was just as devastating,' he bit out harshly.

'Is that why you're so driven?'

'Maybe.' Lucien scowled; he really had talked far too much about his personal life to this woman.

'It was tough for me, after the accident, but I've managed okay,' she added brightly. 'Obviously not as okay as you, but even so… I worked for a couple of years to get my basic tuition fees together, so now I just work to pay the bills.'

He frowned. 'There was no money after your parents died?'

Cyn smiled as she shook her head. 'Not a lot, no. We lived in rented accommodation that was far too big for me once I was on my own,' she dismissed without rancour. 'I've almost finished my course now, anyway,' she added briskly. 'And then I can get myself a real job.'

It all sounded like another world to Lucien. 'As what?'

She shrugged her bare shoulders. 'My degree will be in English Literature, so maybe something in teaching or publishing.'

He frowned. 'It so happens that one of those other Steele Something-or-Others is Steele Publishing, with offices in New York, London and Sydney.'

She smiled ruefully. 'I haven't finished my degree yet. Nor would I aim so high as a job at Steele Publishing once I have,' she added with a frown.

Lucien found himself questioning the sincerity of her refusal. It wouldn't be the first time a woman had downplayed the importance of his wealth in order to try and trap him into a relationship.

Thia had no idea why she had confided in Lucien Steele, of all people, about her parents' death and her financial struggles since then. Maybe as a response to his admission of his own parents' divorce?

She *did* know as she watched the expressions flitting across his for once readable face, noting impatience quickly followed by wariness, that he had obviously drawn his own conclusions—completely wrong ones!—about her reason for having done so!

She turned to look out of the window beside her, stung in spite of herself. 'Just ask your driver to drop me off anywhere here,' she instructed stiffly. 'There are a couple of cheap hotels nearby.'

'I have no intention of dropping you off anywhere!' Lucien Steele rasped. 'This is New York, Cyn,' he added as she turned to protest. 'You can't just walk about the streets at night alone. Especially dressed like that.'

Thia felt the blush in her cheeks as she looked down at her revealing evening gown, acknowledging he was right. She would be leaving herself open to all sorts of trouble if she got out of the car looking like this. 'Then *you* suggest somewhere,' she prompted awkwardly.

'We'll be at Steele Heights in a couple of minutes, at which time I *suggest* you put aside any idea of false pride—'

'There's nothing false about my pride!' Thia turned on him indignantly. 'It's been hard-won, I can assure you.'

'It *is* false pride when you're endangering yourself because of it,' he insisted harshly. 'Now, stop being so damned stubborn and just accept the help being offered to you.'

'No.'

'Don't make me force you, Cyn.'

'I'd like to see you try!' She could feel the heat of her anger in her cheeks.

'Would you?' he challenged softly. 'Is that what all this is about, Cyn? Do you enjoy it…get off on it…when a man bends you to his will, as Miller did earlier?'

'How dare you—?'

'Cyn—'

'My name is *Thia,* damn it!' Her eyes glittered hotly

even as she grappled with the door handle beside her, only to find it was locked.

'Tell Paul to stop the car and unlock this damned door. *Now,*' she instructed through gritted teeth.

'There's no need for—'

'Now, Lucien!' Thia breathed deeply in her fury, not sure she had ever been this angry in her life before.

He sighed deeply. 'Aren't you being a little melodramatic?'

'I'm being a *lot* melodramatic,' she correctly hotly. 'But then you were a lot insulting. I don't— Ah, Paul.' She had at last managed to find what she sincerely hoped was the button for the intercom.

'Miss Hammond…?' the driver answered uncertainly.

'I would like you to stop the car right now, Paul, and unlock the back doors, please,' she requested tightly.

There was a brief pause before he responded. 'Mr Steele…?'

Thia looked across at Lucien challengingly, daring him to contradict her request. She was so furious with him and his insulting arrogance she was likely to resort to hitting him if hc even attempted to do so.

He looked at her for several more minutes before answering his driver. 'Stop the car as soon as it's convenient, Paul. Miss Hammond has decided to leave us here,' he added, and he turned to look out of the window beside him uninterestedly.

As if she were a petulant child, Thia acknowledged. As if he hadn't just insulted her, accused her of—of— She didn't even want to think about what he had accused her of!

She kept her face turned away from him for the short time it took Paul to find a place to safely park the limousine, her anger turning into heated tears. Tears she had no intention of allowing the cynical and insulting Lucien Steele the satisfaction of seeing fall.

'Thank you,' she muttered stiffly, once the car was parked and Paul had got out to open the door beside her. She kept her face averted as she stepped out onto the pavement before walking away, head held high, without so much as a backward glance.

'Mr Steele…?' Dex prompted beside him uncertainly.

Lucien had uncurled himself from the back of the car to stand on the pavement, his expression grim as he watched Cynthia Hammond stride determinedly along the crowded street in her revealing evening gown, seemingly unaware—or simply uncaring?—of the leering looks being directed at her by the majority of the men and the disapproving ones by the women.

'Go,' Lucien instructed the other man tightly; if Cyn—Thia—had so little concern for her own safety then someone else would have to have it for her.

CHAPTER FOUR

A REALLY UNPLEASANT thing about waking up in a strange hotel room was the initial feeling of panic caused by not knowing exactly where you were. Even more unpleasant was noticing that the less-than-salubrious room still smelt of the previous occupant's body odour and cigarette smoke.

But the worst thing—the *very* worst thing—was returning to that disgusting-smelling hotel bedroom after taking a lukewarm shower in the adjoining uncleaned bathroom and realising that you had no clothes to leave in other than the ankle-length blue evening gown you had worn the night before, along with a pair of minuscule blue panties and four-inch-heeled take-me-to-bed shoes.

All of which became all too apparent to Thia within minutes of her waking up in that awful hotel bedroom and taking that shower!

She had been too angry and upset the evening before—too furious with the arrogantly insulting Lucien Steele—to notice how faded and worn the furniture and décor in this hotel room was, how threadbare and discoloured the towel wrapped about her naked body, let alone the view outside the grimy window of a rusted fire escape and a brick wall.

Thia had been sensible enough the night before, after the lone night porter on duty had openly leered at her when she'd booked in, to at least lock and secure the chain on the flimsy door, plus push a chair under and against the door handle, before crawling between the cold sheets and thin blankets on the bed.

Not that it had helped her to fall asleep—she'd still been too angry at the things Lucien Steele had said to be able to relax enough to sleep.

She dropped down heavily onto the bed now and surveyed what that anger had brought her to. A seedy hotel and a horrible-smelling room that was probably usually let by the hour rather than all night. God, no wonder the night porter had leered at her; he had probably thought she was a hooker, waiting for her next paying customer to arrive.

At the moment she *felt* like a hooker waiting for her next paying customer to arrive!

How was she even going to get out of this awful hotel when she didn't even have any suitable clothes to wear?

Thia tensed sharply as a knock sounded on the flimsy door, turning to eye it warily. 'Yes…?'

'Miss Hammond?'

She rose slowly, cautiously, to her feet. 'Dex, is that you…?' she prompted disbelievingly.

'Yes, Miss Hammond.'

How on earth had Lucien Steele's bodyguard even known where to find her…? More to the point, *why* had he bothered to find her?

At that moment Thia didn't care how or why Dex was here. She was just relieved to know he was standing outside in the hallway. She hurried across the room to remove the chair from under the door handle, slide the safety chain across, before unlocking the door itself and flinging it open.

'Oh, thank God, Dex!' She launched herself into his arms as she allowed the tears to fall hotly down her cheeks.

'Er—Miss Hammond...?' he prompted several minutes later, when her tears showed no signs of stopping. His discomfort was obvious in his hesitant tone and the stiffness of his body as he patted her back awkwardly.

Well, of *course* Dex was uncomfortable, Thia acknowledged as she drew herself up straight before backing off self-consciously. What man wouldn't be uncomfortable when a deranged woman launched herself into his arms and started crying? Moreover a deranged woman wearing only a threadbare bathtowel that was barely wide enough to cover her naked breasts and backside!

'I'm so sorry for crying all over you, Dex,' she choked, on the edge of hysterical laughter now, as she started to see the humour of the situation rather than only the embarrassment. 'I was just so relieved to see a familiar face!'

'You—do you think we might go into your room for a moment?' Dex shifted uncomfortably as a man emerged from a room further down the hallway, eyeing Thia's nakedness suggestively as he lingered over locking his door.

'Of course.' Thia felt the blush in her cheeks as she stepped back into the room. 'I—is that my suitcase...?' She looked down at the lime-green suitcase Dex had brought in with him; it was so distinctive in its ugliness that she was sure it must be the same one she had picked up for next to nothing in a sale before coming to New

York. The same suitcase that she had intended collecting, along with her clothes, from Jonathan's apartment later this morning… 'How did you get it?' She looked at Dex suspiciously.

He returned that gaze unblinkingly. 'Mr Steele obtained it from Mr Miller's apartment this morning.'

'Mr Steele did…?' Thia repeated stupidly. 'Earlier this morning? But it's only eight-thirty now…'

Dex nodded abruptly. 'It was an early appointment.'

She doubted that Jonathan would have appreciated that, considering he hadn't emerged from his bedroom before twelve o'clock on a single morning since her arrival in New York. 'And Lu—Mr Steele just asked him for my things and Jonathan handed them over?'

Dex's mouth thinned. 'Yes.'

Thia looked at him closely. 'It wasn't quite as simple as that, was it?' she guessed heavily.

He shrugged broad shoulders. 'I believe there may have been a…a certain reluctance on Mr Miller's part to co-operate.'

Thia would just bet there had. Jonathan had been so angry with her yesterday evening that she had been expecting him to refuse to hand over her things when she went to his apartment for them later. An unpleasant confrontation that Lucien Steele had circumvented for her by making that visit himself. She could almost feel sorry for Jonathan as she imagined how that particular meeting would have panned out. Almost. She was still too disgusted with Jonathan's unpleasant behaviour the previous evening to be able to rouse too much sympathy for him.

But she was surprised at Lucien Steele having bothered himself to go to Jonathan's apartment himself to collect her things; Lucien had let her leave easily enough last night, and he didn't give the impression he was a man who would inconvenience himself by chasing after a woman who had walked away from him as Thia had.

She drew a shaky breath. 'No one was hurt, I hope?'

'I wasn't there, so I wouldn't know,' Dex dismissed evenly.

'I had the impression you accompanied Mr Steele everywhere?' Thia frowned her puzzlement.

'Normally I do.' His mouth flattened. 'I spent last night standing guard in the hallway outside this room, Miss Hammond.' He answered her question before she had even asked it.

Thia took a step back in surprise, only to have to clutch at the front of the meagre towel in order to stop it from falling off completely. Her cheeks blushed a furious red as she tried to hold on to her modesty as well as her dignity. 'I—I had no idea you were out there...' Maybe if she had she wouldn't have spent half the night terrified that someone—that dodgy night porter, for one!—might try to force the flimsy lock on the door and break in.

A suitable punishment, Lucien Steele would no doubt believe, for the way in which she had walked away from him last night! Because there was no way that Dex had spent the night guarding the door to her hotel room without the full knowledge, and instruction of his arrogant employer...

'I doubt you would have been too happy about it if you had.' Dex bared his teeth in a knowing smile before reaching into the breast pocket of his jacket and pulling out an expensive-looking cream vellum envelope with her name scrawled boldly across the front of it. 'Mr

Steele had Paul deliver your suitcase here a short time ago, along with this.'

Thia stared at the envelope as if it were a snake about to bite her, knowing that it had to be Lucien Steele's own bold handwriting on the front of it and dreading reading what he had written inside.

At the same time she felt a warmth, a feeling of being protected, just knowing that Lucien had cared enough to ensure her safety last night in spite of herself...

'A Miss Hammond is downstairs in Reception, asking to see you, Mr Steele. She doesn't have an appointment, of course,' Ben, his PA, continued lightly, 'but she seems quite determined. I wasn't quite sure what I should do about her.'

Lucien looked up to scowl his displeasure at Ben as he stood enquiringly on the other side of the glass-topped desk that dominated this spacious thirtieth-floor office. Lucien wasn't sure himself what to do about Cynthia Hammond.

She was so damned stubborn, as well as ridiculously proud, that Lucien hadn't even been able to guess what her reaction might be to his having had her things delivered to her at that disgustingly downbeat hotel in which she had chosen to stay the night rather than accept his offer of a room at Steele Heights. He certainly hadn't expected that she would actually pay him a visit at his office in Steele Tower.

And he should have done—Cynthia Hammond was nothing if not predictably unpredictable. 'How determined is she, Ben?' He sighed wearily, already far too familiar with Cyn's stubbornness.

'Very.' His PA's mouth twitched, as if he were holding back a smile.

The wisest thing to do—the *safest* thing to do for Lucien's own peace of mind, which would be best served by never seeing the beautiful Cynthia Hammond again—would be to instruct Security to show her the door…as if she didn't already know exactly where it was! But if Cyn was determined enough to see him, then Lucien didn't doubt that she'd just sit there and wait until it was time for him to leave at the end of the day.

He pulled back the cuff on his shirt and glanced at the plain gold watch on his wrist. 'I don't leave for my next appointment for ten minutes, right?'

'Correct, Mr Steele.'

He nodded abruptly. 'Have Security show her up.'

Lucien leant back in his high-backed white leather chair as Ben left the office, knowing this was probably a mistake. He already knew, on just their few minutes' acquaintance the evening before, that Cynthia Hammond was trouble.

Enough to have caused him a night full of dreams of caressing that pearly skin, of making love to her in every position possible—so much so that he had woken this morning with an arousal that had refused to go down until he'd stood under the spray of an ice-cold shower!

He had even had Paul drive by the hotel where he knew she had spent the night on his way to visit Jonathan Miller's apartment this morning. The neighbourhood was bad enough—full of drug addicts and hookers—but the hotel itself was beyond description, and fully explained Dex's concern when he had telephoned Lucien the night before to tell him exactly which hotel Cyn had checked into and to ask what he should do about it. What the hell had possessed her to stay in such a disreputable hovel?

Money. Lucien answered his own question. He knew from his conversation earlier that morning with Jonathan Miller that Cyn really was exactly what she had said she was: a student working as a waitress to put herself through university, and just over here for a week's visit.

Her finances were not Lucien's problem, of course, but he had been infuriated all over again just looking at the outside of that disgusting hotel earlier, imagining that vulnerable loveliness protected only by the flimsy door Dex had described to him. Dex had been so worried about the situation Lucien believed the other man would have decided to stand guard over her for the night whether Lucien had instructed him to do so or not!

Just another example of the trouble Cynthia Hammond caused with her—

'*Wow!* This is a beautiful building, Lucien! And this office is just incredible!'

Lucien also gave a *wow,* but inwardly, as he glanced across the room to where Cynthia Hammond had just breezily entered his office. A Cynthia Hammond whose black hair was once again a straight curtain swaying silkily to just below her shoulders. The beautiful delicacy of her face appeared free of make-up apart from a coral-coloured lipgloss and the glow of those electric blue eyes. She was dressed in a violent pink cropped sleeveless top that left her shoulders and arms bare and revealed at least six inches of her bare and slender midriff—as well as the fact that she wore no bra beneath it. And below that bare midriff was the tightest pair of skinny low-rider blue denims Lucien had ever seen in his life. So tight that he wondered whether Cyn wore any underwear beneath…

And that was just the front view. Ben's admiring glance, as he lingered in the doorway long enough to watch Cyn stroll across the spacious office, was evidence that the back view was just as sexily enticing!

Cyn did casual elegance well—so much so that Lucien felt decidedly overdressed in his perfectly tailored black suit, navy blue silk shirt and black silk tie. 'Don't you have some work to do, Ben?' he prompted harshly as he stood up—and then sat down again as he realised his arousal had sprung back to instant and eager attention. The benefits of his icy cold shower earlier this morning obviously had no effect when once again faced with the enticing Cynthia Hammond.

Trouble with a capital T!

'Thanks, Ben.' Thia turned to smile at the PA before he closed the door on his way out, then returned her gaze to the impressive office rather than the man seated behind the desk, putting off the moment when she would have to face the disturbing Lucien Steele. Just a brief glance in his direction as she had entered the cavernous office had been enough for her to feel as if all the air had been sucked from her lungs, and her nerve-endings were all tingling on high alert.

This black and chrome office was not only beautiful, it was *huge*. Carpeted completely in black, it had an area set aside for two white leather sofas and a bar serving coffee as well as alcohol, and another area with a glass and marble conference table, as well as Lucien Steele's own huge desk, bookshelves lining the wall behind him, and an outer wall completely in glass, giving a panoramic view of the New York skyline.

It really was the biggest office Thia had ever seen, but even so her gaze was drawn as if by a magnet inevitably back to the man seated behind the chrome and black marble desk. The office was easily big enough to accommodate half a dozen executive offices, and yet somehow—by sheer force of will, Thia suspected—Lucien Steele still managed to dominate, to *possess*, all the space around him.

As he did Thia?

Maybe she should have power-dressed for this meeting rather than deciding to go casual? She did have one slim black skirt and a white blouse with her—they would certainly have blended in with the stark black, white and chrome décor of his office. Much more so than her shockingly pink cropped top.

Oh, well, it was too late to worry about that now. She would have to work with what she had.

'Say what you have to say, Cyn, and then go,' Lucien Steele bit out coldly. 'I have to leave for another appointment in five minutes.'

Her breath caught in her throat as she looked at Lucien. A Lucien who was just as knee-tremblingly gorgeous this morning as the previous night. Thia had convinced herself during her restless night of half-sleep that no one could possibly be that magnetically handsome, that she must have drunk too much of the Carews' champagne and imagined all that leashed sexual power.

She had been wrong. Lucien Steele was even more overpoweringly attractive in the clear light of day, with the sun shining in through the floor-to-ceiling windows turning his hair that amazing blue-black, his bronzed face dominated by those silver eyes, and his features so hard and chiselled an artist would weep over his male beauty. And as for the width of those muscled shoulders—!

Time for her to stop drooling! 'Nice to see that you're still living up to my previous description of you as being arrogant and rude,' she greeted with saccharine sweetness.

He continued to look at her coldly with those steel-grey eyes. 'I doubt you want to hear my opinion of *you* after the stunt you pulled last night.'

She felt the colour warm her cheeks and knew he had to be referring to the hotel in which she had spent the night, which Dex would no doubt have described to his employer in graphic detail. 'I didn't have the funds to stay anywhere else.'

'You wouldn't have needed any funds if you had just accepted the room I offered you at Steele Towers,' Lucien reminded her harshly.

'Accepting the room you offered me at Steele Towers would have put me under obligation to you,' she came back, just as forcefully.

Lucien stilled, eyes narrowing to steely slits. 'Are you telling me,' he asked softly, 'that the reason you refused my offer last night was because you believed I would expect to share that bedroom with you for the night as payment?'

'Well, you can't blame me for thinking that after the way you came on to me outside on the balcony and then again in the lift!'

Lucien raised dark brows. 'I can't *blame* you for thinking that?'

'Well…no…' Cyn eyed him, obviously slightly nervous of his quiet tone and the calmness of his expression.

And she was wise to be! Because inwardly Lucien was

seething, furious—more furious than he remembered being for a very long time, if ever. Even during the visit he had paid to Jonathan Miller's apartment earlier this morning he had remained totally in control—coldly and dangerously so. But just a few minutes spent in the infuriating Cynthia Hammond's company and Lucien was ready to put his hands about her throat and throttle her!

If it weren't for the fact that he knew he would much rather put his hands on another part of her anatomy, starting with that tantalisingly bare and silky midriff, and stroke her instead...

Thia took a step back as Lucien Steele stood up and moved round to the front of his desk. His proximity, and the flat canvas shoes she was wearing, meant she had to tilt her head back in order to be able to look him in the face. A face that made her wish she were an artist. What joy, what satisfaction, to commit those hard and mesmerising features to canvas. Especially if Lucien could be persuaded into posing in traditional Apache clout cloth, with oil rubbed into the bare bronzed skin of his chest and arms, emphasising all the dips and hollows of those sleek muscles—

'What are you thinking about, Cyn?'

She looked up guiltily as she realised her appreciative gaze had actually wandered down to that muscled chest as she imagined him bare from the waist up—. 'I—you—nice suit.' She gave him a falsely bright smile.

Lucien Steele's mouth tilted sceptically, as if he knew exactly what she had been thinking. 'Thanks,' he drawled derisively. 'But I believe we were discussing your reckless behaviour last night and your reasons for it?' His voice hardened and all humour left his expression. 'Do you have any idea what could have happened to you if Dex hadn't stayed outside your room all night?'

She had a pretty good idea, yes. 'It was stupid of me. I accept that.'

'Do you?' he bit out harshly.

She nodded. 'That's why I'm here, actually. I wanted to thank you.' She grimaced. 'For allowing Dex to stand guard last night. For having my things delivered to the hotel this morning. And for sending that keycard, in the envelope Dex gave me, for a suite at Steele Heights.'

For all her expectations of what Lucien Steele *might* have put in that vellum envelope Dex had handed her this morning, there had been nothing in it but a keycard for a suite at Steele Heights, which he had obviously booked for her.

Thia had wrestled with her pride over accepting, of course, along with that old adage about accepting sweets from strangers. This was a different sort of suite, of course, but she told herself it was still sensible to be wary. But pride and wariness weren't going to put a roof over her head tonight, and she couldn't possibly go back to Jonathan's.

Lucien leant back against his desk and seemed to guess some of her thoughts. 'I trust you've overcome your scruples and moved in there now?'

'Yes.' Thia grimaced. Just the thought of that luxurious suite—the sitting room, bedroom and equally beautiful adjoining bathroom—was enough for her to know she had done the right thing. It might take her a while, but she fully intended to reimburse Lucien for his generosity.

He quirked one dark brow. 'Does that mean you no longer mind feeling under obligation to me?'

Thia looked up at him sharply, unable to read anything from his mocking expression. 'I think the question should be do *you* believe I'm under any obligation to you?'

'Let me see…' He crossed his elegantly clad legs at the ankles as he studied her consideringly. 'I left a perfectly good party last night because I thought we were going on somewhere to have a drink together. A drink that never happened. You flounced off in a snit after I offered to drive you somewhere, which greatly inconvenienced me as Dex was then forced to stand guard over your room all night. And I was put to the trouble this morning of asking your ex-boyfriend to pack up your belongings in that hideous lime-green suitcase before having my driver deliver it to that seedy hotel.' He gave a glance at the slender gold watch on his wrist. 'Your unexpected visit here this morning means I am now already three minutes late leaving for my next appointment. So what do *you* think, Cyn? *Are* you obligated to me?'

Well, when he put it like that… 'Maybe,' Thia allowed with a pained wince.

'I would say there's no *maybe* about it.' He slowly straightened to his full height of several inches over six feet, that silver gaze fixed on her unblinkingly as he took a step forward.

Thia took a step back as she was once again overwhelmed by the unique lemon and musk scent of Lucien Steele. 'What are you doing?'

'What does it look as if I'm doing?'

He was standing so close now she could feel the warmth he exuded from his body against the bareness of her midriff and arms. His face—mouth—only was inches away from her own as he lowered his head slightly.

She moistened her lips with the tip of her tongue. 'It looks to me as if you're trying to intimidate me!'

He gave a slow and mocking smile as he regarded her through narrowed lids. 'Am I succeeding?'

'You must know that you intimidate everyone.'

'I'm not interested in everyone, Cyn, just you.'

Thia's heart was beating such a loud tattoo in her chest that she thought Lucien must be able to hear it. Or at least see the way her breasts were quickly rising and falling as she tried to drag air into her starved lungs. 'You're standing far too close to me,' she protested weakly.

He tilted his head, bringing those chiselled lips even closer to hers. 'I like standing close to you.'

She realised she liked standing close to Lucien too. That she liked him. That she wanted to do so much more than stand close to him. She wanted Lucien to pull her into his arms and kiss her. To make love to her.

Which was strange when she had never felt the least inclination to make love with any man before now. But Lucien wasn't just any man. He was dark and dangerous and overpoweringly, mesmerisingly, sexually attractive—a combination Thia had never come across before now. She knew her breasts had swelled, the nipples hard nubs, pressing against her cropped top, and between her thighs she was damp, aching. For Lucien Steele's touch!

As if he was able to read that hunger in her face, Lucien's pupils dilated and his head slowly lowered, until those beautiful sculptured lips laid gentle but hungry siege to hers.

Thia felt as if she had been jolted with several thousand volts of electricity. And heat. Such burning heat coursing through her. She stepped in closer to that hard, unyielding body and her arms moved up and over Lucien's wide shoulders as if of their own volition. The warmth of his strong hands spanned the slenderness of her bare waist as her fingers became entangled in that silky black hair at his nape, her lips parting as she lost herself in the heat of his kiss.

Trouble…

Oh, yes, Cyn Hammond, with her black hair, electric-blue eyes, beautiful face and deliciously enticing body, was definitely Trouble with a capital T…

But at this moment, with the softness of her responsive lips parted beneath his, his hands caressing, enjoying the feel of the soft perfection of her bare midriff, Lucien didn't give a damn about that.

Nothing had changed since last night. If anything he wanted her more than he had then.

Again. Right here.

And right now!

Lucien deepened the kiss even as he moulded her slender curves against his own much harder ones, intoxicated, lost in Cyn's taste as he ran his tongue along the pouting softness of her bottom lip. Groaning low in his throat, he let his tongue caress past those addictive lips and into the heat beneath, plunging, possessing that heat as his hands moved restlessly, caressingly, down the length of her spine. Soon Lucien was able to cup that shapely bottom and pull her snugly into and against the pulsing length of his arousal.

The softness of her thighs felt so good against his, so hot and welcoming. He shifted, the hardness of his shaft now cupped and cushioned in that softness, and moved one of his hands to cup her breast through her T-shirt.

It was a perfect fit into the palm of his hand, the nipple hard as an unripe berry as Lucien brushed the soft pad of his thumb across it and heard Cyn's gasp of pleasure, felt her back arching, pressing her breast harder into his cupping hand in a silent plea.

Her skin felt as smooth as silk beneath Lucien's fingertips as he slipped his hand beneath the bottom of her top to cup her bare breast—

Thia wrenched her mouth from Lucien's and pulled out of his arms before taking a stumbling step backwards—as if those few inches in any way nullified Lucien's sexual potency, or the devastation wrought upon her senses by that hungry kiss and those caressing hands!

'No...' she breathed shakily, her cheeks ablaze with embarrassed colour as she attempted to straighten her top over breasts that pulsed and ached for the pleasure she had just denied them.

Lucien's gaze was hooded. There was a flush across those high cheekbones, a nerve pulsing in his clenched jaw. 'No?'

'No,' Thia repeated more firmly. 'This is—I don't do this.'

'"This" being...?'

'Seduction in a zillionaire's office!'

He arched one dark brow. 'How many zillionaires do you know?'

Her cheeks warmed. 'Just the one.'

He nodded. 'That's what I thought.' He crossed his arms in front of his chest and he looked at her from between narrowed lids. 'Just what did you think was going to happen, Cyn, when you came to my office dressed—or rather undressed—like that?' That glittering silver gaze swept appreciatively over her breasts, naked beneath the crop top, her bare midriff and hip-hugging denims.

She hadn't allowed herself to think before coming here—had just acted on impulse, knowing she had to thank Lucien Steele for his help some time today and just wanting to get it over with. But, yes, now that he mentioned it she wasn't exactly dressed for repelling advances. Deliberately if subconsciously so? Lord, she hoped not!

'Stop calling me Cyn,' she snapped defensively.

'But that's what you are to me… Sin and all that word implies.' He all but purred. 'You have all the temptation of a candy bar in that shocking pink top. One that I want to lick all over.'

Thia felt heat in her already blushing cheeks at the provocative imagines that statement conjured in her mind. 'You—I don't—didn't—' She gave a shake of her head. 'Could we get back to our earlier conversation?' *Please,* she added silently, knowing she would have plenty of time later today to think about and to remember with embarrassment the touch of Lucien's lips and hands on her body. 'For one thing, Jonathan was only ever my friend,' she continued determinedly.

'Not any more he isn't.' Lucien nodded with grim satisfaction. 'He made it clear before I left his apartment earlier this morning that he was feeling decidedly less than charitable towards you,' he explained dryly.

Thia's eyes widened. 'What did you say to him?'

'About you?' He shrugged. 'As you have neither a father nor brother to protect you, I thought it necessary that someone should warn Miller against laying so much as a finger on you with the intention of hurting you ever again.'

She gasped. 'I can look after myself!'

'Is that why you spent the night at a less-than-reputable hotel? Why you have bruises on your arm?' Lucien's expression darkened with displeasure as his glittering silver gaze moved to the purple-black smudges at the top of her left arm. 'If I had known the extent of your bruising I would have inflicted a few of my own on him this morning, rather than just firing his ass!'

Thia gasped even as she looked up searchingly into that ruthlessly handsome face, totally unnerved by the dangerous glitter in Lucien's eyes as he continued to glower at the bruises on her arms. 'You fired Jonathan from *Network?*'

He looked up into her face as he gave a humourless smile of satisfaction. 'Oh, yes.'

Oh, good grief...

CHAPTER FIVE

LUCIEN'S HUMOURLESS SMILE became a grimace as he saw the expression of horror on Cyn's face. 'Don't worry. My decision to fire Miller wasn't because of anything he did or said to you. Although that was certainly a side issue in the amount of satisfaction I felt doing it.'

'Then why did you fire him?' She looked totally bewildered.

Lucien gave another impatient glance at his wristwatch. 'Look, can we continue this conversation later? Possibly over dinner? I really do have to leave for my appointment now.' He moved around his desk to pick up the file he needed for his meeting before putting it inside his black leather briefcase and snapping it shut. 'Cyn?' he prompted irritably as she stood as still as an Easter Island statue.

He was more than a little irritated with himself for having suggested the two of them have dinner together when he knew that the best thing for both of them was not be alone together again. His response to Cyn—as he had proved a short time ago!—was so different than to any other woman he had ever met. She was so different from those preening, self-centred, high-maintenance women he usually dated...

'Hmm?' She looked across at him blankly.

'Dinner? Tonight?' he repeated shortly.

'I—no.' She shook her head from side to side. 'You've been very kind to me, but—'

'You consider my almost making love to you just now as being *kind* to you…?' Lucien bit out derisively.

Her cheeks flushed a fiery red. 'No, of course not—'

'Dinner. Tonight,' he said impatiently. He couldn't remember the last time he had been late for a business appointment. Business always came first with him, pleasure second. And making love to Cyn just now had been pure pleasure. 'We can eat at the hotel if that would make you feel…*safer?*' he taunted.

Thia easily heard the mockery in Lucien's voice. A mockery she knew she deserved.

So Lucien had kissed her. More than kissed her. She wasn't a child, for goodness' sake, but a twenty-three-year-old woman, and just because this was the first time that anything like this had happened to her it was no reason for her to go off at the deep end as if she were some scandalised Victorian heroine!

Besides which, it was obvious Lucien wasn't going to tell her any more now about why he had fired Jonathan, and she desperately wanted to know.

Was it even possible for him to dismiss Jonathan so arbitrarily? Admittedly this was Lucien Steele she was talking about—a man who had already proved how much he liked having his own way—but surely Jonathan had a contract that would safeguard him from something like this happening. Besides which, *Network* was the most popular series being shown on US television at the moment; sacking its English star would be nothing short of suicide for both the series *and* Steele Media. And Lucien *was* Steele Media.

'Fine, we'll eat at Steele Heights,' she bit out abruptly. 'What time and which restaurant?' There were three of them, but obviously Cyn hadn't eaten at any.

Lucien moved briskly from behind his desk, briefcase in hand, and took hold of her elbow with the other hand. 'We can talk about that in the car before I drop you off at the hotel.'

'I'm not going back to the hotel just yet.' Thia dug her heels in at being managed again, even as she recognised that familiar tingling warmth where Lucien's fingers now lightly touched her arm. 'I'm going to the Empire State Building this afternoon.'

He raised dark brows. 'Why?'

'What do you mean, *why?*' She looked up at him irritably. 'It's a famous New York landmark, and I've been here five days already and not managed to go to the top of it yet.'

Lucien's mouth twisted derisively. 'I was born in New York, have lived here most of my thirty-five years, and I can honestly say I've never been even to the top of the Empire State Building.'

'You could always come with me—' Thia broke off as she realised the ridiculousness of her suggestion. Of course Lucien Steele, zillionaire entrepreneur, didn't want to do something as mundane as go with her to the top of the Empire State Building any more than Thia really wanted him to accompany her. Did she…? No, of course she didn't. She had succumbed to this man's sexual magnetism enough for one day—made a fool of herself enough for one day—thank you very much.

'Forget it,' she dismissed, with a lightness she was

far from feeling. She wasn't one hundred per cent sure *what* she was feeling at the moment, or thinking. She was too tremblingly aware of Lucien having kissed her just minutes ago to be able to put two coherent thoughts together. 'You said you had a meeting to get to?' she reminded him.

Yes, he did. But strangely, just for a few seconds, Lucien had actually been considering cancelling his business meeting and going with Cyn to visit the Empire State building instead. Unbelievable.

Zillionaires didn't get to be or stay zillionaires, by playing hooky from work to go off and play tourist with a visitor from England. Even if—*especially* if—that visitor was Cyn Hammond. A woman who apparently had the ability to make Lucien forget everything but his desire to be with her and make love to her.

Something that had definitely not happened to him before today.

But, damn it, Cyn really did look like a tempting stick of candy in that pink top... And it took no effort at all on Lucien's part to imagine the pleasure of licking his tongue over every inch of that soft and silky flesh...

He nodded abruptly. 'I can drop you off at the Empire State Building on my way.'

'It's such a lovely day I think I'd rather walk,' she refused lightly, lifting a hand in parting to Ben as they passed through his office and out into the hallway before stepping into the private elevator together.

Just the thought of Cyn wandering the streets of New York dressed in nothing more than that skimpy pink top and those body-hugging denims was enough to bring a dark scowl back to Lucien's brow. 'Do you have *any* sense of self-preservation at all?' he rasped harshly as he released her elbow to press the button for the elevator to take them down to the ground floor.

'It's the middle of the day, for goodness' sake!' She glanced at him with those cobalt blue eyes through lushly dark lashes.

Lucien eyed her impatiently. 'Remind me to tell you later tonight about the statistics for daytime muggings and shootings in New York.'

She chewed on her bottom lip. 'You still have to tell me what time I'm meeting you this evening, and at which restaurant in the hotel,' she said firmly.

'Eight o'clock.' He frowned. 'Go down to the ground floor. I'll have someone waiting to show you to the private elevator that will bring you directly up to the penthouse apartment.'

Her eyes widened. 'The penthouse? You live in an apartment at the top of the Steele Heights Hotel?' Thia was too surprised not to gape at him incredulously.

He gave a smile of satisfaction at her reaction. 'I occupy the whole of the fiftieth floor of Steele Heights when I'm in New York.'

'The whole floor?' she gasped. 'What do you have up there? A tennis court?'

'Not quite.' Lucien smiled tightly. 'There is a full-sized gym, though. A small pool and a sauna. And a games room. A small private cinema for twenty people.' He quirked a dark brow as Cyn gaped at him. 'Changed your mind about having dinner with me at the hotel this evening?' Those silver eyes mocked her.

It didn't take too much effort on Thia's part to realise Lucien was challenging her, daring her. He expected her to baulk at agreeing to have dinner with him now that she knew they would be completely alone in his penthouse apartment. And good sense told Thia that it would be a wise move on her part *not* to rise to this particular challenge, to just withdraw and concede Lucien as being the winner.

Unfortunately Thia had never backed down from a challenge in her life. She wouldn't have been able to survive the death of her parents or worked as a waitress for the past five years in order to support herself through uni if that was the case. And she had no intention of backing down now, either.

Even if she did suspect that Lucien wasn't just challenging her by inviting her to his apartment and that the main reason he wanted them to dine in the privacy of his apartment was because he didn't want to be seen out with her in public.

She knew enough about Lucien Steele to know he was a man the media loved to photograph, invariably entering some famous restaurant or club, and always with a beautiful model or actress on his arm. Being seen with a waitress student from London hardly fitted in with that image.

'Fine.' She nodded abruptly. 'Eight o'clock. Your apartment.'

'No need to dress formally,' Lucien told her dismissively. 'Although perhaps something a little less revealing than what you're currently wearing might be more appropriate,' he added dryly.

'It's a crop top, Lucien. All women are wearing them nowadays.'

'None of the women *I've* escorted have ever done so,' he assured her decisively.

'That's your loss!' Thia felt stung by Lucien's casual mention of those women he'd escorted. Which was ridiculous of her. The fact that they were eating dinner at his apartment told her that this wasn't a date, just a convenient way for the two of them to be able to finish their conversation in private. Well away from the public eye...

'Yes.' He bared his teeth in a wolfish smile as the two of them stepped out of the lift together, causing Thia to blush as he reached out to grasp one of her hands lightly in his before raising it to skim his lips across her knuckles. 'Until later, Cyn.'

Thia snatched her hand from within his grasp, aware of the stares being directed their way by the other people milling about in the lobby of Steele Tower even if he wasn't. 'I hope you're enjoying yourself,' she hissed, even as she did her best to ignore the tingling sensation now coursing the length of her arm. And beyond...

'It has its moments.' His eyes glittered with satisfied amusement as he looked down at her.

Thia glared right back at him. 'You could have told me your reason for firing Jonathan in the time we've been talking together.'

'I do things my own way in my own time, Cyn,' he bit out tersely. 'If you have a problem with that, then I suggest—'

'I didn't say I had a problem with it,' she snapped irritably. 'Only that—oh, never mind!' Lucien had the ability to rob her of her good sense, along with any possibility of withstanding his lethal attraction.

A lethal attraction that affected every other woman in his vicinity, if the adoring glances of the receptionists were any indication, as well as those of the power-dressed businesswomen going in and out of the building.

All of them, without exception, had swept a contemptuous gaze over the casually dressed Thia—no doubt wondering what a man like Lucien Steele was doing even wasting his time talking to someone like her—before returning that gaze longingly, invitingly, to the man at Thia's side. One poor woman had almost walked into a potted plant because she had been so preoccupied with eating Lucien up with her eyes!

It was a longing Thia knew she was also guilty of.

Challenge or no challenge, she really shouldn't have agreed to have dinner alone with him in his apartment this evening…

Thia looked in dismay at the chaos that was her bedroom in the suite on the tenth floor of the Steele Heights Hotel. Clothes were strewn all over the bed after she had hastily tried them on and then as quickly discarded them. Finding exactly the right casual outfit to wear to have dinner with the dangerously seductive Lucien Steele in— oh, hell—fifteen minutes' time was proving much more difficult than she had thought it would. And she hadn't dried her hair yet, or applied any make-up.

She had been late getting back to the hotel as the long queues at the Empire State Building had meant she'd had to wait in line for a long time before getting to the top. It had been worth the wait when she finally got there, of course, but by that time it had been starting to get late.

She'd also had the strangest feeling all afternoon that she was being followed…

Lucien's warnings earlier had made her paranoid. That was more than a possibility. Whatever the reason, Thia had felt so uncomfortable by the time she'd come down from the top of the Empire State Building and stepped back out into the street that she had decided to treat herself and take a taxi back to the hotel.

She had taken out her laptop and gone online for half an hour once she was back in the hotel suite, determined to know at least a little more about the enigmatic Lucien Steele before they met again this evening.

Unfortunately the moment she'd come offline and lain back on the bed she had fallen asleep, tired from her outing, and also exhausted from the previous sleepless night she had spent at that awful hotel. No surprise, then, that she hadn't woken up again until almost seven-thirty!

Which now meant she was seriously in danger of being late—and she still hadn't found anything to wear that she thought suitable for having dinner with a man like Lucien Steele!

Oh, to hell with it. Black denims and a fitted blouse the same colour blue as her eyes would have to do; she simply didn't have any more time to waste angsting over what she should or shouldn't wear to have dinner with a zillionaire. And the blue blouse also had the benefit of having elbow-length sleeves, meaning those bruises Jonathan had inflicted on her arm the previous evening, which had so angered Lucien earlier, would be safely hidden from his piercing gaze.

Jonathan....

If she concentrated on the fact that it was only because she wanted to know exactly why Lucien had decided to fire Jonathan from *Network* that she had agreed to have dinner with Lucien—even if she no longer believed that!—then maybe she would be able to get through this evening.

The butterflies fluttering about in her stomach didn't seem to be listening to her assurances as she stood alone in the private lift minutes later, on her way up to the penthouse apartment. Her hair still wasn't completely dry and her face felt flushed. No doubt it looked it too, despite her application of a light foundation.

The manager of the hotel himself had been waiting on the ground floor to show her into the private coded lift. The sheer opulence of the lift in which she was now whizzing up fifty floors to the penthouse apartment— black carpet, plush bench seat along one mirrored wall, a couple of pot plants—and the thought of the overwhelmingly sexy man who would be waiting up there for her were so far beyond what was normal for Thia, was it any wonder she was so nervous she felt nauseous?

Or maybe it was just the thought of being alone with Lucien again that was making her feel that way... Her online snooping about him earlier had informed her that he was thirty-five years old—something Lucien had already told her—and the only child of New Yorker Howard Steele and Parisian Francine Maynard. Educated at private school and then Harvard, he had attained a law degree and in his spare time designed a new gaming console and graphics for many computer games, enabling him to make his first million— or possibly billion?—before he was twenty-one. That was something else Lucien had already told her. He had taken full advantage of this success by diversifying those millions into any number of other successful businesses.

There had also, depressingly, been dozens of photographs of him with dozens of the women he had escorted at some time or other during the past fifteen years: socialites, actresses, models. All of them, without exception, were extremely beautiful, as well as being tall and blond.

And this was the man that Thia, five-foot-two, raven-haired and merely pretty, had agreed to have dinner alone with this evening...

Knowing she simply wasn't his type should have made her feel less nervous about the evening ahead. Should have. But it didn't. How could it when she only had to think of the way Lucien had kissed her so intensely this afternoon, of his caressing hands on her bare midriff—and higher!—to know that he had felt desire for her then, even if she *was* five-foot-two and raven-haired!

After all her apprehension, the man who had caused all those butterflies in her stomach was nowhere to be seen when Thia stepped out of the lift into the penthouse apartment seconds later. The apartment itself was everything she had thought it would be—white marble floors, original artwork displayed on ivory walls. She walked tentatively down the hallway to the sitting room in search of Lucien. It was a spaciously elegant room, with the same minimalist white, black and chrome décor of Lucien's office. Had the man never heard of any other colours but white, black and chrome?

The view from the floor-to-ceiling windows was even more spectacular than the one from the Carews' apartment—

'I'm sorry I wasn't here to greet you when you arrived, Cyn. My meeting ran much later than I had anticipated and I only got back a few minutes ago.'

Thia turned almost guiltily at the sound of Lucien's voice, very aware of the fact that she had just walked into his private apartment and made herself at home, only to stand and stare, her mouth falling open, blue eyes wide and unblinking, as she took in his rakishly disheveled and practically nude appearance.

Lucien had obviously just taken a shower. His black

hair was still damp and tousled, a towel was draped about his shoulders, and he wore only a pair of faded blue denims sitting low down on the leanness of his hips, leaving that glistening bronzed chest and shoulders—the same ones Thia had fantasised about earlier this afternoon!—openly on view. Revealing he was just as deliciously muscled as she had imagined he would be. His nipples were the size and colour of two dark bronze coins amongst the dusting of dark hair that dipped and then disappeared beneath the waistband of his denims.

If Lucien had wanted to lick her all over this afternoon then Thia now wanted to do the same to him… Dressed in those low-slung denims, with his bronzed shoulders and chest bare, overlong blue-black hair sexily dishevelled, his bare feet long and elegant, Lucien definitely looked good enough to eat!

'Cyn…?' Lucien eyed her questioningly as she made no response.

Or perhaps she did…

She was wearing another pair of those snug-fitting denims this evening—black this time—with a fitted blouse the same electric blue colour as her sooty-lashed eyes. The material of the blouse was so sheer it was possible for Lucien to see that she wore no bra beneath it. Her breasts were a pert shadow, nipples plump as berries as they pressed against the soft gauzy material. Hard and aroused berries…

'I—er—shouldn't you go and finish dressing…?'

Lucien dragged his gaze slowly, reluctantly away from admiring those plump, nipple-crested breasts to look up into Cyn's face, instantly noting the flush to her cheeks and the almost fevered glitter to her eyes as she shifted uncomfortably from one booted foot to the other. As if her breasts weren't the only part of her body that was swollen with arousal...

Instead of doing as she suggested Lucien stepped further into the sitting room. 'I'll get you a drink first.' He threw the damp towel down onto a chair as he strolled over to the bar in the corner of the room. 'Bottled water, white wine, red wine...something stronger...?' He arched a questioning brow.

Was Lucien strutting his bare, bronzed stuff deliberately? Thia wondered. As a way of disconcerting her? If he was then he was succeeding. She had never felt so uncomfortably aware of a man in her life as she was now by all his warm naked flesh. Or so aroused!

The man should have a public health warning stamped on his chest. Something along the lines of 'Danger to all women with a pulse' ought to do it. And Thia was the only woman with a pulse presently in Lucien Steele's disturbing vicinity! Her throat felt as if it had closed up completely, and her chest was so tight she could barely breathe, let alone speak.

She cleared her throat before even attempting it. 'Red wine would be lovely, thank you,' she finally managed to squeak, in a voice that sounded absolutely nothing like her own, only to draw a hissing breath into her starved lungs as Lucien turned away from her. The muscles shifted in his back beneath that smooth bronzed skin as he bent to take a bottle of wine from the rack beside the bar, and even more muscles flexed in his arms as he straightened to open it, the twin dips at the base of his spine clearly visible above the low-riding denims.

Twin dips Thia longed to stroke her tongue over, to

taste, before working her way slowly up the length of that deliciously muscled back…!

'Here you go.' Lucien strolled unconcernedly across the room carrying two glasses of red wine—one obviously meant for Thia, the other for himself.

Evidence that he didn't have any intention of putting any more clothes on in the immediate future? And why should he? This was his home, after all!

His close proximity now meant that Thia was instantly overwhelmed by that smell of lemons and the musky male scent she now associated only with this man, and her hand was trembling slightly as she reached out to take one of the wine glasses from him—only to spill some of the wine over the top of the glass as a jolt of electricity shot up her arm the moment her fingers came into contact with his.

'Sorry,' she mumbled self-consciously, passing the glass quickly into her other hand with the intention of licking the spilt wine dripping from her fingers.

'Let me…' Lucien reached out to catch her hand in his before it reached her parted lips, his gaze easily holding hers as he carried her fingers to his own mouth before lapping up the wine with a slow and deliberate rasp of his tongue. 'Mmm, delicious.' He licked his lips. 'Perhaps I should consider always drinking wine this way…?' His shaft certainly thought it was a good idea as it rose up hard and demanding inside his denims!

'Lucien—'

'Hmm?' He continued to lick the slenderness of Cyn's silky fingers even after all the wine had gone, enjoying the way her hand was trembling in his and watching the slow rise and fall of those plumped breasts and aroused nipples, his erection now almost painful in its intensity.

She snatched her hand away from his to glare up at him. 'Are you doing this on purpose?'

'Doing what…?'

Her eyes narrowed. 'Would you please go and put some clothes on?'

Lucien straightened slowly to look at her from between narrowed lids. 'You seem a little…tense this evening, Cyn. Didn't the Empire State live up to your expectations?'

'The Empire State was every bit as wonderful as I always imagined it would be. And I'm not in the least tense!' She moved away jerkily until she stood apart from him.

Far enough that she thought she had put a safe distance between them.

Lucien was so aroused right now he didn't think the other side of the world would be far enough away to keep Cyn safe from him…

His meeting that afternoon had not gone well. No, that wasn't accurate. It hadn't been the meeting that was responsible for his feelings of impatience and dissatisfaction all afternoon. That had been due to the intrusive thoughts he'd had of Cyn all through that lengthy meeting—not just the silkiness of her skin, her responsive breasts, the delicious taste of her mouth, but also the fact that he *liked* her…her sense of humour, the way she answered him back, everything about her, damn it! It had caused Lucien to finally call a halt to negotiations and reschedule the meeting for another day next week.

Needless to say he had not been best pleased that he had allowed the distraction of those thoughts of Cyn to infringe on his business meeting, but one look at her tonight, dressed in those snug-fitting black denims and the delicate blue blouse, with the silky darkness of her hair loose about her shoulders, and his earlier feeling of irritated dissatisfaction had instantly been replaced by desire.

'I thought that I had been invited up here for dinner,' she snapped now. 'Not to witness a male strip show!'

Lucien made no effort to hold back his grin of satisfaction at her obvious discomfort at seeing his bare chest. It seemed only fair when he had thought of her all afternoon. When his shaft was now an uncomfortable, painful throb against his denims. 'I'm wearing more now than I would be on a beach,' he reasoned.

'Unless you haven't noticed, we don't happen to *be* on a beach.' She frowned. 'And I do not have any intention of providing your amusement for the evening.'

He eyed her mockingly. 'Oh, I haven't even begun to be amused yet, Cyn.'

'And as far as I'm concerned you aren't going to be, either!' She placed her glass down noisily on the coffee table before straightening and turning, with the obvious intention of walking out on him.

Lucien reached out and grasped her arm as she would have stormed past him—only to ease up on the pressure of that grasp as he saw the way she winced. 'Are your wrist and arm still hurting you?' he rasped.

'No. I—they're fine.' She gave a dismissive shake of her head, her eyes avoiding meeting his piercingly questioning gaze. 'You just caught me unawares, that's all.'

'I don't believe you.'

She sighed her impatience. 'I don't care whether or not— What are you doing?' she demanded as Lucien released her arm before moving his hands to the front of

her blouse, his fingers unfastening the tiny blue buttons.
'Lucien? Stop it!' She slapped ineffectually at his hands.

'I don't trust your version of "fine", Cyn. I intend to
see for myself,' Lucien muttered grimly as he continued
unfastening those buttons.

'Stop it, I said!' She pulled sharply away from him—a
move immediately followed by a delicate ripping sound
as Lucien refused to release his hold. The gauzy blouse
ripped completely away from the last remaining buttons,
leaving Cyn's breasts completely bared to his heated
gaze.

Full and beautifully sloping breasts…tipped by two
perfect rosy-red nipples…those nipples were plumping
and hardening in tempting arousal as Lucien continued
to look down at them appreciatively.

CHAPTER SIX

'I CAN'T BELIEVE you just did that!' Thia was the first to recover enough to speak, staring accusingly at Lucien even as her shaking hands scrabbled desperately to pull the two sides of her blouse together over her bared breasts, feeling mortified by her nakedness in front of a man she already found far too overpoweringly attractive for comfort.

Her knees had once again turned to the consistency of jelly at the heat she saw in those silver eyes...!

'I believe, if you think about it, you'll find that *we* just did that,' Lucien drawled hardly. 'You pulled away. I didn't let go.' He shrugged.

Thia bristled indignantly, clutching on to anger as a means of hiding her embarrassment—and arousal—at the continued heat in Lucien's gaze. 'You shouldn't have been unbuttoning my blouse in the first place!'

'I wanted to see your bruises. I still want to see them,' he added determinedly.

'You saw a lot more than my bruises!' she snapped. 'And I believe we've already had one discussion about my feelings concerning what you do or don't want. In this instance what you wanted resulted in the ruination of a blouse I was rather fond of and saved for weeks to buy.'

'I'll replace it for you tomorrow.'

'Oh, won't that be just wonderful?' She huffed her exasperation. 'I can hear your telephone conversation with the woman in the shop now—*Send a blue blouse round to Miss Hammond's suite at Steele Heights Hotel. I ripped the last one off her!*' She attempted to mimic his deep tones. 'Are you laughing at me, Lucien?' Thia eyed him suspiciously and she thought—was *sure*!—she saw his lips twitch.

He chuckled softly. 'Admiring the way you sounded so much like me.'

'Well, I certainly can't stay and have dinner with you *now*.'

'Why not?' All amusement fled and his expression darkened.

'Hello?' She gave him a pitying look. 'Ripped blouse and no bra?'

'I noticed that.' Lucien nodded, silver eyes once again gleaming with laughter even if his expression remained hard and unyielding. 'We've met three times now, and on none of those occasions have you been wearing a bra,' he added curiously.

Thia's cheeks blushed a fiery red as she thought of the revealing gown she had been wearing last night— no way could she have been wearing a bra beneath *that*. And the intimacy of Lucien's caresses in his office earlier today had shown him that she hadn't been wearing a bra under her pink crop top, either. As for ripping her blouse just now and baring her breasts…!

'I—the uniform I have to wear when I'm working at the restaurant is of some heavy material that makes me really hot, so I usually go without one and it's just become a habit,' she explained defensively.

'Don't get me wrong. I'm not complaining.'

'Why am I not surprised?' If she were honest, Thia's initial shock and anger were already fading and she now felt a little like laughing herself—slightly hysterically—at this farcical situation. Hearing her blouse rip, seeing the initial shock on Lucien's face, had been like something out of a sitcom. Except Thia didn't intend letting him off the hook quite that easily...

Oh, she had no doubt that ripping her blouse had been an accident, and that she was as much to blame for it as Lucien was. But if he hadn't been behaving quite so badly by insisting on having his own way—again!—he would never have been in a position to rip her blouse in the first place. Or to bare her breasts. And that really had been embarrassing rather than funny.

Besides, she really did find Lucien far too disturbing when he was only wearing a pair of faded denims and showing lots of bare, muscled flesh. Her ripped blouse was the perfect excuse for her to cry off having dinner with him this evening.

'We haven't talked about the Jonathan Miller situation yet.'

Lucien had just—deliberately?—said the one thing guaranteed to ensure Thia stayed exactly where she was!

Lucien had found himself scowling at the idea of Thia working in a public restaurant night after night, wearing no bra, with those delicious breasts jiggling beneath her uniform for all her male customers to see and ogle.

Just as it now displeased him that Cyn was so obviously rethinking her decision about not having dinner with him only because he had mentioned the Jonathan Miller situation.

The other man had physically hurt her, was responsible for her having had nowhere to sleep last night other
than that disreputable hotel, and yet Miller hadn't given
a damn what had happened to her when he'd thrown her
belongings haphazardly into a suitcase this morning and
handed them over to Lucien.

Worst of all, Lucien now knew, from his conversation with Miller, that the other man had been using Cyn
for his own purposes. He had believed—wrongly, as it
happened—that her presence in his apartment in New
York would give the impression that his affair with Simone Carew, was over. Something Cyn was still totally
unaware of…

'Well?' he rasped harshly.

She gave a pained frown. 'Perhaps you have a T-shirt
I could wear? And maybe you could find one for yourself while you're at it?' she added hopefully.

How did this woman manage to deflate his temper, to
make him want to smile, when just seconds ago he had
been in a less than agreeable mood at how distracted he
had been all afternoon? Because of this woman…

But smile he did as he crossed his arms in front of his
chest. 'It really bothers you, doesn't it?'

'All that naked manly chest stuff? Yes, it does.' She
nodded. 'And it isn't polite, either.'

'That was a rebuke worthy of my mother!' Lucien was
no longer just smiling. He was chuckling softly.

'And?'

'And far be it from me to disobey any woman who
can scold like my mother!'

'You're so funny.' She eyed him irritably.

He gave an unconcerned shrug. 'I'll get you one of

my T-shirts.' No doubt Cyn would look sexy as hell in one of his over-large tops!

Her eyes narrowed suspiciously. 'You're being very obliging all of a sudden.'

Lucien quirked a dark brow. 'As opposed to...?'

'As opposed to your usual bossy and domineering self—' She broke off to eye Lucien warily as he dropped his arms back to his sides before stepping closer to her.

'You know, Cyn,' he murmured softly, 'it really isn't a good idea to insult your dinner host.'

'Would that be the same dinner host who almost ripped my blouse off me a few minutes ago?'

The very same dinner host who would enjoy nothing more than ripping the rest of that blouse from her body! The realisation made Lucien scowl again.

This woman—too young for him in years and experience, and far too outspoken for her own good—made him forget all his own rules about the women in his life—namely, only older, experienced women, who knew exactly what they were getting—or rather what they were not going to get from him, such as marriage and for ever—when they entered into a relationship with him.

He'd had little time even for the *idea* of marriage after his parents had separated and then divorced so acrimoniously, and making his own fortune before he was even twenty-one had quickly opened his eyes to the fact that most women saw only dollar signs when they looked at him, not the man behind those billions of dollars.

So far in their acquaintance Cyn Hammond had resisted all his offers of help, financial or otherwise, and that pride and independence just made him like her more.

'Good point.' He straightened abruptly. 'I'll be back in a few minutes.'

* * *

Thia admired Lucien's loose-limbed walk as he left the room, only able to breathe again once she knew she was alone. She knew from that determined glitter in Lucien's eyes just now that she had only barely—literally!—managed to avert a possibly physically explosive situation. Just as she knew she wasn't sure if she had the strength of will to resist another one…

The truth was her breasts tingled and she grew damp between her thighs every time she so much as dared a glance at all that fascinating naked and bronzed flesh!

Lucien was without doubt the most nerve-sizzling and gorgeous man Thia had ever seen. His whole body was muscled and toned but not too much so, in that muscle-bound and unattractive way some men were. And as for the strength and beauty of that perfectly chiselled face…!

All that wealth and power, and the man also had a face and body that would make poets of both sexes wax lyrical. Hell, *she* was writing a sonnet in her head about him!

And now she was completely alone with him, in his fiftieth floor apartment, with her tattered and ripped blouse pulled tightly across her bare breasts…

She should have kept to her earlier decision to leave. Should have made her escape as quickly and as—

'Here you go—what is it?' Lucien questioned sharply, having come back into the room and seen how pale Cyn's face had become in his absence. Her eyes were dark and troubled smudges between those sooty lashes. 'Cyn?' he prompted again concernedly as she only continued to look at him nervously, with eyes so dark they appeared navy blue.

Her creamy throat moved as she swallowed before

speaking. 'I think it would be better if I left now, after all…'

Lucien frowned. 'What have you eaten today?'

She looked puzzled by the change of subject. 'No breakfast, but I bought a hot-dog from a street vendor on the way to the Empire State Building for lunch.'

'Then you need to eat. Put this T-shirt on and then we'll go into the kitchen and see what Dex has provided us with to cook for dinner.' He held out the white T-shirt he had brought back for her to wear, having pulled on a black short-sleeved polo shirt over his own naked chest. A naked chest that had seemed to bother her as much as she bothered him…

Her eyes widened. 'Does Dex do your food shopping for you, too?'

'When necessary, yes.'

'What else does he do for you…?'

'Many, many things,' Lucien drawled derisively.

'You probably wouldn't know how to go about buying your own groceries anyway,' she dismissed ruefully.

'Probably not,' he acknowledged easily. 'Does it bother you that we're eating here?'

Cyn shrugged. 'I just assumed you would be ordering hotel room service this evening.'

'Most of the time I do.' He nodded.

'But you decided tonight would be an exception?' she said knowingly.

'I just thought you would prefer to eat here. Don't tell me.' He grimaced. 'You don't know how to cook?'

'Of course I know how to—' She broke off, eyes narrowing suspiciously. 'You're challenging me to get your own way again, aren't you?'

He quirked a brow. 'Is it working?'

Some of the tension eased from her expression. 'Yes.'

He nodded. 'Then that's exactly what I'm doing.'

Cyn eyed him frustratedly. 'Why are you so determined to keep me here?'

Lucien had absolutely no idea! Especially when he had initially made the suggestion of dinner in his apartment just to see what Cyn's reaction would be. Boy, had *that* backfired on him! 'Why are you so determined to leave?' he came back challengingly.

'Yep, the face of an angel and the wiles of the devil...'

Lucien heard her mutter the words irritably. 'Sorry?' he said. He knew exactly what Cyn had said—he just wanted to see if he could get her to say it again. Especially the part where she said he had the face of an angel...

'Nothing.' Cyn refused to humour him and gave a rueful shake of her head. 'Okay, give me the T-shirt.' She took it out of his outstretched hand before holding it up defensively in front of her breasts. 'Why don't you just disappear off into the kitchen while I slip off my blouse and put this on?' she prompted as he made no effort to leave.

'And if I'd rather stay here and watch you slip off your blouse...'

He enjoyed the flush that instantly coloured her cheeks. Enjoyed teasing Cyn, full-stop. So much so that, despite her being so disruptive and stubborn, teasing her was fast becoming one of Lucien's favourite pastimes. Exclusively so.

'Life is just full of little disappointments!' she came back, with insincere sweetness.

'Oh, it wouldn't be a *little* disappointment, Cyn,' he assured her huskily. And it wouldn't be; Lucien could imagine nothing he would enjoy more than to see Cyn strip out of her blouse, allowing him to look his fill of those pert little breasts and plump, rose-coloured nipples.

'Go,' she instructed firmly.

'And you accuse *me* of being bossy...'

'You've made a fine art of it. I'm just doing it out of self-defence.'

Lucien gave a wicked 'wiles of the devil' grin. 'Do you need defending from me?'

She eyed him irritably. 'Now you're deliberately twisting my words.'

He shrugged. 'Maybe that's because you're trying to spoil my fun.'

She gasped. 'Because I won't let you stand there and gawp at me while I change my blouse?'

'I never *gawp,* Cyn,' he drawled derisively. 'If I stayed I would just stand here quietly and appreciate.'

Her face warmed. 'You aren't staying.'

Lucien gave another appreciative grin; she really was cute when she got her dander up.

Cute? He had never found a woman *cute* in his life! Until now...

Because Cyn, all hot and bothered and clutching his T-shirt tightly to her as if it were her only defence, was most definitely cute.

'Okay, I'll leave you to change,' he murmured dryly. 'I'll take the bottle of wine and glasses through with me.'

'Fine.' She nodded distractedly.

Anything to get him out of the room while she changed her top, Lucien acknowledged ruefully as he collected up the bottle of wine and glasses before leaving. As if such a flimsy barrier—*any* barrier!—could have stopped him if he had decided he wanted her naked!

* * *

'Did you have Dex follow me today…?' Thia prompted huskily when she entered the kitchen.

Lucien turned from taking food out of the huge chrome refrigerator that took up half the space of one wall in what was a beautiful kitchen—white marble floors again, extensive kitchen units a pale grey, a black wooden work table in the middle of the vast room, silver cooking utensils hanging from a rack next to a grey and white cooker. No doubt there was a dishwasher built into one of those cabinets, too.

He hadn't answered her question yet…

'Lucien?' she said softly as she lifted her replenished glass from the table and took a sip of red wine.

'I got so distracted by how sexy you look in my T-shirt that I've forgotten what the question was,' he came back dryly.

No, he hadn't. This man didn't forget anything. *Ever.* And his prevarication was answer enough. He *had* instructed Dex to follow her this afternoon. And Thia wasn't sure how she felt about that. Annoyed that he had dared to have her followed at all, but also concerned as to why he continued to feel it necessary…

And sexy was the last thing she looked in Lucien's white T-shirt. The shoulder seams hung halfway down her arms, meaning that the short sleeves finished below her elbows, and it was so wide across the chest it hung on her like a sack, so long it reached almost to her knees. Well…it didn't hang *completely* like a sack, Thia realised as she glanced down. Colour once again warmed her cheeks as she saw the way the T-shirt skimmed across the tips of her breasts. Across the hard, aroused thrust of her nipples!

Even so, *ridiculous* was the word Thia would have used to describe her current appearance, not sexy.

'*Did* you have Dex follow me today?' she repeated determinedly.

'I did, yes.'

'Can I ask why?' she prompted warily.

'You can if you can make salad and ask at the same time.' Lucien seemed totally relaxed as he placed the makings of a salad down on the kitchen table before returning to the fridge for steaks.

Thia rolled her eyes. 'I'm a woman, Lucien. Multitasking is what we do best.' She took the salad vegetables out of the bags and put them in the sink to wash them.

'That sounds…interesting.' He turned to arch mocked brows.

She was utterly charmed by this man when he became temptingly playful. And she shouldn't allow herself to be.

It wasn't just those twelve years in age that separated them, it was what Lucien had done in those twelve years that set them so far apart—as evidenced by all those photographs of him online, taken with the multitude of women he had briefly shared his life with. Or, more accurately, his bed.

And at the grand age of twenty-three Thia was still a virgin. Not deliberately. Not even consciously as in 'saving herself' for the man she loved and wanted to marry.

She had just been too busy keeping her life together since her parents died to do more than accept the occasional date, and very rarely a second from the same man. Jonathan had been the exception, but even he had become just a friend rather than a boyfriend. Thia had never been even slightly tempted to deepen their relationship into something more.

And yet in the twenty-four hours she had known Lucien Steele she seemed to have thought of nothing else but how it would feel to go to bed with him. To make love with him.

Weird.

Dangerous!

Because Lucien might desire her, but he didn't do falling in love and long-term relationships. And why should he when he could have any woman—as many women as he wanted? Except…

'What are you thinking about so deeply that it's making you frown…?' he asked huskily.

Thia snapped herself out of imagining how it would feel to have Lucien Steele fall in love with her. A ridiculous thought when she so obviously wasn't his type.

And yet here she was, in this apartment, with a relaxed and charming Lucien, and the two of them intended to cook dinner together just like any other couple spending the evening at home together.

She took another sip of wine before answering him. 'Nothing of any importance,' she dismissed brightly as she put the wine glass down to drain the vegetables. 'Do you have any dressing to go with the salad or shall I make some?'

'Can you do that?'

Thia gave him a scathing glance as she crossed the room to open the vast refrigerator and look inside for ingredients for a dressing. 'I'm a waitress, remember?'

'You're a student, working as a waitress in your spare time,' he corrected lightly.

She straightened slowly. 'No, I'm actually a waitress who's working for a degree in my spare time,' she insisted firmly. 'And you still haven't answered my original question.'

'Which was…?'

'Why did you have Dex follow me today?' she repeated determinedly, knowing that Lucien was once again trying to avoid answering one of her questions.

He shrugged. 'Dex suggested it was necessary. I agreed with him.'

'What does that mean?'

'It means that he was obviously as concerned about your walking about New York on your own as I was. You might have been robbed or attacked. Speaking of which…' Lucien strolled across the kitchen, checking her wrist first, which was only slightly reddened from where Jonathan's fingers had twisted it, before gently peeling back the sleeve of the white T-shirt. He drew in a hissing breath as he saw the livid black and blue bruises on the top of her arm.

'They look worse than they feel.' Thia pulled out of his grasp before turning to take down a chopping board and starting to dice vegetables for the salad. 'Isn't it time you started cooking the steaks…?' she prompted dryly.

'Deflection is only a delaying tactic, Cyn. Sooner or later we're going to talk about those bruises,' he assured her grimly.

'Then let's make it later,' she dismissed. 'Steaks, Lucien?' she repeated pointedly when she turned to find him still watching her from between narrowed lids.

He gave a deep sigh. 'Okay, Cyn, we'll do this your way for now,' he conceded. 'We'll eat first and then we'll talk.'

'It really is true what they say—men don't multi-task!' She smiled teasingly.

'Maybe we just prefer to do one thing at a time and ensure that we do it really, really well?' Lucien murmured huskily, suggestively, and made a determined effort to damp down the renewed anger he felt at seeing those bruises on Cyn's delicately lovely skin.

Colour washed over her cheeks. 'You're obviously wasting your talents as an entrepreneur, Lucien; you should have been a comedian.'

But what Lucien was actually doing was mirroring her own deflection...

Because he was once again so angry after seeing Cyn's bruises—bruises inflicted by Miller—that he didn't want to have to answer her question as to why he'd had Dex follow her on her outing this afternoon just yet.

Oh, he accepted that he would have to answer it some time—just not yet. Talking about the reason Dex had followed her to the Empire State Building earlier, and how his concern was directly linked to Jonathan Miller, was not conducive to the two of them being able to enjoy cooking and eating a meal together. And, despite Lucien's earlier irritation, he was totally enjoying Cyn's company.

'How do you like your steak?' he prompted as he moved to turn up the heat beneath the griddle, hoping he remembered how to cook steaks. Cyn's assumption earlier had been a correct one: it had been years since Lucien had cooked for himself or anyone else.

'Medium rare, please,' she answered distractedly as she put the salad into a wooden bowl. 'Are we eating in here or in the dining room?'

'Which would you prefer?'

Her brows rose. 'You're actually asking for my opinion about something now?'

Lucien turned to lean back against one of the kitchen cabinets. 'Smart-mouthed young ladies are likely to get their bottoms spanked!'

Her eyes widened. 'Dinner hosts who threaten their female guests are likely to get cayenne pepper sprinkled on their half of the salad dressing. What is it?' she questioned curiously as Lucien began to chuckle. 'You aren't used to being teased like this, are you?' she realised slowly.

'No, I'm not,' he conceded ruefully, unable to remember the last time anyone had dared to tease him, let alone argue with him in the way that Cyn so often did. 'My mother does it occasionally, just to keep it real, but only mom/son stuff.' He shrugged.

Cyn eyed him wistfully. 'Have you remained close to both your parents?'

He nodded. 'I don't see either of them as often as I could or should—but, yeah, I've stayed close to both of them.'

'That's nice.'

Lucien looked at her searchingly. 'Don't you have any family of your own?'

'None close, no.' She grimaced. 'Don't feel sorry for me, Lucien,' she added lightly as he still frowned. 'I had great parents. I lost them a little earlier than I would have wished or wanted, but I still count myself lucky to have had them to love and be loved by for seventeen years.'

The more Lucien came to know about Cynthia Hammond, the more he came to appreciate that she really was unlike any other woman he had ever known. So obviously beautiful—inside as well as out. And that outward beauty she could so easily have used to her advantage these past six years, if she had wanted to, by snaring herself a rich husband to support her. Instead she had chosen independence.

No feeling sorry for herself at the premature death of her parents. She was just grateful to have had them for as long as she had. And instead of bitching about the necessity to fend for herself after their deaths she had picked herself up and started working her way through university. And instead of bemoaning the fact that Jonathan Miller, a man she had believed to be her friend, had let her down royally since she'd come to New York she had done all she could to remain loyal to him.

It was fast becoming an irresistible combination to Lucien when coupled with the fact that she was so bright and bubbly she made him laugh, was mouthwateringly beautiful, and obviously intelligent.

She also, Lucien discovered a short time later—once the two of them were seated opposite each other at the small candlelit table in the window of the dining room, where they could look out over the city—ate with such passionate relish that he found himself enjoying watching her, devouring her with his eyes rather than eating his own food.

The expression of pleasure on her face as she took her first forkful of dessert—a New York cheesecake from a famous deli in the city—was almost orgasmic. Her eyes were closed, cheeks flushed, pouting lips slightly moist as she licked her tongue across them.

Lucien groaned inwardly as his erection, having remained painfully hard and throbbing inside his denims during the whole of dinner, rose even higher, seeming to take on a life of its own. To such a degree that he had to shift on his seat in order to make himself more comfortable!

Not that he was complaining. No, not at all. His thoughts had turned to the possibility of taking Cyn to his bed, of making love to her until he saw that same look on her face over and over again as he pleasured her to orgasm after orgasm.

'That was…indescribably good.' Thia sighed her pleasure as she placed her fork down on her empty dessert plate. 'Aren't you going to eat yours…?' She hadn't realised until now that Lucien was watching her rather than eating his own cheesecake.

Dinner with Lucien Steele had been far more enjoyable than she had thought it would be. The food had been good, and the conversation even more so as they'd discussed their eclectic tastes in books, films, television and art. Surprisingly, their opinions on a lot of those subjects had been the same, and the times when they hadn't been they had argued teasingly rather than forcefully. Thia liked this more relaxed Lucien. Too much so!

Lucien pushed his untouched dessert plate across the table towards her. 'You have it.'

'I couldn't eat another bite,' Thia refused, before chuckling huskily. 'I bet you're doubly glad now not to be seen out in public with me. I've realised since I've been here that it isn't really the done thing in New York for a woman to actually *enjoy* eating. We're supposed to just pick at the food on our plate before pushing it away uninterestedly. I've always enjoyed my food too much to be able to do that.' She gave a rueful shake of her head. 'Besides, it's rude not to eat when someone has taken you out for a meal or cooked for you. And I've enjoyed this much more than going out, anyway. Cooking dinner is probably the first normal thing I've done since coming to New York! Do you think…?' Her voice trailed off as she realised that Lucien had gone very quiet.

An unusual occurrence for him, when he seemed to have something to say on so many other subjects!

'Lucien…?' Thia eyed him warily as she saw the way his eyes glittered across at her with that intense silver light. His mouth had thinned, his jaw tensed—all signs, she recognised, of his displeasure.

What had she said to annoy him? Perhaps he hadn't liked her comment on the expectations of New York society? After all, he was a member of that society.

Whatever she had said, Lucien obviously wasn't happy about it…

CHAPTER SEVEN

THERE WAS A cold weight of anger in Lucien's chest, making it difficult for him to breathe, let alone speak. Cyn actually thought—she believed that he—

Lucien stood up abruptly, noisily, from the table, thrusting his hands into his pockets as he turned to look sightlessly out of the window, breathing deeply through his nose in an effort to control that anger. If he said anything now he was only going to make the situation worse than it already was.

'Lucien?'

The uncertainty, hesitation in Cyn's voice succeeded in annoying him all over again. Just minutes ago they had been talking so comfortably together—occasionally arguing light-heartedly about a book, a film or a painting they had both read or seen, but for the most part finding they shared a lot of the same likes and dislikes.

That easy conversation, coupled with Cyn's obvious enjoyment of the food they had prepared, had resulted in Lucien feeling relaxed in her company in a way he never had with any other woman. Not completely relaxed. He was too aware of everything about her for that: her silky midnight hair, those beautiful glowing cobalt blue eyes, her flushed cheeks, the moist pout of her lips, the way his borrowed T-shirt hugged the delicious uptilting curve of her breasts whenever she moved her arms to emphasise a point in conversation… But Cyn's complete lack of awareness of Lucien's appreciation of those things had been another part of his enjoyment of the evening. There had been none of the overt flirting that he experienced with so many other women, or the flaunting of her sexuality in an effort to impress him. Cyn had just been her usual outspoken self. An outspoken self that he found totally enticing…

And now this!

He drew a deep breath into his starved lungs before turning back to face her, his own face slightly in shadow as he stood out of the full glow of the flickering candlelight. 'You believe I made a conscious decision not to take you out to a restaurant for dinner this evening because I didn't want to be seen publicly in your company?'

Ah. That was the comment that had annoyed him…

Thia gave a dismissive shrug. 'It's no big deal, Lucien. Believe me, I've seen photos of the women you usually escort, and I don't even come close—'

'Seen how?' he prompted suspiciously.

She gave a self-conscious grimace. 'I—er—checked you out online earlier this evening,' she admitted reluctantly, wishing Lucien wasn't standing in the shadows so that she could see the expression on his face.

'Why did you do that?'

'Because I wanted to know more about the man I had agreed to have dinner with, alone in his apartment,' she came back defensively. 'I was using that sense of self-preservation you seem to think I have so little of.'

He gave a terse inclination of his head. 'And after

reading about me online, seeing photographs of the women I usually escort, you came to the conclusion I was deliberately keeping you hidden away in my apartment this evening because I didn't want to be seen out in public with you?'

'Oh, no. I decided that after you made the invitation earlier today,' Thia dismissed easily.

His brows rose. 'Can I ask why?'

She sighed heavily. 'When was the last time you cooked dinner for a woman in your apartment?'

'What does that—?'

'Just answer the question, please, Lucien,' she cajoled teasingly.

He shrugged. 'I think tonight is the first time I've cooked dinner in my apartment at all—let alone for or with a woman.'

'Exactly.' Thia had noticed earlier that none of the state-of-the-art equipment in the kitchen looked as if it had ever been used.

His mouth thinned. 'If you must know, I made the invitation initially because I suspected your having dinner alone with me here would throw you into something of a panic, and I wanted to see what you would do.'

'And I called your bluff and accepted.' She gave a rueful shake of her head.

'Yes, you did.' He nodded slowly.

'Probably best not to challenge me again, hmm?'

'I don't regret a single moment of this evening.'

Thia's cheeks bloomed with heated colour as she recalled the earlier part of the evening, when Lucien had ripped her blouse. 'You were also aware, because I told you so last night, that New York society has absolutely no interest in furthering its acquaintance with a wait-

ress from London. Just think how shocked they would
have been to see Lucien Steele in a restaurant with *me!*'

He breathed his impatience. 'I don't give a damn what
anyone else thinks.'

'I'm really not in the least offended by any of this,
Lucien.' Thia smiled. 'I had a good time this evening.
As for New York society…I don't enjoy their company
either, so why should it bother me what any of them
think of me?'

'Do you have so little interest in what *I* might think
of you?' he prompted softly.

That was a difficult question to answer. Thia was
so attracted to Lucien that of course it mattered to her
whether or not he liked her—just as it mattered what
he thought of her. But by the same token it also didn't.
Because they wouldn't ever see each other again after
tonight. Even the money for the suite, which Thia was
so determined to pay back to him, no matter how long
it took her to do so, could be sent to his office at Steele
Tower when the time came. They had no reason to see
each other again once she left here this evening. Which,
although disappointing, was just a fact of life. Their totally different lives…

'I like to think I'm a realist, Lucien,' she answered
lightly. 'Zillionaire Lucien Steele—' she pointed to him
'—and Cynthia Hammond, waitress/student, living from
payday to payday.' She pointed to her own chest. 'Not
exactly a basis for friendship.'

'I have no interest in being your *friend!*' he rasped
with harsh dismissal.

She flinched at the starkness of his statement. 'I believe I just said that—'

'I have no interest in being your friend because I want

to be your lover. Touch me.' Lucien stepped forward to grasp her hand impatiently in his before lifting it to the bulge at the front of his denims.

Evidence of an arousal that Thia had been completely unaware of until that moment. She couldn't possibly remain unaware of it now—not when she could feel the long, hard length of Lucien's swollen shaft, the heat of it burning her fingertips as she stroked them tentatively against him. Her eyes widened as she felt the jolt, the throb, of that arousal in response to her slightest caress.

She moistened her lips with the tip of her tongue and looked up at Lucien. 'Does one preclude the other…?'

His mouth twisted derisively. 'In my experience, yes.'

In Thia's limited experience too…

She'd only dated maybe half a dozen times these past six years, and had always ended up being friends with those men rather than lovers. Including Jonathan. Although she suspected that their friendship had ceased after his behaviour yesterday, and yet again this morning, when he had packed her belongings into her suitcase and handed it over to Lucien seemingly without a second thought as to where or how she was.

'Stop thinking about Miller,' Lucien rasped.

She blinked. 'How did you know—?'

'I think I'm intelligent enough to know when the woman I'm with is thinking about another man,' he bit out harshly, having known from the way Cyn's gaze had become slightly unfocused that her attention was no longer completely here with him. Which, considering her hand was currently pressed against his pulsing erection, was less than flattering.

She gave a rueful smile. 'I sincerely doubt it's happened to you often enough for that to be true.'

'It's never happened to me before, as far as I'm aware,' he grated.

He lifted her hand away impatiently before pulling her to her feet, so that she now stood just inches in front of him. His other hand moved beneath her chin to raise her face, so that she had no choice but to look up at him. 'And, yes, I was challenging you earlier. I wanted to unnerve you a little by inviting you to my apartment. But I did *not* have dinner with you here as a way of hiding you away. I'm insulted that you should ever have thought that I did.' He was more than insulted—he actually felt hurt that Cyn could believe him capable of behaving in that way where she was concerned...

Thia could see that he was. His eyes glittered dangerously, there was angry colour along those high cheekbones, his lips had thinned and his jaw thrust forward forcefully.

'I apologise if I was mistaken.'

'You were,' he bit out. 'You still are.'

She nodded; Lucien was too upset not to be telling her the truth.

'Have I succeeded in ruining the evening?' She looked up at him through long dark lashes.

Lucien eyed her impatiently. 'I have absolutely no idea.'

She drew in a shaky breath. 'How about we clear away in here while you decide?'

His eyes narrowed. 'Are you humouring me, Thia?'

The fact that Lucien had called her Thia for the first time was indicative of how upset he was. 'Is it working?' she deliberately used the same phrase he had to her earlier, when she had challenged him about always wanting his own way.

Some of the tension left his shoulders. 'Maybe a little,' he conceded dryly. 'And we can just blow out the candles in here and leave all this for housekeeping to clear away in the morning.' He indicated the dinner table beside them.

Thia's stomach did a somersault. 'Oh…'

He gave a rueful shake of his head. 'I have no idea how you do that…'

'Do what?' She looked up at him curiously.

'Make me want to laugh when just seconds ago I was so angry with you I wanted to kiss you senseless!' He gave a self-disgusted shake of his head as the last of his earlier tension eased from his expression.

'Senseless, hmm?' Thia eyed him teasingly. 'According to you, that wouldn't be too difficult!'

'See?' Lucien chuckled wryly, shaking his head.

The sudden hunger in Lucien's gaze told Thia this was the ideal time for her to suggest she return to her own suite in the hotel, to thank Lucien for dinner, and his company and conversation, and then leave, never to see or hear from him again.

It was the latter part of that plan that stopped her from doing any of those things… 'Does one preclude the other?' she repeated provocatively, daringly.

'You *want* me to kiss you senseless…?' he prompted gruffly.

She drew in a sharp breath, knowing this was a moment of truth. 'Even more than I enjoy watching you laugh,' she acknowledged shyly.

Lucien's piercing gaze narrowed on her searchingly. 'Be very sure about this, Thia,' he finally warned her. 'I want you so badly that once I have you in my bed I'm unlikely to let you out of it again until I've made love to you at least half a dozen times.'

Thia's heart leapt as he jumped from kissing her senseless to taking her to his bed. Her heart pounded loudly in her chest at the thought of all that currently leashed but promised passion. Of having this man— having *Lucien Steele!*—want to make love to her with such an intensity of feeling. It was an intensity of passion she didn't know, in her inexperience, that she could even begin to match…

But she would at least like to the opportunity to try!

'Can you do that? I thought that men needed to…to rest for a while…recuperate before…well, you know…'

He arched dark brows. 'Let's give it a try, shall we? Besides, I don't recall giving any time limit for making love to you those half a dozen times.'

No, he hadn't, had he? Thia acknowledged even as her cheeks burned. In embarrassment or excitement? She really wasn't sure! 'I only have one more full day left before I leave New York, and don't you have to go to work tomorrow?'

'Not if I have you in my bed, no,' Lucien assured her softly.

Thia's heart was now beating a wild tattoo in her chest and she breathed shallowly, feeling as if she were standing on the edge of a precipice: behind her was the safety of returning to her own hotel suite, in front of her the unknown of sharing Lucien's bed for the night.

She drew in a shaky breath. 'Well, then…'

Lucien's control was now so tightly stretched that he felt as if the slightest provocation from Cyn would make it snap. That *he* would snap, and simply rip that T-shirt off her in the same way he had her blouse earlier.

It was an uncomfortable feeling for a man who never lost control. Of any situation and especially of himself. But this woman—barely tall enough to reach his shoulders, so slender he felt as if he might crush her if he held her too tightly—had thrown him off balance from the moment he first saw her.

Just twenty-four admittedly eventful hours ago…!

'Well, then…what…?' he prompted slowly.

The slenderness of Cyn's throat moved as she swallowed before answering him. 'Let's go to bed.'

'No more arguments or questions? Just "Let's go to bed"?' He raised dark brows.

She moistened her lips with the tip of her tongue before replying huskily. 'I—if that's okay with you, yes.'

If it was okay with him?

If Cyn only knew how much he wanted to rip her clothes off right now, before laying her down on the carpet and just taking her, right here and right now, plunging into the warmth of her again and again, then she would be probably be shocked out of her mind. *He* was out of his mind—for this woman.

Which was the reason Lucien was going to do none of those things. He was balanced on the edge of his self-control right now, and needed to slow things down. For Cyn's sake rather than his own. Because he didn't want to frighten her with the intensity of the desire she aroused in him.

'It's more than okay with me, Cyn,' he assured her gruffly, blowing out the candles on the table and throwing the room into darkness before putting his arm about the slenderness of her waist as he guided her out of the dining room and down the hallway towards his bedroom.

Thia's nervousness deepened with each step she took down the hallway towards sharing Lucien's bed. To sharing Lucien Steele's bed!

Those other women—the ones she had seen online, photographed with Lucien—had all looked sophisticated and confident, and they no doubt had the physical experience, the confidence in their sexuality, to go with those looks. Whereas she—

For goodness' sake, she was twenty-three years old and she was going to lose her virginity some time—so why not with Lucien, a man she found as physically exciting as she did knee-meltingly attractive. A man who made her feel safe and protected as well as desired.

Was that *all* she felt for Lucien?

Or was she already a little—more than a little!—in love with him?

And wouldn't that be the biggest mistake of her life—in love with a man whose relationships never seemed to last longer than a month?

'Cyn?'

She blinked as she realised that while she had been so lost in thought they had already entered what must be the master bedroom—Lucien's bedroom. A huge four-poster bed dominated the shadowed room, and those shadows made it impossible for her to tell whether the black, white and chrome décor Lucien seemed to prefer had spilt over into his bedroom. The carpet beneath her feet was certainly dark, as were the curtains and the satin cover and cushions piled on the bed, but the actual colours eluded her in the darkness…

'Say now if you're feeling…less than sure about this,' Lucien prompted gruffly, his hands resting lightly on her waist as he turned her so that she was looking up at him.

The one thing Thia was totally sure about was that she wanted Lucien. Her body ached with that longing; her breasts were swollen and tingling, nipples hard and aroused, and there was a heated dampness between her thighs. At the same time she *so* didn't want to be a disappointment to him!

It would have been better if he had just made love to her right there in the dining room. If he hadn't given her time to think, to become so nervous.

But this was Lucien Steele, a man of sophistication and control. He wasn't the type of man to be so desperate for a woman he would rip her clothes off—well, apart from Thia's blouse earlier. But that had been an accident rather than passion! Or the type of man to make wild and desperate love to her.

Thia chewed worriedly on her bottom lip as she looked up into his hard and shadowed face, at those pale eyes glittering down at her intently in thc darkness. 'I am a little nervous,' she admitted softly. 'I'm not as experienced as you are, and there have been all those other women for you—' She broke off as he placed silencing fingertips against her lips.

'I'm clean medically, if that's what's bothering you.'

'It isn't,' she assured him hastily, her cheeks blushing a fiery-red. 'And I—I'm—er—clean too.' How could she be anything else when she had never been to bed with anyone?

He nodded abruptly. 'And that's the last time I want to talk about other people for either of us.'

'But—'

'Cyn, neither of us is experienced when it comes to each other.' He moved his hand to gently cup her cheek. 'Half the fun will be in learning which caress or touch pleases the other,' he added huskily.

Fun? Going to bed with a man, making love with him, was *fun?* Thia had never thought of it in quite that light before, but she had no reason to doubt what Lucien said. He had always been totally, bluntly honest when he spoke to her.

'You're right.' She shook off her feelings of nervousness and straightened determinedly. 'Is it okay if I just use the bathroom?'

'Of course.' Lucien released her before stepping back. 'Don't be long,' he added huskily as he opened the door to the adjoining bathroom and switched on the light for her.

Thia leant back weakly against the door the moment it closed behind her and she was alone in the bathroom, her legs shaking so badly she could no longer stand without that support at her back.

Lucien stared at that closed bathroom door for several seconds after Cyn had closed it so firmly behind her, a frown darkening his brow as he considered her behaviour just now. She was more than just nervous. She seemed almost afraid. Just of him? Or of any man?

Why? Had something happened to her in the past? Maybe even with Miller? Something to make her nervous about going to bed with another man? It seemed highly possible, when she'd admitted she *had* been thinking of the other man when he'd called her on it a few minutes ago. It made Lucien wish now that he had given in to the impulse he'd had this morning to punch the other man in the face as Miller threw Cyn's belongings into her suitcase without so much as a thought or a question as to what was going to happen to her.

Whatever the reason for Cyn's nervousness, Lucien didn't intend adding to it. He was glad now that he had shown such restraint a few minutes ago. He wanted to make slow and leisurely love to her, no matter the cost to his own self-control. Wanted to touch and pleasure Cyn until she could think of nothing else, no one else, but him and their lovemaking— —

Lovemaking? Was he actually falling in love with Cyn?

It was an emotion he had always avoided in the past, and his choice of women—experienced and self-absorbed —was probably a reflection of that decision. Until now. Cyn was like no other woman he had ever known. And, yes, she was slipping—already *had* slipped?—beneath his defences.

None of which he wanted to explore too deeply right now.

Lucien crossed the bedroom to turn on the bedside lamp before turning back the bedcovers and quickly removing his clothes. His shaft bobbed achingly now that it was free of the confines of his denims.

He lingered beside the bed, looking down at the black silk bedsheets as he imagined how right Cyn would look lying there, with that beautiful, pale, luminescent body spread out before him like a feast he wanted to gorge himself on. Just the thought of it was enough to cause his aching erection to throb eagerly, releasing pre-cum onto the bulbous tip before it spilt over and dripped slowly down his length.

Sweet heaven!

Lucien grasped his length before smoothing that liquid over it with the soft pad of his thumb, knowing he had never been this aroused before, this needy of any woman. Not in the way he now needed—desired— Cyn...

Thia studied herself critically in the mirror over the bathroom sink once she had taken her clothes off. Her face was pale, eyes fever-bright, her hair a silky black curtain across her bared shoulders. Her skin was smooth and unblemished, breasts firm and uptilting, tipped by engorged rosy-red nipples. Her waist was slender, hips flaring gently around the dark thatch of curls between her thighs, her legs long and slender.

She was as ready as she was ever going to be to walk out of here and go to bed with Lucien!

That courage didn't include walking out stark naked, though, and quickly she pulled on the black silk robe she had found hanging behind the bathroom door, tying the belt of what was obviously Lucien's own bathrobe tightly about the slenderness of her waist before taking a deep breath and opening the bathroom door, switching off the light...

Only to come to an abrupt halt in that doorway as she realised that Lucien had turned on a single lamp on the bedside table, allowing her to see that the bedroom was indeed decorated in those black, white and chrome colours Lucien favoured. Lucien himself was already lying in the bed, that bronzed chest bare, only a black silk sheet draped over him and concealing his lower body.

She had thought they would make love in the darkness—had imagined slipping almost anonymously beneath the bedcovers and then—

'Take off the robe, Cyn.'

She raised a startled gaze to Lucien and saw he was leaning up on his elbow, causing the muscles to bulge in his arm, as he looked across at her with those glittering silver eyes. The darkness of his overlong hair was now tousled and falling rakishly over his forehead, probably after he had removed his T-shirt.

He was utterly beautiful in the same way that a deadly predator was beautiful—with all the power in that sleek and muscled body just waiting to be unleashed.

'I want to look at you,' he encouraged gruffly.

Thia's throat had gone so dry she could barely speak. 'Doesn't that work both ways?'

'Sure.' The intensity of his gaze never left hers as he slowly kicked down the black silk sheet.

Thia's breath caught in her throat and she could only stand and stare. At the width of his shoulders. At his muscled chest covered in that misting of dark hair. She could now see that it trailed down over his navel and grew thicker at the base of his arousal.

Oh. Good. Grief.

That was never going to fit inside her!

Lucien was a tall man, several inches over six feet and his bronze-skinned body was deeply muscled, so it was no surprise that his aroused shaft was in perfect proportion to the rest of him—at least nine, possibly ten inches long, and so thick and wide Thia doubted her fingers would meet if she were to clasp them around it as she so longed, ached to do. Just as she longed to caress, to touch and become familiar with every perfect inch of him!

Even so, her wide gaze moved back unerringly to the heavy thrust of his arousal.

Maybe it was like those 'one size fits all' pairs of socks or gloves you could buy? Hadn't she read somewhere, in one of those sophisticated women's magazines often left lying around in a dentist's waiting room, that if a woman was prepared properly, with lots of foreplay, she was capable of stretching *down there,* accommodating any length or thickness—

'Cyn?'

Her startled gaze moved back up to Lucien's face and, her cheeks flamed with colour as she met the heat in his eyes. He looked across at her expectantly, his hand held out to her invitingly, obviously waiting for her to unfasten the robe and remove it completely before joining him in the bed…

CHAPTER EIGHT

LUCIEN TAMPED DOWN the urgency he felt to get out of bed and go to Cyn and instead waited patiently, allowing Cyn to take her time, to adjust. Allowing her to be the one to come *to* him.

They had all night—hours and hours for him to pleasure her into coming *for* him!

Right now her face was so pale that her ivory skin appeared almost translucent. Blue veins showed at the delicacy of her temples and her cobalt-blue eyes were dark and shadowed as she continued to look across at him, cheeks pale, her lips slightly parted, as if she were having trouble breathing.

'I'm starting to get a complex, Cyn,' he murmured ruefully.

Her startled gaze was quickly raised to his. 'You are…? But you're beautiful, Lucien,' she murmured huskily.

'So are you.' Lucien slowly lifted his arm to hold out his hand to her again, holding his breath as the nervousness in Cyn's gaze told him that she might turn tail and run if he made any sort of hasty move in her direction. Something he found surprisingly endearing rather than irritating.

Cyn was so different from the women he had been with in the past. Beautiful women, certainly, but it was usually a pampered and sometimes enhanced beauty, after hours spent at beauty salons and spas or beneath a plastic surgeon's knife. And all those women, without exception, had been confident of their perfectly toned bodies, of their sexual appeal.

Cyn, on the other hand, obviously had no time or money to spend at beauty salons or spas. The sleekness of her body was just as nature had intended it, as was her breathtaking beauty. A beauty that was all the more appealing because Cyn seemed so completely unaware of it, of its effect on him and every other man she came into contact with. The women in New York society might have no interest in furthering the acquaintance of student/waitress Cynthia Hammond from England, but Lucien very much doubted the men felt the same way!

And Lucien was the lucky man who had her all to himself—for tonight, at least…

Thia was frozen in place—couldn't move, couldn't speak, could only continue to stand in the bathroom doorway as she stared across at Lucien in mute appeal, inwardly cursing herself for her gauche behaviour but unable to do anything about it.

'Please, Cyn!' he said gruffly.

It was the aching need that deepened Lucien's voice to a growl which finally broke her out of that icy cage, causing Thia to take one step forward, and then another, until she finally stood beside the bed, allowing Lucien to reach out and enfold one of her trembling hands in his much warmer one.

He lifted it slowly to his lips, his gaze still holding

hers as those lips grazed the back of her knuckles, tongue rasping, tasting. 'You are so very beautiful, Cyn.'

The warmth of his breath brushed lightly against her over-sensitised skin. She swallowed. 'I believe you'll find the saying is *Beautiful as sin...*'

'Nothing could be as beautiful as you.' He gave a slow shake of his head.

At this moment in time, Thia finished ruefully inside her head. Right here and right now she had Lucien's complete attention. But tomorrow it would be different—

Oh, to hell with tomorrow!

For once in her carefully constructed life she was going to take not what was safe, or what she could afford, but what she *wanted.*

And tonight she so very much wanted to be here with Lucien.

She lowered her lashes and pulled her hand gently from his grasp, before moving to unfasten the belt of the robe, shrugging the black silk from her shoulders and hearing Lucien's breath catching in his throat as she allowed the robe to slide down her arms to fall onto the carpet at her feet. She was completely naked in front of him as she finally raised her lashes to look at him.

'You're exquisite,' Lucien groaned, taking the time to admire each and every curve and dip and hollow of her naked body before moving smoothly up onto his knees at the edge of the bed, nullifying the difference in their heights, putting his face on a level with hers as his arms moved about the slenderness of her waist.

Her hands moved up to clasp onto his shoulders as he pulled her in closer to him. Her skin felt so soft and she was so slender Lucien felt as if he could wrap his arms about her twice. His palms spread, fingers splayed across her shapely bottom, as he settled those slender curves into his much harder ones before touching his mouth lightly against hers.

Lucien moved his lips across her creamy soft cheek to the softness beneath her ear, along the column of her throat. The rasp of his tongue tasted the shady hollows at the base of her throat as one of his hands curled about the gentle thrust of her breast, the soft pad of his thumb unerringly finding, stroking the aroused nipple.

'Look at the two of us, Cyn,' he groaned throatily. 'See how beautiful we are together,' he encouraged as she looked down to where his hand cupped her breast. He looked at that contrast himself. Ivory and bronze…

Her skin looked so white against the natural bronze tone of Lucien's. Ice and fire. And fire invariably melted ice, didn't it?

Thia's inhibitions were melting, and her earlier apprehension along with it, as she twined her arms over those strong, muscled shoulders, her fingers becoming entangled in silky dark hair as she initiated a kiss between them this time—gentle at first, and then deeper, hungrier, as their passion flared out of control.

Lucien continued to kiss her even as Thia felt his arms move beneath her knees and about her shoulders. He lifted her easily up and onto the bed, lying her down almost reverently onto the black silk sheets before stretching his long length beside her, his gaze holding hers before his head lowered, lashes falling down against those hard cheekbones, and his lips parted. He drew her nipple into his mouth, gently suckling, licking that aroused nub, even as his hands caressed the ribcage beneath her breasts, the slender curve of her waist, before moving lower still.

Thia arched into his caresses as her nervousness faded completely and pleasure coursed through her—building, building, until she moved restlessly against him, needing more, wanting more. She was groaning low in her throat as she felt Lucien's fingers against the silky curls between her thighs, seeking and finding the nubbin hidden there and moving lower still, to where the slickness of her juices had made her wet, so very wet, circling, moistening her swollen lips.

His thumb pressed delicately against the nubbin above and still she wanted more, needed more. She felt as if she were poised on the edge of a precipice, one that burned. Flames were licking up and through her body, sensitising her to every touch of Lucien's hands, to every sweep of his tongue across the swollen hardness of her nipples, as he divided his attentions between the two, first licking, then suckling. Each lick and suck seemed to increase the volcanic pleasure rising between her thighs.

'Please, Lucien!' Her fingers tightened in his hair and she pulled his head up, forced him to look at her with eyes that glittered pure silver. His lips were swollen and moist. 'Please…!' she groaned beseechingly. 'Lucien…'

He moved so swiftly, so urgently, that Thia barely had time to realise he now lay between her parted thighs.

'You are so beautiful *here,* Cyn,' he murmured. His breath was a warm caress as the soft pads of his thumbs slicked her juices over those plump folds and the sensitive knot of flesh above. 'Look at us, Cyn,' he encouraged gruffly. 'Move up onto your elbows and show me those pretty breasts.'

Thia would have done anything Lucien asked of her at

that moment. Her cheeks were flushed, eyes fever-bright, as she looked down at him, at his hair midnight-black against the paleness of her skin, bronzed back long and muscled, buttocks taut.

His gaze held hers as he cupped his hands beneath her bottom and held her up and open to him. 'I'm going to eat you up, Cyn,' he promised, and his head lowered and his tongue swept, rasped against her slick folds.

Over and over again he lapped her gently, and then harder, until Thia was no longer able to hold herself up on her elbows as the pleasure grew and grew inside her. Lucien's fingers were digging almost painfully into the globes of her bottom as he thrust a tongue deep inside her slick channel, sending her over that volcanic edge as the pleasure surged and swelled, surged and swelled again and again, taking Thia into the magic of her first ever climax.

It was the first of many. Lucien continued to pleasure her, taking her up to that plateau again and again, each time ensuring that he took her over the edge and into the maelstrom of pleasure on the other side, until Thia's throat felt ragged and sore from the sobbing cries of each climax. Her body was becoming completely boneless as those releases came swifter and fiercer each time, and Lucien's arms were looped beneath her thighs now, holding her wider to allow for the ministrations of his lips and tongue, increasing her pleasure each and every time she came.

'No more, Lucien!' Thia finally gasped, her fingers digging into his muscled shoulders. Blackness had begun to creep into the edges of her vision and she knew she couldn't take any more. There was foreplay and then there was hurtling over the edge into unconsciousness.

Which was exactly what was going to happen if her body was racked by one more incredible climax! 'Please, Lucien. I just can't...' She looked at him pleadingly as he raised his head to look at her, his cheeks flushed, lips swollen and moist.

'I'm sorry—I got carried away. Are you okay?' He gave a shake of his head.

'Yes...'

'You just taste so delicious...' He groaned achingly as he moved up beside her, his hands shaking slightly as he cupped the heat of her cheek. 'Like the finest, rarest brandy. I just couldn't stop drinking your sweet essence. Taste yourself, Cyn,' he encouraged huskily, and brushed his lips lightly against hers.

The taste was sweet and slightly salty, with an underlying musk. Thia's cheeks blazed with colour at the knowledge that Lucien now knew her body inside and out, more intimately than she did. That he—

She tensed to stillness as the telephone began to ring on the bedside table. Lucien scowled his displeasure and didn't even glance at the telephone. 'Ignore it,' he rasped.

'But—'

'Nothing and no one is going to intrude on the two of us being together tonight. I won't allow it,' he stated determinedly.

'But it could be important—'

'Obviously not,' he murmured in satisfaction as the telephone fell quiet after the sixth ring, allowing him to reach out and remove the receiver to prevent it from ringing and disturbing them again.

He rolled onto his back, hands firm on Cyn's hips, and lifted her up and over him. Her thighs now straddled his, and the dampness of her folds pressed against the hardness of his shaft as she sat upright, the swell of her breasts, tipped by strawberry-ripe nipples, peeping through the dark swathe of her hair.

'Do you have birth control, Cyn?'

'I didn't think…' she groaned. 'I—no, I don't.' Her cheeks were fiery red. 'Do you?'

Lucien would have preferred there to be nothing between him and Cyn the first time he entered her, but at the same time he liked that her lack of protection indicated she wasn't involved sexually with any other man right now.

He reached out and opened a drawer on the side table before taking out a silver foil packet and opening it. 'Would you…?' he invited huskily.

'Me?' Her eyes were wide.

'Perhaps not.' Lucien chuckled softly before quickly dealing with it himself. 'I want to be inside you now, Cyn…' he said huskily. 'In fact if I don't get inside you soon I think I'm going to spontaneously combust.' He settled her above him. 'I promise I'll go slower next time, but for the moment I just need—'

'Next time…?' Cyn squeaked.

'You said earlier that you would stay with me until I had made love to you half a dozen times, remember?' Lucien gave a hard, satisfied smile.

She gasped. 'But I—I already—I've lost count of how many times I've already—'

'Foreplay doesn't count,' he dismissed. 'When I'm inside you and we climax together—something I'm greatly looking forward to, by the way—that's when it counts. And I want you so badly this time I'm not going to last,' he acknowledged.

He knew it was true. His liking for Cyn, his enjoyment of her company as well as her body, had enhanced their lovemaking to a pitch he had never known before...

Thia gasped. All those incredible, mind-blowing climaxes didn't *count?* He couldn't truly think that she was going to be able to repeat this past hour—or however long it had been since Lucien had started making love to her. She had completely lost track of time! If they did she wouldn't just lose consciousness, she would surely die. And wouldn't that look great on her headstone— *Here lies Cynthia Hammond, dead from too much pleasure!*

But what a wonderful way to go...

Emotion—love...?—swelled in Thia's chest as she looked down at the man sprawled beneath her on the bed. Lucien really was the most gorgeous, sexy man she had ever met- –breathtakingly handsome, elegantly muscled and loose-limbed. And he was all hers.

For the moment, that taunting little voice whispered again inside her head.

This moment was all that mattered. Because it was all there was for her and Lucien. They had no tomorrow. No future. Just here and now.

And she wanted it. Wanted Lucien.

She held that silver gaze with her own and eased up on her knees before reaching down between them, fingers light, as she guided his sheathed length to the slickness of her channel—only to freeze in place as she suddenly heard the unexpected sound of Mozart's *Requiem* playing!

'It's my mobile,' Lucien explained impatiently when he saw Cyn's dazed expression. 'Damn, it!' His hands slapped down forcefully onto the mattress beside him. He should have turned the damn thing off before making love with Cyn. Should have—

'You need to answer it, Lucien.' A frown marred Cyn's brow. 'It must be something important for someone to call again so quickly—and on your mobile this time.'

Nothing was more important at this moment than his need to make love with Cyn. *Nothing!*

'Lucien…?' she prompted huskily as his damned mobile just kept on playing Mozart's *Requiem*.

Which, in the circumstances, was very apt…

Talk about killing the moment! One interruption was bad enough. Lucien had managed to save the situation the first time, but he doubted he would be able to do so a second time.

A sentiment Cyn obviously echoed as she slid off and away from him, over to the side of the bed, before bending down to pick up the black silk robe from the floor. Her back was long and slender, ivory skin gleaming pale and oh-so-beautiful in the glow of the lamp, before she slipped her arms into the robe, pulling it about herself and then standing up to fasten the belt. She turned to face him.

'You have to answer the call, Lucien.' Her gaze remained firmly fixed on his face rather than lower, where he was still hard and wanting.

Oh, yes, there was no doubting he had to answer the call—and whoever was on the other end of it was going to feel the full force of his displeasure!

He slid to the side of the bed before reaching for his denims and taking his mobile out of the pocket to take the call. 'Steele,' he rasped harshly.

Thia winced at the coldness of Lucien's voice, feeling sorry for whoever was on the other end of that line. At the same time she couldn't help but admire the play of muscles across the broad width of Lucien's shoulders and back beneath that bronzed skin as he sat on the other side of the bed, his black hair rakishly tousled from her fingers earlier.

Earlier...

Her cheeks warmed as she thought of those earlier intimacies. Lucien's hands, lips and tongue caressing her, touching her everywhere. Giving pleasure wherever they touched. Taking her to climax again and again.

Her legs trembled just at remembering that pleasure—

'I'll be down in five minutes,' Lucien grated harshly, before abruptly ending the call and standing up decisively to cross the room and collect up the clothes he had taken off earlier, his eyes cold, his expression grimly discouraging.

Thia looked at him dazedly. He seemed almost unaware of her presence. 'Lucien...?'

He was scowling darkly as he turned to look at her. 'That was Dex,' he bit out economically. 'It appears that your ex-boyfriend is downstairs in Reception and he's been making a damned exhibition of himself!'

She gasped. 'Jonathan?'

Lucien nodded sharply. 'Unless you have any other ex-boyfriends in New York?'

She gave a pained wince at the harsh anger she heard in his tone. Misdirected anger, in her opinion. 'I told you—Jonathan was never my boyfriend. And isn't it more likely he's making an exhibition of himself in *your* hotel because you fired him from *Network* this morning?'

It was a valid, reasoned argument, Lucien acknowledged impatiently—but at the same time he knew he was just too tense at the moment to be reasoned with. Even by Cyn.

He had enjoyed this evening with her more than he had enjoyed being with a woman for a very long time— if ever. Not just making love to her, but cooking dinner with her, talking freely about everything and nothing, when usually he was careful of how much he revealed about himself to the women he was involved with—a self-defence reflex that simply hadn't existed with Cyn from the beginning.

And now *this*.

His mouth thinned with his displeasure. 'I apologise for being grouchy. I just—' He ran his hand through the dark thickness of his hair. 'I'll get dressed and go down and sort this situation out. I shouldn't be long. What are you doing…?' He frowned as Cyn turned towards the bathroom.

'Getting dressed so that I can come with you.'

'You aren't coming downstairs with me.'

'Oh, but I am,' she assured him.

'No—'

'Yes,' she bit out firmly, her hands resting on her hips as she raised challenging brows.

Lucien's nostrils flared. 'My hotel. My problem.'

'Your hotel, certainly. But we don't know yet whose problem it is,' she insisted stubbornly.

His jaw clenched. 'Look, Cyn, there are some things about Miller I don't believe you're aware of—'

'What sort of things?' She looked at him sharply.

'Things,' Lucien bit out tersely. This evening had already gone to hell in a handbasket. Cyn did not need to know about all of Jonathan Miller's behaviour, or the reason the other man had been using her, which was sure to come out if Miller was as belligerent as Dex had said he was. 'In the circumstances, the best thing you can do is—'

'Please don't tell me that the best thing I can do is to stay up here and make coffee, like a good little woman, and wait until the Mighty Hunter returns!' Her eyes glowed deeply cobalt.

Apart from the good little woman and Mighty Hunter crack, that was exactly what Lucien had been about to say. 'Well…maybe you could forget the coffee,' he said dryly.

'And maybe I can forget the whole scenario—because it isn't going to happen!' She thrust her hands into the pockets of his silk robe.

Lucien noted that it was far too big for her; it was wrapped about her almost twice, with the sleeves turned up to the slenderness of her wrists, and the length reached down to her calves—altogether making her look like a little girl trying to play grown-up.

'Dex has managed to take Miller to a secure room for the moment, but it could get nasty, Cyn.'

'I've been a waitress for six years; believe me, I know how to deal with *nasty*,' she assured him dryly.

Lucien was starting to notice that Cyn seemed to use the waitress angle as a defence mechanism. As if in constant reminder to herself, and more probably Lucien, of who and what she was…

Who she was to Lucien was Cynthia Hammond—a beautiful and independent young woman whom he admired and desired.

What she was to Lucien was also Cynthia Hammond—a beautiful and independent young woman whom Lucien admired as well as desired.

The rest, he realised, had become totally unimportant to him—was just background noise and of no consequence.

Not true of Cyn, obviously…

He drew in a deep breath. 'I would really rather you didn't do this.'

'Your opinion is noted.' She nodded.

'But ignored?'

'But ignored.'

'Fine,' he bit out between clenched teeth, knowing he couldn't like Cyn's independence of spirit on the one hand and then expect her not to do exactly as she pleased on the other. 'I'll be leaving in about two minutes. If you aren't ready—'

'I'll be ready.'

She hurried into the bathroom and closed the door behind her.

Lucien drew in several controlling breaths as he glared at that closed bathroom door, knowing that the next few minutes' conversation with Miller would in all probability put an end to Lucien and Cyn spending the rest of the night together…

CHAPTER NINE

'MAKING AN EXHIBITION of himself how?' Thia prompted softly.

Lucien was scowling broodingly where he stood on the other side of the private lift as it descended to the ground floor.

He was once again dressed in those casual denims and black T-shirt, although the heavy darkness of his hair was still tousled —from Thia's own fingers earlier, and also Lucien's own now as he ran his hands through it in impatient frustration. Probably because of her stubbornness in insisting on accompanying him downstairs rather than Jonathan's behaviour, Thia acknowledged ruefully.

Silver eyes glittered through narrowed lids. 'He came in and demanded to see me. According to Dex, once both the receptionist and the manager had told him I wasn't available this evening, Miller then decided to start shouting and hurling the potted plants about. When that failed to get him what he wanted he resorted to smashing up the furniture, which was when Security arrived and took charge of the situation.'

'How...?'

'Two of them lifted him up and carried him away to

a secure room before calling Dex,' Lucien explained grimly.

Thia winced as she pictured the scene. 'I can imagine Jonathan might be upset after what happened this morning, but surely this isn't normal behaviour?'

Lucien gave her an irritated frowning glance. 'Cyn, have you *really* not noticed anything different about him since you came to New York?'

Well…she *had* noticed that Jonathan was more self-absorbed than he'd used to be. That he slept the mornings away and barely spoke when he did emerge, sleepy-eyed and unkempt, from his bedroom. And he had insisted on the two of them attending those awful parties together every night, at which he usually abandoned her shortly after they had arrived. And he had been extremely aggressive at the Carews' party last night—she had the sore wrist and the bruises on her arms to prove that!

She chewed on her bottom lip. 'Maybe he's a little more…into himself than he used to be.'

'That's one way of describing it, I suppose.' Lucien nodded grimly, standing back as the lift came to a halt and allowing her to step out into the marbled hallway first.

Thia eyed him guardedly as she walked along the hallway beside him; Lucien obviously knew which room Jonathan had been secured in. 'How would *you* describe it?'

Lucien's mouth thinned. 'As the classic behaviour of an addict.'

She drew in a sharp breath as she came to an abrupt halt in the hallway. 'Are you saying that Jonathan is—that he's taking drugs?'

'Amongst other things.' Lucien scowled.

'He's drinking too?'

'Not that I know of, no.'

'Then what "other things" are you talking about…?' Thia felt dazed, disorientated, at Lucien's revelation about Jonathan. Admittedly Jonathan hadn't seemed quite himself since she arrived in New York, but she had put that down to reaction to his sudden stardom. It must be difficult coping with being so suddenly thrust into the limelight, finding himself so much in demand, as well as having so many beautiful women throwing themselves at him.

Lucien grimaced. 'This is not a good time for me to discuss this with you.'

'It's exactly the time you should discuss this with me,' Thia insisted impatiently. 'Maybe if someone had thought to discuss it with me earlier I might have been able to talk to him about it—perhaps persuaded him to seek help.' She gave a shake of her head. 'As things now stand he's not only messed up his career, but the rest of his life as well!'

Lucien frowned as he heard the underlying criticism in her tone. 'Damn it, Cyn, do *not* turn this around on me. Miller was given a warning about his behaviour weeks ago. In fact he's been given two warnings.'

'When, exactly?'

'The first was two months ago. And again about five weeks ago, when it became obvious he had taken no notice of the first warning. I have a strict no-drugs policy on all contracts,' he added grimly.

'What sort of warn—? Did you say *five weeks* ago…?' she prompted guardedly.

Lucien quirked dark brows. 'Mean something to you?'

'Jonathan visited me in London a month ago…' She chewed on her bottom lip. 'I hadn't seen him for almost three months, and he had only telephoned me a couple of times since he'd left for New York, and then he—he just turned up one weekend.'

Lucien nodded. 'And subsequently invited you to come and stay with him in New York?'

'How do you know that?'

He scowled. 'I just did the math, Cyn.'

'I don't understand…'

Lucien didn't see why he should be the one to explain Miller's behaviour, either. Cyn already considered him callous for firing Miller. He wasn't going to be the one to tell her that Miller had only invited her to New York as a cover for his affair with another—married!—woman!

The fact that Cyn was with him now would probably be enough for Miller to realise she must have been with Lucien in his apartment when Dex telephoned a short time ago. Add that to the fact that she was so obviously wearing a man's oversized T-shirt and Miller was sure to add two and two together and come up with the correct answer of four!

Which was precisely the reason Lucien hadn't wanted Cyn with him during this confrontation. Well, okay, it wasn't the whole reason. He really would have preferred it that Cyn stayed in his apartment, made coffee, like the good little woman, and waited for the Mighty Hunter to return. He wanted to protect her from herself, if necessary. As it was, he somehow doubted that Cyn would be returning to his apartment tonight at all…

'Could we get a move on, do you think?' Lucien snapped tersely, giving a pointed glance at his wristwatch. 'I told Dex I'd be there in five minutes and it's been over ten.'

Cyn blinked at his vehemence. 'Of course. Sorry.'

She grimaced as she once again fell into step beside him, leaving Lucien feeling as if he had just delivered a kick to an already abused and defenceless animal.

Not that he thought of Cyn as defenceless—she was too independent, too determined ever to be completely that. But he had no doubt that Miller's real reason for inviting her to come to New York was going to upset her.

It was hard to believe, considering the tension between them now, that the two of them had been making love just minutes ago—that he now knew Cyn's body intimately, and exactly how to give her pleasure.

On the plus side, his erection had got the message that the night of pleasure was over and had deflated back to normal proportions. Not that it would take much to revive his desire…just a sultry look from cobalt blue eyes, the merest touch of Cyn's hand anywhere on his body. Which Lucien already knew wasn't going to happen in the immediate future. If ever again.

Another reason for Lucien to be displeased at Miller's increasingly erratic behaviour. If he needed another reason. Which he didn't. Forget the drugs and the affair with Simone Carew; the man was an out-and-out bastard for attempting to use Cyn as a shield for that affair. Not that the ruse had worked, but that didn't excuse Miller's callous behaviour towards a woman who had thought he was her friend. Or the fact that the other man had held Cyn so roughly the evening before he had succeeded in badly bruising her.

And Cyn was annoyed with *him*, because he had fired Miller for blatant and continuous breach of contract!

'Dex.' He greeted the other man grimly as they turned a corner and he saw his bodyguard standing outside a door to the right of the hallway. 'He's in there?' He nodded to the closed door.

Dex scowled. 'Yes.'

'And has he quietened down?'

'Some.' Dex nodded grimly before shooting Cyn a frowning glance. 'I don't think it's a good idea for Miss Hammond to go in with you. Miller is violent, and he's also throwing out all sorts of accusations,' he warned with a pointed glance at Lucien.

'I'm going in,' Cyn informed them both stubbornly.

Lucien's mouth tightened. 'As you can see, Dex, Miss Hammond insists on accompanying me.'

'It's really not a good idea, Miss Hammond,' Dex warned her gently.

It was a gentleness Lucien hadn't even known the other man was capable of. No doubt Dex found Cyn's beauty and her air of fragility appealing—but the fragility was deceptive. There was a toughness beneath that fragile exterior that made Lucien think Cyn would be capable of stopping a Humber in its tracks if she chose to do so! Hopefully Dex was concerned in a fatherly sort of way, because Lucien knew he wouldn't be at all happy with his bodyguard having a crush on the woman he—

The woman he what…? Was falling in love with? Was already in love with?

Now was hardly the time for Lucien to think about what he might or might not be feeling for Cyn. Damn it, they had met precisely three times now, and shared one evening together. Admittedly it had been the most enjoyable—and arousing!—evening Lucien had ever spent with a woman…

The depth of his desire for Cyn was unprecedented—

to the point that Lucien really had thought he was going to come just at the taste of her on his tongue.

And for the early part of the evening she had believed him to have deliberately hidden her away in his apartment because he didn't want to be seen in public with her. She may still believe that, for all he had denied it.

Damn it, he should have tanned her backside earlier rather than making love to her!

'I appreciate your concern, Dex.' Thia answered the older man softly. 'But Jonathan is my friend—'

'No. He really isn't,' Lucien rasped harshly.

'And I have every intention of speaking with him tonight,' she continued firmly, at the same time giving Lucien a reproving frown.

'I agree with Mr Steele,' Dex murmured regretfully. 'Mr Miller's behaviour earlier was…out of control,' he added.

Thia had come to like and trust this man over the past couple of days—how could she *not* like and trust a man who had stood guard all night outside her bedroom in that awful hotel in order to ensure she came to no harm from any of the staff or other guests staying there? In fact she felt slightly guilty now, for thinking Dex looked like a thug the first time she had seen him. He might look tough, but she didn't doubt there was a heart of gold under that hard exterior.

And she valued his advice now—as she did Lucien's. Although his scowling expression indicated he thought otherwise! She just didn't feel she could abandon Jonathan when he so obviously needed all the friends he could get. She had no doubt that all those shallow people who had been all over Jonathan at those celebrity parties would drift away the moment they knew he had been dropped as the star of *Network*.

'I appreciate your concern, Dex.' She smiled her gratitude as she placed a hand lightly on his muscled forearm. 'I really do.'

'But she's going to ignore it,' Lucien said knowingly.

Her smile faded as she turned to face him, knowing how displeased he was with her by the coldness in his eyes as he looked down the length of his nose at her, but unable to do anything about it.

She accepted, despite that interruption to their lovemaking, that Lucien had become her lover this evening—was closer to her and now knew her more intimately than any other man ever had. But by the same token she had been friends with Jonathan for two years now, and she didn't desert her friends. Especially when one of those friends was so obviously in trouble.

She drew in a deep, steadying breath. 'Yes, I'm afraid I am.'

Lucien had known she would. She had to be the most irritatingly stubborn woman he had ever known!

As well as being the most beautiful—inside as well as out. And the funniest. Her comments were sometimes totally outrageous. She was also the sexiest woman Lucien had ever known. And definitely the most responsive!

That in itself was such a turn-on—an aphrodisiac. Lucien was an accomplished lover, and had certainly never had any complaints about his sexual technique, his ability to bring a woman to climax, or in finding his own release. But with Cyn there had been no need for that measured and deliberate technique—just pure pleasure as, after her initial shyness, she had held absolutely nothing back and responded to his lightest touch, at the same time heightening his own pleasure and arousal.

To such an extent that Lucien knew Cyn was fast becoming his own addiction…

And yet here they were at loggerheads again, just minutes later—and over Jonathan Miller, of all people. A man Lucien didn't consider as being good enough to lick Cyn's boots, let alone to deserve her loyalty and friendship.

'Fine,' he bit out harshly before turning away. 'You had better unlock the door and let us in, then, Dex. The sooner we get this over and done with the better for all of us,' he added grimly.

'Lucien…?' Cyn prompted almost pleadingly.

'You've made your decision, Cyn.' He rounded on her angrily, hands clenching at his sides. 'I only hope you don't live to regret it. No, damn it, I *know* you're going to regret it!' He glared down at her.

Thia had a sinking feeling she would too… Both Dex and Lucien seemed convinced of it, and she had no reason to distrust the opinion of either man.

Yes, Jonathan had been less than a polite host since she'd arrived in New York—to the point where his behaviour the previous evening meant she'd had no choice but to move out of his apartment. She just couldn't quite bring herself to turn her back on him if he needed a friend.

Lucien followed Dex into the room, the two of them blocking her view of Jonathan until they moved aside and Thia finally saw him where he stood silhouetted against the darkness of the window. He looked a mess: his denims were covered in soil—from the pot plants he had thrown about the hotel reception?—his T-shirt was ragged and torn, but it was the bruises on his face and the cut over one eye that dismayed her the most.

His lips curled back into a sneer as he saw the shocked expression on her face. 'You should see the other guy!'

'The "other guy" is at the hospital, having stitches put in the gash to the head he received when you smashed a lamp over him,' Lucien rasped harshly.

Jonathan turned that sneering expression onto the older man. 'He shouldn't have got in my way.'

'Watch your mouth, Miller. Unless you want him to press charges for assault,' Lucien warned grimly.

Thia paled at the knowledge that Jonathan had attacked another man with a lamp, necessitating that man needing to go to the hospital for stitches. 'You're just making the situation worse, Jonathan—'

'Exactly what are *you* doing here, Thia?' Jonathan turned on her, eyeing her speculatively as he took in the whole of her appearance in one sweeping glance. 'You look as if you just fell out of bed. Oh. My. God.' He gave a harsh laugh as he turned that speculative gaze on Lucien and then back to Thia. 'You just fell out of *his* bed! How priceless is that—'

She winced. 'Jonathan, don't.'

'Shut up, Miller,' Lucien bit out coldly at the same time.

'The prudish Thia Hammond and the almighty Lucien Steele!' Jonathan ignored them both as he laughed all the harder at a joke obviously only he appreciated.

Thia felt numb. Lucien was obviously icily furious. Dex remained stoically silent.

Jonathan's humour was so derisive and scathing Thia felt about two inches high—as he no doubt intended her to do. 'You aren't helping, Jonathan.'

'I have nothing left to lose,' he assured her scornfully as he gave a shake of his head. 'You stupid little fool—don't you know that he's just using you to get back at me?' He looked at Thia pityingly.

'You're the one who used her, Miller,' Lucien scorned icily.

Jonathan glared. 'I tried to convince you that Thia and I were involved, yes. In the futile hope of getting you off my back. But what you've done tonight—seducing Thia—is ten times worse than anything I did!' He gave a disgusted shake of his head before turning to Thia with accusing eyes. 'Damn it, Thia, we actually dated for a while two years ago—until you made it obvious you weren't interested in me in that way. And yet you only met Steele yesterday and already you've been to bed with him! Un-bloody-believable!' He eyed her incredulously.

When he put it like that it *was* pretty incredible, Thia acknowledged with an inner wince. Not that she and Lucien had completely consummated their lovemaking, but that was pure semantics. After the number of times Lucien had brought her to sobbing orgasm he was definitely her lover. A man, as Jonathan had just pointed out, she had only known for twenty-four hours…

Lucien had heard enough—seen enough. Cyn's face was tinged slightly green and she was swaying slightly, as if she was about to pass out! 'I suggest we talk about this again tomorrow, Miller,' he snapped icily. 'When you've had a chance to…calm down.' He eyed the other man disgustedly, knowing by Miller's flushed cheeks and over-bright eyes that he was high on something—something he needed to sleep off overnight. Preferably with Dex keeping a sharp eye on him to ensure he didn't take anything else.

'You would no doubt prefer it if Thia didn't hear all the sordid details?' the younger man taunted.

Lucien shrugged. 'They're your sordid details.'

'Not all of them,' Miller challenged. 'Something I'm pretty sure you won't have shared with Thia either.'

Lucien's mouth tightened. 'Not only do your empty threats carry no weight with me, but they could be decidedly dangerous. To your future career,' he added softly.

'You don't think Thia has a right to know that the *real* reason you've been trying to break my contract the last couple of months—the reason for your being with her tonight—is because I've been having an affair with the woman I seduced out of *your* bed?'

'We both know that isn't true, Miller.' Lucien's teeth were clenched so tightly his jaw ached.

'Do we?'

'Yes!' he rasped. 'Something I will discuss with you in more detail tomorrow,' he added determinedly.

'And will you also fill me in on all the juicy details of how you succeeded in seducing and deflowering the Virgin Queen?' Miller came back tauntingly.

'What the hell...?' Lucien muttered.

'It's what I've always called Thia in my mind.' The other man grinned unrepentantly.

Lucien stilled as all thought of Miller's accusations fled his mind. Barely breathing, he felt his heart pounding loudly in his chest as he gave Cyn a brief disbelieving glance—just long enough to show him that she had somehow managed to go even paler. Her cheeks were now paper-white.

The Virgin Queen?

Was it possible that on this subject at least Miller might be telling the truth and Cyn had been a virgin?

Correction: she was still technically a virgin—despite the intensity of their lovemaking earlier.

Had Lucien taken a virgin to his bed and not even known it? Would he only have realised it the moment he ripped through that delicate barrier?

Lucien was the one who now felt nauseous. Sick to his stomach, in fact, at how close he had come to taking Cyn's innocence without even realising until it was too late.

Perhaps he should have known.

He had noted that disingenuous air about her the first time they met. There had also been her shyness earlier, in regard to her own nudity as much as his. Her confusion when he had assured her he had a clean bill of health and her hesitant confirmation that she did too. And the glaringly obvious fact that Cyn wasn't on any birth control.

Because she was a virgin.

Even during the wildness of his youth Lucien had never taken a virgin to his bed—had stayed well away from any female who looked as if she might still be one. A woman's virginity was something to be valued—a gift—not something to be thrown away on a casual relationship, and Lucien had never felt enough for any of the women he had been involved with to want to take a relationship any further.

What had Cyn been thinking earlier?

Maybe she hadn't been thinking at all? Lucien knew he certainly hadn't. He had been too aroused, too caught up in the intensity of his desire for Cyn—of his growing addiction to her—to be able to connect up the dots of her behaviour and their conversation and realise exactly how innocent she was. As it was, he had been on the point of thrusting into her, of taking her innocence, when the ringtone of his mobile had interrupted them.

Sweet, merciful heaven…!

CHAPTER TEN

'LUCIEN—'

'Not now, Thia.'

She almost had to run to keep up with Lucien's much longer strides, and Jonathan's mocking laughter followed them as they walked down the deserted marble hallway towards where the main lifts were situated, in the reception area of the hotel. The lifts Thia would need to use if she was returning to her suite on the tenth floor. Which it seemed she was about to do...

'Is Dex going to stay with Jonathan tonight?' Thia hadn't been able to hear all the softly spoken conversation that had taken place between Lucien and Dex before Lucien had taken a firm hold of her arm and escorted her from the room, but she had gathered that Dex intended taking Jonathan out of the back entrance of the hotel and then driving him to his apartment.

Lucien nodded abruptly. 'If only to make sure he stays out of trouble for the rest of the night.'

She winced. 'Is the drug thing really that bad?'

'Yes,' he answered grimly.

Thia frowned. 'Lucien, what did Jonathan mean? He seemed to be implying that there was a woman involved in your decision to fire him from *Network*?'

Lucien turned to look down at her with icy silver eyes. 'I don't think that's the conversation we should be having right now, Thia.'

The fact that he kept calling her Thia in that icily clipped tone was far from reassuring... Not that she wasn't totally aware of the reason for Lucien's coldness. It was as if an arctic chill had taken over the room the moment Jonathan had so baldly announced her virginity. Lucien's shocked reaction to that statement had been unmistakable. As if she had a disease, or something equally as unpleasant! Good grief, he had been a virgin himself once upon a time—many years ago now, no doubt, but still...

'I don't understand why you're so annoyed.' She frowned. 'It's my virginity, and as such I can choose to lose it when I damn well please. It's no big deal.'

'I'm guessing that's why you've waited twenty-three years to even think about doing so?'

Thia smarted at his scathing tone. 'It isn't the first time I've considered it—and that's my bruised arm, Lucien!' she complained, when his fingers tightly grasped the top of her arm as he came to a halt in the deserted hallway before swinging her round to face him.

He released her as abruptly, glaring down at her, nostrils flaring as he breathed deeply. 'What the hell were you thinking, Thia? What were you doing going alone to a man's apartment at all?'

'Accepting an invitation to dinner in a man's apartment isn't saying *Here I am—take me to bed!*'

'It's been my experience that that depends on the woman and her reasons for accepting the invitation.'

She bristled. 'I don't think I like the accusation in your tone.'

'Well, that's just too bad,' he bit out harshly. 'Because my tone isn't going to change until I know exactly why you went to bed with me earlier this evening!'

Her cheeks blazed with colour. 'I thought I was making love with a man whom I desired and who also desired me!'

His jaw tightened. 'Not good enough, Thia—'

'Well, it's the only explanation I have. And stop calling me that!' Tears stung her eyes.

'It's your name,' he dismissed curtly.

'But *you've* never called me by it.' She blinked back those heated tears. 'And I—I liked it that only you had ever called me Cyn,' she admitted huskily, realising it was the truth. She had found Lucien's unique name for her irritating at first, but had very quickly come to like that uniqueness.

His nostrils flared in his impatience. 'Answer the damned question, Thia!'

'Which one?' she came back just as angrily. He'd called her that name again. 'Why did I decide to have dinner alone with you in your apartment this evening? Or why did I choose you as the man to whom I wanted to lose my virginity? Or perhaps to you they're one and the same question?' she challenged scornfully. 'You obviously think that I had pre-planned going to bed with you this evening! That I was attempting to—to entrap you into—into *what*, exactly?' Thia looked at him sharply.

Lucien was still too stunned at the knowledge of Cyn's virginity—at the thought of her never having been with anyone else—to be able to reason this situation out with his usually controlled logic. As a consequence he was talking without thinking about what he was saying, uncharacteristically shooting straight from the hip. But, damn it, if his mobile had rung even a few seconds later—!

'Damned if I know,' he muttered exasperatedly.

'Oh, I think you *do* know, Lucien.' Cyn's voice shook with anger. 'I think you've decided—that you believe—I deliberately set out to seduce you this evening.'

'I believe *I* was the one who did the seducing—'

'Ah, but what if I'm clever enough to let you *think* you did the seducing?' she taunted, eyes glittering darkly.

He gave a rueful shake of his head. 'You aren't—'

'It's a pity you asked about birth control, really,' she continued without pause. 'Otherwise I might even have discovered I was pregnant in a few weeks' time. And wouldn't that have been wonderful? I can see the headlines in the newspapers now—*I had Lucien Steele's lovechild!* Except we aren't in love with each other, and there isn't ever going to be a child—'

'Stop it, Cyn!' he rasped sharply, reaching up to grasp her by the shoulders before shaking her. 'Just *stop* it!'

'Let me go, Lucien,' she choked. 'I don't like you very much at the moment.' Tears fell unchecked down the paleness of her cheeks, her eyes dark blue pools of misery.

Lucien didn't like himself very much at the moment either. And it was really no excuse that he was still in shock from Miller's 'Virgin Queen' comment. His knee-jerk angry comments had now made Cyn think—believe—that he was angry about her virginity. When in actual fact he felt like getting down on his knees and worshipping at her beautiful feet. A woman's virginity was a gift. A gift Cyn had been about to give to *him* this evening. The truth was he was in total awe at the measure of that gift.

And he had made her cry. That was just unacceptable.

He released her shoulders before pulling her into his arms—a move she instantly fought against as she tried to push him away, before beating her fists against his chest when she failed to release herself.

'I said, let me go, Lucien!' She glared up at him as he still held her tightly against his chest.

'Let me explain, Cyn—'

'I have questions I want answered too, Lucien. And so far you've refused to answer any of them. Including explaining about this woman Jonathan reputedly stole from you—'

'I don't consider Miller's fantasies as being relevant to our present conversation!' He scowled darkly.

'And I disagree with that opinion. Jonathan said that the two of us making love together this evening was deliberate on your part—that you seduced me to get back at him—'

'Does that *really* sound like something I would do?' he grated, jaw clenched.

'Any more than entrapment sounds like something I would do?' she came back tauntingly. 'I don't really know you, Lucien...'

'Oh, you know me, Cyn,' Lucien assured her softly. 'In just a few short days I've allowed you to know me better than anyone else ever has. And the conversation we need to have is about what happened between the two of us this evening.'

'I think we—you, certainly—have already said more than enough on that subject!' she assured him firmly.

'Because I was understandably stunned at learning of your—your innocence?'

'Was that you being stunned? It looked more like shock to me!'

'You're being unreasonable, Cyn—'

'Probably because I *feel* unreasonable!' Cyn gave another push against his chest with her bent elbows, those tears still dampening her cheeks. 'So much has happened this evening that I—Lucien, if you don't release me I'm going to start screaming, and I think the other guests staying at the hotel have already witnessed enough of a scene for one evening!'

'You're upset—'

'Of *course* I'm upset!' Cyn stilled to look up at him incredulously. 'I've just learnt that the friend I came to New York to visit has not only become involved in taking drugs, but has also been using me to hide his affair with another woman. Add to that the fact that the man I had dinner with and made love with earlier this evening also seems to have been involved with that woman—'

'I'm not involved with anyone but you.'

'I think that gives me the right to be upset, don't you?' she continued determinedly.

Lucien frowned his own frustration with the situation as he released her, before allowing his arms to drop slowly back to his sides, knowing he had handled this situation badly, that his first instinct—to kneel and worship at Cyn's feet—was the one he should have taken.

'I apologise. It— I— It isn't every day a man learns that the woman he has just made love with is a virgin.'

'No, I believe we're becoming something of an endangered species.' She nodded abruptly. 'Thank you for the fun of cooking dinner together this evening, Lucien. I enjoyed it. The sex too. The rest of the evening… Not quite so much.' She stepped back. 'I'll make sure I have your T-shirt laundered and returned to you before I leave on Saturday—'

'Do you think I give a damn about my T-shirt?' he bit out in his frustration with her determination to leave him.

'Probably not.' She grimaced. 'I'm sure you have dozens of others just like it. Or you could *buy* another dozen like it! I would just feel better if I had this one laundered and returned to you.'

So that she didn't even have *that* as a reminder of him once she had returned to her life in London, Lucien guessed heavily.

Lucien wouldn't need anything to remind him of Cyn once she had gone.

He had spoken the truth when he'd told her that he had been more open, more relaxed in her company, than he ever had with any other woman.

As for the sex…!

He'd had good sex in his life, pleasurable sex, and very occasionally mechanical sex, when mutual sexual release had been the only objective, but he'd never had such mind-blowing and compatible sex as he'd enjoyed tonight with Cyn, where the slightest touch, every caress, gave them both unimagined pleasure.

He had always believed that sort of sex had to be worked at, with the two people involved having a rapport that went beyond the physical to the emotional.

He and Cyn had something between them beyond the physical. Lucien had known Cyn a matter of days, and yet the two of them had instinctively found that rapport. In and out of bed. Only to have it all come crashing down about their heads the moment Dex rang to tell them of Miller's presence downstairs in the hotel reception area.

Not only that, but Cyn was a virgin, and now that Lucien knew that he realised that her shyness earlier was an indication that she was an inexperienced virgin. A *very* inexperienced virgin, who had climaxed half a dozen times in his arms. Which was surely unusual— and perhaps an indication that she felt more for him than just physical attraction?

Or was that just wishful thinking on his part...?

Lucien didn't know any more. Had somehow lost his perspective. On everything. A loss that necessitated in him needing time and space in which to consider exactly what he felt for Cyn. Time the mutinously angry expression on Cyn's face now told him he simply didn't have!

'Fine.' He tersely accepted her suggestion about returning the T-shirt. 'But I'll see you again before you leave—'

'I don't think that's a good idea.' She backed up another step, putting even more distance between the two of them.

Lucien scowled darkly across that distance. 'You're being unreasonable—'

'Outraged virgin unreasonable? Or just normal female unreasonable?' she taunted with insincere sweetness.

'Just unreasonable,' he grated between clenched teeth, not wanting to lose his temper and say something else he would have cause to regret. The fact that he was in danger of losing his temper at all was troubling. He *never* lost his control—let alone his temper. Tonight, with Cyn, he had certainly lost his control, and his temper was now seriously in danger of following it. 'You're putting words into my mouth now, Cyn,' he continued evenly. 'And we *will* see each other again before you leave. I'll make sure of it.'

She raised midnight brows. 'I'd be interested to know how.'

Lucien gave a humourless smile. 'I believe, ironically, that you're travelling back to London on Saturday on the Steele Atlantic Airline.'

'How on earth did you know that?' She stared at him incredulously.

'I checked.' He shrugged. 'I thought it would be a nice gesture to bump your seat up to First Class. Miller was a cheapskate for not booking you into First Class in the first place!'

'He did,' she snapped. 'I'm the one who insisted he change it to Economy.'

'No doubt because you have every intention of paying the money back to him.' Lucien sighed, only too well aware of Cyn's fierce independence. It was a knowledge that made his earlier comments—accusations!—even more ridiculous. And unforgivable.

'Of course.' She tilted her chin proudly.

Lucien nodded. 'Nevertheless, if you avoid seeing me again before you leave for the airport on Saturday, one telephone call from me and the flight gets delayed...or cancelled altogether.'

Cyn gasped. 'You wouldn't seriously do that?'

He raised a mocking brow. 'What do you think?'

'I think you're way way out of line on this—that is what I *think*!' she hissed forcefully.

He shrugged. 'Your choice.'

'You—you egomaniac!' Thia glared at him. Arrogant, manipulative, *impossible* ego-maniac!

Lucien gave a hard, humourless smile. 'As I said, it's up to you. We either talk again before you leave or you don't leave.'

'There are other airlines.'

He shrugged. 'I will ensure that none are available to you.'

She gasped. 'You can't do that—'

'Oh, but I can.'

Her eyes widened. 'You would really stop me from leaving New York until we've spoken again...?'

His mouth thinned. 'You aren't giving me any alternative.'

'We all have choices, Lucien.' She gave a shake of her head. 'And your overbearing behaviour now is leaving *me* with no choice but to dislike you intensely.'

He sighed. 'Well, at least it's *intensely;* I would hate it to be anything so insipid as just mediocre dislike! Look, I'm not enjoying backing you into a corner, Cyn,' he reasoned grimly as she glared at him. 'All I'm asking for is that we both sleep on this situation and then have a conversation tomorrow. Is that too much to ask?'

Was it? Could Thia even bear to be alone with him again after all that had been said?

Oh, she accepted that Lucien had been shocked at the way Jonathan had just blurted out her physical innocence. But Lucien's response to that knowledge had been—damned painful. That was what it had been!

'Okay, we'll talk again tomorrow.' She spoke in measured tones. 'But in a public place. With the agreement that I can get up and leave any time I want to.'

His eyes narrowed. 'I'm not sure I like your implication...'

'And my answer to that is pretty much the same as the one you gave me a few minutes ago—that's just too bad!' She looked at him challengingly.

Lucien gave a slow shake of his head. 'How the hell

did we get into this situation, Cyn? One minute I have my mouth and my hands all over you, and the next—'

'You don't,' she snapped, the finality of her tone implying he never would again.

Except…it was impossible for Lucien not to see the outline of her nipples pouting hard as berries against the soft material of his T-shirt. Or not to note the way an aroused flush now coloured her throat and up into her cheeks. Or see the feverish glitter in the deep blue of her eyes.

Cyn was angry with him right now—and justifiably so after his own train-wreck of a conversation just now—but that hadn't stopped her from remembering the fierceness of the desire that had flared between them earlier, or prevented the reaction of her body to those memories.

'Tomorrow, Cyn?' he encouraged huskily. 'Let's both just take a night to calm down.'

She frowned. 'It's my last day and I'd planned on taking a boat ride to see the Statue of Liberty. Don't tell me!' She grimaced as she obviously saw his expression. 'You've never been there, either!'

He smiled slightly. 'You live in London—have *you* ever been to the Tower of London and Buckingham Palace?'

'The Palace, yes. The Tower, no.' She shrugged. 'Okay, point taken. But tomorrow really is my last chance to take that boat trip…'

'Then we'll arrange to meet up in the evening.' Lucien shrugged.

Cyn eyed him warily. 'You're being very obliging all of a sudden.'

He grimaced. 'Maybe I'm trying to score points in

the hope of making up for behaving like such a jackass earlier?'

'And maybe you just like having your own way,' she said knowingly. 'Okay, Lucien, we'll meet again tomorrow evening. But I'll be out most of the day, so leave a message for me at the front desk as to where we're supposed to meet up.'

He grimaced. 'Not the most gracious acceptance of an invitation I've ever received, but considering the jackass circumstances I'll happily take it.'

'This isn't a date, Lucien.' Cyn snapped her impatience.

She was doing it again—making him want to laugh when the situation, the strain that now existed between the two of them, should have meant he didn't find any of this in the least amusing! Besides which, Lucien had no doubt that if he *did* dare to laugh Cyn would be the one throwing potted plants around the hotel's reception—in an attempt to hit him with one of them!

Just thinking of Miller's behaviour earlier tonight was enough to dampen Lucien's amusement. 'I want your word. I would *like* your word,' he amended impatiently, bearing in mind Cyn's scathing comment earlier about his always wanting to have his own way, 'that you will stay away from Miller's apartment tomorrow.'

'I thought I might just—'

'I would really rather you didn't,' Lucien said frustratedly. 'You saw what he was like this evening, Cyn. His behaviour is currently unpredictable at best, violent at worst. You could get hurt. Far worse than just those bruises on your arm,' he added grimly.

She looked pained as she shook her head. 'Jonathan's life is in such a mess right now—'

'And it's a self-inflicted mess. Damn it, Cyn.' He scowled. 'He's already admitted he was only using you as a shield for his affair with another woman when he invited you to stay with him in New York!'

'Even so, it doesn't seem right—my just leaving without seeing him again.' She gave a sad shake of her head. 'I would feel as if I were abandoning him… Not everyone is as capable of handling sudden fame and fortune as you were,' she defended, when Lucien looked unimpressed.

'Damn it, Cyn.' He rasped his impatience with her continued concern for a man who didn't deserve it. 'Okay, if I see what can be done about getting Miller to accept help, maybe even going to a rehab facility, will you give me your promise not to go to his apartment tomorrow?'

'And you'll reconsider firing him from *Network*?'

'Don't push your luck, Cyn,' Lucien warned softly.

To his surprise, she gave a rueful grin. 'Okay, but it was worth a try, don't you think, as you're in such an amenable mood?'

Some of the tension eased from Lucien's shoulders as he looked at her admiringly. 'You are one gutsy lady, Cynthia Hammond!'

Thia was feeling far from gutsy at the moment. In fact reaction seemed to be setting in and she suddenly felt very tired, her legs less than steady. A reaction no doubt due to that fierceness of passion between herself and Lucien earlier as much as Jonathan's erratic, and…yes, she admitted *dangerously* unbalanced behaviour.

She was willing to concede that Lucien was right about that, at least; she had hardly recognised Jonathan this evening as the man she had known for two years.

But there were still so many questions that remained unanswered. The most burning question of all, for Thia, being the name of the woman Jonathan claimed to have seduced out of Lucien's bed.

Mainly because Thia simply couldn't believe that any woman would be stupid enough ever to prefer Jonathan over Lucien…

CHAPTER ELEVEN

'YOU JUST NEVER listen, do you? Never heed advice when it's given, even when it's for your own safety!'

Lucien's expression was as dark as thunder as he strode past Thia and into her hotel suite early the following evening, impressively handsome in a perfectly tailored black evening suit with a snowy white shirt and red silk bow-tie—making it obvious he had obviously only called to see her on his way out somewhere.

'Do come in, Lucien,' she invited dryly, and she slowly closed the door behind him before following him through to her sitting room. Her hair was pulled back in a high ponytail and she was wearing a pale blue fitted T-shirt and low-rider denims. 'Make yourself at home,' she continued as he dropped a large box down onto the coffee table before sitting down in one of the armchairs. 'And do please help yourself to a drink,' she invited.

He bounced restlessly back onto his feet a second later to cross the room and open the mini-bar, taking out one of the miniature bottles of whisky and pouring it into a glass before throwing it to the back of his throat and downing the fiery contents in one long swallow.

'Feeling better?'

Lucien turned, silver eyes spearing her from across

the room. 'Not in the least,' he grated harshly, taking out another miniature bottle of whisky before opening it and pouring it into the empty glass.

'What's wrong, Lucien?' Thia frowned.

His eyes narrowed to glittering silver slits. 'You gave me your word last night that you wouldn't see Miller today—'

'I believe I said that I wouldn't go to his apartment,' she corrected with a self-conscious grimace, knowing exactly where this conversation was going now.

'So you invited him to come here instead?'

Thia sighed. 'I didn't *invite* him anywhere, Lucien. Jonathan turned up outside my door. You only just missed him, in fact...'

His jaw tightened. 'I'm well aware of that!'

She arched a brow. 'Dex?'

Lucien's eyes narrowed. 'It was totally irresponsible of you to be completely alone with Miller in your suite—'

'But I wasn't completely alone with him, was I?' Thia said knowingly. 'I'm pretty sure Dex followed me to the docks today, and that he was standing guard outside the door to this suite earlier. And no doubt he ratted me out by telephoning you and telling you Jonathan was here.'

Lucien's eyes glittered a warning. 'Dex worries about your safety almost as much as I do.'

'Who's watching your back while Dex is busy watching mine?'

'I can take care of myself.'

'So can I!'

Lucien gave a disgusted snort. 'I discovered the first grey hair at my temple when I looked in the mirror to shave earlier—I'm damned sure it's appeared since yesterday.'

'Very distinguished,' she mocked. 'But there is absolutely no need for either you or Dex to worry about me,' she dismissed lightly. 'Jonathan only came by to apologise for the way he's behaved these past few weeks. He also said that when the two of you spoke earlier today you offered to give him another chance on *Network* if he agrees to go to rehab.'

'An offer I am seriously rethinking.'

She sighed. 'Don't be petty, Lucien.'

An angry flush darkened his cheeks. 'I made the offer because you asked me to, Cyn. Not for Miller's sake.'

'And because you know it makes good business sense,' she pointed out ruefully. 'It would be indescribably bad business for you to sack the star of *Network* when the programme—and Jonathan—are obviously both so popular.'

Lucien's mouth thinned. 'And you seriously think losing a few dollars actually *matters* to me?'

Thia slipped her hands into the back pockets of her denims so that Lucien wouldn't see that they were shaking slightly—evidence that she wasn't feeling as blasé about this conversation and Jonathan's visit earlier as she wished to give the impression of being.

She had seen Lucien in a variety of moods these past few days: the confident seducer on the evening they met, the focused billionaire businessman at his office the following day, playful and then seductive in his apartment yesterday evening, before he became cold and dismissive towards Jonathan, and then a total enigma to her after Jonathan deliberately dropped the bombshell of her virginity into the conversation.

But Lucien's mood this evening—a mixture of anger and concern—was as unpredictable as the man himself.

Her chin rose. 'I thought we had agreed to meet in a public place this evening?'

'I decided to come here after Dex called up to the penthouse and informed me of Miller's visit.'

'You could have just telephoned.'

'I could have *just* done a lot of things—and, believe me, my immediate response was to do what I've threatened to do several times before and put you over my knee for having behaved so damned irresponsibly,' he bit out harshly.

Thia frowned. 'Correct me if I'm wrong, but shouldn't *I* be the one who's feeling angry and upset?' she challenged.

Lucien's expression became wary. 'About what?'

'About *everything!*' she burst out.

He stilled. 'What else did Miller tell you earlier?' Lucien's expression was enigmatic as he picked up the whisky glass and moved to stand in the middle of the room—a move that instantly dominated the space.

'Nothing I hadn't already worked out for myself,' Thia answered heavily. She had realised last night, as she'd lain alone in her bed, unable to sleep, exactly who the woman involved in the triangle must be. There had been only one obvious answer—only one woman Jonathan had spent any amount of time alone with over the past few days. And it wasn't a triangle but a square. Because Simone Carew, Jonathan's co-star in *Network,* also had a husband…

And if, as Jonathan claimed, he had seduced Simone away from Lucien's bed several months ago, then Jonathan's assertion that Lucien, believing Thia was Jonathan's English lover, had seduced her as a way of getting back at Jonathan, it all made complete sense.

Painfully so.

Perhaps it was as well she would be leaving New York tomorrow, with no intentions of seeing Lucien or Jonathan ever again.

Not seeing Jonathan again didn't bother her in the slightest—they had said all they had to say to each other earlier.

Not seeing Lucien again—that was something else entirely.

Because Thia had realised something else as she'd lain alone in her bed the previous night. Something so huge, so devastating, that she had no idea how she was going to survive it.

She was in love with Lucien Steele.

Thia had heard of love at first sight, of course. Of how the sound of a particular voice could send shivers of awareness down the spine. How the first sight of that person's face could affect you so badly that breathing became difficult. Of how their touch could turn your legs to jelly and their kisses make you forget everything else but being with them.

Yes, Thia had heard of things like that happening—and now she realised that was exactly what had happened to her!

The worst of it was that the man she was in love with was Lucien Steele—a man who might or might not have been deliberately using her but who certainly wasn't in love with her.

'Such as?' Lucien prompted harshly as he saw the pained look on Cyn's face. 'Damn it, Cyn, even the con-

demned man is given an opportunity to defend himself!'
he said as she remained silent.

She looked up, focusing on him with effort. 'You're
far from being a condemned man, Lucien.' She gave a
rueful shake of her head. 'And I think it's for the best if
we forget about all of this and just move on.'

'Move on to where?' he prompted huskily.

She gave a pained frown. 'Well, Jonathan to rehab,
hopefully. Me back to England. And you—well, you to
whatever it is you usually do before moving on to another relationship. Not that we actually *had* a relationship,' she added hurriedly. 'I didn't mean to imply that—'

'You're waffling, Cyn.'

'What I'm doing is trying to allow both of us to walk
away from this situation with a little dignity.' Her eyes
flashed a deep dark blue.

'I don't remember saying I wanted to walk away.' He
quirked one dark brow.

She gave a shake of her head. 'I know the truth now,
Lucien. I worked out most of it for myself—Simone
Carew. Jonathan filled in the bits I didn't know, so let's
just stop pretending, shall we? The condensed version
of what happened is that you gave Jonathan two sepa-
rate verbal warnings, about Simone and the drugs, he
invited me over here in an attempt to mislead you about
his continuing relationship with Simone at least, and
you—you flirted with me to get back at him for taking
Simone from you. End of story.'

'That's only Miller's version of the story, Cyn...'
Lucien murmured softly as he placed his whisky glass
carefully, deliberately, down on the coffee table before
straightening.

His deliberation obviously didn't fool Cyn for a moment, as she now looked across at him warily. 'I told you—some of it I worked out for myself and the rest... It really isn't that important, Lucien.' She gave a dismissive shake of her head.

'Maybe not to you,' he bit out harshly. 'I, on the other hand, have no intention of allowing you to continue believing I have ever been involved with a married woman. It goes against every code I've ever lived by.' He drew in a sharp breath. 'My parents' marriage ended because my mother left my father for someone else,' he stated flatly. 'I would never put another man through the pain my father went through after she left him.'

Cyn's eyes widened. 'I didn't realise... Did your relationship with Simone happen *before* she married Felix?'

Lucien gave an exasperated sigh. 'It never happened at all!'

She winced at his vehemence. 'Then why did Jonathan say that it did...?'

'I can only assume because that's what Simone told him—probably as a way of piquing his interest.'

'I— But— *Why?* No, strike that question.' Cyn gave an impatiently disgusted shake of her head. 'I've met Simone Carew a few times over the past few days and she's a very silly, very vain woman. So, yes, I can well believe she's capable of telling Jonathan something like that just for the kudos. It isn't enough that she's married to one of the most influential directors in television— she also had to claim to having had a relationship with the richest and most powerful man in New York!'

Lucien gave a humourless smile. 'I knew you would get there in the end!'

'This isn't the time for your sarcasm, Lucien.' Cyn

glared. 'And if you knew she was going around telling such lies why didn't you stop her?'

'Because I didn't know about it until Miller blurted it out to me a few weeks ago.' He scowled. 'And once I did know it didn't seem particularly important—'

'Simone Carew was going around telling anyone who would listen that the two of you'd had an affair, and it didn't seem particularly important to you?' Cyn stared at him incredulously. 'What about her poor husband?'

Lucien gave a weary sigh. 'Felix is thirty years older than Simone and he knew exactly what he was getting into when he married her. As a result, he chooses to look the other way when she has one of her little extra-marital flings.'

'Big of him.'

'Not really.' Lucien grimaced. 'He happens to be in love with her. And there are always rumours circulating in New York about everyone—most of them untrue or exaggerations of the truth. So why would I have bothered denying the ones about Simone and me? Have you never heard people say the more you deny something the more likely people are to believe it's the truth?'

'I wouldn't have!'

'That's because *you* are nothing like anyone else I have ever met,' Lucien dismissed huskily.

Thia didn't know what to say in answer to that comment. Didn't know what to say, full-stop.

Oh, she believed Lucien when he said he hadn't ever had an affair with Simone—why wouldn't she believe him when he had no reason to bother lying to her? It was totally unimportant to Lucien what *she* believed!

It did, however, raise the question as to why Lucien had pursued *her* so determinedly…

'What's in the box, Lucien?' Thia deliberately changed the subject as she looked down at the box Lucien had dropped down onto the coffee table when he first entered the suite.

'End of subject?'

She avoided meeting his exasperated gaze. 'I can't see any point in talking about it further. It's—I apologise if I misjudged you.' She gave a shake of her head. 'Obviously I'm not equipped—I don't understand the behind-the-scenes machinations and silly games of your world.'

'None of that is *my* world, Cyn. It's an inevitable part of it, granted, but not something I have ever chosen to involve myself in,' he assured her softly. 'As for what's in the box…why don't you open it up and see?'

Thia eyed the box as if it were a bomb about to go off, having no idea what could possibly be inside.

'It's a replacement for the blouse that was ripped!' she realised with some relief, her cheeks warming as she recalled exactly how and when her blouse had been ripped. And what had followed.

She couldn't think about that now! *Wouldn't* think about that now. There would be time enough for thinking about making love with Lucien, of being in love with him, in all the months and years of her life yet to come…

'Open it up, Cyn,' Lucien encouraged gruffly as he moved to sit down on the sofa beside the coffee table.

'Before I forget—I had your T-shirt laundered today—'

'Will you stop delaying and open the damned box, Cyn?'

'I can do it later,' she dismissed. 'You're obviously on

your way out somewhere.' She gave a pointed look at his evening clothes. 'I wouldn't want to delay you any more than I have already—'

'You aren't delaying me.'

'But—'

'What is so difficult about opening the box, Cyn?' He barked his impatience with her prevarication.

Thia worried her bottom lip between her teeth. 'I just—I'm sorry if I'm being less than gracious. I'm just a little out of practice at receiving gifts…'

Lucien's scowl deepened as he realised the reason for that: Cyn's parents had died six years ago and she'd admitted to having no other family. And her relationship with Miller obviously hadn't been of the gift-giving variety—he was a taker, not a giver!

'It isn't a gift, Cyn,' Lucien assured softly. 'I ruined your blouse. I'm simply replacing it.'

A delicate blush warmed the ivory of her cheeks, emphasising the dark shadows under those cobalt blue eyes. Because Cyn hadn't slept well the night before?

Neither had Lucien. His thoughts had chased round and round on themselves as he'd tried to make sense, to use his normal cold logic, to explain and dissect his feelings for Cyn. In the end he had been forced to acknowledge, to accept, that there was no sense or reason to any of it. It just was.

There was now a dull ache in his chest at the realisation he wanted to shower Cyn with gifts, to give her anything and everything she had ever wanted or desired. At the same as he knew that her fierce independence would no doubt compel her to throw his generosity back in his face!

Lucien was totally at a loss to know what to do about this intriguing woman. Was currently following a previously untrodden path—one that had no signs or indications to tell him where to go or what he should do next. Except he knew he wasn't going to allow her to just walk out of his life tomorrow.

He took heart from the blush that now coloured her cheeks at the mention of her blouse ripping the night before. 'I would like to know if you approve of the replacement blouse, Cyn,' he encouraged gruffly.

'I would love to have been a fly on your office wall during *that* telephone conversation!' she teased as she finally moved forward to loosen the lid of the box before removing it completely.

'I went to the store this morning and picked out the blouse myself, Cyn.'

She gave him a startled look. 'You did?'

'I did,' he confirmed gruffly.

'I— But— Why…?'

He shrugged. 'I didn't trust a store assistant to pick out a blouse that was an exact match in colour for your eyes.'

'Oh…'

'Yes…oh…' Lucien echoed softly as he looked into, held captive, those beautiful cobalt blue eyes. 'Do you like it?' he prompted huskily as she folded back the tissue paper and down looked at the blouse he had chosen for her.

Did Thia *like* it?

Even if she hadn't this blouse would have been special to her, because Lucien had picked it out for her personally. As it was, Thia had never seen or touched such a beautiful blouse before. The colour indeed a perfect match for her eyes, and the material softer, silkier, than anything else she had ever owned.

Tears stung her eyes as she looked up. 'It's beautiful, Lucien,' she breathed softly. 'Far too expensive, of course. But don't worry,' she added as a frown reappeared between his eyes, 'I'm not going to insult you by refusing to accept it!'

'Good, because it certainly isn't going back to the store, and it really isn't my size or colour.'

'Very funny.' Thia picked up the blouse carefully, not sure when she would ever find the opportunity to wear something so beautiful—and expensive!—but loving it anyway. 'I—there appears to be something else in the box…' she breathed softly as she realised the blouse had been hiding the fact that there was another article wrapped in tissue beneath it. 'Lucien?' She looked up at him uncertainly.

'Ah. Yes.' He looked less than his usual confident self as he gave a self-conscious grimace. 'That's for you to wear this evening—unless you already have something you would prefer. You looked lovely in the gown you were wearing the evening we met, for example, although you might feel happier wearing something new.'

Thia eyed him warily. 'And where am I going this evening that I would need to wear something new?'

'To a charity ball.' He stood up restlessly, instantly dwarfing the room—and Thia—with the sheer power of his personality. 'With me. It's the reason I'm dressed like this.' He indicated his formal evening clothes.

'A charity ball…?' Thia echoed softly.

He nodded. 'I thought we could spend a couple of hours at the ball and then leave when you've had enough.'

She looked at him sharply. 'Is this because of what I said to you last night?'

He grimaced. 'You said a lot of things to me last night, Cyn.'

Yes, she had—and quite a lot of them had been insulting. Most especially the part where she had suggested Lucien was hiding her away because he didn't want to be seen in public with a waitress student from London… 'There's really no need for you to do this, Lucien. I was out of line, saying what I did, and I apologise for misjudging you—'

'You apologised for that last night,' he dismissed briskly. 'Tonight we're going out to a charity ball. Most, if not all of New York society will be there too.' Lucien met her gaze unblinkingly.

'Exactly how much per ticket is this charity ball?' Thia had seen several of these glittering affairs televised, and knew that they cost thousands of dollars to attend.

'What the hell does that have to do with—?'

'Please, Lucien.'

His mouth thinned. 'Ten thousand dollars.'

'For *both?*' she squeaked.

'Per ticket.'

'Ten thous…?' Thia couldn't even finish the sentence—could only gape at him.

He shrugged. 'The proceeds from the evening go towards the care of abused children.'

Even so… Ten thousand dollars a ticket! It was—'I can't allow you to spend that sort of money on me.' She gave a determined shake of her head.

'It isn't for you. It's for abused children. And I've already bought the tickets, whether we attend or not, so why not use them?'

'Because—because I—' She gave a pained wince. 'Why don't you just take whoever you were originally going to take?'

'I bought the extra ticket today, Cyn. You *are* the person I was originally going to take.' His gaze was compelling in its intensity.

Maybe so, but that didn't mean Thia had to go to the charity ball with him.

Did it…?

CHAPTER TWELVE

'THAT WASN'T SO bad, was it…?' Lucien turned to look at Cyn as the two of them sat in the back of the limousine, driven by Paul, with Dex seated beside him, and they left the charity ball shortly before midnight.

'It wasn't bad at all. Everyone was so…nice.' She looked at him from beneath silky dark lashes.

'They can be.' Lucien nodded.

'It probably helped that I was being escorted by the richest and most powerful man in New York!'

'I didn't notice any pitying glances being directed my way,' he teased huskily.

'If there were, they were kept well hidden!'

Lucien reached across the distance between them to lift up one of her hands before intertwining his fingers with hers—ivory and bronze. 'Will you come up to my apartment for a nightcap when we get back to the hotel?' he invited gruffly.

Thia gave him a shy glance in the dimly lit confines of the back of the limousine. The privacy partition was up between them and the front of the car. To her surprise, she had enjoyed the evening much more than she had thought she would, meeting so many more people than just the celebrity side of New York society. Such was the force of Lucien's personality that all of them had accepted her place at his side without so much as a raised eyebrow.

The only moment of awkwardness for Thia had been when they had spoken briefly to Felix and Simone Carew. The older woman had avoided meeting Thia's gaze—that fact alone telling Thia that Jonathan must have spoken to the actress today, and that Simone knew Thia now knew about the two of them.

Lucien's manner had been extremely cool towards the other woman, and his arm had stayed possessively about Thia's waist as he spoke exclusively to Felix, before making their excuses so that he could introduce Thia to some friends of his across the room. That arm had remained firmly about her waist for the rest of the evening.

She had even worn the gown Lucien had selected and bought for her. A bright red figure-hugging, ankle-length dress that left her shoulders and the swell of her breasts bare. And she had secured the darkness of her hair at her crown. The appreciation in Lucien's eyes when she'd rejoined him in the sitting room of her suite had been enough to tell her that he approved of her appearance.

She moistened her lips with the tip of her tongue now. 'Is that a good idea?'

His fingers tightened about hers. 'We can go to your suite if you would prefer it?'

'I've had a lovely time this evening, Lucien, but—'

'This sounds suspiciously like a brush-off to me.' He had tensed beside her.

Thia gave a shake of her head. 'I'm leaving in the morning, Lucien. Let's not make things complicated.'

His eyes glowed in the dim light. 'What if I want to complicate the hell out of things?'

She smiled sadly. 'We both know that isn't a good idea. I'm…what I am, and you're…what you are.'

'And didn't tonight prove to you that I don't give a damn about the waitress/student/billionaire/businessman thing?'

Thia chuckled huskily. 'The difference between us I was referring to was actually the virgin and the man of experience thing!'

'Ah.'

'Yes—*ah*. A difference that horrified you last night,' she reminded him huskily.

'It didn't horrify me. I was just surprised,' he amended impatiently. 'But I'm over the surprise now, and—'

'And you want to continue where we left off last night?' Thia arched her brows.

'You know, Cyn, when—if—I've ever thought of proposing marriage to a woman, I certainly didn't envisage it would be in the back of a car. Even if that car *is* a limousine! But if that's how it has to be, then I guess—'

'Did you say you're proposing marriage…?' Thia turned fully on the leather seat to look at him with wide disbelieving eyes. Lucien couldn't really mean he was proposing marriage to *her*!

'Well, no,' he answered predictably. 'Because I haven't actually got around to asking you yet,' he added dryly. 'I believe I need to get down on one knee for that, and although the back of this car is plenty big enough I think you would prefer that Paul and Dex didn't make their own assumptions as to exactly what I'm doing when I drop down onto my knees in front of you!'

Thia felt the warm rush of colour that heated her cheeks just at the thought of what the other two men might think about seeing their employer falling to his knees in the back of the car.

She snatched her hand out of his. 'Stop teasing me, Lucien— What are you doing?' she gasped as he moved down onto his knees in front of her after all, before taking both of her hands in his. 'Lucien!'

What *was* he doing?

How the hell did Lucien know? He was still travelling that untrodden path with no signs or indications to guide him.

Thia had obviously enjoyed herself this evening, and he could only hope part of that enjoyment had been his own company.

She looked so beautiful tonight Lucien hadn't been able to take his eyes off her. The fact that other men had also looked at her covetously had been enough for Lucien to keep his arm possessively about her waist all evening, rather than just accepting the glances of admiration his dates usually merited. He didn't want any other man admiring Thia but him.

He knew it was probably too soon for Cyn. That the two of them had only known each other a couple of days. But what a couple of days they had been!

That first evening, when he had literally looked across a crowded room and seen her for the first time, she'd been so beautiful she had taken his breath away. And he had felt as if she had punched him in the chest later on, when she'd preferred to walk away from him, in the middle of a crowded New York street, rather than accompany him to Steele Heights Hotel. The following morning, when he had seen the disreputable hotel where she had spent the night, he'd actually had palpitations! And when she had arrived at his office later that afternoon, wearing that cropped pink T-shirt and those figure-hugging low-rider denims, his physical reaction had been so wonderfully different…!

Cooking dinner last night with Cyn had been fun, and their conversation stimulating, while at the same time Lucien had felt more comfortable, more at ease in her company than he had ever been before. And she had looked so cute in his over-sized T-shirt. He had even enjoyed shopping for the blouse and gown for her earlier today. As for making love with her last night… How Cyn had responded, the way she had given herself to him totally, only for him to learn later that she was inexperienced, an innocent, had literally brought him to his knees.

And he had been on his knees ever since.

He was on his knees again now…

'I'm really not insane, Cyn.' His hands tightened about hers as he looked up intently into her beautiful pale face. 'I am, however, currently shaking in those handmade Italian leather shoes you mentioned at our first meeting,' he admitted ruefully.

She blinked. 'Why?'

'I've never proposed to a woman before, and the thought of having you refuse is enough to make any man shake.'

Cyn gave a pained frown. 'I don't—this is just—'

'Too soon? Too sudden? I know all that, Cyn.' He grimaced. 'I've been telling myself the same thing all day. But none of it changes the fact that I've fallen in love with you—that the thought of you going back to London tomorrow, of never seeing you again, is unacceptable to me. I don't just love you, Cyn, I adore you. I love your spirit, your teasing, your intelligence, your kindness, your loyalty, the way you give the whole of yourself, no matter what the situation. I had no idea how empty my life and heart were until I met you, but you've filled both of them in a way I could never have imagined. In a way I never want to live without,' he added huskily.

Thia stared at him incredulously. Had Lucien just said—? Had he really just told her that he loved her? He adored her?

Maybe she was the one who was insane—because he really couldn't have said those things. Not to *her*. Not Lucien Steele, American zillionaire, the richest and most powerful man in New York.

And yet there he was, on his knees in front of her, her hands held tightly in his as he gazed up at her with such a look of love Thia thought her heart had actually stuttered and then stilled in her chest.

'Hey, look…you don't have to answer me now.' He'd obviously mistaken her look of disbelief for one of panic. 'There's no rush. I realise that it's too much for me to expect you to know if you'll ever feel the same way about me, but we can spend as long as you like getting to know each other better. You'll want to go back to London anyway, to finish your degree. I'll buy an apartment there, or maybe a house, so that we can spend as much time together as you have free, and then, after a few months, if you—'

'Yes.'

'If you still don't think you could ever love me the way I love you, then I'll—'

'Yes.'

'I'll somehow have to learn to accept it, to live with that. I won't like it, but—'

'I said *yes,* Lucien.' Thia squeezed his hands to pull him up so that she could look directly into his face. 'I said yes, Lucien…' she repeated softly as he returned her gaze questioningly.

'Yes, what…?'

Her breath caught in her throat, tears stinging the backs of her eyes. But they were tears of happiness. Lucien loved her. He really loved her. He knew that she had struggled to finance her degree and understood she was determined to finish it. He was going to buy a home in London so that he could be close to her while she did so. He had asked her to *marry* him!

Yes, it was too soon.

For other people.

Not for Lucien and Thia.

Because they were a result of their past—people who had both lost the security of their parents in different ways, at a vulnerable time in their lives. As a result they were two people who didn't love or trust easily—and the fact that they had fallen in love with each other surely had to be fate's reward for all those previous years of loneliness.

Thia slid forward on the leather seat and then down onto her knees in the carpeted footwell beside him. 'I said yes, Lucien.' She raised her hands to cup each side of his beloved and handsome face. 'Yes, I love you, too. Yes, I'll marry you. Tomorrow, if you like.'

'I— But—'

'Or maybe we can wait a while, if that's too soon for you. Lucien!' She gasped as he pulled her tightly against him before his mouth claimed hers hungrily.

* * *

'I'll take that as a yes to us getting married, then,' Lucien murmured a long time later, when the two of them were cuddled up together on one of the sofas in the sitting room of his penthouse apartment at Steele Heights, with only a side lamp to illuminate the room.

Cyn stirred beside him. 'I still think you're mean to make me wait for you until our wedding night.'

'Shouldn't that be my line?' he came back indulgently, more relaxed, happier than he had ever been in his life before. How could he feel any other way when he had the woman he loved beside him?

'It should, yes.' She pouted up at him. 'But you're the one who's gone all "not until we're married" on me.'

Lucien chuckled softly, trailing her loosened hair like midnight silk over his fingers. 'That doesn't mean we can't...*be* together before then. I would just prefer that we left things the way they are for now. I can't wait to see you walk down the aisle to me, all dressed in white and all the time knowing that I'm going to undress you later that night and make love to you for the first time.'

When he put it like that...

Cyn moved up on her elbow to look down at him, loving how relaxed Lucien looked, how *loved* he looked. 'What do you mean, we can *be* together before then...?'

His mouth quirked seductively. 'You enjoyed what we did last night, didn't you?'

'Oh, yes.' Her cheeks grew hot at the memory of their lovemaking.

'Would you like to repeat it tonight?'

'That depends...'

His smile faded to a frown. 'On what?'

Thia gave a rueful smile. 'On whether or not you'll

allow me to…reciprocate. You'll have to show me how, of course, but I'm sure I'll quickly get the hang of it—'

'Dear God…!' Lucien gave a pained groan and closed his eyes briefly, before opening them again, those same eyes narrowing as he saw how mischievously she returned his gaze. 'You're teasing me again!' he realised self-derisively.

'Only partly.' She wrinkled her nose at him. 'I know the mechanics, of course, but I'm guessing that doesn't mean a whole lot when it comes to the real thing?'

'Let's go and see for ourselves, shall we…?' Lucien stood up, bending down to lift her up into his arms and cradling her tenderly against his chest.

Thia wrapped her arms about his shoulders and gazed up at him adoringly. 'I could get used to this.'

'I very much hope that you do—because I intend spoiling and petting you for the rest of your life.' That same love glowed in Lucien's eyes as he looked down at her. 'I love you very much, Cynthia Hammond. Thank you for coming into my life.'

Her lips trembled with emotion. 'I love *you* very much, Lucien Steele. Thank *you* for coming into my life.'

It was everything.

Now.

Tomorrow.

Always.

* * * * *

The Talk of Hollywood

CHAPTER ONE

'IT WOULD APPEAR that your guest has finally arrived, Gramps,' Stazy said as she stood stiffly beside one of the bay windows in the drawing room, facing towards the front of Bromley House and watching the sleek black sports car as it was driven down the gravel driveway of her grandfather's Hampshire estate. She was unable to make out the features of the driver of the car behind the tinted windows; but, nevertheless, she was sure that it was Jaxon Wilder, the English actor and director who for the past ten years had held the fickle world of Hollywood in the palm of his elegant hand.

'Don't be so hard on the man, Stazy; he's only five minutes late, and he did have to drive all the way from London!' her grandfather chided indulgently from the comfort of his armchair.

'Then maybe it would have been a good idea on his part to take into account the distance he had to travel and set out accordingly.' Stazy had made absolutely no secret of her disapproval of Jaxon Wilder's visit here, and found the whole idea of his wanting to write and direct a film about the life of her deceased grandmother totally unacceptable. Unfortunately, she hadn't been able to persuade her grandfather into dismissing the idea as readily—which was why Jaxon Wilder was now parking that sleek black sports car on the driveway outside her grandfather's home.

Stazy turned away before she saw the man in question alight from the car; she already knew exactly what Jaxon Wilder looked like. The whole world probably recognised Jaxon Wilder after he had completely swept the board at every awards ceremony earlier in the year with his recent film, in which he had once again acted and directed.

Aged in his mid-thirties, he was tall and lean, with wide and powerful shoulders, slightly overlong dark hair, and piercing grey eyes set either side of an aristocratic nose. His mouth was sculptured and sensual, his chin square and determined, and the deep timbre of his voice had been known to send quivers of pleasure down the spines of women of all ages. Jaxon Wilder was known to be the highest paid actor and director on both sides of the pond.

His looks and appeal had often led to his being photographed in newspapers and magazines with the latest beautiful woman to share his life—and his bed! And his reason for coming here today was to use that charm in an effort to persuade Stazy's grandfather into giving his blessing—and help—to the writing of a screenplay about the adventurous life of Stazy's grandmother, Anastasia Romanski. A woman who, as a young child, had escaped the Russian Revolution with her family by fleeing to England, and as an adult had been one of the many secret and unsung heroines of her adopted country.

Anastasia had died only two years ago, at the age of ninety-four. Her obituary in the newspaper had drawn the attention of a nosy reporter who, when he had looked deeper into Anastasia's life, had discovered that there had been far more to Anastasia Bromley than the obscure accolades mentioned. The result had been a sensationalised biography about Anastasia, published six months ago, and the ensuing publicity had caused her grandfather to suffer a mild heart attack.

In the circumstances, was it any wonder that Stazy had been horrified to discover that Jaxon Wilder intended to make a film of Anastasia's life? And, even worse, that the film director had an appointment with her grandfather in order to discuss the project? Stazy had decided it was a discussion she had every intention of being a part of!

'Sir Geoffrey.' Jaxon moved smoothly forward to shake the older man's hand as the butler showed him into the drawing room of Bromley House.

'Mr Wilder.' It was hard to believe that Geoffrey Bromley was a man aged in his mid-nineties as he returned the firmness of Jaxon's handshake. His dark hair was only lightly streaked with grey, his shoulders still stiffly erect in his tailored dark three-piece suit and snowy white shirt with a meticulously tied grey tie.

'Jaxon, please,' he invited. 'May I say how pleased I am that you agreed to see me today—?'

'Then the pleasure would appear to be all yours!'

'Stazy!' Geoffrey Bromley rebuked affectionately as he turned towards the woman who had spoken so sharply.

Jaxon turned to look at her too as she stood in front of the bay window. The sun shining in behind her made it hard for him to make out her features, although the hostility of her tone was enough of an indication that she, at least, wasn't in the least pleased by Jaxon's visit!

'My granddaughter Stazy Bromley, Mr Wilder,' Sir Geoffrey introduced lightly.

Jaxon, having refreshed his memory on the Bromley family before leaving his London hotel earlier that morning, already knew that Stazy was short for Anastasia—the same name as her grandmother. Information that had in no way prepared him for Stazy Bromley's startling resemblance to her grandmother as she stepped out of the sunlight.

About five-six in height, with the same flame-coloured hair—neither red nor gold, but a startling mixture of the two—and a pale and porcelain complexion, she had a wide, intelligent brow above sultry eyes of deep emerald-green. Her nose was small and perfectly straight, and she had full and sensuous lips above a stubbornly determined chin.

The hairstyle was different, of course; Anastasia had favoured shoulder-length hair, whereas her granddaughter's was stylishly cut in an abundance of layers that was secured at her nape and cascaded down to the middle of her back. The black, knee-length sheath of a dress she wore added to the impression of elegant chic.

Other than those minor differences Jaxon knew he might have been looking at the twenty-nine-year-old Anastasia Romanski.

Green eyes raked over Jaxon dismissively. 'Mr Wilder.'

Jaxon gave an inclination of his head. 'Miss Bromley,' he returned smoothly.

'That would be *Dr* Bromley,' she corrected coolly.

Stazy Bromley had the beauty and grace of a supermodel rather than the appearance of a dusty doctor of Archaeology, as Jaxon knew her to be. Maybe, faced with her obvious antagonism towards him, Jaxon should have had Geoffrey Bromley's granddaughter investigated more thoroughly than simply making a note of her age and occupation...

'Stazy, perhaps you would like to go and tell Mrs Little we'll have tea now...?' her grandfather prompted, softly but firmly.

Those full and sensuous lips thinned. 'Is that an unsubtle hint for me to leave you and Mr Wilder alone for a few minutes, Gramps?' Stazy Bromley said dryly, those disapproving green eyes remaining firmly fixed on Jaxon.

'I think that might be best, darling,' her grandfather encouraged ruefully.

'Just try not to let Mr Wilder use his reputed charm to persuade you into agreeing to or signing anything before I get back!' she warned, with another cold glance in Jaxon's direction.

'I wouldn't dream of it, Dr Bromley,' Jaxon drawled. 'Although I'm flattered that you think I have charm!' Mockery perhaps wasn't the best line for him to take when Stazy Bromley was obviously so antagonistic towards him already, but then Jaxon couldn't say he particularly cared for being treated as if he were some sort of trickster, trying to dupe her grandfather into selling off the family jewels!

Obviously the subject of her grandmother's past was a sensitive one to Stazy Bromley.

'I don't know you well enough as yet to have decided exactly what you are, Mr Wilder,' Stazy Bromley assured him distantly.

But she obviously didn't number his 'charm' as one of his more obvious attributes, Jaxon recognised ruefully. That was a pity, because her physical similarities to her grandmother were already enough to have him intrigued. Similarities that she seemed to deliberately downplay with her lack of make-up and the confinement of her riotous red-gold hair.

If that really was Stazy's intention then she had failed miserably. As if those sultry green eyes and that poutingly sensuous mouth weren't enough of an attraction, her curvaceous figure in that fitted black dress certainly was!

Stazy had only ever seen Jaxon Wilder on the big screen before today, where he invariably appeared tall and dark and very powerful. It was an image she had believed to be magnified by the size of that screen. She had been wrong. Even dressed formally, in a tailored black suit, snowy-white silk shirt and silver tie, Jaxon Wilder was just as powerfully charismatic in the flesh.

'That really is enough, darling,' her grandfather rebuked. 'And I have no doubt that Mr Wilder and I will manage perfectly well for the short time you're gone,' he added pointedly.

'I have no doubt you will, Grandfather.' Her voice softened as she smiled affectionately at her aged grandparent before leaving.

Her grandfather was now the only family Stazy had, her parents having both died fifteen years ago, when their light aeroplane had crashed into the sea off the coast of Cornwall.

Despite already being aged in their early eighties, Anastasia and Geoffrey had been wonderful to their traumatised granddaughter, taking fourteen-year-old Stazy into their home and their lives without a second thought. As a result Stazy's protectiveness where they were both concerned was much stronger than it might otherwise have been.

To the point where she now saw Jaxon Wilder's plans to make a film about her deceased grandmother as nothing more than Hollywood sensationalism—no doubt inspired by that dreadful biography, in which her grandmother had been portrayed as the equivalent of a Russian Mata Hari working for British Intelligence!

No doubt Jaxon Wilder also saw the project as a means of earning himself yet another shelf of awards to add to his already considerable collection. That was a pity—for him!—because Stazy saw it as her mission in life to ensure that film was never made!

'I'm afraid Stazy doesn't approve of your making a film of my late wife's life, Jaxon,' Sir Geoffrey murmured wryly.

He gave a rueful smile. 'One would never have guessed!'

The older man smiled slightly. 'Please, sit down and tell me exactly what it is you want from me,' he invited smoothly as he resumed his seat in the armchair beside the unlit fireplace.

'Shouldn't we wait for your granddaughter to return before we discuss this any further?' Jaxon grimaced as he lowered his lean length down on to the chair opposite, already knowing that Stazy Bromley's attitude was going to be a problem he hadn't envisaged when he had flown over to England yesterday with the express purpose of discussing the details of the film with Geoffrey Bromley.

Jaxon had first written to the older man several months ago—a letter in which he had outlined his idea for the film. The letter he had received back from

Geoffrey Bromley two weeks later had been cautiously encouraging. The two men had spoken several times on the telephone before Jaxon had suggested they meet in person and discuss the idea more extensively.

In none of those exchanges had Sir Geoffrey so much as hinted at his granddaughter's antagonism to the film being made!

Sir Geoffrey smiled confidently. 'I assure you that ultimately Stazy will go along with whatever I decide.'

Jaxon had no doubt that when necessary the older man could be as persuasive as his wife was reputed to have been, but in a totally different way—the part Geoffrey Bromley had played in the events of the previous century were even more shrouded in mystery than those of his now deceased wife. But from the little Jaxon knew the other man had held a very high position of authority in England's security at the time of his retirement twenty-five years ago.

Was it any wonder that Stazy Bromley had the same forceful determination as both her grandparents?

Or that his own visit here today promised to be a battle of wills between the two of them!

A battle Jaxon ultimately had every intention of winning…

'I trust the two of you didn't discuss anything of importance during my absence…?' Stazy said softly as she came back into the room, closely followed by the butler. He was carrying a heavily laden silver tray, the contents of which he proceeded to place on the low coffee table in front of the sofa where Stazy now sat, looking enquiringly at the two men seated opposite.

Her grandfather gave her another of those censorious

glances as Jaxon Wilder answered. 'I'm sure that neither of us would have dared to do that, Dr Bromley...' he said dryly.

Stazy was just as sure that the forceful Jaxon Wilder would pretty much dare to do anything he damn well pleased! 'Do you care for milk and sugar in your tea, Mr Wilder?' she prompted lightly as she held the sugar bowl poised over the three delicate china cups.

'Just milk, thanks.'

Stazy nodded as she added two spoonfuls of sugar to her grandfather's cup before commencing to pour the tea. 'No doubt it becomes more difficult, as you get older, to maintain the perfect bodyweight.'

'Darling, I really don't think this constant bickering with Jaxon is necessary,' her grandfather admonished affectionately as she stood up to carry his cup and saucer over to him after handing Jaxon his own cup.

'Perhaps not,' Stazy allowed, her cheeks warming slightly at the rebuke. 'But I'm sure Mr Wilder is equally capable of defending himself if he feels it necessary.'

Jaxon was fast losing his patience with Stazy Bromley's snide comments. She might appear delicately beautiful in appearance, but as far as he could tell, where this particular woman was concerned, that was exactly where the delicacy ended.

'Undoubtedly,' he bit out abruptly. 'Now, if we could perhaps return to discussing *Butterfly*...?'

'"Butterfly"...?' his adversary repeated slowly as she resumed her seat on the sofa before crossing one silkily elegant knee over the other.

'It was your grandmother's code name—'

'I'm aware of what it was, Mr Wilder,' she cut in crisply.

'It's also the working title of my film,' Jaxon explained tersely.

'Isn't that rather presumptuous of you?' She frowned. 'As far as I'm aware,' she continued warily, 'there has been no agreement as yet to there even *being* a film, let alone it already having a working title!' She turned enquiring eyes to her grandfather, her tension palpable.

Sir Geoffrey shrugged. 'I don't believe there is any way in which we can stop Mr Wilder from making his film, Stazy.'

'But—'

'With or without our co-operation,' Sir Geoffrey added firmly. 'And personally—after the publication of that dreadful biography!—I would rather be allowed to have some say in the content than none at all.'

Stazy Bromley's eyes glittered with anger as she turned to look at Jaxon. 'If you've dared to threaten my grandfather—'

'Of course Jaxon hasn't threatened me, darling—'

'And Jaxon resents the hell—excuse my language, sir—' Jaxon nodded briefly to the older man before turning his chilling gaze back to the bristling Stazy Bromley '—out of the implication that he might have done so!'

Stazy had the good sense to realise that she just might have been out of line with that last remark. It was really no excuse that she had been predisposed to dislike Jaxon Wilder before she had even met him, based purely on the things she had read about him. Especially when he had been charm itself since his arrival. To her grandfather, at least. Stazy was pretty sure, after her barely veiled remarks, that the antagonism now went both ways!

But exactly what had Jaxon Wilder expected to happen when he had arranged to come here? That he would meet alone with a man aged in his mid-nineties who had recently suffered a heart attack? That the two of them would exchange pleasantries before he walked away with Geoffrey's complete co-operation? If that was what he'd thought was going to happen then he obviously didn't know Stazy's grandfather very well; even twenty-five years after his supposed retirement Geoffrey was a power to be reckoned with! And Stazy considered herself only one step behind him...

Not only was she a highly qualified London university lecturer, it had been hinted at by the powers that be that she was in line to become head of the department when her professor stepped down next year—and Stazy hadn't put herself in that position at only twenty-nine by being shy and retiring.

'I apologise if I was mistaken,' she murmured softly. 'Mr Wilder's use of the term "working title" seemed to imply that things had already been settled between the two of you.'

'Apology accepted,' Jaxon Wilder grated, without even the slightest lessening of the tension in those broad shoulders. 'Obviously I would rather proceed with your blessing, Sir Geoffrey.' He nodded to the older man, at the same time managing to imply that he didn't give a damn whether or not he had Stazy's!

'And his co-operation?' she put in dryly.

Cool grey eyes turned back in her direction. 'Of course.'

Stazy repressed the shiver that threatened to run the length of her spine—of alarm rather than the pleasure she imagined most women felt when Jaxon Wilder looked at them! As his icy gaze raked over her with slow criticism Stazy knew exactly what he would see: a woman who preferred a no-nonsense appearance. Her lashes were naturally long and dark, requiring no mascara, and in fact her face was completely bare of make-up apart from a pale peach lipgloss. Her hands, throat and ears were completely unadorned with jewellery.

Certainly Stazy knew herself to be nothing in the least like the beautiful and willowy actresses in whose company Jaxon Wilder had so often been seen, photographed for newspapers and magazines during the last dozen years or so. She doubted the man would even know what to do with an intelligent woman...

What on earth—?

Why should she care what Jaxon Wilder thought of her? As far as Stazy was concerned there would be absolutely no reason for the two of them ever to meet again after today—let alone for her to care what he thought of her as a woman...

She straightened determinedly. 'I believe you are not only wasting your own time, Mr Wilder, but also my grandfather's and mine—'

'As it happens, I'm willing to give Jaxon my blessing and my co-operation. I will allow him to read letters and personal papers of Anastasia's.' Geoffrey spoke firmly over Stazy's scathing dismissal. 'But only under certain conditions.'

Stazy's eyes widened as she turned to look at her grandfather. 'You can't be serious!'

Her grandfather gave a slight inclination of his head. 'I believe you will find, darling, that it's called controlling a situation that one knows is inevitable, rather than attempting a futile fight against it.'

Jaxon felt none of the exhilaration he might have expected to feel at Sir Geoffrey not only giving his blessing to the making of the film, but also offering him access to certain of Anastasia's personal papers in order to aid in the writing of the screenplay. Inwardly he sensed that whatever Geoffrey's conditions were, Jaxon wasn't going to like them...

Stazy Bromley obviously felt that same sense of unease as she stood up abruptly, a frown between those clear green eyes as she stared down at her grandfather for several long seconds before her expression softened slightly.

'Darling, remember what happened after that awful book was published—'

'I'm insulted that you would even *think* of comparing the film I intend to make with that sensationalised trash!' Jaxon rose sharply to his feet.

She turned to look at him coolly. 'How can I think otherwise?'

'Maybe by giving me a chance—'

'Now, now, you two.' Sir Geoffrey chuckled softly. 'It really doesn't bode well if the two of you can't even be in the same room together without arguing.'

Jaxon's earlier feeling of trepidation grew as he turned to look down at the older man, not fooled for a moment by the innocence of Sir Geoffrey's expression. 'Perhaps you would care to explain your conditions...?' he prompted slowly, warily. Whatever ace Geoffrey Bromley had hidden up his sleeve Jaxon was utterly convinced he wasn't going to like it!

The older man gave a shrug. 'My first condition is that there will be no copies made of my wife's personal papers. In fact they are never to leave this house.'

That was going to make things slightly awkward. It would mean that Jaxon would have to spend several days—possibly a week—here at Bromley House in order to read those papers and make notes before he was able to go away and write the screenplay. But, busy schedule permitting, there was no real reason why it couldn't be done. Over the years he had certainly stayed in infinitely less salubrious places than the elegant comfort of Bromley House!

'My second condition—'

'Exactly how many conditions are there?' Jaxon prompted with amusement.

'Just the two,' Sir Geoffrey assured him dryly. 'And the first condition will only apply if you agree to the second.'

'Fine.' Jaxon nodded ruefully.

'Oh, I wouldn't give me your agreement just yet, Jaxon,' the older man warned derisively.

Stazy didn't at all like the calculating glint she could clearly see in her grandfather's eyes. His first condition made a certain amount of sense—although there was no guarantee, of course. But at least Jaxon Wilder having access to her grandmother's personal papers might mean there was a slight chance his screenplay would have some basis in truth. Not much, but some.

That only left her grandfather's second condition…

'Go ahead, Gramps,' she invited softly.

'Perhaps you should both sit down first…?'

Stazy tensed and at the same time sensed Jaxon's own increased wariness as he stood across the room from her. 'Do we need to sit down…?'

'Oh I think it might be advisable,' her grandfather confirmed dryly.

'I'll remain standing, if you don't mind,' Jaxon Wilder rasped gruffly.

'Not at all.' Geoffrey chuckled. 'Stazy?'

'The same,' she murmured warily.

'Very well.' Her grandfather relaxed back in his chair as he looked up at the two of them. 'I have found your conversation today highly…diverting, shall we say? And I assure you there is really very little that a man of my age finds in the least amusing!' her grandfather added ruefully.

He was playing with them, Stazy recognised frustratedly. Amusing himself at their expense. 'Will you just spit it out, Gramps!'

He smiled slightly as he rested his elbows on the arms of the chair before linking his fingers together in front of his chest. 'Stazy, you obviously have reservations about the content of Jaxon's film—'

'With good reason!'

'With no reason whatsoever,' Jaxon corrected grimly. 'I am not the one responsible for that dreadful biography—nor have I ever written or starred in a film that twists the truth in order to add sensationalism,' he added hardly.

'I doubt most Hollywood actors would recognise the truth if it jumped up and bit them on the nose!' Those green eyes glittered with scorn.

Jaxon wasn't sure which one of them had closed the distance between them—was only aware that they now stood so close that their noses were almost touching as she glared up at him and Jaxon scowled right back down at her.

He was suddenly aware of the soft insidiousness of Stazy's perfume: a heady combination of cinnamon, lemon and—much more disturbing—hotly enraged woman…

Close to her like this, Jaxon could see that those amazing green eyes had a ring of black about the iris, giving them a strangely luminous quality that was almost mesmerising when fringed with the longest, darkest lashes he had ever seen. Her complexion was the pale ivory of fine bone china, with the same delicacy of appearance.

A delicacy that was completely at odds with the sensual fullness of her mouth.

Her lips were slightly parted now, to reveal small and perfectly straight white teeth. Small white teeth that Jaxon imagined could bite a man with passion as easily as— What the…?

Jaxon stepped back abruptly as he realised he had allowed his thoughts to wander way off the reservation, considering the antagonism the two of them clearly felt towards each other. Not only that, but Stazy Bromley was exactly like all the buttoned-down and career-orientated women he knew who had clawed themselves up the professional ladder so that they might inhabit the higher echelons of certain film studios. Hard, unfeminine women, whom Jaxon always avoided like the plague!

He eased the tension from his shoulders before turning back to face the obviously still amused Geoffrey Bromley. 'I agree with Stazy—'

'How refreshing!' she cut in dryly.

'You may as well just get this is over with,' Jaxon finished ruefully.

'Let's hope the two of you are in as much agreement about my second condition.' Sir Geoffrey nodded, no longer smiling or as relaxed as he had been a short time ago. 'I've given the matter some thought, and in view of Stazy's lack of enthusiasm for the making of your film, and your own obvious determination to prove her suspicions wrong, Jaxon, I feel it would be better for all concerned if Stazy were to assist you in collating and researching Anastasia's personal papers.'

'What…?'

Jaxon was completely in agreement with Stazy Bromley's obvious horror at the mere suggestion of the two of them working that closely together even for one minute, let alone the days or weeks it might take him to go through Anastasia Bromley's papers!

CHAPTER TWO

STAZY WAS THE first to recover her powers of speech. 'You can't be serious, Gramps—'

'I assure you I am perfectly serious.' He nodded gravely.

She gave a disbelieving shake of her head. 'I can't just take time off from the university whenever I feel like it!'

'I'm sure Jaxon won't mind waiting a few weeks until you finish for the long summer break.'

'But I've been invited to join a dig in Iraq this summer—'

'And I sincerely doubt that any of those artifacts having already been there for hundreds if not thousands of years, are going to disappear overnight just because you arrive a week later than expected,' her grandfather reasoned pleasantly.

Stazy stared down at him in complete frustration, knowing that she owed both him and her grandmother so much more than a week of her time. That if it wasn't for the two of them completely turning their own lives upside down fifteen years ago she would never have coped with her parents deaths as well as she had. It had also been their encouragement and support that had helped her through an arduous university course and then achieving her doctorate.

Stazy's thoughts came to an abrupt halt as she suddenly became aware of Jaxon Wilder's unnatural silence.

Those silver-grey eyes were narrowed on her grandfather, hard cheekbones thrown into sharp prominence by the clenching of his jaw, and his mouth was a thin and uncompromising line. His hands too were clenched, into fists at his sides.

Obviously not a happy bunny, either, Stazy recognised ruefully.

Although any satisfaction she might have felt at that realisation was totally nullified by her own continued feelings of horror at her grandfather's proposal. 'I believe you will find Mr Wilder is just as averse to the idea as I am, Gramps,' she drawled derisively.

He shrugged. 'Then it would appear to be a case of film and be damned,' he misquoted softly.

Stazy drew in a sharp breath as she remembered the furore that had followed the publication of the unauthorised biography six months ago. The press had hounded her grandfather for weeks afterwards—to the extent that he had arranged for round-the-clock guards to be placed at Bromley House and his house in London. And he had suffered a heart attack because of the emotional strain he had been put under.

Stazy had even had one inventive reporter sit in on one of her lectures without detection, only to corner her with a blast of personal questions at the end—much to her embarrassment and anger.

The thought of having to go through all that again was enough to send cold shivers of dread down Stazy's spine. 'Perhaps you might somehow persuade Mr Wilder into not making the film at all, Gramps?' Although her own behaviour towards him this past hour or so certainly wasn't conducive to Jaxon Wilder wanting to do her any favours!

Probably she should have thought of that earlier. Her grandmother had certainly believed in the old adage, 'You'll catch more with honey than with vinegar…'

The derision in Jaxon Wilder's piercing grey eyes as he looked at her seemed to indicate he was perfectly aware of Stazy's belated regrets! 'What form of…persuasion did you have in mind, Dr Bromley?' he drawled mockingly.

Stazy felt the colour warm her cheeks. 'I believe I referred to my grandfather's powers of persuasion rather than my own,' she returned irritably.

'Pity,' he murmured softly, those grey eyes speculative as his gaze moved slowly over Stazy, from her two-inch-heeled shoes, her curvaceous figure in the black dress, to the top of her flame-coloured head, before settling on the pouting fullness of her mouth.

She frowned her irritation as she did her best to ignore that blatantly sexual gaze. 'Surely you can appreciate how much the making of this film is going to upset my grandfather?'

'On the contrary.' Jaxon deeply resented Stazy Bromley's tone. 'I believe that a film showing the true events of seventy years ago can only be beneficial to your grandmother's memory.'

'Oh, please, Mr Wilder.' Stazy Bromley eyed him pityingly. 'We both know that your only interest in making this particular film is in going up on that stage in a couple of years' time to collect yet another batch of awards!'

Jaxon drew in a sharp breath. 'You—'

'Enough!' Sir Geoffrey firmly cut in on the conversation before Jaxon had the chance to finish his blistering reply. Eyes of steely-blue raked over both of them as he stood up. 'I believe that for the moment I have heard quite enough on this subject from both of you.' He gave an impatient shake of his head. 'You'll be staying for dinner, I hope, Jaxon...?' He raised steel-grey brows questioningly.

'If you feel we can make any progress by my doing so—yes, of course I'll stay to dinner,' Jaxon bit out tensely.

Sir Geoffrey gave a derisive smile. 'I believe it will be up to you and Stazy as to whether any progress will or can be made before you leave here later today,' he said dryly. 'And, with that in mind, I am going upstairs to take a short nap before dinner. Stazy, perhaps you would like to take Mr Wilder for a walk in the garden while I'm gone? My roses are particularly lovely this year, Jaxon, and their perfume is strongest in the late afternoon and early evening,' he added lightly, succeeding in silencing his granddaughter as she drew in another deep breath with the obvious intention of arguing against his suggestion.

Jaxon was reminded that the older man had once been in a position of control over the whole of British Intelligence, let alone one stubbornly determined granddaughter! 'A walk in the garden sounds...pleasant,' Jaxon answered noncommittally, not completely sure that Stazy Bromley wouldn't use the opportunity to try and stab him with a garden fork while they were outside, and so put an end to this particular problem.

'That's settled, then,' Sir Geoffrey said heartily. 'Do cheer up, darling.' He bent to kiss his granddaughter on the forehead. 'I very much doubt that Jaxon has any intention of attempting to steal the family silver before he leaves!'

The sentiment was so close to Jaxon's own earlier thoughts in regard to Stazy's obviously scathing opinion of him that he couldn't help but chuckle wryly. 'No, Sir Geoffrey, I believe you may rest assured that all your family jewels are perfectly safe where I'm concerned.'

The older man placed an affectionate arm about his granddaughter's slender shoulders. 'Stazy is the only family jewel I care anything about, Jaxon.'

'In that case, they're most *definitely* safe!' Jaxon assured him with hard dismissal.

'And on that note…' Sir Geoffrey smiled slightly as his arm dropped back to his side. 'I'll see both of you in a couple of hours.' He turned and left the room. Leaving a tense and awkward silence behind him…

Stazy was very aware of the barely leashed power of the man walking beside her across the manicured lawn in the warmth of the late-afternoon sunshine, and could almost feel the heated energy radiating off Jaxon Wilder. Or perhaps it was just repressed anger? The two of them had certainly got off to a bad start earlier—and it had only become worse during the course of the next hour!

Mainly because of her own less-than-pleasant attitude, Stazy accepted. But what else had this man expected? That she was just going to stand by and risk her grandfather becoming ill again?

She gave a weary sigh before breaking the silence between them. 'Perhaps we should start again, Mr Wilder?'

He raised dark brows as he looked down at her. 'Perhaps we should, Dr Bromley?'

'Stazy,' she invited abruptly.

'Jaxon,' he drawled in return.

He obviously wasn't going to make this easy for her, Stazy acknowledged impatiently. 'I'm sure you are aware of what happened five months ago, and why I now feel so protective towards my grandfather?'

'Of course.' Jaxon gave a rueful smile as he ducked beneath the trailing branches of a willow tree, only to discover there was a wooden swing chair beneath the vibrant green leaves. 'Shall we…?' he prompted lightly. 'I resent the fact,' he continued once they were both seated, 'that you believe he might need any protection from me.'

That was fair enough, Stazy acknowledged grudgingly. Except she still believed this man was in a position to cause her grandfather unnecessary distress. 'He and my grandmother were totally in love with each other until the very end…'

Jaxon heard clearly the pain of loss underlying her statement. 'I'm not about to do anything to damage either Geoffrey's or your own treasured memories of Anastasia,' he assured her huskily.

'No?'

'No,' Jaxon said evenly. 'On the contrary—I'm hoping my film will help to set the record straight where your grandmother's actions seventy years ago are concerned. I don't believe in making money—or in acquiring awards—' he gave her a pointed look '—by causing someone else unnecessary pain.'

Stazy felt her cheeks warm at the rebuke. 'Perhaps we should just draw a veil over our previous conversation, Jaxon…?'

'Perhaps we should.' He chuckled wryly.

Stazy's eyes widened as she saw that a cleft had appeared in Jaxon's left cheek as he smiled, and those grey eyes were no longer cold but the warm colour of liquid mercury, his teeth very white and even against his lightly tanned skin.

Stazy had spent the past eleven years acquiring her degree, her doctorate, and lecturing—as well as attending as many archaeological digs around the world as she could during the holidays. Leaving very little time for such frivolities as attending the cinema. Even so, she had seen several of Jaxon Wilder's films, and was able to appreciate that the man in the flesh was very much more…*immediate* than even his sexy screen image portrayed. Mesmerisingly so…

Just as she was aware of the heat of his body as he sat beside her on the swing seat—of the way his lightly spicy aftershave intermingled with the more potent and earthy smell of a virile male in his prime.

That was something of an admission from a woman who over the years had eschewed even the suggestion of a personal relationship in favour of concentrating on her career. And now certainly wasn't the time for Stazy to belatedly develop a crush on a film star!

Even one as suavely handsome as Jaxon Wilder…

Especially one as suavely handsome as Jaxon Wilder! What could a London university lecturer in archaeology and an award-winning Hollywood actor/director possibly have in common? *Nothing*, came the clear answer!

Was she disappointed at that realisation? No, of course she wasn't! Was she…?

Stazy got abruptly to her feet. 'Shall we continue with our walk?' She set out determinedly towards the fishpond, without so much as waiting to see if he followed her.

Jaxon slowly stood to stroll along behind Stazy, not quite sure what had happened to make her take off so abruptly, only knowing that something had. He also knew, after years of spending time with women who were totally fixated on both their career and their appearance—and not necessarily in that order! —that Stazy Bromley was so much more complex than that. An enigma. One that was starting to interest him in spite of himself, Jaxon acknowledged ruefully as he realised he was watching the way her perfectly rounded bottom moved sensuously beneath her black fitted dress as she walked...

Even Stazy's defence of her grandparents, although an irritation to him, and casting aspersions upon his own character as it undoubtedly did, was still a trait to be admired. Most of the women Jaxon was acquainted with would sell their soul to the devil—let alone their grandparents' reputations!—if it meant they could attract even a little publicity for themselves by doing so!

Stazy Bromley obviously did the opposite. Even that inaccurate biography had only fleetingly mentioned that Anastasia had had one child and one grandchild, and any attempt to talk to Stazy after the publication of that book had been met with the response that 'Dr Stazy Bromley does not give personal interviews'.

'So,' Jaxon began as he joined her beside a pond full of large golden-coloured fish, 'what do you think of your grandfather's idea that the two of us meet here in the summer and research your grandmother's personal papers together...?'

She gave a humourless smile as she continued to watch the fish lazing beneath the water in the warmth of the early-evening sunshine. 'If I didn't know better I would say it was the onset of senility!'

Jaxon chuckled appreciatively. 'But as we both do know better…?'

She gave a shrug. 'You really can't be persuaded into dropping the film idea altogether?'

He drew in a sharp breath. 'Stazy, even if I said yes I know for a fact that there are at least two other directors with an interest in making their own version of what happened.'

Stazy turned to look at him searchingly, knowing by the openness of his expression as he returned her gaze that he was telling her the truth. 'Directors who may not have your integrity?' she questioned flatly.

'Probably not.' He grimaced.

'So, what you're saying is it's a question of going with the devil we know, or allowing some other film director to totally blacken my grandmother's name and reputation?' Stazy guessed heavily.

Jaxon nodded abruptly. 'That about sums it up, yes.'

Damned if they did—double damned it they didn't. 'You do realise that if I agree to do this I would be doing so under protest?'

His mouth twisted derisively. 'Oh, I believe you've made your feelings on that particular subject more than clear, Stazy,' he assured her dryly.

She shot him an irritated glance before once again turning to walk away, this time in the direction of the horses grazing in a corner of the meadow that adjoined the garden. One of those horses, a beautiful chestnut stallion, ambled over to stretch its neck across the fence, so that Stazy could stroke absently down the long length of his nose as she continued to consider the options available to her.

There really weren't any.

She either agreed to help Jaxon Wilder in his research or she refused, and then he'd go ahead and make the film without any input from her grandfather or Anastasia's private papers.

Her uncharacteristic physical awareness of this man was not only unacceptable but also baffling to Stazy, and even now, standing just feet away from him as she continued to stroke Copper's nose, she was totally aware of Jaxon's disturbing presence. Too much for her not to know that spending a week in his company was simply asking for trouble.

It was all too easy for Jaxon to see the riot of emotions that flashed across Stazy Bromley's expressive face as she considered what to do about this situation: impatience, frustration, anger, dismay—

Dismay...?

Jaxon raised dark brows as he wondered what *that* was all about. Obviously Stazy would rather this situation didn't exist at all, but she didn't appear to be the type of woman who would allow anything to get the better of her... And exactly *why* was he even bothering to wonder what type of woman Stazy Bromley was? Jaxon questioned self-derisively.

Her physical resemblance to her grandmother had aroused his interest initially, but this last hour or so of being insulted by her—both for who and what he was—had surely nullified that initial spark of appreciation?

Jaxon studied Stazy from beneath lowered lids. That wonderful hair gleamed fiery-gold in the sunlight, her eyes were a sultry and luminescent green, and there was a slight flush to her cheeks from walking in the sunshine. Her full and sensuous lips curved into an affectionate smile as the stallion nudged against her shoulder for attention.

He drew in a deep breath. 'It must have been a difficult time for you after your parents died—'

'I would rather not discuss my own private life with you, if you don't mind,' she said stiffly.

'I was only going to say that this must have been a wonderful place to spend your teenage years,' Jaxon murmured as he turned to lean his elbows on the fence and look across at the mellow-stoned house.

'It was—yes,' Stazy confirmed huskily. She looked up at him curiously. 'Whereabouts in England are you from?'

'Cambridgeshire.'

'And do you still go home?' she prompted curiously.

'Whenever I can.' Jaxon nodded. 'Which probably isn't as often as my family would like. My parents and younger brother still live in the small village where I grew up. But it's nowhere near as nice as this.'

It really was idyllic here, Jaxon appreciated, with horses gently grazing behind them, birds singing in the trees in the beautiful wooded area surrounding Bromley House and the coastline edging onto the grounds. The slightly salty smell of the sea was just discernible as waves gently rose and fell on the distant sand.

'I had forgotten that places like this existed,' he added almost wistfully.

'Nothing like it in LA, hmm?' Stazy mocked as she turned to look at him.

He shot her a rueful smile. 'Not exactly, no.' The place he had bought on the coast in Malibu several years ago was too huge and modern to feel in the least homely. 'Although I do own a place in New England—very rustic and in the woods—where I go whenever I get the chance.' Which, he realised, hadn't been all that often during recent years...

He had been busy filming and then editing his last film most of the previous year, then caught up in attending the premieres and numerous awards ceremonies since—including those that Stazy had mocked earlier! All of that had left him little time in which to sit back and smell the roses. Here at Bromley House it was possible to do that. Literally.

But the serpent in this particular Eden appeared to be the tangible antagonism of the beautiful and strangely alluring woman standing beside him...

Jaxon breathed deeply. 'For your grandfather's sake, couldn't we at least try to—?' He broke off as Stazy gave a derisive laugh. 'What?' he prompted irritably.

'My grandfather has taught me never to trust any statement that begins with "for whoever or whatever's sake"!' she revealed. 'He assures me it's usually a prefix to someone imposing their will by the use of emotional blackmail!'

Jaxon gave a rueful shake of his head. 'I would have thought you were old enough to make up your own mind about another person's intentions!'

Stazy felt the sting of colour in her cheeks at this obvious challenge. 'Oh, I am, Jaxon,' she assured him derisively.

He arched dark brows. 'And you decided I was going to be trouble before you even met me?' he guessed easily.

'Yes.' A belief that had been more than borne out these past few minutes as Stazy had become more physically aware of this magnetically handsome man in a way she wasn't in the least comfortable with! 'Shall we go back to the house?' It was a rhetorical and terse suggestion on Stazy's part, and she gave Copper one last affectionate stroke on his velvet-soft nose before walking away.

Jaxon fell into step beside her seconds later. 'And is that your final word on the subject?'

Stazy eyed him derisively. 'Don't be misled by my grandfather's social graciousness or his age, Jaxon. If you do come here to stay for a week to do your research then I believe you will very quickly learn that he always has the last word on any subject!'

Jaxon Wilder wouldn't be here at all if Stazy had her way!

A fact he was well aware of if his rueful smile was any indication. He shrugged those impossibly wide shoulders. 'Then I guess the outcome of all this is completely in your grandfather's hands.'

'Yes,' she acknowledged heavily, knowing her grandfather had left her in no doubt earlier as to what he had already decided...

Geoffrey was his usual charming self when he returned downstairs a short time later, obviously refreshed and alert from his nap. He took charge of the conversation as they all ate what on the surface appeared to be a leisurely dinner together.

Beneath that veneer of politeness it was a different matter, of course: Stazy still viewed Jaxon Wilder with suspicion; and on his part she was sure there was amusement, at her expense, glittering in those mercu-

rial grey eyes every time he so much as glanced in her
direction!

By the time they reached the coffee stage of the meal
Stazy could cheerfully have screamed at the underlying
tension in the air that surrounded them.

'So.' Her grandfather finally sat back in his chair at
the head of the table. 'Did the two of you manage to come
to any sort of compromise in my absence?'

Jaxon gave a derisive smile as he saw the way Stazy's mouth had thinned into stubbornness. 'I believe my
conclusion is that all the talking in the world between
the two of us won't make the slightest bit of difference
when you are the one to have the final say in the matter!'

'Indeed?' the older man drawled. 'Is that what you
believe, too, Stazy?'

She shrugged slender shoulders. 'You know that I will
go along with whatever you decide, Gramps.'

'I would rather have your co-operation, darling,'
Geoffrey prompted gently.

Jaxon watched Stazy from beneath lowered lids as he
took a sip of his brandy, knowing her initial antagonism
towards him hadn't lessened at all over the hours. That
if anything Stazy seemed even more wary of him now
than she had been earlier—to the point where she had
avoided even looking at him for the past half an hour or
so, let alone making conversation with him.

Could that possibly be because she was as physically
aware of him as Jaxon was of her…?

Doubtful!

She grimaced before answering her grandfather. 'Mr
Wilder has very kindly pointed out to me that he isn't
the only film director interested in making a film about

Granny.' The coldness of Stazy's tone implied she considered Jaxon anything but kind.

'So I believe, yes.' Geoffrey nodded.

Stazy's eyes widened. 'You knew that?'

'Of course I knew, darling,' her grandfather dismissed briskly. 'I may not be in the thick of things nowadays, but I still make it my business to know of anything of concern to my family or myself.'

Jaxon frowned. 'In my defence, I would like you to know that I have every intention of giving a fair and truthful version of the events of seventy years ago.'

'You wouldn't be here at all if I wasn't already well aware of that fact, Jaxon.' Steely-blue eyes met his unblinkingly. 'If I had believed you were anything less than a man of integrity I would never have spoken to you on the telephone, let alone invited you into my home.'

His respect and liking for the older man deepened. 'Thank you.'

'Oh, don't thank me too soon.' Sir Geoffrey smiled. 'I assure you, you've yet to convince my granddaughter!' he drawled, with an affectionate glance at Stazy's less than encouraging expression.

Jaxon grimaced. 'Perhaps the situation might change once we've worked together…?'

'Stazy…?' Geoffrey said softly.

Stazy was totally aware of being the focus of both men's gazes as they waited for her to answer—her grandfather's encouraging, Jaxon Wilder's much more guarded as he watched her through narrowed lids.

But what choice did she have, really…?

Her own feelings aside, her grandfather might have said he would have to accept Jaxon's film and 'be damned', but Stazy wasn't fooled for a moment. She knew of her grandfather's deep and abiding love for her grandmother, and of how much it would hurt him—perhaps fatally—if the film about Anastasia were to be in any way defamatory. And the only way to guarantee that didn't happen was if she agreed to work with Jaxon Wilder.

'Okay,' Stazy agreed heavily. 'I can give you precisely one week of my time at the beginning of my summer break.' She glared across at Jaxon as she recognised the triumphant gleam that had flared in his gaze at her capitulation. 'But only on the condition.'

'Another condition?' Jaxon grimaced.

She nodded. 'My grandfather has to give his full approval of the screenplay once it's been written,' she added firmly.

Working here with the prickly Stazy Bromley for a week was far from ideal as far as Jaxon was concerned. But not impossible when he considered the alternative...

'Fine.' He nodded abrupt agreement.

The tension visibly left Sir Geoffrey's shoulders, and Stazy saw this as evidence that he hadn't been as relaxed about this situation as he wished to appear. 'In that case, shall we expect to see you back here the first week of July, Jaxon?'

'Yes.' Even if that would involve reshuffling his schedule in order to fit in with Stazy Bromley's.

She still looked far from happy about the arrangement...

Her next comment only confirmed it. 'A word of warning, though, Jaxon—if anything happens to my grandfather because of this film then I am going to hold you totally responsible!'

Great.

Just great!

CHAPTER THREE

'WHAT'S WITH ALL the extra security at the front gates?'

Much as six weeks previously, Stazy had been prowling restlessly up and down in the drawing room of Bromley House as she waited for Jaxon Wilder. Her stomach had tightened into knots when she'd finally seen their visitor had arrived. Not in the expensive black sports car she had been expecting, but on a powerful black and chrome motorbike instead.

Convinced Jaxon Wilder couldn't possibly be the person riding that purring black machine, and confused as to why the guards had let a biker through the front gates at all, Stazy had continued to frown out of the window as the rider had brought the bike to a halt outside the drawing room window, before swinging off the seat and straightening to his full, impressive height.

The man was completely dressed in black—black helmet with smoky-black visor, black leathers that fitted snugly to muscled shoulders and back, narrowed waist and taut backside, and long, powerful legs. Black leather gloves. And heavy black biker boots.

He—it was definitely a he, with that height and those wide and muscled shoulders—had had his back turned towards her as he'd removed his gloves, before unfastening and removing the helmet and shaking back his almost shoulder-length dark hair as he placed the helmet on top of the black leather seat.

Stazy had felt the colour drain from her cheeks as the rider had turned and she had instantly recognised him. Jaxon Wilder. Almost instantly he had looked straight up into the window where she stood staring down at him, leaving her in absolutely no doubt as to his knowing he was being watched.

Staring?

Gaping at him was probably a more apt description!

All her defences had gone—crumbled—with the disappearance of the sophisticated man she had met six weeks ago, wearing a discreetly tailored suit, silk shirt and tie, with his dark hair slightly long but nevertheless neatly styled. In his place was a rugged and dangerous-looking man who looked as if he would be completely at home at a Hell's Angels reunion!

Stazy had left all the details of Jaxon's visit to her grandfather, knowing from conversations with Geoffrey that the two men had been in contact by telephone on several occasions during the last six weeks, and that the date for Jaxon to arrive at Bromley House had been fixed for today—the day after Stazy had driven herself down from London.

That initial meeting with Jaxon, the sizzling awareness she had felt, had seemed like something of a dream once Stazy had been back in London. So much so that she hadn't even mentioned her encounter to any of her friends at the university. Besides, she very much doubted that her work colleagues would have been interested in knowing she had spent part of the weekend with the famous Hollywood actor and director Jaxon Wilder.

But that didn't mean Stazy hadn't thought about him. About the way he looked. The aura of male power that was so much a part of him. The mesmerising grey of his eyes. The sensual curve of those chiselled lips. The deep and sexy timbre of his voice…

That aura was even more in evidence today—dangerously so!—as he looked up at her and gave her a slow and knowing grin.

Stazy had been completely flustered at being caught staring at him. Damn it, just because the man had arrived today looking like testosterone on legs, it didn't mean she had to behave as though she were no older than one of her students. She was virtually drooling, with her tongue almost hanging out, and she found it impossible to look away from how hot Jaxon looked in biker's leathers!

He had become no less imposing when the butler had shown him into the drawing room. Those leathers fitted Jaxon's muscled body like a second skin, the black boots added a couple of inches to his already considerable height, and that overlong dark hair fell softly onto his shoulders.

Already feeling something of a fool for being caught staring out of the window at him in that ridiculous way, Stazy was in no mood to repeat the experience.

'And a good afternoon to you, too, Jaxon,' she drawled pointedly.

Humour lightened his eyes. 'Are we aiming at playing nice this time around?'

'I thought we might give it a try, yes.' The tartness in her voice totally belied that.

Jaxon grinned, totally appreciative of how good Stazy looked in a white blouse that fitted snugly to the flatness of her abdomen and the fullness of her breasts, with faded denims fitting just as snugly to her curvaceous bottom and long and slender legs. Her glorious red-gold hair tumbled in loose layers over her shoulders and down the slenderness of her back today. And those sultry green eyes glowed like twin emeralds in the sun-kissed beauty of her delicately beautiful face.

She looked far younger and sexier today than the twenty-nine Jaxon knew her to be. In fact if any of his own university lecturers had ever looked this good then he doubted he would ever have been able to concentrate on attaining his degree. 'In that case, good afternoon, Stazy,' he drawled.

She gave him a slow and critical perusal, from the soles of his booted feet to his overlong hair. 'Are you on your way to a fancy dress party?'

He raised derisive brows. 'Whatever happened to playing nice...?'

She shrugged. 'It seems a perfectly reasonable question, considering the way you're dressed today. Or not, as the case may be.' She grimaced.

After the way she had stared wide-eyed at him out of the window earlier, Jaxon wasn't at all convinced by Dr Stazy Bromley's condescending tone in regard to the way he was dressed. He returned her shrug. 'I keep an apartment for my use when I'm in London, and the car and the bike are kept there too. As it's such a beautiful day, and I've been stuck on a plane for hours, I decided a ride down on the bike was called for.' He gave an appreciative smile. 'Have you ever been on a bike before, Stazy?'

'No,' Stazy answered huskily, her cheeks blazing with colour as she was assailed with the idea of wrapping her legs around that monstrous machine, feeling its vibration between her legs even as her arms were tightly clasped about the strength of Jaxon's waist, her breasts pressed against the warmth of that muscled back—

'Would you like to…?'

Stazy straightened abruptly, completely nonplussed at the way her thoughts kept wandering down a sensual path that was totally alien to her. Especially as she had managed to convince herself these last six weeks that she had imagined finding this man in the least attractive! 'No, thanks,' she dismissed coolly.

'You only have to say so if you should change your mind…'

'I won't,' she assured firmly. 'Is the bike also the reason for the long hair?' she prompted abruptly, fighting the uncharacteristic longing to run her fingers through those silky dark locks…

She had dated very little during the past eleven years, and the few men she had been out with had always possessed intellect rather than brawn. She had never particularly cared for long hair on men—had always thought it rather effeminate.

Jaxon had shown on the last occasion they had met that he was a man of intellect as well as brawn. And as for his being effeminate—the man was so blatantly male there was no possibility of ever doubting his masculinity!

'The long hair is for a pirate movie I start filming next month.' He ran his fingers ruefully through the length of that hair.

In exactly the same way Stazy's fingers itched to do!

She clasped her wayward hands firmly together behind her back. 'I'd always assumed actors wore a wig or extensions for those sorts of roles?'

He grimaced. 'I've always preferred to go with the real thing.'

Just the thought of Jaxon as a pirate, sweeping his captive—*her*!—up into his arms, was enough to make Stazy's palms feel damp. 'Whatever,' she snapped.

What on earth was wrong with her?

She'd never had fantasies about being swept off her feet by a marauding pirate before, so why now?

The disturbing answer to that question unfortunately stood only feet away from her…

'So, you didn't answer me—what's with the added security at the front gates?' Jaxon prompted lightly.

'I'm afraid it's all over the estate—not just the front gates.' Stazy shrugged. 'My grandfather arranged it.'

That didn't sound good. 'To keep the two of us in or other people out?' he asked.

'Very funny.' Those full and sensuous lips thinned at his teasing. 'Gramps received a telephone call late last night and the security guards arrived almost immediately afterwards. I believe he did attempt to call you and give you the option to postpone your visit until a later date, but he couldn't reach you on any of the telephone numbers you'd given him…' She arched red-gold brows.

'As I said earlier, I only arrived in England a few hours ago. I was probably in transit,' Jaxon dismissed distractedly. 'Any idea what the problem is?'

'Gramps never discusses matters of security with me.' She shook her head. 'Unfortunately you won't be able to discuss it with him either,' she added unapologetically, 'because he left for London very early this morning.'

Meaning that, apart from the household staff, the two of them were currently alone here together.

Probably not a good idea, when Jaxon was totally

aware of Stazy's femininity today in the fitted blouse
and tight denims. And that glorious unconfined red-gold
hair was a temptation he was barely able to resist reaching out and touching.

What would it feel like, he wondered, to entangle his
fingers in that silky hair? Or, even more appealing, to
have the length of that gorgeous hair tumbling sensuously about his thighs as a naked Stazy knelt between
his parted legs, her fingers curled about his throbbing
shaft as she bent forward to taste him…?

'He did say he would try to telephone you later today
to explain,' she added dismissively.

'Fine,' Jaxon accepted tersely, aware that his erotic
imaginings had produced a bulge of arousal beneath the
fitted leathers. Something Stazy was going to become
aware of too if he didn't get out of here soon!

'I'm sure he'll understand if, under the circumstances,
you decide you would rather leave the research for now
and come back another time…'

Was that hope he heard in Stazy's voice? Probably,
Jaxon acknowledged ruefully. Despite her casual appearance, she didn't seem any more pleased to see him this
time around than she had six weeks ago. 'Sorry to disappoint you, Stazy, but I don't have any other time free.'

'I assure you it makes absolutely no difference to me
whether you stay or go,' she dismissed scathingly.

Nope, Stazy wasn't pleased to have him here at all.
'In that case, I'm staying,' he drawled.

Stazy nodded tersely. 'Gramps left all the necessary
papers in the library for us to look through, if you would
like to get started?'

Jaxon shook his head. 'I've been travelling for almost twenty-four hours. What I would really like to do

is shower and change out of these leathers.' All of that should give enough time for his wayward arousal to ease!

Unfortunately Jaxon's request instantly gave Stazy an image of Jaxon stripped out of those decadent leathers, standing naked beneath a hot shower, the darkness of his hair wet and tousled as rivulets of soapy water ran down his hard and tanned torso—

'Would you like some tea before you go upstairs?' she bit out abruptly, inwardly cursing the way her breasts felt fuller just at her thinking about a naked Jaxon in the shower.

This was ridiculous, damn it! She had never been a sensual being—had certainly never—*ever*!—reacted like this in her life before, let alone found her imagination wandering off into flights of fantasy about a man whose reputation with women was legendary!

'Just the shower and a change of clothes, thanks.'

She nodded. 'I'll have Little take you up to the suite of rooms my grandfather has had prepared for your arrival.'

'Why put the butler to all that trouble when you're already here…?' Jaxon asked huskily.

Stazy stilled, her finger poised over the button that would summon the butler back to the drawing room, before slowly turning to look at Jaxon. The mockery in those assessing grey eyes and the challenging expression on his ruggedly handsome face indicated that he was aware of exactly how much his suggestion had disconcerted her.

Her mouth thinned. 'Fine.'

Jaxon realised this was going to be a long week if the two of them were going to get into a battle of wills over something as small as Stazy showing him up to his suite of rooms!

'I trust you didn't have too much of a problem rearranging your departure for Iraq to next week instead of this?' He attempted conversation as the two of them walked up the wide staircase together.

She gave him the briefest of glances from those emerald-green eyes. 'Would it bother you if I had?'

'Honestly? Not really.' He grimaced, only to raise surprised brows as she gave a laugh. A husky laugh that brought a warm glow to those sultry green eyes. A dimple appeared in her left cheek as the parted fullness of her lips curved into a smile.

Strangely, Jaxon had found himself thinking about those sensuous lips more often than he would have liked these past six weeks. Full and luscious lips that were at odds with the rest of Stazy's buttoned down, no-nonsense appearance... The sort of lips that would be delicious to kiss and taste, and to have kiss and taste him in return...

Something he probably shouldn't think of again when he was already so hard his erection was pressing painfully against the confines of his leathers!

'Which isn't to say I don't appreciate your having—'

'Oh, don't go and spoil it by apologising, Jaxon.' Stazy still chuckled softly as they reached the top of the stairs and she turned right to walk down the hallway ahead of him. 'If we're to spend any amount of time together then you need to know that I'll appreciate your honesty much more than I would any false charm.'

'My charm is never false,' he snapped irritably.

Stazy turned to quirk a teasing brow. 'Never? Be warned, Jaxon, I'm guilty of having watched film awards on television in the past!'

'Guilty...?'

She snorted. 'Oh, come on, Jaxon—it's all so much glitzy hype, isn't it?'

'I believe the newspapers praised me for the shortness of my acceptance speech this year,' he drawled.

'I'm not surprised; I thought your co-star was never going to get off the podium!'

'She can be…a little emotional,' Jaxon allowed reluctantly.

'A little…?' Stazy raised mocking brows. 'She thanked everyone but the man who sweeps the studio floor!'

His eyes narrowed. 'You really can be a—' He broke off with an impatient shake of his head. 'Never mind,' he muttered tersely.

Stazy pushed open the door to the suite of rooms she knew her grandfather had allocated to his guest. The green and cream decor and dark furniture there was more obviously masculine than in some of the other guest suites, as was the adjoining cream and gold bathroom visible through the open doorway. But it was the massive four-poster bed that dominated.

'The sitting room is through here.' She turned away from the intimacy of the bedroom to walk through to the adjoining room with its green carpet and cream sofa. A mahogany desk placed in front of the bay window looked out over the gardens at the back of the house, with the blue of the sea visible above the high wall that surrounded the grounds.

'This is very nice,' Jaxon murmured evenly.

Stazy eyed him derisively. 'You seem a little…tense?'

Those grey eyes narrowed. 'I wonder why!'

She shrugged. 'Can I help it if the much publicised Wilder charm doesn't work on me?'

Jaxon's mouth thinned at the deliberate insult. 'You shouldn't believe everything you read in trashy magazines!'

Her eyes flashed deeply green. 'I've never read a trashy magazine in my life, thank you very much!'

'Too lowbrow for you?' he taunted.

She drew in a sharp breath. 'My grandfather made it clear to me before he left that he expected me to be polite to a guest in his home during his absence—'

'I hate to be the one to tell you—but so far today you've failed. Miserably!' Jaxon bit out.

Stazy eyed him coolly. 'Being polite doesn't mean I have to be insincere.'

'If you wouldn't mind...?' He began to unzip those body-moulding leathers. 'I would like to take my shower now.' He arched mocking brows.

Stazy had no doubt that Jaxon's challenging attitude now was in return for her earlier scathing comments about 'the much-published Wilder charm'. But as he continued to move that zip further and further down his hard muscled chest she knew it was a challenge she simply didn't have the sophistication—or the experience!—to meet.

'Come downstairs when you're ready and I'll show you the library where we're to work,' she said stiltedly, before turning sharply on her booted heels and hurrying over to the doorway.

Totally aware of the sound of Jaxon's throaty laughter behind her...

'Where do you want to start?'

'I have absolutely no idea.' Jaxon looked down in some dismay at the copious amount of documents and notebooks Geoffrey Bromley had left neatly stacked on the desktop in the library for him to look through. Jaxon wasn't sure he would be able to get through them all in just the week Stazy had agreed to give him.

The library itself was full of floor to ceiling mahogany bookcases stacked mainly with leather-bound books, although some of the shelves near the door seemed to be full of more modern hardbacks that he might like to explore another time.

Jaxon felt somewhat refreshed after a long cold shower and a change of clothes, and thankfully had succeeded in dissipating the last of his erection as well as washing off the travel dust.

The erection was something—despite their sharp exchange in his suite earlier—that was guaranteed not to stay away for very long if Stazy was going to continue bending over the desk in that provocative way, her denims clearly outlining the perfect curve of her bottom.

'Maybe we should just sort them out year by year today, and start looking through them properly tomorrow?' he prompted tersely.

'Sounds logical.' Stazy nodded.

Jaxon regarded her through narrowed lids. 'And are you big on logic?'

She looked irritated by the implied criticism. 'I've always found it's the best way to approach most situations, yes.'

'Hmm.' He nodded. 'The problem with logic is that it leaves no room for emotion.'

'Which is precisely the point,' Stazy reasoned shortly.

No doubt—but Jaxon didn't work that way. 'Are these Anastasia's diaries?' He ran awed fingers lightly over a pile of a dozen small notebooks.

'They certainly look like them, yes…' Stazy frowned down at them as if they were a bomb about to go off.

He glanced up as he sensed her tension. 'You didn't know there were diaries?'

She gave a pained wince. 'No.'

Jaxon breathed deeply. 'Stazy, as much as you may choose not to think so, I *do* appreciate that none of this can be easy for you—'

Those green eyes flashed in warning. 'I doubt you have any idea how much I hate doing this!'

'Obviously Anastasia was your grandmother, and you only knew her during her latter years, but—'

'But even then she would still have known exactly how to deal with someone like *you*!' Stazy assured him dismissively. Even that red-gold hair seemed to crackle with her repressed anger.

'Like me?' he said softly.

'You know exactly what I mean!'

'I do,' he acknowledged, with that same deceptive mildness. 'I'd just like to hear you say it,' he added challengingly.

She glared her frustration. 'Jaxon, you've known from the first that nothing is going to make me like you *or* your damned film!'

'Nothing…?'

Stazy stilled as she looked up at him guardedly. The darkness of that overlong hair was still damp and slightly tousled from his shower. His jaw was freshly shaven, and he had changed out of the black leathers into a tight-fitting white short-sleeved tee shirt that revealed the tanned strength of his arms and black denims that rested low down on the leanness of his waist.

He looked, in fact, every inch Jaxon Wilder—sex

symbol of both the big and little screen. A stark reminder—if Stazy had needed one—of just how little it actually mattered to this man whether or not she liked or approved of him and what he was doing.

Her chin rose determinedly. 'I'm sorry to disappoint you, Jaxon, but I have absolutely no interest in…in providing you with a—a romantic diversion to help while away your leisure time during your week-long stay here,' she assured him derisively.

'What on earth makes you think I would be in the least interested in having you as "a romantic diversion"—now or at any other time…?' His expression was amused as he leant back against the desk and looked down at her with mocking grey eyes, his arms folded across the powerful width of his chest, revealing the bulge of muscle at the tops of his tanned arms.

Stazy's cheeks heated with embarrassed colour at this deliberate set-down. What on earth had she been thinking? Of *course* Jaxon's challenge hadn't been hinting he was in the least interested in her in a personal way!

'But just to set my mind at ease, if things *should* go that way between us I'd be interested to know whether or not you're involved with someone at the moment…?'

When had Jaxon moved so that he now stood only inches away from her? Stazy wondered warily. He was pinning her as he looked down at her with piercing grey eyes.

She moistened her lips with the tip of her tongue. 'I don't see what that has to do with anything…'

'Humour me, hmm?' he encouraged gruffly.

The more immediate problem for Stazy—the whole root of the problem between the two of them—was that from their first meeting she had realised his magnetism was such that she wanted to do so much more than humour this man!

It was totally illogical. Ridiculous. Not only that, but it went totally against everything she had said and thought about this man!

And yet at this moment she literally *ached* to curve her body into his as she ran her hands lightly up the warmth of that muscled chest, over the broad expanse of his shoulders, before allowing her fingers to become entangled in the heavy thickness of that overlong dark hair to pull his head down and have those sensually chiselled lips claim hers…

This wasn't just ridiculous—it was dangerous!

And so completely out of character that Stazy barely recognised herself. Damn it, she didn't even *want* to recognise herself as this woman who couldn't seem to stop fantasising about the two of them in one clinch or another!

She had taken precisely two lovers in her twenty-nine years. The first had been one of her university lecturers, twenty years her senior, on a single night ten years ago. The second one had been a man on a summer dig in Tunisia four years ago—a man who had a wife and children back home in England. Admittedly that was something Stazy had only learnt *after* spending the night with him, when his wife had telephoned to inform him that one of his three children was in hospital and he was needed back home immediately!

Neither of those experiences had resulted in Stazy feeling any warmth or pleasure in the act, let alone having an orgasm. They certainly hadn't prepared her for the seductively lethal charm and good looks of Jaxon Wilder!

She stepped back abruptly. 'As it happens I'm not involved with anyone at the moment. Nor do I wish to be,' she added with cold dismissal.

It was a coldness so at odds with the quickened rise and fall of her breasts, the deepening in colour of those sultry green eyes and the soft swelling of poutingly moist lips, that Jaxon wanted nothing more than to take Stazy in his arms and prove her wrong!

That need hovered in the air between them for several long, tense seconds.

Stazy's chin rose as she deliberately tilted her head back in order to meet his gaze.

Did she have any idea how tempted Jaxon was by that challenge? Of how he wanted nothing more at that moment than to pull her into his arms and kiss the hell out of her?

Stazy was a beautiful woman in her late twenties, and as such she had to be aware of exactly what she was doing. Which begged the question—did she actually *want* him to kiss the hell out of her...?

CHAPTER FOUR

STAZY TOOK A STEP back as she saw the look of sexual interest that had entered Jaxon's narrowed eyes. 'Perhaps you would like to concentrate on the papers and I'll sort out the diaries?' To her dismay she sounded slightly breathless, and Jaxon was still standing close enough that she was aware of the heat of his body and the tantalising smell of his aftershave.

'Fine,' he agreed huskily, that smoky-grey gaze unblinking.

She continued to eye him warily, very aware that something—she wasn't quite sure what—hung in the balance in these tension filled minutes. Something deep and almost primal. Something so nerve-tinglingly huge that Stazy feared it threatened to tear down the structured life of academia that she had so carefully surrounded herself with these past eleven years!

Jaxon felt as if he could have reached out and touched the sudden and obvious panic that spiked through Stazy as her eyes widened and the slenderness of her body trembled. The very air between them seemed to shimmer with that same emotion.

The question was *why*? What was so wrong with a

man finding Stazy attractive enough to want to kiss her? Maybe even make love to her?

Had she been hurt in the past to the extent that it had made her wary of all men? Or did she only feel that wariness where Jaxon was concerned? She had certainly seemed to imply as much earlier!

Admittedly the newspapers had seemed to take great delight in photographing him with the beautiful actresses he'd been involved with during the past ten years; but in reality they really hadn't been that numerous—and a lot of the photographs that had appeared had actually been publicity shots, usually for the film he was currently working on.

Even so, he didn't feel that was any reason for Stazy to look at him in that wary and suspicious way. Almost as if she feared that at any moment he might rip her clothes off before throwing her across the desk and having his wicked way with her!

It was an idea that might merit further investigation, but certainly wasn't something Jaxon thought was likely to happen in the next few minutes!

He eased the tension from his shoulders. 'Shall we make a start then…?'

'Why not?' Stazy felt as if she were emerging from a dream as she forced herself to reply with the same lightness of tone, before ignoring him completely to concentrate all her attention on the piles of papers.

On the surface, at least. Inwardly, it was a different matter!

What had happened just now?

Had *anything* happened…?

Maybe she had just imagined the physical tension that had seemed to crackle briefly in the air between Jaxon

and herself? Or—worse—maybe that physical awareness had only been on her side?

No, Stazy was sure it hadn't been. But, as she had assured him earlier, she certainly knew better than to take
seriously any emotional or physical games a man as experienced as Jaxon might decide to play. He was only
here for a week, and then he would depart to commence
making his pirate film, at which time he would probably
forget Dr Stazy Bromley even existed.

As long as she kept reminding herself of that fact she
should escape from their week's confinement together
unscathed…

'Geoffrey seemed more than a little…evasive as to his
reason for the need for extra security when I spoke to
him on the telephone earlier…?' Jaxon looked across the
dinner table at Stazy. The butler had served them their
first course of prawns with avocado before once again
leaving them alone together in the small and sunlit family dining room.

Stazy looked extremely beautiful this evening, having changed into a knee-length red sheath of a dress that
should have clashed with that red-gold hair and yet instead somehow managed to add vibrancy to the unusual
colour. Her legs were long and shapely in high-heeled
red sandals, and her sun-kissed face was once again bare
of make-up except for a red gloss on the fullness of her
lips. A light dusting of endearing freckles was visible
across the bridge of her tiny nose.

It had only taken one look at her when they'd met up
in the drawing room before dinner for Jaxon to once
again become aroused, quickly bringing him to the con-

clusion that suffering a whole week of this torment might just be the death of him.

'I did try to warn you that until Gramps has something he thinks we should know he'll play whatever this is pretty close to his chest,' Stazy answered unsympathetically.

Jaxon arched dark brows as she continued to eat her prawns and avocado. 'You seem to be taking it all very calmly?' It 'all' included those security guards at the main gates, as well as half a dozen more he had seen patrolling the grounds when he'd looked out of his bedroom window earlier—several of them accompanied by dogs.

She shrugged slender shoulders. 'I lived here with Granny and Gramps for almost ten years.'

'And you've had other security scares in the past?'

'Once or twice, yes,' Stazy said lightly.

'But—'

'Jaxon, if you're that worried about it you always have the option of leaving,' she reasoned softly.

Great—now she'd managed to make him sound like a complete wuss! 'I'm happy where I am, thanks,' he dismissed—or at least he would be if he didn't feel so on edge about his constant state of arousal whenever he was in Stazy's company!

Admittedly Stazy was beautiful, but she was nowhere near as beautiful as some of the women Jaxon had been involved with in the past. Nor did she make any attempt to hide her distrust of him. In fact the opposite.

Which was perhaps half the attraction…?

Maybe—although somehow Jaxon doubted it. Stazy was like no other woman he had ever met. For one thing she didn't even seem aware of her own beauty. Add that to her obvious intelligence and it was a pretty potent mix.

Jaxon had never been attracted to a woman simply on her looks alone, and he liked to be able to talk to a woman out of bed as well as make love with her in it. Stazy Bromley obviously ticked all the boxes as far as his raging libido was concerned.

Stazy wasn't sure she particularly cared for the way in which Jaxon was looking at her from between those hooded lids—almost as if he were thinking of eating *her* for his dinner rather than the food on his plate!

She had deliberately put on her favourite red dress this evening, in order to give herself the boost in confidence she had felt she lacked earlier. After those tension-filled minutes in her grandfather's library she had felt in need of all the armour she could get where Jaxon Wilder was concerned, and feeling confident about her own appearance was definitely a good place to start.

Or at least it would have been if the moment she'd seen him again she hadn't been so completely aware of how dangerously attractive Jaxon looked this evening, in a loose white silk shirt and those black denims that fitted snugly to the leanness of his muscled thighs and long, long legs…

His shirt was unbuttoned at his throat to reveal the beginnings of a dusting of dark hair that no doubt covered most of his chest. And lower. That 'lower' being exactly where Stazy had forced her thoughts to stop earlier today. Unfortunately she didn't seem to be having the same success this evening!

This just wasn't *her*, damn it. Those two attempts at taking a lover had not only proved completely unsatisfactory but had also firmly put an end to any illusions she might have had where she and men were concerned. She certainly didn't indulge in erotic fantasies about movie stars—or any other man, come to that!—and the sooner her grandfather returned from London and put a stop to this cosy intimacy for two the better!

'So…' Jaxon waited until the butler had been in to clear away their used plates before leaning forward. 'Have I told you how lovely you're looking this evening…?'

That air of intimacy between them became even cosier—in fact the temperature in the room seemed to go up several degrees! 'No, you haven't—and I would prefer that you didn't do so now, either,' Stazy bit out determinedly.

He raised dark brows. 'I thought you asked me for honesty earlier…?'

'Not that sort of honesty!' Her eyes flashed a deep disapproving green. 'We're work colleagues, Jaxon, and work colleagues do not comment on each other's appearance if they are to maintain a proper working relationship.'

'You sound as if you're speaking from experience…?'

Colour warmed her cheeks. 'Perhaps.'

'Feel like telling me about it…?'

Her mouth firmed. 'No.'

Pity, because Jaxon would have liked to know more—a lot more!—about Stazy's personal life. 'Most of the actresses I've worked with would be insulted if I didn't mention their appearance at least once a day.'

Stazy shot him an impatient frown. 'Well, I assure you in my case it isn't necessary. Or appreciated.'

He smiled ruefully. 'I thought all women liked to receive compliments?'

'I would rather be complimented on my academic ability than the way I look,' she stated primly.

Jaxon might have been more convinced of that if Stazy's hand hadn't trembled slightly as she picked up her glass and took a sip of the red wine. 'That's a little difficult for me to do when I know next to nothing about your academic ability—other than you're obviously good at what you do—but I can clearly see how beautiful you look in that red dress.'

Those green eyes darkened. 'We aren't out on a date, Jaxon, and no amount of compliments from you is going to result in the two of us ending up in bed together at the end of the evening, either— Damn, damn, *damn*!' she muttered, with an accusing glare in his direction as the butler returned to the dining room just in time to hear that last outburst.

Jaxon barely managed to keep his humour in check as Stazy studiously avoided so much as looking at him again as Little hastily served their food before beating an even hastier retreat. 'Guess what the gossip in the kitchen is going to be about later this evening…' he murmured ruefully.

'This isn't funny, Jaxon,' she bit out agitatedly. 'Little has worked for my grandfather for years. I've known him all my life. And now he's going to think that I— that we—' She broke off with a disbelieving shake of her head.

'Oh, cheer up, Stazy.' Jaxon smiled unconcernedly. 'Look on the bright side—at least I now know where I stand in regard to the possibility of sharing your bed tonight. With any luck, after hearing your last remark, Little will decide to put lighted candles on the dinner table for us tomorrow evening, in an attempt to heat up the romance!'

Much as she hated to admit it, Stazy knew she didn't

need any 'heating up' where this man was concerned! And considering it was now July, and the evenings stayed light until after ten o'clock at night, she didn't think there was much chance of any candles appearing on the dinner table—tomorrow night or any other. In fact it was still so light at the moment that the curtains hadn't even been drawn over the floor-to-ceiling windows yet, and the view of a beautiful sunset was certainly adding to the air of romance.

Whatever cutting reply Stazy might have wanted to make to Jaxon's suggestion was delayed as Little returned with a laden tray, his face completely expressionless as he served their main course without meeting the gaze of either one of them before quietly departing again.

'You're enjoying yourself, aren't you?' Stazy eyed Jaxon impatiently as he grinned across the table at her.

Jaxon chuckled softly. 'So would you be if you would just lighten up a little. Oh, come on, Stazy—just think about it for a minute and then admit it *was* funny,' he cajoled irritably as she continued to frown.

'I'll admit no such thing! You—'

'Ever heard the saying about the lady protesting too much…?' He raised mocking brows. 'I've been told that when a lady does that, it usually means she wants you to do the opposite of what she's saying.'

'Whoever told you that was an idiot!' She gave an impatient shake of her head. 'And if you weren't my grandfather's guest I would ask you to leave!'

'Pity about that, isn't it?' he murmured dryly.

Stazy threw her napkin down on the tabletop before standing up and moving away from the table. 'If you will excuse me—'

'No.'

She stilled. 'What do you mean, no?'

'Exactly what I said—no.' The humour had gone from Jaxon's voice and expression, and there was a dark scowl on his brow as he threw down his own napkin before standing up to move purposefully around the table towards her.

Stazy raised a protesting hand even as she instinctively took a step backwards—only to find herself trapped between a looming Jaxon in front of her and a glass cabinet containing china ornaments behind her. 'Stop this right now, Jaxon—'

'Believe me, I haven't even started yet,' he growled, a nerve pulsing in his tightly clenched jaw as he towered over her. 'In fact I think maybe we should just get this over with and then maybe we can move on!' he muttered impatiently.

Stazy looked up at him with startled eyes. 'Get what over with…?'

He gave a shake of his head and lifted his arms to place them either side of her head so that his hands rested on the doors of cabinet behind her, his body almost, but not quite, touching hers. 'For some reason you seem to have decided that at some time during my stay here I'm going to try and seduce you into my bed, so I thought we might as well make a start!'

'You—' Stazy's protest came to an abrupt end as she realised that lifting her hands and placing them against Jaxon's chest, with the intention of pushing him away from her, had been a bad idea. A *very* bad idea…

Her hands lingered. His chest felt very warm to her touch through the soft material of his shirt—like steel encased in velvet as his muscles flexed beneath her fingers. The smell of his cologne—cinnamon and sandalwood—

combined with hot, hot male was almost overwhelming to the senses.

Almost?

Stazy ceased to breathe at all as she stared up at Jaxon with wide, apprehensive eyes. Was he right? *Had* she been 'protesting too much'? When in reality she had been longing for this to happen?

God, yes…!

Much as it pained her to admit it, Stazy knew she had thought about Jaxon far too often for comfort in the last six weeks. Damn it, she had even fantasised earlier about what it would be like to be naked with Jaxon, making love with him…

But wanting something and getting it weren't the same things, were they? For instance she had wanted an expensive microscope when she was ten years old— had been convinced at the time that she intended to be a medical doctor when she was older. Her parents had bought her a less expensive microscope, equally convinced that it was just a fad she was going through, with the promise of buying her the more expensive microscope one day if she ever *did* become a doctor.

Maybe not the best analogy, but Stazy no more needed Jaxon in her bed now than she had really needed that very expensive microscope nineteen years ago.

In other words, allowing Jaxon Wilder to kiss her would be an extravagance her emotions just didn't want or need!

Stazy liked her life ordered. Structured. Safe!

Most of all safe…

She had learnt at a very young age that caring for someone, loving them, needing a special someone in your life, was a guarantee of pain in the future when that person either left or—worse—died. As her parents had died. As Granny had died. As her grandfather, now in his nineties, and with that heart attack only a few months ago behind him, would eventually die.

Stazy didn't want to care about anyone else, to need anyone else—couldn't cope with any more losses in her life.

'Don't do that!' Jaxon groaned huskily.

She raised startled lids. 'Do what?'

'Lick your lips.' The darkness of his gaze became riveted on the moistness of those lips as Stazy ran her tongue nervously between them. 'I've been wanting to do exactly the same thing since the moment we first met,' Jaxon admitted gruffly.

Her eyes were wide. 'You have…?'

He rested his forehead against hers, his breath a warm caress across her already heated cheeks. 'You have the sexiest mouth I've ever seen…'

She gave a choked laugh. 'I thought it was universally acknowledged that that was Angelina Jolie?'

'Until six weeks ago I thought so too.' Jaxon nodded.

He had fantasised about Stazy's mouth these past six weeks. Imagined all the things she could do to him with those deliciously full and pouting lips. Grown hard with need just thinking of that plump fullness against his flesh, kissing him, tasting him. As he now longed to taste her…

'I'm going to kiss you now, Stazy,' Jaxon warned harshly.

'Jaxon, no…!' she groaned in protest.

'Jaxon, yes!' he contradicted firmly, before lowering his head and capturing those full and succulent lips with his own, groaning low in his throat as he found she felt and tasted as good as he had imagined she would!

If Jaxon's mouth had been demanding or rough against hers then Stazy believed she might have been able to resist him. She *hoped* she would have been able to resist him! As it was he kissed her with gentle exploration, sipping, tasting, as his mouth moved over and against hers with a slow languor that was torture to the senses. Taste as well as touch.

Those chiselled lips were surprisingly soft and warm against her own, his body even hotter as Jaxon lowered himself against her with a low groan, instantly making her aware of the hardness of his arousal pressing against her own aching thighs.

Unbidden, it seemed, her hands glided up his chest and over his shoulders, until her fingers at last became entangled with the overlong thickness of that silky dark hair.

He pulled back slightly, and Stazy at once felt bereft without the heat of those exploring lips against her own.

'Say so now if you want me to stop…'

'No…' She was the one to initiate the kiss this time, as she moved up onto her tiptoes, her lips parting to deepen the kiss rather than end it as she held him to her.

It was all the invitation Jaxon needed. He pressed himself firmly against the warm softness of her body as his hands moved to cup either side of her face so that he could explore that delicious mouth more deeply, tongue dipping between her parted lips to enter and explore the moist and inviting heat beneath.

Her taste—warmth and the sweetness of honey, and something indefinably feminine—was completely intoxicating. Like pure alcohol shooting through Jaxon's bloodstream, it threw him off balance, ripping away any awareness of anything other than the taste and feel of Stazy's mouth against his and her warm and luscious body beneath him.

He could only *feel* as Stazy wrapped her arms more tightly about his shoulders and arched her body up and into his, her soft breasts against the hardness of his chest, the heat of her thighs against the hot throb of his arousal. His hands moved down to her waist before sliding around to cup the twin orbs of her bottom to pull her up closer to him.

Jaxon kissed her hungrily, his arousal a fierce throb as Stazy returned the hunger of that kiss, lips hot and demanding, tongues duelling, bodies clamouring for even closer contact.

As Stazy had expected—feared—the tight control she usually exerted over her emotions had departed the moment Jaxon began to kiss her. Her nipples had grown hard and achingly sensitised, and the heat from their kisses was moving between her thighs—a feeling she hadn't experienced even when fully making love with those two men in her past.

She didn't want Jaxon ever to stop. Every achingly aroused inch of her cried out for more. One of his hands moved to cup the fullness of her breast, sending hot rivulets of pleasure coursing through her as his thumb grazed across the aching nipple. Stazy pressed into the heat of his hand, wanting more, needing more, and Jaxon lifted her completely off the floor to wrap her legs about his waist.

She no longer cared that they were in her grandfather's family dining room, or that Little could walk back into the room at any moment to remove their dinner plates.

All she was aware of was Jaxon—the heat of his arousal pressing into her softness, the pleasure that curled and grew inside her as he squeezed her nipple between thumb and finger, just enough to increase her pleasure but not enough to cause her pain, the hardness of him sending that same pleasure coursing through her.

She whimpered in protest as Jaxon broke the kiss, that protest turning to a low and aching moan of pleasure as his mouth moved down the length of her throat, his tongue a hot rasp against her skin as he tasted every hot inch of her from the sensitivity of her earlobe to the exposed hollow where her neck and shoulder met. And all the time his thighs continued that slow and torturous thrust against her.

Stazy still felt as if she were poised on the very edge of a precipice, but no longer cared if she fell over the edge. She wanted this. Wanted Jaxon. He felt so good, so very, very good, that she never wanted this to end…

Jaxon pulled back with a groan, his forehead slightly damp as it rested against hers. 'Lord knows I don't want us to stop, but Little is sure to come back in a few minutes…'

Stazy stared up at him blankly for several seconds, and then her face paled, her eyes widening with dismay as she took in the full import of what had just happened. 'Oh-my-God…!' Her expression was stricken as she struggled to put her feet back onto the floor, her face averted as she pulled out of Jaxon's arms to hastily straighten and pull her dress back down over the silkiness of her thighs.

'Stazy—'

'I think it's best if you don't touch me again, Jaxon,' she warned shakily, even as Jaxon would have done exactly that.

His arms dropped back to his sides as he saw the bewilderment in her eyes. His tone was reasoning. 'Stazy, what happened just now was perfectly normal—'

'It may be "normal" for you, Jaxon, but it certainly isn't normal for me!' she assured tremulously.

'Damn it, I *asked* you if you wanted me to stop!'

'I know…!' she groaned. 'I just— This must never happen again, Jaxon.' She looked up at him with tear-wet eyes.

'Why not…?'

'It just can't,' she bit out determinedly.

'That isn't a reason—'

'I'm afraid it's the only one you're going to get at the moment,' she confirmed huskily, giving him one last pleading look before turning to hurry across the room to wrench open the door, closing it firmly behind her several seconds later.

Leaving Jaxon in absolutely no doubt that the passionately hot Stazy—the woman he had held in his arms only minutes ago—would be firmly buried beneath cool and analytical Dr Anastasia Bromley by the time the two of them met again…

CHAPTER FIVE

'IF YOU HAD LET me know you were going out riding earlier this morning then I would have come with you, rather than just sat and watched you out of the window as I ate my breakfast...'

Stazy's gaze was cool when she glanced across at Jaxon as he entered the library the following morning. 'To have invited you to accompany me would have defeated the whole object.' Having to accept one of her grandfather's security guards accompanying her, and in doing so severely curtailing where she rode, had been bad enough, without having Jaxon trailing along as well!

After last night he was the last person she had wanted to be with when she'd got up this morning!

Neither of her two experiences had prepared her in the least for the heat, the total wildness, of being in Jaxon's arms the previous evening.

It had been totally out of control. *She* had been out of control!

Her two sexual experiences had been far from satisfactory, and yet she had almost gone over the edge just from having her legs wrapped around Jaxon's waist while he thrust against the silky barrier of her panties!

Having escaped to her bedroom the previous evening, Stazy had relived every wild and wanton moment of being in Jaxon's arms. The thrumming excitement. The arousal. And—oh, God!—the pleasure! She had trembled from the force of that pleasure, the sensitive ache still between her thighs, her breasts feeling full and sensitised.

She had been so aroused that she dreaded to think what might have happened if Jaxon hadn't called a halt to their lovemaking. Would Jaxon have stripped off her clothes? Worse, would she have ripped off her own clothes? And would he have made love to her on the carpeted floor, perhaps? Or maybe he would have just ripped her panties aside and taken her against the cabinet? Having either of those two things happen would have been not only unacceptable but totally beyond Stazy's previous experience.

'Am I wrong in sensing the implication that you much preferred to go out riding rather than having to sit and eat breakfast with me…?' Jaxon prompted dryly.

She looked across at him. 'Is that what I implied…?'

He eyed her frustratedly. Knowing that beneath Stazy's exterior of cool logic was a woman as passionate as the fiery red-gold of her hair, a woman who had become liquid flame in his arms as she absorbed—*consumed*!—the blazing demand of his desire before giving it back in equal measure didn't help to ease that frustration in the slightest.

'Besides which,' she continued briskly, 'I was up at six, as usual, and breakfasted not long after.'

Jaxon closed the door behind him before strolling over to sit on the edge of the table where Stazy sat. 'I'll have to remember that you're an early riser if I ever want the two of us to breakfast together.'

Stazy could think of only one circumstance under which that might be applicable—and it was a circumstance she had no intention of allowing to happen! That didn't mean to say she wasn't completely aware of Jaxon's muscled thigh only inches away from her where he perched on the edge of the table…

He looked disgustingly fit and healthy this morning for a man who had flown over from the States only yesterday: the sharp angles of his face were healthily tanned, that overlong dark hair was slightly damp from the shower, his tee shirt—black today—fitted snugly over his muscled chest and the tops of his arms, and faded denims outlined the leanness of his waist and those long legs. There was only a slightly bruised look beneath those intelligent grey eyes to indicate that Jaxon suffered any lingering jet lag.

'I shouldn't bother for the short amount of time you'll be here,' she advised dryly.

He gave a relaxed smile. 'Oh, it's no bother, Stazy,' he assured her huskily.

She shifted restlessly. 'Considering your time here is limited, shouldn't we get started…?'

Jaxon didn't need any reminding that he now had only six days left in which to do his research. Just as he didn't need to be told that it was Stazy's intention to keep her distance from him for those same six days…

There had been a few moments of awkwardness the previous evening, when he'd told Little that Stazy wasn't feeling well enough to finish her meal and had gone upstairs to her bedroom. The knowing look in the older man's eyes, before he'd quietly cleared away her place setting had been indicative of his scepticism at that explanation. But, being the polite English butler that he was, Little hadn't questioned the explanation—or Jaxon's claim that *he* didn't want any more to eat either.

Food, at least…

Jaxon's appetite for finishing what he and Stazy had started had been a different matter entirely!

Once upstairs, despite feeling exhausted, he had paced the sitting room of his suite for hours as he thought of Stazy's fiery response to his kisses, his shaft continuing to throb and ache as he remembered having her legs wrapped about his waist, the moist heat between her thighs as he pressed against her.

A virtually sleepless night later he only had to look at her again this morning to recall the wildness of their shared passion. The fact that her appearance was every inch the prim and cold Dr Anastasia Bromley again today—hair pulled back and plaited down the length of her spine, green blouse loose rather than fitted over tailored black trousers, and flat no-nonsense shoes—in no way dampened the eroticism of last night's memories.

In fact the opposite; if anything, that air of cool practicality just made Jaxon want to kiss her until he once again held that responsive woman in his arms!

'Fine.' He straightened abruptly before taking the seat opposite hers and concentrating on the pile of papers Geoffrey Bromley had left for him to look through.

That was not to say he wasn't completely aware of Stazy as she sat opposite him. He could smell her perfume—a light floral and her own warm femininity—and the sunlight streaming through the window was turning her hair to living flame. A flame Jaxon wanted to wrap about his fingers as he once again took those full and pouting lips beneath his own…

'Have you heard from Geoffrey this morning?' he

prompted gruffly after several minutes of torturous silence—minutes during which he was too aware of Stazy to be able to absorb a single thing he had read.

She shook her head. 'As I've already told you, my grandfather has become a law unto himself since Granny died.'

Jaxon sat back in his chair. 'And before that…?'

Her gaze instantly became guarded. 'What exactly is it you want to know, Jaxon?'

He shrugged. 'All my own research so far gives the impression their long marriage was a happy one.'

'"So far"?'

Discussing Stazy's grandparents with her had all the enjoyment of walking over hot coals: one wrong step and he was likely to get seriously burned! 'You know, we're going to get along much better if you don't keep reading criticism into every statement I make.' He sighed.

It wasn't in Stazy's immediate or long term plans to 'get along' with Jaxon. In fact, after her uncharacteristic behaviour last night, she just wanted this whole thing to be over and done with. 'Sorry,' she bit out abruptly.

'So?'

'So, yes, their marriage was a long and happy one,' she confirmed evenly. 'Not joined at the hip,' she added with a frown. 'They were both much too independent in nature for that. But emotionally close. Always.'

'That's good.' Jaxon nodded, making notes in the pad he had brought downstairs with him.

Stazy regarded him curiously. 'You mentioned your own parents when you were here last…are they happily married?'

'Oh, yes.' An affectionate smile curved Jaxon's lips as he looked up. 'My brother, too. One big happy family, in fact, and all still living in Cambridgeshire. I'm the only one in the family to have left the area and avoided the matrimonial noose,' he added dryly.

Stazy doubted that he was in any hurry to marry, considering the amount of women reputedly queuing up to share the bed of Jaxon Wilder. Something she had been guilty of herself the previous evening…!

'I don't suppose your lifestyle is in any way…conducive to a permanent relationship,' she dismissed coolly.

Jaxon studied her through narrowed lids. 'Any more than your own is. An archaeologist who travels around the world on digs every chance she gets…' he added with a shrug as she looked at him enquiringly.

She smiled tightly. 'That's one of the benefits of being unattached, yes.'

'And what do you consider the other advantages to be?' he prompted curiously.

She gave a lightly dismissive laugh. 'The same as yours, I expect. Mostly the freedom to do exactly as I wish *when* I wish.'

'And the drawbacks…?'

A frown creased the creaminess of her brow. 'I wasn't aware there were any…'

'No…?'

'No.'

He raised dark brows. 'How about no one to come home to at the end of the day? To talk to and be with? To share a meal with? To go to bed with?' He smiled ruefully. 'I suppose it can all be summed up in one word—loneliness.'

Was she ever lonely? Stazy wondered. Probably. No—definitely. And for the reasons Jaxon had just stated. At the end of a long day of teaching she always returned home to her empty apartment, prepared and ate her meal alone, more often than not spending the evening alone, before sleeping alone.

That was exactly how she preferred it! Not just preferred it, but had deliberately arranged her life so it would be that way. Apart from her grandfather, she didn't want or need anyone in her life on a permanent basis. Didn't want or need the heartache of one day losing them—to death or otherwise.

She eyed Jaxon teasingly. 'I find it difficult to believe that you ever need be lonely, Jaxon!'

He gave a tight smile. 'Never heard the saying "feeling alone in a crowd"?'

'And that describes you?'

'Sometimes, yes.'

'I somehow can't see that…' she dismissed.

'Being an actor isn't all attending glitzy parties and awards ceremonies, you know.'

'Let's not forget you get to escort beautiful actresses to both!' she teased.

'No, let's not forget that,' he conceded dryly.

'And you get to go to all those wonderful places on location too—all expenses paid!'

Jaxon smiled wryly. 'Oh, yes. I remember what a wonderful time I had being in snake and crocodile infested waters for days at a time during the making of *Contract with Death*!'

Her eyes widened. 'I'd assumed you had a double for those parts of the film…'

And from the little Stazy had said during that first meeting six weeks ago Jaxon had assumed *she* was far too much the academic to have ever bothered to see a single one of his films! 'I don't use doubles any more than I do hair extensions.'

'You must be a nightmare for film studios to insure.'

'No doubt.'

'What about the flying in *Blue Skies*…?'

He shrugged. 'I went to a village in Bedfordshire where they have a museum of old working planes and learnt to fly a Spitfire.'

A grudging respect entered those green eyes. 'That was…dedicated. What about riding the elephant in *Dark Horizon*?'

He grinned. 'Piece of cake!'

'Riding a horse bareback in *Unbridled*?'

He gave her a knowing look. 'A blessed relief after the elephant!'

'Captaining a boat in *To the Depths*?'

So Stazy obviously hadn't seen just one of his films, but several. Although Jaxon was sure that Stazy had absolutely no idea just how much she was revealing by this conversation. 'I used to spend my summers in Great Yarmouth, helping out on my uncle's fishing boat, when I was at university.'

Her eyes widened. 'You attended university?'

Jaxon was enjoying himself. 'Surprised to learn I'm not just a pretty face, after all?'

If Stazy was being honest? Yes, she *was* surprised. 'What subject did you take?'

He quirked a teasing brow. 'Are you sure you really want me to answer that?'

She felt a sinking sensation in her chest. 'Archaeology?'

'History and archaeology.'

She winced. 'You have a degree in history and archaeology?'

He gave a grin. 'First-class Masters.'

'With what aim in mind…?'

He shrugged. 'I seriously thought about teaching before I was bitten by the acting bug.'

'Why didn't you tell me that before?' Before she'd made a fool of herself and treated him as if he were just another empty-headed movie star. That, in retrospect, had not only been insulting but presumptuous…

Jaxon shrugged wide shoulders. 'You didn't ask. Besides which,' he continued lightly, 'you were having far too much fun looking down your nose at a frivolous Hollywood actor for me to want to spoil it for you.'

Because it had been easier to think of Jaxon that way than to acknowledge him as not only being a handsome movie star but also an intelligent and sensitive man. Which he obviously was…

A dangerous combination, in fact!

Stazy straightened briskly. 'Shall we get on?'

In other words: conversation over, Jaxon acknowledged ruefully. But, whether she realised it or not, he had learnt a little more about Stazy this morning; it was a little like extracting teeth, but very slowly he was learning the intricacies that made up the personality of the beautiful and yet somehow vulnerable Stazy Bromley.

And finding himself intrigued and challenged by all of them…

'Time for lunch, I believe…'

Stazy had been so lost in reading one of her grandmother's diaries that she had momentarily forgotten that Jaxon sat across the table from her, let alone noticed the passing of time. Surprisingly, it had been a strangely companionable morning, that earlier awkwardness having dissipated as they both became lost in their individual tasks.

She gave a shake of her head now. 'I rarely bother to eat lunch.'

'Meaning that I shouldn't either?' Jaxon teased.

'Not at all,' she told him briskly. 'I'll just carry on here, if you would like to go and— What are you doing...?' She frowned across at Jaxon as he reached across the table to close the diary she was reading before rising to his feet and holding out his hand to her expectantly.

'Ever heard the saying "all work and no play..."'?'

Her mouth firmed as she continued to ignore his outstretched hand. 'I've never pretended to be anything other than dull.'

'I don't find you in the least dull, Stazy,' Jaxon murmured softly.

She raised startled eyes. 'You don't?'

'No,' he assured her huskily; having spent the past three hours completely aware of Stazy sitting across the table from him, how could he claim otherwise? She was a woman of contradictions: practical by nature but delicately feminine in her appearance. Her hands alone seemed proof of that contradiction. Her wrists were fragile, her fingers slender and elegant, but they were tipped with practically short and unvarnished nails. He had spent quite a lot of the last three hours looking at Stazy's hands as she turned the pages of the diary she was reading and imagining all the places those slender fingers tipped by those trimmed nails might linger as she caressed him...

'Let's go, Stazy,' he encouraged her now. 'I asked Little earlier if he would provide us with a lunch basket.'

She frowned. 'You expect me to go on a picnic with you?'

'Why not?' Jaxon asked softly.

Probably because Stazy couldn't remember the last time she had done anything as frivolous as eating her lunch *al fresco*—even in one of the many cafés in England that now provided tables for people to eat outside. When she was working she was too busy during the day to eat lunch at all, and when she came here her grandfather preferred formality. Occasionally Granny had organised a picnic down on the beach at the weekends, but that had been years ago, and—

'You think too much, Stazy.' Jaxon, obviously tired of waiting for her to make up her mind, pulled her effortlessly to her feet.

Stazy couldn't think at all when she was standing close to Jaxon like this, totally aware of the heat of his body and the pleasant—*arousing*—smell of the cologne he favoured. 'Aren't we a little old to be going on a picnic, Jaxon?'

'Not in the least,' he dismissed easily. Not waiting to hear any more of her objections, his hand still firmly clasping hers, he pulled her along with him to walk out into the cavernous hallway. 'Ah, Little, just in time.' He smiled warmly at the butler as he appeared from the back of the house with a picnic basket in one hand and a blanket in the other. 'If Mr Bromley calls we'll be back in a couple of hours.'

Jaxon handed Stazy the blanket before taking the picnic basket himself, all the time retaining that firm grasp on Stazy's hand as he kept her at his side. He strode out of the front doorway of the house and down the steps onto the driveway.

The warm and strong hand totally dwarfed Stazy's, and at the same time she was tinglingly aware of that warmth and strength. The same strength that had enabled him to ride an elephant, go bareback on a horse, to handle the controls of a Spitfire and captain a fishing boat, and do all of those other stunts in his films that Stazy had assumed were performed by someone else.

Making Jaxon far less that 'pretty face' image she had previously taken such pleasure in attributing to him...

If she were completely honest with herself Jaxon was so much more than she had wanted him to be before meeting him, and as such had earned—albeit grudgingly!—her respect. It would have been far easier to simply dismiss the pretty-faced Hollywood actor of her imaginings; but the real Jaxon Wilder was nothing at all as Stazy had thought—hoped—he would be. Instead, he had a depth and intelligence she found it impossible to ignore.

Add those things to the way he looked—to the way he had kissed her and made her feel the previous evening—and Stazy was seriously in danger of fighting a losing battle against this unwanted attraction.

That was why it really wasn't a good idea to go on a picnic with him!

He turned to look down at her from beneath hooded lids. 'Beach or woody glade?'

'Neither.' Stazy impatiently pulled her hand free of his. 'I really don't have time for this, Jaxon—'

'Make time.'

She eyed him derisively. 'Did you need to practise that masterful tone or does it just come naturally?'

Jaxon grinned unconcernedly. 'Just getting into character for next week, when I become captain of a pirate ship and need to keep my female captive in line.'

'Seriously?'

The look of total disbelief on Stazy's face was enough to make him chuckle out loud. 'Seriously.' He grinned. 'That's before I have my wicked way with her about half-way through the movie, of course.'

She winced. 'After which she no doubt keeps *you* in line?'

'I seem to recall I then become her willing slave in the captain's cabin, yes,' Jaxon allowed dryly, enjoying the delicate blush that immediately coloured Stazy's cheeks; for a twenty-nine-year-old woman she was incredibly easy to shock. 'So, Stazy—beach or woody glade?' He returned to their original conversation.

Stazy's thoughts had briefly wandered off to images of herself as Jaxon's captive on his pirate ship, where he swept her up in his arms. Her hair was loose and wind-swept, and she was wearing a green velvet gown that revealed more than it covered as he lowered his head and his mouth plundered hers.

Just imagining it was enough to cause her body to heat and her nipples to tingle and harden inside her bra as the warm feeling between her thighs returned.

Good grief…!

She gave a self-disgusted shake of her head as she dismissed those images. 'I think you'll find that my grandfather's security guards might have something to say about where we're allowed to go for our picnic.' She grimaced as she recalled how her ride this morning had been decided by one of those attentive guards.

'Let's walk down to the beach and see if anyone tries

to stop us.' Once again Jaxon took a firm hold of her hand, before walking towards the back of the house and the pathway down to the beach.

Dragging a reluctant Stazy along with him...

CHAPTER SIX

No one tried to stop them, but Jaxon noted the presence of the two black-clothed men who moved to stand at either end of the coved beach that stretched beyond the walled gardens of Bromley House, positioning themselves so that they faced outwards rather than watching the two of them as he and Stazy spread the blanket on the warmth of the sand.

The sun was shining brightly and a breeze blew lightly off the sea.

'Little seems to have thought of everything,' Jaxon murmured appreciatively as he uncorked a bottle of chilled white wine before pouring it into the two crystal glasses he had unwrapped from tissue paper.

'Years of practice, I expect.' There was a wistful note in Stazy's voice as she knelt on the blanket, arranging the chicken and salad onto plates.

His expression was thoughtful as he sipped his wine. 'You used to come here with your grandparents.' It was a statement rather than a question.

She nodded abruptly. 'And my parents when they were still alive.'

'I hadn't realised that.' He winced. 'Would you rather have gone somewhere else?'

'Not at all,' she dismissed briskly. 'I'm sure you know me well enough by now, Jaxon, to have realised I have no time for sentimentality,' she added dryly.

No, Jaxon couldn't say he had 'realised' that about her at all. Oh, there was no doubting that Stazy liked to give the impression of brisk practicality rather than warmth and emotion; but even in the short time Jaxon had spent in her company he had come to realise that was exactly what it was—an impression. Even if she hadn't responded to him so passionately—so wildly—the evening before he would still have known that about her. Her defence of her grandparents, everything she said and did in regard to them, revealed that she loved them deeply. And as she had no doubt loved her parents just as deeply...

'Where were you when your parents died...?' He held out the second glass of chilled wine to her.

Her fingers trembled slightly as she took the glass from him. 'At boarding school.' Her throat moved convulsively as she swallowed. 'My father was flying the two of them to Paris to celebrate their twentieth wedding anniversary.'

'Do you know what went wrong...?'

Her eyes were pained as she looked up at him. 'Are you really interested, Jaxon, or are these questions just out of a need for accuracy in your screenplay—'

'I'm really interested,' he cut in firmly, more than a little irritated that she could ask him such a question. Admittedly they had only met at all because of the film he wanted to make about her grandmother, but after their closeness last night he didn't appreciate having Stazy still view his every question with suspicion. 'I've already decided that neither you nor your parents will feature in the film, Stazy.'

She raised red-gold brows. 'Why not?'

Jaxon shook his head. 'There's only so much I can cover in a film that plays for a couple of hours without rushing it, so I've more or less decided to concentrate on the escape of Anastasia's family from Russia, her growing up in England, and then the earlier years of the love story between Anastasia and Geoffrey.'

Her expression softened. 'It really was a love story, wasn't it?'

Again there was that wistful note in Stazy's voice. Jaxon was pretty sure she was completely unaware of it. An unacknowledged yearning, perhaps, for that same enduring love herself…? Yet at the same time Stazy was so determined to give every outward appearance of not needing those softer emotions in her life.

She seemed to recognise and shake off that wistfulness as she answered him with her usual briskness. 'There's no mystery about my parents' deaths, Jaxon. The enquiry found evidence that the plane crashed due to engine failure—possibly after a bird flew into it. One of those one in a million chances that occasionally happen.' She shrugged dismissively.

It *was* a one in a million chance, Jaxon knew, and it had robbed Stazy of her parents and completely shattered her young life. A one in a million chance that had caused her to build barriers about her emotions so that her life—and her heart?—would never suffer such loss and heartache again…

He was pretty sure he was getting close to the reason for Stazy's deliberate air of cold practicality. A coldness and practicality that he had briefly penetrated when the two of them had kissed so passionately the evening before…

He reached out to lightly caress one of her creamy cheeks. 'Not everyone leaves or dies, Stazy—'

He knew he had made a mistake when she instantly flinched away from the tenderness of his fingers, her expression one of red-cheeked indignation as she rose quickly to her feet.

'What on earth do you think you're doing, Jaxon?' She glared down at him, her hands clenched into fists at her sides, her breasts rapidly rising and falling in her agitation. 'Did you really think all you had to do was offer a few platitudes and words of understanding in order for me to tumble willingly into your arms? Or is it that your ego is so big you believe every woman you meet is going to want to fall into bed with you?'

Jaxon drew his breath in sharply at the deliberate insult of her attack, his hand falling back to his side as he rose slowly to his feet to look down at her gloweringly. 'It's usually polite to wait until you're asked!'

'Then I advise you not to put yourself to the trouble where I'm concerned!' she bit out dismissively, two bright spots of angry colour in her cheeks, green eyes glittering furiously as she glared up at him. 'I may have made the mistake of allowing you to kiss me last night, but I can assure you I don't intend to make a habit of it!'

Jaxon gave a frustrated shake of his head. 'You kissed me right back, damn it!'

Stazy knew that! Knew it, and regretted it with every breath in her body. At the same time as she wanted to kiss Jaxon again. To have him kiss her. Again. And again…!

She ached for Jaxon to kiss her. To more than kiss

her. Had been wanting, aching for him to kiss her again ever since the two of them had parted the night before. So much so that right now she wanted nothing more than for the two of them to lie down on this blanket on the sand—regardless of the presence of those two guards!—and have him make love to her.

That was precisely the reason she wouldn't allow it to happen!

Jaxon was only staying here at Bromley House for a week. Just one week. After which time he would leave to make his pirate movie, before returning to the States and his life there. It would be madness on Stazy's part to allow herself to become involved with him even for that short length of time.

Why would it? The only two relationships she'd previously had in her life had been with men she had known were uninterested in a permanent relationship. Surely making Jaxon the perfect candidate for a brief, week-long affair…

No, she couldn't do it! She sensed—knew—from the wildness of her response to him yesterday evening that Jaxon represented a danger to all those barriers she had so carefully built about her emotions. So much so that she knew even a week of being Jaxon's lover would be six days and twenty-three hours too long…!

'Where are you going?' Jaxon reached out to firmly grasp Stazy's arm as she would have turned and walked away.

'Back to the house—'

'In other words, you're running away?' he scorned. 'Again,' he added, those grey eyes taunting.

Just the touch of his fingers about her arm was enough to rob Stazy of her breath. For her to be completely aware of him. Of his heat. His smell. For her fingers to itch, actually ache to become entangled in the long length of his hair as his lips, that sensuously sculptured mouth, claimed hers.

What was it about this man, this man in particular, that made Stazy yearn to lose herself in his heat? To forget everything and everyone else as she gave in to the rapture of that sensuous mouth, the caresses of his strong and capable hands?

Danger!

To her, Jaxon represented a clear and present danger.

Physically.

Emotionally.

At the same time Stazy knew she had no intention of revealing her weakness by running away from the challenge of his taunt. She pulled her arm free of his steely grasp. 'I happen to be *walking* away, Jaxon, not running. And I'm doing so because I'm becoming bored by the constant need you feel to live up to your less than reputable image!'

The hardness of his cheekbones became clearly defined as his jaw tightened harshly. 'Really?'

'Really,' she echoed challengingly.

Jaxon continued to meet the challenge in those glittering green eyes for several long seconds as he fought an inner battle with himself, knowing the wisest thing he could to do was to let Stazy go, while at the same time wanting to take her in his arms and kiss her into submission. No—not submission; he wanted Stazy to take as much from him as he would be asking of her.

In your dreams, Wilder!

Stazy might have had a brief lapse in control the evening before, but he had no doubt it was that very lapse that made her so determined not to allow him to get close to her again. If he even attempted to kiss her now she would fight him with every part of her. And he didn't want to fight Stazy. He wanted to make love to her...

He also had no doubt that at the first sign of a struggle between the two of them those two watching bodyguards would decide that Stazy was the one in need of protection. From him...

He stepped back. 'Then I really mustn't continue to bore you any longer, must I?' he drawled dryly.

Stazy looked up at him wordlessly for several seconds, slightly stunned at his sudden capitulation. What had she expected? That Jaxon would ask—plead—for her not to go back to the house just yet? To stay and have lunch with him here instead? That he would ask her for more than just to have lunch with him? If she had thought—hoped for—that then she was obviously going to be disappointed. Jaxon Wilder could have any woman he wanted. He certainly didn't need to waste his time charming someone who continued to claim she wasn't interested.

'Fine,' she bit out tautly. 'Enjoy your lunch.' Her head was held high as she turned and walked away.

Jaxon watched her leave through narrowed lids, knowing that he had allowed Stazy to get to him with those last cutting remarks, and feeling slightly annoyed with himself for allowing her to do so. And, damn it, what 'less than reputable image' was she referring to?

Okay, so over the past ten years or so he'd had his share of relationships with beautiful women. But only two or three in a year. And only ever one at a time. He certainly wasn't involved with anyone at the moment.

He was allowing Stazy's remark to put him on the

defensive, when there was nothing for him to feel defensive about!

Jaxon turned slightly as he saw the nearest guard had moved off the headland and was now following Stazy back to the house. His smile became rueful as he watched the second guard leave his position in order to follow behind them, nodding curtly to Jaxon as he passed by several feet away, at the same time letting him know *he* wasn't the one being protected.

Just watching the way the two men moved so stealthily told Jaxon they were attached to one of the Special Forces, and even though neither man carried any visible weapon Jaxon was certain that they were both probably armed.

That knowledge instantly brought back the feelings of unease Jaxon had felt when he had arrived yesterday...

'Ready to call it a day...?'

Stazy had been wary of Jaxon's mood when he'd returned to the house an hour after she had left him so abruptly on the beach, but her worries had proved to be unfounded. Whatever Jaxon felt about that heated exchange, it was hidden beneath a veneer of smooth politeness she found irritating rather than reassuring; either Jaxon had a very forgiving nature, or her remarks had meant so little to him he had totally dismissed them from his mind!

She glanced at the plain gold watch on her wrist now, as she leant against the back of her chair, surprised to see it was almost half past six in the evening.

'Jaxon, I—' She drew in a deep breath before continuing. 'I believe I owe you an apology for some of the things I said to you earlier...'

'You do?' Jaxon raised dark brows as he flexed his shoulder in a stretch after hours of sitting bent over the table, the two of them having only stopped work briefly when Little had brought in a tray of afternoon tea a couple of hours ago.

Stazy had been just as distracted by Jaxon's physical proximity this afternoon as she had this morning, and now found herself watching the play of muscles beneath his tee shirt as he stretched his arms above his head before standing up. His waist was just as tautly muscled above those powerful thighs and long legs. Damn it, even that five o'clock shadow looked sexy on Jaxon!

And she was once again ogling him like some starstruck groupie, Stazy realised self-disgustedly.

'My grandfather would be…disappointed if he were to learn I had been rude to a guest in his home,' she said.

'I'm not about to tell him, Stazy.' Jaxon gave a rueful shake of his head. 'And technically we weren't *in* your grandfather's home at the time.'

'Nevertheless—'

'Just forget about it, okay?' he bit out tautly, no longer quite as relaxed as he had been. 'But, for the record, that disreputable image you keep referring to is greatly overstated!'

Obviously she had been wrong. It hadn't been a case of Jaxon having a forgiving nature *or* her remarks meaning so little to him he had dismissed them at all; Jaxon was just better at hiding his annoyance than most people!

'I only said that because—' She broke off the explanation as she remembered exactly why she had felt defensive enough to make that less than flattering remark earlier. Because she had once again been completely physically aware of Jaxon. Because she had been terrified of her own aching response to that physical awareness, of the danger Jaxon represented to her cool control...

She gave a shake of her head. 'Did you find anything interesting in my grandmother's papers?'

Stazy's attempt at an apology just now had gone a long way to cementing the fragile truce that had existed between the two of them this afternoon, and in the circumstances Jaxon wasn't sure this was the right time to discuss anything he might or might not have read in Anastasia's private papers.

'A couple of things I'd like to discuss with Geoffrey when I see him next.'

'Such as?'

'It can wait until Geoffrey comes back,' he dismissed.

Stazy's mouth firmed. 'I thought the whole reason for my being here was so that you didn't need to bother my grandfather with any questions...?'

Jaxon gave a rueful smile. 'And I thought the reason you had decided to be here was to make sure I didn't decide to run off with any of any of these private papers!'

'I'm sure the security guards would very much enjoy ensuring you weren't able to do that!' she came back dryly.

'Thanks!' Jaxon grimaced.

She gave him a rueful smile of her own. 'You're welcome!'

That smile transformed the delicacy of her features into something truly beautiful: her eyes glowed deeply green, there was a becoming flush to her cheeks, and her lips were full, curved invitingly over small and even white teeth.

An invitation, if Jaxon should decide to risk taking it up, that would no doubt result in those teeth turning around and biting him.

Now, *there* was a thought guaranteed to ensure he didn't sleep again tonight!

Stazy's smile slowly faded as she saw the flare of awareness in the sudden intensity of Jaxon's gaze fixed on her parted lips. 'I think I'll go upstairs for a shower before dinner,' she said briskly.

'I'd offer to come and wash your back for you if I didn't already know what your answer would be,' he finished mockingly.

Stazy looked up into that lazily handsome face—warm and caressing grey eyes, those sculptured lips curved into an inviting smile, that sexy stubble on the squareness of his chin—and briefly wished that her answer didn't have to be no. That she really was the sophisticated woman she tried so hard to be—the woman capable of just enjoying the moment by separating the physical from the emotional.

The same woman she had succeeded in being during those other two brief sexual encounters in her past...

But not with Jaxon, it seemed.

Because her reaction to him was frighteningly different...

He quirked one expectant dark brow. 'You seem to be taking a while to think it over...?'

'Not at all.' Stazy shook herself out of that confusion of thoughts. 'I'm just amazed—if not surprised!—at your persistence in continuing to flirt with me.'

He gave an unconcerned shrug. 'It would appear I have something of a reputation to live up to.'

Stazy gave a pained wince. 'I have apologised for that remark.'

'And I've accepted that apology.' He nodded.

'But not forgotten it...?'

No, Jaxon hadn't forgotten it. Or stopped questioning as to the reason why Stazy felt the need to resort to insulting him at all...

Did he make her feel threatened in some way? And, if so, why? Once again he acknowledged that Stazy Bromley had to be one of the most complex and intriguing women he had ever met. On the outside beautiful, capable and self-contained. But beneath that cool exterior there was a woman of deep vulnerability who used that outer coldness to avoid any situation in which her emotions might become involved. Including physical intimacy. *Especially* physical intimacy!

Not that Jaxon thought for one moment that Stazy was still a virgin. But she would have chosen her lovers carefully. Coolly. Men who were and wished to remain as unemotionally involved as she was.

Had she found enjoyment in those encounters? Had she managed to maintain those barriers about her emotions even during the deepest of physical intimacy?

The cool detachment of her gaze as she looked at him now seemed to indicate those relationships hadn't even touched those barriers, let alone succeeded in breaching them.

As Jaxon so longed to do...

Last night he had briefly seen a different Stazy—a Stazy who had become a living flame in his arms as she met and matched his passion, her fingers entangled in his hair as she wrapped her legs about his waist to meet each slow and pleasurable thrust of his erection against the moist arousal nestled between her thighs.

Jaxon's hands clenched at his sides as he fought against taking her in his arms and kissing her until she once again became that beautiful and intoxicating woman.

'I think I'll go outside for a stroll before dinner.' And hope that the fresh air would dampen down his renewed arousal!

If not, there was always the coldness of the English Channel he could throw himself into to cool off…!

CHAPTER SEVEN

'I'VE INVITED AN old friend of my grandfather's to join us for dinner this evening,' Stazy informed Jaxon when he came into the drawing room an hour later.

'Really?' He strolled further into the room. He was wearing a black silk shirt unbuttoned at the throat this evening, with black tailored trousers. His hair was once again damp from the shower, the square strength of his chiselled jaw freshly shaven.

Stazy was quickly coming to realise that Jaxon used that noncommittal rejoinder when he was less than pleased with what had been said to him. 'I thought you might be getting a little bored here with just me for company,' she came back lightly as she handed him a glass of the dry martini she now knew he preferred before dinner.

'Did you?' he drawled softly.

She felt the warmth of colour enter her cheeks at his continued lack of enthusiasm. 'Obviously you're used to more sophisticated entertainments—'

'All the more reason for me to enjoy a week of peace and quiet.' Jaxon met her gaze steadily.

'I was only trying to be hospitable—'

'No, Stazy, you weren't,' he cut in mildly.

She stiffened. 'Don't presume to tell me what my motives are, Jaxon.'

'Fine.' He shrugged before strolling across the room to sit down in one of the armchairs, placing his untouched drink down on a side table before resting his elbows on the arms of the chair and steepling his fingers together in front of his chest. 'So who is this "old friend" of your grandfather's?'

Stazy's heart was beating so loudly in her chest she thought Jaxon must be able to hear it all the way across the room. He was right, of course; she hadn't invited Thomas Sullivan to dinner because she had thought Jaxon might be bored with her company—she had invited the other man in the hope he would act as a buffer against this increasing attraction she felt for Jaxon!

For the same reason she was wearing the same plain black shift dress she had worn six weeks ago, when she and Jaxon had first met, with a light peach gloss on her lips and her hair secured in a neat chignon.

She moistened dry lips. 'He and my grandfather were at university together.'

Jaxon raised dark brows. 'That *is* an old friend. And your grandfather's...outside employees are okay with his coming here this evening?'

'I didn't bother to ask them,' she dismissed.

'Then perhaps you should have done.'

Stazy frowned. 'We aren't prisoners here, Jaxon.'

He gave a slight smile. 'Have you tried leaving?'

'Of course not—' Her eyes widened as she broke off abruptly. 'Are you saying that you tried to leave earlier and were prevented from doing so...?'

Jaxon wasn't sure whether Stazy was put out because he might have tried to leave, or because he had been stopped from doing so. Either way, the result was the same: it appeared that for the moment neither of them were going anywhere.

'I had half an hour or so to spare before dinner and thought I would go for a ride—enjoy looking at some of the scenery in the area. I was stopped at the main gate and told very firmly that no one was allowed in or out of Bromley House this evening. Which probably means your grandfather's old friend isn't going to get in either,' he added derisively.

'But that's utterly ridiculous!' She looked totally bewildered as she placed her glass down on a side table before turning towards the door. 'I'll go and speak to one of them now.'

'You do that.' Jaxon nodded. 'And while you're at it maybe you can ask them what that flurry of activity was half an hour or so ago.'

Stazy stopped in her tracks and turned slowly back to face him. 'What flurry of activity?'

He shrugged. 'Extra chatter on the radios, and then about half a dozen more guards arrived fifteen minutes or so later—several of them with more dogs.'

Her cheeks were now the colour of fine pale porcelain. 'I wasn't aware of any of that...'

'No?' Jaxon stood up abruptly, frowning as Stazy instinctively took a step backwards. 'I think you have a much bigger problem here to worry about than me, Stazy,' he said harshly.

She looked even more bewildered. 'I'll telephone my grandfather and ask him what's going on—'

'I already tried that.' A nerve pulsed in Jaxon's clenched jaw. 'I even explained to the woman who answered my call that I was staying here with you at

Bromley House at Sir Geoffrey's invitation. It made absolutely no difference. I was still politely but firmly told that Sir Geoffrey wasn't able to come to the telephone at the moment, but that she would pass the message along.'

Stazy gave a slow shake of her head. 'That doesn't sound like my grandfather...'

'I thought so too.' Jaxon nodded tersely. 'So I tried calling him on the mobile number he gave me. It was picked up by an answering service. Needless to say I didn't bother to leave another message— Ah, Little.' He turned to the butler as the other man quietly entered the drawing room. 'Dr Bromley and I were just speculating as to the possible reason for the extra guards in the grounds...'

To his credit, the older man's expression remained outwardly unchanged by the question. But years of acting, of studying the nuances of expression on people's faces, of knowing that even the slightest twitch of an eyebrow could have meaning, had resulted in Jaxon being much more attuned than most to people's emotions.

Even so, if he hadn't actually been looking straight at the older man he might have missed the slight hardening of his brown eyes before that emotion was neatly concealed by the lowering of hooded lids. Leaving Jaxon to speculate whether that small slip might mean that Little was more than just a butler.

'It seems that several teenagers were apprehended earlier today, trying to climb over the walls of the estate with the idea of throwing a party down on the beach,' Little dismissed smoothly.

'Really?' Jaxon drawled dryly.

'Yes,' the older man confirmed abruptly, before turning to Stazy. 'Dinner is ready to be served, Miss Stazy.

Mr Sullivan telephoned a few minutes ago to extend his apologies. Due to a slight indisposition he is unable to join the two of you for dinner this evening after all.'

'What a surprise!' Jaxon looked across at Stazy knowingly.

To say *she* was surprised by all of this was putting it mildly. In fact she had been more than willing to dismiss Jaxon's earlier claims as nonsense until Little came into the room and confirmed at least half of them. That made Stazy question whether or not Jaxon might not be right about the other half too...?

'Little, do you have any idea why my grandfather might be unavailable this evening?'

The butler raised iron-grey brows. 'I had no idea that Sir Geoffrey was unavailable...'

She had known Little for more years than she cared to acknowledge, and had always found him to be quietly efficient and totally devoted to the comfort of both her grandmother and grandfather. Never, during all of those years, had Stazy ever doubted Little's word.

She doubted it now...

There was something about Little's tone—an evasiveness that caused a flutter of sickening unease in the depths of Stazy's stomach. 'Could you please ask Mrs Harris to delay dinner for fifteen minutes or so?' she requested briskly. 'I have several things I need to do before we go through to the dining room.'

This time she was sure that she wasn't imagining it when Little's mouth tightened fractionally in disapproval. 'Very well, Miss Stazy.' He gave her a formal bow before leaving.

But not, Stazy noted frowningly, before he had sent a slightly censorious glance in Jaxon's direction!

'Not a happy man,' Jaxon murmured ruefully as he stood up.

'No,' Stazy agreed softly.

She was obviously more than a little puzzled by this strange turn of events—to the point that Jaxon now felt slightly guilty for having voiced his concerns and causing Stazy's present confusion. Maybe he should have just kept quiet about the arrival of the extra guards and his not being allowed to leave the grounds of Bromley House earlier? And the fact that Geoffrey had been unable to come to the telephone when he'd called. Whatever that obscure statement might mean…

Jaxon certainly regretted the worry he could now see clouding Stazy's troubled green eyes, and the slight pallor that had appeared in the delicacy of her cheeks. 'I'm sure there's no real need for concern, Stazy—'

'You're sure of no such thing, Jaxon, so please stop treating me as if I were a child,' she dismissed. 'Something is seriously wrong here, and I intend to find out exactly what it is!'

After only two days of being in close proximity to Stazy he knew better than to argue with her. Or offer her comfort. He was only too well aware that she was a woman who liked to give the outward appearance of being in control of her emotions, at least.

'And how do you intend to do that…?' he prompted softly.

'By telephoning my grandfather myself, of course.' She moved to where her handbag lay on the floor beside one of the armchairs, taking her mobile from its depths before pressing the button for one of the speed dials. 'I've never been unable to talk to my grandfather— Is that you, Glynis…?' She frowned as the call was obviously answered not by Geoffrey, as she had hoped, but probably the same woman Jaxon had spoken to earlier. 'Yes. Yes, it is. Where—? Oh. I see. Well, do you have any idea when he will be out of the meeting?' She shot Jaxon a frowning glance.

Jaxon gave her privacy for the call by strolling across the room to stand in front of one of the bay windows that looked over the long driveway. The same window, he realised, where Stazy had been standing six weeks ago, and again two days ago, as she had waited for him to arrive...

He had certainly been aware of the existence of Geoffrey and Anastasia Bromley's granddaughter before coming here, but he had in no way been prepared for Stazy's physical resemblance to her grandmother. Since his return to Bromley House he had become aware that that resemblance was more than skin deep; Stazy had the same confidence and self-determination that his earlier research had shown Anastasia to have possessed in spades.

It appeared that the only way in which the two women differed was emotionally...

Not even that self-confidence and strong outer shell were able to hide Stazy's inner emotional vulnerability. A vulnerability that for some reason brought forth every protective instinct in Jaxon's body...

That was pretty laughable when Stazy had made it clear on more than one memorable occasion that he was the last person she wanted to get close to her—emotionally or otherwise!

He turned back into the room now, as he heard her ending the call.

'Everything okay?' he prompted lightly.

She seemed preoccupied as she slipped her mobile back into her bag before straightening. 'My grandfather is in a meeting,' she explained unnecessarily; Jaxon had already ascertained that much from listening to the beginning of Stazy's telephone conversation. 'Glynis will get him to call me back as soon as he comes out.'

'And Glynis is…?'

The frown deepened between Stazy's delicate brows. 'She was his personal secretary until his retirement twenty-five years ago…'

Considering the speed with which those guards had appeared outside Bromley House following the late-night telephone call that had taken Geoffrey up to London two days ago, Jaxon would be very surprised if Geoffrey had ever fully retired.

He gave a shrug. 'Then we may as well go and have dinner while we wait for him to return your call.' He held his arm out to Stazy.

Stazy didn't move, more than a little unsettled by everything that had happened this evening. Those extra guards and her grandfather's unavailability. Little's careful evasion of her questions. Her own feelings of unease at Glynis's claim that her grandfather couldn't speak to her because he was in a meeting. Not once in the fifteen years since Stazy's parents had died had her grandfather ever been too busy to talk to her on the telephone. And why would Glynis be answering Geoffrey's personal mobile at all…?

'It's probably best if you try not to let your imagination run away with you, Stazy.'

She drew herself up determinedly as she realised Jaxon had moved to stand in front of her—so close she could see the beginnings of that dark stubble returning to the squareness of his jaw, and each individual strand of dark hair on his chest revealed by the open neck of his black silk shirt. She could feel the heat of his body, smell the lemon shampoo he had used to wash his hair, and the sandalwood soap he had showered with, all over-laid with a purely male smell that she had come to know was uniquely Jaxon. A smell that always succeeded in making Stazy feel weak at the knees…!

Unless that was just a result of the tensions of these past few minutes?

Who was she trying to fool with these explanation? Herself or Jaxon? If it was herself then she was fail-ing miserably; once again she found it difficult even to breathe properly with Jaxon standing this close to her. And if it was Jaxon she was trying to convince of her uninterest, then the simple act of accepting his arm to go through to the dining room would reveal just how much she was shaking just from his close proximity.

She nodded abruptly as she chose to ignore that proffered arm. 'I'll just go and tell Little we're ready to eat now—if you would like to go through to the din-ing room?'

Another moment of vulnerability firmly squashed beneath that determined self-control, Jaxon thought rue-fully as he gave a brief nod, before lowering his arm and following her from the drawing room. Except Jaxon didn't consider it a vulnerability to acknowledge con-cern for someone you loved as much as Stazy obviously loved her grandfather…

'Sir Geoffrey is on the telephone,' Little informed them loftily as he came in to the dining room an hour and a half later to remove their dessert plates. 'I took the liberty of transferring the call to his study.'

Stazy stood up abruptly. 'I'll go through immediately—'

'It was Mr Wilder that Sir Geoffrey asked to speak with.' The butler straightened, his gaze fixed steadily on Jaxon rather than on Stazy.

'Mr Wilder?' she repeated dazedly. 'You must be mistaken, Little—'

'Not at all,' the butler assured her mildly. 'I believe you telephoned Sir Geoffrey earlier this evening, sir...?'

Jaxon had to admire the other man's stoicism in the face of Stazy's obvious disbelief of his having correctly relayed the message from Geoffrey Bromley. At the same time he recognised that Stazy's reaction was completely merited; what possible reason could Geoffrey have for asking to speak to Jaxon rather than his own granddaughter? Whatever that reason was, Jaxon doubted it was anything good!

'I did, yes,' he acknowledged lightly as he placed his napkin on the table before standing up. 'If you could just show me to Sir Geoffrey's study...?'

'Certainly, Mr Wilder.'

'Jaxon!'

His shoulders tensed as he turned slowly back to face an obviously less than happy Stazy. Justifiably so, in Jaxon's estimation. Geoffrey had to know that his granddaughter wouldn't just accept his asking to speak with Jaxon rather than her without comment.

'I'm coming with you,' she informed him determinedly.

'I believe Sir Geoffrey wishes to speak with Mr Wilder alone,' Little interjected—bravely, in Jaxon's estimation.

Stazy looked ready to verbally if not physically rip anyone who stood in the way of her talking with her grandfather to shreds. And at the moment Little was definitely attempting to do just that!

Her eyes flashed deeply green as she turned to the butler. 'Sir Geoffrey can wish all he likes, Little,' she assured him firmly. 'But I'm definitely accompanying Mr Wilder to the study!'

Jaxon managed to stand back just in time as Stazy swept past him and out of the room. 'I think that was a pretty predictable reaction, don't you?' he drawled ruefully to the watching butler. 'And, on the positive side, at least I actually got to eat this time before she walked out on me!' The food had been untouched when he had handed the picnic basket back to Little earlier.

'There are times when it is almost possible to believe Lady Anastasia is back with us again…' the other man murmured admiringly as he looked down the hallway at Stazy's retreating and stiffly determined back.

Jaxon nodded. 'Perhaps you had better bring a decanter of brandy and a couple of glasses through to Sir Geoffrey's study in about five minutes…?'

'Certainly, sir.' Little nodded smoothly.

Jaxon strolled down the hallway to where he had seen Stazy enter what had to be Geoffrey Bromley's study, sure that the next few minutes were going to be far from pleasant…

'You heard your grandfather, Stazy,' Jaxon reminded her gently. 'He said there's absolutely no reason for you to rush up to London just now.'

Stazy was well aware of what her grandfather had said on the telephone, once she had managed to wrest the receiver out of Jaxon's hand and talked to her grandfather herself. Just as she was aware that she had no intention of taking any notice of her grandfather's instruction for her to wait to hear from him again before taking any further action.

Mainly because her grandfather's telephone call had revealed that he had rushed up to London two days ago, and security here had been increased, because he and some members of one of his previous security teams had been receiving threats. That threat had somehow escalated in the past twenty-four hours, and now her grandfather expected—instructed—that she just calmly sit here at Bromley House and await further news!

No way. Absolutely no way was Stazy going to just sit here waiting to see if someone succeeded in attacking her grandfather.

She turned to look at Little as he quietly entered the study with a silver tray containing a decanter of brandy and two glasses. 'I suppose *you* already knew what was going on before we spoke to my grandfather?'

'Stazy,' Jaxon reproved softly from where he sat in the chair facing her grandfather's desk.

'I'm sorry, Little.' Stazy sighed. 'Did you happen to know about these threats to my grandfather?' she asked, less challengingly but just as determinedly, as she watched the butler carefully and precisely place the decanter and glasses on the desktop.

Again Jaxon was sure that he hadn't imagined the butler's reaction—a slight but nevertheless revealing tic in his cheek—before the other man covered his emotion with his usual noncommittal expression as he answered Stazy. 'I believe the increased security measures here are only a precaution, Miss Stazy.'

'I'm not concerned about myself—'

'That will be all, thank you, Little.' Jaxon gave the older man a reassuring smile as he stood up to cross the room and usher the butler out into the hallway before closing the door firmly behind him. 'Taking out your worry concerning your grandfather on one of the people who works for him isn't going to make you feel any better, Stazy.' He spoke mildly as he moved to the front of the desk to pour brandy into the two glasses.

'Is it too much to expect you to understand how worried I feel?' A nerve pulsed in her tightly clenched jaw, and her cheeks were once again pale, her eyes suspiciously over-bright.

With anger or tears, Jaxon wasn't sure…

He straightened slowly to hand her one of the glasses of deep amber liquid. 'No, of course it isn't. I just don't believe insulting Little or me is going to help the situation.'

'Then what is?' She threw the contents of the glass to the back of her throat before moving to refill it.

Jaxon winced. 'Expensive brandies like this one are meant to be breathed in, sipped and then savoured—not thrown down like a pint of unimpressive warm beer!'

'I know that.' She picked up the second glass and took a healthy swallow of the contents of that one too, before slamming it back down on the desk to look up challengingly at Jaxon.

'Stazy, I really wouldn't advise you pushing this situation to a point where I have to use extreme measures in order to calm you down,' Jaxon said softly as he saw the reckless glint in her eyes had deepened.

'Such as what?' she prompted warily. 'Are you

going to put me over your knee and spank me for being naughty? Or will just slapping me on the cheek suffice?'

He shrugged. 'I'm not about to slap you anywhere—but the first suggestion has a certain merit at this moment!' Ordinarily Jaxon wouldn't dream of using physical force of any kind on a woman. But this situation was far from ordinary. Stazy was way out of her normally controlled zone. Almost to the point of hysteria. Rightly so, of course, when her grandfather was all the family she had left in the world...

In these unusual circumstances Jaxon didn't at all mind being used as Stazy's verbal punchbag, but he knew her well enough to know that she would be mortified at her treatment of the obviously devoted Little once she had calmed down enough to recognise how she had spoken to him just now—out of love and worry for her grandfather or otherwise.

The uncharacteristic tears glistening in those eyes were his undoing. 'Oh, Stazy...!' he groaned, even as he took her gently into his arms. 'It's going to be okay—you'll see.'

'You don't really know that,' she murmured against his chest as she choked back those tears.

'No, I don't,' Jaxon answered honestly. 'But what I do know is that Geoffrey is a man who knows exactly what he's doing. If he says this problem is going to be handled, then I have no doubt that it will be. And, as you know him much better than I do, you shouldn't either,' he encouraged softly as he ran comforting hands up and down the length of her back.

'You're right. I know you are.' She nodded against him. 'I just—I can't help feeling worried.'

'I know that.' Jaxon's arms tightened about her as

the softness of her body rested against the length of his.
'And so does Geoffrey. Which is why he asked me to
take care of you.'

She raised her head to look at him, her smile still tear-
ful. 'And this is you taking care of me…?'

'I could possibly do a better job of it if I thought you
wouldn't object…?'

Stazy groaned low in her throat as Jaxon slowly lowered his head and slanted his mouth lightly against hers,
her body instantly relaxing into his and her fingers becoming entangled in his hair as her lips parted to deepen
that kiss.

It felt as if Stazy had been waiting for this to happen
since the last time Jaxon had kissed her. Waiting and
longing for it. Instantly she became lost to the pleasure
of those exploring lips and the caress of Jaxon's hands
as they roamed her back before cupping her bottom and
pulling her into him.

She was achingly aware of every inch of the lean
length of Jaxon's body against hers—his chest hard and
unyielding against the fullness of her breasts, the hardness of his erection caught between her stomach and
thighs, living evidence of his own rapidly escalating
arousal.

Stazy gave another groan as Jaxon's hands tightened
about her bottom and he lifted her up and placed her on
the edge of the desk. His knees nudged her legs apart,
pushing her dress up to her thighs as he stepped between
them, and she felt the heat of his erection against the
lace of her panties. That groan turned into a low moan
of heated pleasure as he pressed into her, applying just
the right amount of pressure.

Her neck arched and her fingers clung to the broad

width of Jaxon's shoulders when his lips left hers to
kiss across her cheek before travelling the length of her
throat—kissing, gently biting, as he tasted her creamy
skin before his tongue plundered and rasped the sensitive hollows at the base of her neck.

Her back arched as Jaxon's hand moved to cup beneath one of her breasts. The soft material of her dress
was no barrier to the pleasure that coursed through her
hotly as his thumb moved lightly across the roused and
aching nipple, and she was only vaguely aware of it when
his other hand slowly lowered the zip of her dress down
the length of her spine before his hand touched the naked
flesh beneath, revealing that she wasn't wearing a bra.

Jaxon heard the voice in his head telling him to stop
this now. Offering Stazy comfort was one thing—what
he wanted was something else entirely. He heard that
voice and ignored it—had no choice but to ignore it when
he could feel how Stazy's pleasure more than matched
his own.

He reached up to ease the dress down her arms, baring her to the waist before he moved his hands to cup
beneath the swell of her breasts. Such full and heavy
breasts, when the rest of her body was so slender. Full
and heavy breasts that Jaxon wanted in his mouth as he
tasted and pleasured her.

His hands remained firmly on her waist and he moved
back slightly to look down at her nakedness. The heat of
his gaze on those uptilting breasts tipped by rosy pink
and engorged nipples stayed for long, admiring seconds
before he lowered his head to take one in his mouth.

Stazy moved her arms so that her hands were flat on
the desk behind her, supporting her as the pleasure of
having Jaxon's mouth and tongue on her coursed hotly

from her breasts to between her thighs. She felt herself tingle there as he took her nipple fully into the heat of his mouth and began to suckle, gently at first, and then more greedily, as his hand cupped her other breast and began to caress her in that same sensuous rhythm.

She was on fire, the ache between her thighs almost unbearable now, building higher and higher, until she knew Jaxon held her poised on the edge of release. 'Please, Jaxon…!' she groaned weakly.

He ignored that plea and instead turned the attentions of his lips, tongue and teeth to her other breast. His lips clamped about the fullness of the nipple as his tongue and teeth licked and rasped against that sensitive bud, driving Stazy wild as she moved her thighs restlessly against his in an effort to ease her aching need for the release that was just a whisper of pleasure away.

She trembled all over with that need, her breath a pained rasp in her throat as she looked down at Jaxon with hot and heavy eyes. Just the sight of his lips clamped about her, drawing her nipple deeper and deeper into his mouth with each greedy suck, caused another rush of heat between her restless and throbbing thighs.

'Jaxon…!' Instead of deepening that pleasure, as she so wanted him to do, it seemed as if Jaxon began to ease away from her, gently kissing her breasts now, his hands once again a soft caress against her back. 'Stop playing with me, please, Jaxon!' she pleaded throatily.

'This isn't a sensible idea, Stazy,' he groaned achingly, even as his arms dropped from about her waist before he straightened away from her.

Stazy looked at him searchingly for several long seconds, easily seeing the regret in his eyes before a shutter came down over those twin mirrors into his emotions. 'Jaxon…?' she breathed softly.

He gave a shake of his head, his expression grim. 'We both know that you're going to end up hating me if I take this any further…'

'You're wrong, Jaxon.' She gave a disbelieving shake of her head, continuing to stare up at him dazedly as she pulled her dress back up her arms to hold it in front of the bareness of her breasts with one hand while she pulled the material down over her naked thighs with the other.

'I am?' he prompted huskily.

'Oh, yes,' Stazy breathed softly. 'Because I couldn't possibly hate you any more than I do at this moment!' Her eyes glittered with humiliated anger now, rather than tears.

Jaxon knew he fully deserved that anger—that he had allowed things to go much further between them just now than was wise when Stazy was already feeling so emotionally vulnerable. But he also knew that Stazy was wrong—she would definitely have hated him more if they had taken their lovemaking to its inevitable conclusion. And on the plus side—for Geoffrey and Little, that was!—Stazy was now far more angry with him than she had been earlier with either of them!

That, in retrospect, was probably the best outcome. He was scheduled to leave here at the end of the week, whereas Geoffrey and Little would both be around for much longer than that.

Jaxon kept his expression noncommittal as he stepped fully away from Stazy, his shaft throbbing in protest as he did so. No doubt another cold shower—a very *long* cold shower!—would be in order when he got back to his suite of rooms. 'There's the possibility you might even thank me for my restraint in the morning…' he murmured ruefully.

'I shouldn't hold your breath on that happening, if I were you!'

'Stazy—'

'I think you should leave now, Jaxon.' It was definitely anger that now sparkled in her eyes.

'Fine,' he accepted wearily. 'But you know where I am if you can't sleep and feel like—'

'Like what?' she cut in sharply. 'I thought we had both just agreed that this was a very bad idea?'

'I was going to say if you feel like company,' Jaxon completed firmly. 'And I don't remembering saying it was a bad idea—just not a very sensible one, given the circumstances.'

'Well, "given the circumstances", I would now like you to leave.' Her chin rose proudly as she held his gaze.

Jaxon gave her one last regretful glance before doing exactly that, knowing that to stay would only make the situation worse.

If that was actually possible…

CHAPTER EIGHT

'THAT REALLY WASN'T very clever, now, was it?' Jaxon looked at Stazy impatiently as he entered the drawing room almost two hours later, to see her pacing in front of the bay windows, now dressed in a thick green sweater and fitted black denims, with her red-gold hair neatly plaited down the length of her spine.

She shot him only a cursory glance as she continued to pace restlessly. 'Shouldn't you be fast asleep?'

He closed the door softly behind him. 'Little came and knocked on my bedroom door. He seemed to think I might like to know that you had tried to take my Harley in an attempt to go and see your grandfather tonight.'

'The traitor…'

Jaxon gave a rueful shake of his shaggy head, having quickly pulled on faded denims and a black tee shirt before coming downstairs. 'Exactly when did you take the keys to the Harley off my dressing table…?'

'When I heard the shower running in your bathroom.' She had the grace to look a little guilty. 'I am sorry I took them without your permission, but at the time I didn't feel I had any other choice.'

'Is that your idea of an apology?'

'No.' She sighed. 'It was very wrong of me, and I do

apologise, Jaxon. My grandfather would be horrified if he knew!'

'I'm horrified—but probably not for the same reason!' Jaxon gave her an exasperated glance as he too easily imagined what might have happened if she had managed to ride the Harley. 'How could you even have *thought* taking my motorbike was going to work, Stazy, when there are enough guards patrolling the grounds for them to hear a mouse squeak let alone the roar of an engine starting up?'

'I didn't even get the bike out of the garage,' Stazy acknowledged self-disgustedly.

There had been no excuse for what she had allowed to happen in her grandfather's study earlier that evening, and just thinking about those intimacies once Stazy reached the privacy of her bedroom had been enough to make her want to get as far away from Bromley House—and Jaxon—as possible!

Admittedly it had taken a little time on her part, but once it had occurred to her that she could 'borrow' the keys to Jaxon's Harley and then take the less used and hopefully less guarded back road out of the estate to leave, she hadn't been able to rid herself of the idea.

Unfortunately, as Jaxon had already pointed out, just starting up the engine had brought three of her grandfather's guards running to where the motorbike was parked at the back of the house. Quickly followed by the humiliation of having the keys to the motorbike taken from her before being escorted back inside.

With the added embarrassment that Jaxon now knew exactly what she had planned on doing too. 'Obviously I didn't really think beyond the idea of going to London to see my grandfather,' she accepted guiltily.

'Obviously!' Jaxon gave a disgusted shake of his head. 'You could have been killed, damn it!'

In retrospect Stazy accepted that her method of leaving Bromley House really hadn't been a good plan at all. Not only had starting the engine sounded like the roar of an angry lion in the stillness of the night, but there had still been no guarantee that she would have found it any easier to leave by the back road. She would never know now...

No, in retrospect, taking the Harley hadn't been a good plan at all. And, if Stazy was being honest, she now admitted it had also been an extremely childish one...

Why, oh, why did just being around Jaxon make her behave in this ridiculous way...?

She gave an impatient shake of her head. 'I just feel so—so useless, having to sit here and wait for news from my grandfather.'

Jaxon's expression softened. 'I'm sure Geoffrey is well aware of exactly how you feel, Stazy—'

'Are *you*?' she said warily.

'Yes.' He sighed. 'Look, it's almost one o'clock in the morning, and no doubt the kitchen staff all went to bed hours ago. So why don't the two of us go down to the kitchen and make a pot of tea or something?'

She smiled ruefully. 'Tea being the English panacea for whatever ails you?'

He shrugged. 'It would seem to work in most situations, yes.'

It certainly couldn't do any harm, and Stazy knew she was still too restless to be able to sleep even if she went up to bed now. 'Why not?' she said softly as she crossed the room to precede him out into the hallway.

The house was quiet as Jaxon and Stazy crossed the

cavernous entrance hall on their way to the more shadowy hallway that led down to the kitchen, with only the sound of the grandfather clock ticking to disturb that eerie silence.

A stark reminder, if Jaxon had needed one, that it was very late at night and he and Stazy were completely alone...

And if Stazy believed there had been no repercussions for him after having to walk away from her earlier this evening then she was completely mistaken!

A fifteen-minute cold shower had done absolutely nothing to dampen Jaxon's arousal. Nor had sitting at the desk in his bathrobe to read through the notes he had already accumulated for the screenplay. Or telephoning his agent in LA and chatting to him about it for ten minutes.

None of those things had done a damned thing to stop Jaxon's mind from wandering, time and time again, to thoughts of making love with Stazy in Geoffrey's study.

As he was thinking about it still...

Self-denial wasn't something Jaxon enjoyed. And walking away from Stazy—not once, but twice in the past two days!—was playing havoc with his self-control!

The cosy intimacy of the warm kitchen and working together to make tea—Jaxon finding the cups while Stazy filled the kettle with water and switched it on—did nothing to lessen his awareness of her. Not when his gaze wandered to her constantly as the slender elegance of her hands prepared and warmed the teapot and he all too easily imagined the places those hands might touch and caress. The smooth roundness of her bottom in those black fitted denims wasn't helping either!

'Feeling any better?' Jaxon prompted gruffly, once

he was seated on the other side of the kitchen table from Stazy, two steaming cups of tea in front of them.

'Less hysterical, you mean?' She grimaced.

He shook his head. 'You weren't hysterical, Stazy, just understandably concerned about your grandfather.'

'Yes,' she acknowledged with a sigh. 'Still, I didn't have to be quite so bitchy about it.'

'You? Bitchy?' Jaxon gave an exaggerated gasp of disbelief. 'Never!' He placed a dramatic hand on his heart.

She smiled ruefully. 'You aren't going to win any awards with *that* performance!'

'No,' he acknowledged with a wry chuckle.

Stazy sobered. 'Do you think my grandfather is telling us the truth about this threat?' She looked across at him worriedly. 'It occurred to me earlier that he could be using it as a smokescreen,' she continued as Jaxon raised one dark brow. 'That maybe this screenplay and the making of the film might have brought on another heart attack…?'

'Why am I not surprised!' Jaxon grimaced ruefully. 'Do you seriously believe your grandfather would lie to you in that way?'

'If he thought I would worry less, yes,' she confirmed unhesitantly.

Unfortunately, so did Jaxon…

Although he honestly hoped in this instance that wouldn't turn out to be the case. 'Then it's one of those questions where I can't win, however I choose to answer it. If I say no, I can't see that happening, then you aren't going to believe me. And if I say it's a possibility, you'll ask me to consider dropping the whole idea.'

Stazy was rational enough now to be able to see the

logic in Jaxon's reply. 'Maybe we should just change the subject…?'

'That might be a good idea,' he drawled ruefully.

She nodded. 'As you probably aren't going to be able to speak to my grandfather about it for several days yet, perhaps you would like to tell *me* what it is you found earlier and wanted to talk to him about…?'

Jaxon gave a wince. 'Another lose/lose question as far as I'm concerned, I'm afraid. And it seems a pity to spoil things when we have reached something of a truce in the last few minutes…'

'It's probably an armed truce, Jaxon,' Stazy said dryly. 'And liable to erupt into shots being exchanged again at any moment!'

'Okay.' He grimaced. 'Curiously, what I've found is something the reporter who wrote the biography seems to have missed altogether…'

'Hmm…'

Jaxon raised one dark brow at that sceptical murmur. 'You don't think he missed it?'

'What I think,' Stazy said slowly, 'is that, whatever you found, my grandfather will have ensured the reporter didn't find it.'

'You believe Geoffrey has that much power…?'

'Oh, yes.' She smiled affectionately.

Jaxon shook his head. 'You don't even know what this is about yet.'

She shrugged. 'I don't need to. If my grandfather left some incriminating papers in the library for you to look at then he meant for you to find them.'

That made Jaxon feel a little better, at least. 'There were two things, actually, but they're related.'

Stazy looked down at her fingertip, running it distractedly around the rim of her cup as she waited for him to continue.

He sighed. 'I found your grandparents' marriage certificate for February 1946.'

'Yes?'

'And your father's birth certificate for October 1944.'

'Yes?'

'Leaving a discrepancy of sixteen months.'

'Two years or more if you take into account the nine months of pregnancy,' she corrected ruefully.

'Yes…'

The tension eased out of Stazy's shoulders as she smiled across at him. 'I'm sure that there are always a lot of children born with questionable birth certificates during war years.'

'No doubt.' Jaxon was literally squirming with discomfort now. 'But—'

'But my father's place of birth is listed as Berlin, Germany,' she finished lightly.

'Yes.' Jaxon breathed his relief.

'With no name listed under the "Father" column.'

'No…'

'Meaning there's no way of knowing for certain that Geoffrey was actually his father.'

'I didn't say that—'

'You didn't have to.' Stazy chuckled. 'It would have looked a little odd, don't you think, to have the name of an Englishman listed as the father of a baby boy born in Berlin in 1944?'

'Well, yes… But—'

'More tea, Jaxon?' She stood up to put more hot water into the teapot before coming back to stand with the pot poised over his cup.

'Thanks,' he accepted distractedly. He had been dreading having to talk to any of the Bromley family about his discovery earlier today, and especially the unpredictable Stazy. Now, instead of being her usual defensive self, she actually seemed to find the whole thing amusing. To the point that he could see laughter gleaming in those expressive green eyes as she refilled his cup before sitting down again. 'Like to share what's so amusing…?'

'You are.' She gave a rueful shake of her head as she resumed her seat. 'You're aged in your mid-thirties, Jaxon, a Hollywood A-list actor and director, and yet you seem scandalised that there might have been babies born out of wedlock seventy years ago!' She grinned across at him.

'I'm not in the least scandalised—'

'Um…protesting too much, much?' she teased, in the manner of one of her students.

Jaxon eyed her frustatedly. 'These are your grandparents we're talking about. And your father.'

'Geoffrey and Anastasia never tried to hide from me that my father was actually present and sixteen months old at the time of their wedding,' she assured him gently. 'We have the photographs to prove it. Which I can show you tomorrow—later today,' she corrected, after a glance at the kitchen clock revealed it was now almost two o'clock in the morning. 'If you would like to see them?'

'I would, yes.'

She nodded. 'I'll look them out in the morning.'

'So what happened?' Jaxon said slowly. 'Why didn't the two of them marry when Anastasia knew she was expecting Geoffrey's child?'

'They didn't marry earlier because Anastasia didn't know she was pregnant when she was dropped behind enemy lines in late February 1944. By the time she realised her condition she had already established her cover as a young Austrian woman, recently widowed and bitterly resentful of the English as a result, and it was too late for her to do anything but remain in Berlin and continue with the mission she had been sent there to complete. She always maintained her pregnancy actually helped to confirm that identity.'

'My God…' Jaxon fell back against his chair.

'Yes.' Stazy smiled affectionately. 'Of course my grandfather, once informed of Anastasia's condition, ensured that she was ordered out of Berlin immediately.'

'And she refused to leave until she had finished what she went there to do?' Jaxon guessed.

Stazy met his gaze unblinkingly. 'Yes, she did.'

'She went through her pregnancy, gave birth to her son, cared for him, all the while behind enemy lines under a false identity that could have been blown apart at any moment?'

Her chin tilted. 'Yes.'

He gave an incredulous shake of his head. 'God, that's so—so—'

'Irresponsible? Selfish?' There was a slight edge to Stazy's voice now.

'I was going to say romantic.' Jaxon grinned admiringly. 'And incredibly brave. What a woman she must have been!'

Stazy relaxed slightly as she answered huskily, 'I've always believed so, yes.'

Jaxon nodded. 'And so you should. You're very like her, you know,' he added softly.

'I don't think so, Jaxon.' Stazy gave a choked laugh. 'Even in her nineties Anastasia would have made sure she got on that Harley tonight and somehow managed to ride it out of here, despite all those guards trying to stop her!'

'Maybe,' he acknowledged dryly. 'But you definitely gave it your best shot.'

She shrugged. 'Not good enough, obviously.'

'Choosing the Harley for your first attempt was extremely gutsy.' In fact Stazy's behaviour tonight was so much more than Jaxon would ever have believed possible of that stiffly formal and tightly buttoned down Dr Anastasia Bromley he had been introduced to six weeks ago. 'So you think Geoffrey meant for me to find the marriage and birth certificates…?'

She nodded. 'I'm sure of it.'

'Why?'

Stazy gave a rueful smile. 'For some reason he seems to trust you to do the right thing…' she said slowly, knowing there was no way her grandfather would ever have put the reputation of his darling Anastasia in the hands of a man he didn't trust implicitly.

Something she should probably have appreciated more while resenting Jaxon these past six weeks…

He leant across the table now, to take one of her hands gently in both of his. 'And do *you* trust me to do that too, Stazy?'

She did trust him, Stazy realised as she looked across the table at him. That silver-grey gaze was unmistakably sincere as it met hers unwaveringly.

Yes, she trusted Jaxon—it was herself she didn't trust whenever she was around him!

Even now, worried about her grandfather, frustrated

at not being able to leave the estate, Stazy was totally aware of Jaxon as he held her hand in both of his. Of the roughness of his palm, the gentleness of his fingers as they played lightly across the back of her hand, sending a quiver of awareness through her arm and down into the fullness of her breasts and between her thighs. Warming her. Once again arousing her…

'I trust my grandfather's judgement in all things,' she finally said huskily.

'But not mine?' Jaxon said shrewdly.

Stazy pulled her trembling hand out of his grasp before pushing it out of sight beneath the table, very aware of the heat of awareness singing through her veins. 'It's late, Jaxon.' She stood up abruptly. 'And tomorrow looks as if it's going to be something of a long and anxious day. We should at least try to get some sleep tonight.' She picked up their empty cups and carried them over to the sink to rinse them out before placing them on the rack to dry.

All the time she was aware of Jaxon's piercing gaze on her. Heating her blood to boiling point. Her legs trembled slightly, so that she was forced to resort to leaning against the sink unit for support.

'Stazy…?'

She drew in a deep breath, desperately searching for some of the coolness and control that had stood her in such good stead these past ten years. Searching and failing.

'If something I've said or done has upset you, then I apologise…'

Stazy had been so deeply entrenched in fighting the heat of her emotions that she hadn't even been aware that Jaxon had moved to stand behind her. The warmth of his breath was now a gentle caress as it brushed against the tendrils of hair at her nape that had escaped the neatness of her plait. If he should so much as touch her—!

She slipped away from that temptation before turning to face him. 'You haven't done anything to upset me, Jaxon,' she assured him crisply. 'I think it's as you implied earlier—I'm just emotionally overwrought.'

Jaxon could see the evidence of exhaustion in the dark shadows beneath her eyes. Her cheeks were pale, those full and vulnerable lips trembling slightly as she obviously fought against giving in to that exhaustion. 'Time for bed,' he agreed firmly, before taking a tight grip of her hand and leading her gently across the room to the doorway, switching off the kitchen light on his way out.

He retained that firm grip on the delicacy of her hand as the two of them walked down the shadowed hallway and up the wide staircase together, allowing him to feel the way her fingers tightened about his and her steps seemed to slow as they approached the top of the stairs.

Jaxon turned to look at Stazy in the semi-darkness. Her eyes were deeply green and too huge in the paleness of her face. 'Stazy, would you rather have company tonight…?' Even though he spoke softly his voice still sounded over-loud in the stillness of the dark night surrounding them.

Stazy came to an abrupt halt at the top of the stairs, frowning as she turned to look at him searchingly, the contours of his face sharply hewn in the moonlight, the expression in his eyes totally unreadable with those grey eyes hooded by long dark lashes and lowered lids. 'Exactly what are you suggesting, Jaxon…?' she finally murmured warily.

'I'm asking if you would like me to come to your

bedroom and spend the rest of the night with you,' he bit out succinctly.

Exactly what Stazy had thought he was offering! 'Why?'

Jaxon chuckled softly. 'How about because I know how the hours between two o'clock in the morning and five o'clock can sometimes be tough to get through if you have something on your mind.'

Stazy raised auburn brows. 'Are you talking from personal experience?'

He gave a hard grin. 'Difficult as you obviously find that to believe, yes, I am. Never anything as serious as your present concerns over your grandfather, but I've definitely had my fair share of worries over the years.'

'Things like looking in the mirror for the first grey hair and wrinkle?' she came back teasingly.

'Hair dye and botox injections,' Jaxon came back dismissively.

Her eyes widened. 'Have you ever—?'

'No, I can honestly say I've never resorted to using either one of those things!' he assured her irritably, seeing her obvious humour at his expense.

'Yet.'

'Ever,' Jaxon assured firmly. 'I'm going to live by the adage and grow old gracefully.'

Stazy knew he was teasing her—was very aware that these last few minutes they'd both been talking only for the sake of it. Delaying as they waited to see what her answer was going to be to Jaxon's offer to spend the night with her…

'Well?' Jaxon prompted huskily.

He claimed he was making the offer so that she didn't have to spend the hours before dawn alone; and God knew Stazy didn't want to *be* alone, knowing that once she was in her bedroom her imagination was going to run riot again in regard to her grandfather's safety. Did that mean she was actually thinking of *accepting* Jaxon's offer to spend the night with her...?

CHAPTER NINE

'I PREFER TO SLEEP on the right side of the bed.'

'So do I.'

'It's my bedroom.'

'And, as your guest, don't you think I should be allowed first choice as to which side of the bed I would like to sleep on?'

'Not if my guest is a gentleman.'

As conversations before leaping into bed with a man went, this one was pretty pathetic, Stazy acknowledged self-derisively. No doubt due in part to the fact that now they were actually at the point of getting into bed she was awash with flustered embarrassment.

To a degree that she questioned which part of her brain had actually been functioning when she had accepted Jaxon's offer to spend the night in her bedroom with her. Certainly not the logical and ordered Dr Stazy Bromley part! And even the less logical, easily-aroused-by-Jaxon-Wilder, Stazy Bromley now questioned the sanity of that decision too!

It had been an impulsive decision at best, made out of a desire not to lie alone in the darkness for hours with her own worried thoughts.

Having just returned from the adjoining bathroom

in a white vest top and the grey sweats she slept in, she saw the soft glow of the bedside lamp revealed that Jaxon wore only a pair of very brief black underpants that clearly outlined the enticing bulge beneath. His bare shoulders were wide and tanned, chest muscled and abdomen taut, his legs long and muscular and equally tanned, allowing Stazy to fully appreciate just how ridiculously naive that decision had been.

Especially when her clenched fingers actually itched with the need she felt to touch the fine dark hair that covered his chest before it arrowed down in an enticing vee to beneath those fitted black underpants…

'Perhaps you should go to your bedroom first and get some pyjamas…' she said doubtfully—as if Jaxon wearing pyjamas was *really* going to make her any less aware of his warmth in the bed beside her!

'That would probably be a good idea if I actually wore pyjamas.' Jaxon eyed her mockingly across the width of the double bed.

Right. Okay. Definitely time to regroup, Stazy. 'In that case you can have the right side of the bed—'

'I was just kidding about that, Stazy,' Jaxon drawled softly when she would have walked around to the side of the bed where he stood. 'The left side of the bed is fine.'

To say he had been surprised by her acceptance of his offer was putting it mildly. That only went to prove that Stazy was even more complex than he had thought she was. To the point that Jaxon had no idea what she was going to do or say next. That was very refreshing from a male point of view, but damned inconvenient when a man was only supposed to be acting as a concerned friend…

For some reason he had expected her to be wearing one of those unbecoming nightgowns that covered a woman from neck to toe when she came back from the bathroom. Instead she wore a thin white fitted top with narrow shoulder straps, clearly outlining her upthrusting and obviously naked breasts, and in the process allowing Jaxon to see every curve and nuance of her engorged nipples, along with a pair of loose grey soft cotton trousers that rested low down on her hips and gave him the occasional glimpse of the flat curve of her stomach. The cherry on top of the cake—as if he needed one!—was that she had released the long length of her red-gold hair from its plait and it now lay in a soft and silky curtain across her shoulders and down her back.

All of them were things that were pure purgatory for any man who was expected to behave only as a friend...

He should be grateful Stazy had a double bed in her room, he supposed; just think how cosy the two of them would have been in a single bed! Even so, Jaxon was well aware of how much space he was going to take up, so it was perhaps as well that Stazy was so slender.

He quirked one dark brow as he looked across the bed at her. 'Are we going to get in and get warm, or just stand here looking at each other all night?'

Stazy drew in a slightly shaky breath. 'Perhaps your spending the night here wasn't such a good idea, after all— Oh!' She broke off as Jaxon lifted his side of the duvet before sliding in beneath it to look up at her expectantly.

'It's much warmer in here than it is out there...' he encouraged, and turned the duvet back invitingly.

Stazy wasn't sure any extra warmth was necessary. She already felt inwardly on fire, her cheeks flushed, the palms of her hands slightly damp.

Oh, for goodness' sake—

'Better,' Jaxon murmured as Stazy finally slid into the bed beside him.

She turned to look at him as she straightened the duvet over her. 'Is that a statement or a question?'

'Both,' he assured her softly, before reaching out to turn off the bedside lamp and plunge the room into darkness. His arms moved about her waist as he pulled her in to his side and gently pressed her head down onto the warmth of his shoulder.

Stazy didn't feel in the least relaxed. How could she possibly relax when she was snuggled against Jaxon's warm and almost naked body, her fingers finally able to touch the silkily soft hair on his chest as her hand lay against that hardness encased in velvet, her elbow brushing lightly against that telling bulge in his underpants?

This had *so* not been a good idea. She was never going to be able to relax, let alone—

'Just close your eyes and go to sleep, Stazy,' Jaxon instructed huskily in the darkness.

Her throat moved as she swallowed before answering him softly. 'I'm not sure that I can.'

'Close your eyes? Or go to sleep?'

'Either!'

'I could always sing you a lullaby, I suppose...'

'I didn't know you could sing...'

'I can't.' His chest vibrated against her cheek as he chuckled, then Jaxon's hand moved up to cradle the back of her head as it rested against his shoulder. He settled more comfortably into the pillows. 'This is nice.'

Nice? It was sheer heaven as far as Stazy was concerned! Decadent and illicit pleasure. A time out of time, when it felt as if only the two of them existed. Those 'witching hours' between dusk and dawn when any-thing—everything!—seemed possible.

'Stop fidgeting, woman,' Jaxon instructed gruffly when she shifted restlessly beside him.

Or not, Stazy acknowledged ruefully. 'I was just get-ting comfortable.'

When a man wanted a woman as much as Jaxon wanted Stazy, her 'getting comfortable' could just be the last straw in the breaking of his self-control. Es-pecially when that 'getting comfortable' involved her hair spilling silkily across his chest, the softness of her breasts pressing into his side, and the draping of one of her legs over the top of his.

Her hand rested lightly on his stomach as she snug-gled closer to his warmth... 'What's that noise...?' she murmured sleepily minutes later.

'Probably my teeth grinding together.'

'Why—?'

'Will you please just go to sleep!' Jaxon's jaw was tightly clenched as he determinedly held his desire for her in check.

'I thought people were usually grouchy when they woke up in the morning, not before they've even gone to sleep...'

Jaxon had a feeling he was going to be grouchy in the morning too—probably more so than he was now, if he had been lying beside Stazy all night with a throbbing erection! Worst of all, he had brought all this on him-self, damn it. 'I'll try not to disappoint,' he murmured self-derisively.

Stazy chuckled sleepily, and the evenness of her breathing a few minutes later told him that she had man-aged to fall asleep after all.

Leaving Jaxon awake and staring up at the ceiling in the darkness, in the full knowledge that he wasn't going to be able to find the same release from his own self-imposed purgatory…

Arousal.

Instant.

Breathtaking.

Joyous!

'Are you awake…?' Jaxon prompted softly.

'Mmm…' Stazy kept her eyes closed as she relished the sensation of Jaxon's large and capable hands moving lightly, slowly over her and down her body, as if he intended to commit every curve and contour to memory.

Her back. The soft curve of her bottom. Skimming across her hips. The gentle slope of her waist. Her ribcage and up over her breasts. Until he cupped the side of her face, his fingertips moving lightly across the plumpness of her parted lips before running lightly down the length of her throat to dip into the hollows at its base. Those same fingers ran a light caress over her clavicle, before pushing the thin strap from her shoulder and down her arm, tugging gently on the material of her top until one plump, aroused breast popped free of its confinement.

Stazy gave a breathless gasp as she arched into that large and cupping hand, its thumb and index finger lightly rolling the engorged bud at its tip before tugging gently. Pleasure coursed through her hotly as Jaxon alternated those rhythmic caresses for several agonisingly pleasurable minutes before the hot and moist sweep of his tongue laved that throbbing nipple.

'Jaxon…!' Her eyes were wide open now, and she looked down at him in the early-morning sunlight, the darkness of his hair a tousled caress against her flesh, those grey eyes smoky with arousal as he glanced up at her. 'Please don't stop this time…!' she encouraged achingly.

One of her hands moved up to cradle the back of his head and her fingers became entangled in the overlong darkness of his hair as she held him to her.

Pleasure lit his eyes before he turned his attention back to her breast, alternately licking, biting and gently suckling, before moving across to bestow that same pleasure upon its twin.

His skin was so much darker than hers as he nudged her legs apart and moved to settle between her parted thighs, all hard muscle and sinew where her hands moved caressingly down the length of his spine. Stazy was totally aware of the long length of his arousal pressing into her as her hands dipped beneath his black underpants to cup the muscled contours of his bottom.

Jaxon's hands tightly gripped Stazy's hips as he raised his head to draw in a hissing breath. Those slender hands squeezed and caressed him, turning his body slightly, and he encouraged those hands to move to the front of his body, ceasing to breathe at all as long and slender fingers curved around his shaft and the soft pad of her thumb ran lightly over the moisture escaping its tip.

He had fallen asleep fitfully, only to wake mere hours later. Stazy had continued to sleep. His body had been hard and aching, and finally he hadn't been able to resist waking her. He had needed to touch her—just a light caress or two, he had promised himself. And so he had caressed her hips. Her stomach. Her throat.

That was when he had lost it, Jaxon acknowledged achingly. The arching of Stazy's body into that caress had been more than his control could withstand, and the pulse of his shaft grew harder as he'd suckled her greedily into his mouth.

And now, at the first touch of her fingers on him, Jaxon felt as if he was about to explode—

'Lie back, Jaxon, and let me take these off for you,' Stazy encouraged huskily, and she pushed him back against the pillows before moving up onto her knees beside him, pulling off the tangle of her top to ease her movements before sitting forward to slowly pull his black underpants down over his hips and thighs. His eyes were riveted on her naked breasts as they bobbed forward enticingly, and he groaned low in his throat as his throbbing shaft was at last allowed to jut free as she discarded his underpants completely before looking down at him with greedy eyes.

Jaxon groaned again as he saw her tongue appear between those pouting lips before moving over them moistly. If Stazy so much as touched him with those wet and pouting lips then he was going to—

'Oh, dear God...!' Jaxon's hips lifted up off the bed as Stazy lowered her head, one of her hands once again firmly grasping his shaft and the other cupping him beneath, and her lips parted widely as she took him completely into the heat of her mouth, licking, sucking, savouring...

He could smell Stazy's arousal now—a hot and musky scent that drove his own pleasure higher than ever as her tongue laved him, fingers lightly pumping, before she took him fully into her mouth and sucked him deep into the back of her throat.

It was too much—Stazy was too much!

'You have to stop. Now!' Jaxon gripped her shoulders as he pulled her up and away from him, allowing the full heaviness of his shaft to fall damply against the hardness of his stomach. 'It's my turn,' he assured her huskily as he saw the questioning disappointment in her eyes, and he laid her gently back against the pillows and moved to roll the last piece of clothing from her body, sitting back on his haunches to look down at the pearly perfection of her naked body: pale ivory skin, the fullness of her breasts tipped with those ruby-red nipples, a red-gold thatch of curls between her thighs.

His nudge was gentle as he parted her legs to kneel between her thighs and reveal her hidden beauty to him. He enjoyed Stazy's groan of pleasure as he ran the tips of his fingers over and around her sensitive bud before lowering his head to move his tongue against her, again and again, until she arched into him as he gently suckled her into his mouth.

Stazy gave a low and torturous moan as Jaxon's finger caressed and probed her moist and swollen opening before sliding gently inside her, quickly joined by a second. Those muscled walls clasped around him and he began to thrust into her with the same rhythm as his suckling mouth. Stazy arched into those thrusts, needing, wanting—

Pleasure coursed hotly, fiercely through her as she began to orgasm. There was a loud roaring sound in her ears and a kaleidoscope of coloured lights burst behind her eyelids as ecstatic release ripped through her for long, relentless minutes. Jaxon gave no quarter as he coaxed the last shuddering spasm of pleasure from her boneless and replete body before finally releasing her, to lay his head against her thigh.

That was when Stazy became aware she still had that

loud roaring noise in her ears. Her eyes opened wide as she looked down at Jaxon dazedly. 'What…?'

He raised his head lazily, eyes dark, lips moist and full. 'I'd really like to take credit for being the cause of that phenomena, but I'm afraid I can't,' he murmured ruefully.

Stazy looked about the bedroom dazedly, completely disorientated—both by the satiated weakness she felt following the fierceness of her first ever orgasm, and by that loud, inexplicable roaring in her ears.

Her gaze returned to Jaxon when she could find no possible reason for that noise in the neatness of her bedroom. 'What is it?' she breathed huskily.

Jaxon had a feeling he knew exactly what it was. *Who* it was. Just as he knew it was a presence guaranteed to wipe away that look of satiation from the relaxed beauty of Stazy's face!

He gave Stazy's naked and satisfied body one last regretful glance before levering up onto his elbows and knees and crawling off the end of the bed to stroll over to the window. He twitched aside one of the curtains to look down on to the manicured lawn below.

'Yep, I was afraid of that.' He grimaced, letting the curtain fall back into place as he turned back to where Stazy now sat on the side of the bed, looking across at him with wide, still slightly dazed eyes.

'Afraid of what?' She gave a puzzled shake of her head.

Jaxon drew in a heavy breath before answering her. 'It's your grandfather. He's just arrived by helicopter,' he added, as Stazy still looked completely dazed.

Her eyes widened in alarm. 'He— I— You— We—' She threw back the bedclothes to stand up abruptly, completely unconcerned by her nakedness—and Jaxon's, regrettably!—as she hurried across the room to pull one of the curtains aside for herself. 'Oh, dear Lord…!' she groaned, obviously in a complete panic as she quickly dropped the curtain back over the window and turned to grasp Jaxon's arm. 'We have to get dressed! No—first you need to go back to your own bedroom!' She released his arm to commence frantically gathering his discarded clothes up off the carpet, before screwing them up into a bundle and shoving them at his chest. 'You need to take these with you—'

'Will you just calm down, Stazy?' Jaxon took the clothes from her and placed them on the bedside chair, before reaching out to grasp both her arms and shake her gently. 'You're twenty-nine years old, for goodness' sake—'

'And that's my grandfather out there!' Her eyes had taken on a hunted look.

'We haven't done anything wrong,' he said soothingly.

'If this were my apartment, or a hotel, then I would be inclined to agree with you—but this is *Gramps'* home!' She was breathing hard in her agitation, her face white against the deep green of her eyes as she hurried through to the adjoining bathroom to return with her robe seconds later.

'Stazy, I very much doubt that the first thing Geoffrey is going to do when he enters the house is come up to your bedroom to see if by some chance we might have spent the night together in his absence—'

'Please don't argue any more—just go, Jaxon!' She looked up at him pleadingly after tying the belt to her robe.

'I have every intention of going back to my own bedroom, Stazy,' he assured gruffly. 'But I think I should dress first, don't you? Rather than risk bumping into your grandfather or one of the household staff in the hallway when I'm completely naked...?'

He had a point, Stazy accepted with a pained wince. She hadn't expected— It hadn't even occurred to her— She hadn't been thinking clearly at all last night when she had agreed to Jaxon's coming to her bedroom and spending the night with her!

And her explanation—her excuse for what had happened with Jaxon this morning...?

She didn't have one. At least not one that she wanted to think about right now. She couldn't think at all now— not with her grandfather about to enter Bromley House!

'Nor,' Jaxon continued grimly, 'do I find it in the least acceptable to sneak out of your bedroom like a naughty schoolboy caught in the act!'

Stazy winced at the obvious displeasure in his tone. 'I wasn't implying that—'

'No?' He turned away to sort impatiently through the pile of clothes on the bedroom chair, giving Stazy a breathtaking view of the bare length of his back and the tautness of his buttocks as he pulled on those fitted black underpants. 'It seems to me that's exactly what you're implying.' His expression was bleak as he unhurriedly pulled on the rest of his clothes before sitting down on the side of the bed to lace his shoes.

'Look, we can talk about this later, Jaxon—?'

'What is there to talk about?' He stood up, towering over Stazy as she stood barefoot in front of him. 'In my profession I've learnt that actions invariably speak louder than words, Stazy,' he bit out harshly. 'And your

actions, your haste to get rid of me, tell me that you regret what just happened—'

'And *you're* behaving like that ridiculous schoolboy—' She broke off as she saw the thunderous darkness of Jaxon's frown. His eyes were a pale and glittering
grey as he looked down the length of his nose at her, a
nerve pulsed in his tightly clenched jaw.

'Just forget it, Stazy,' he bit out bleakly.

Forget it? Forget that amazing, wonderful lovemaking? Forget that she had wanted Jaxon enough, trusted
him enough, to share her first ever orgasm with him…?

That alone was enough to tell Stazy how inconsequen-
tial her two sexual experiences had been. Just how much
of herself she had held back from those other men…

Just now, with Jaxon, she had been completely open.
The barriers that she had kept erected about her emotions
for so many years had come crashing down around her
ears as she gave herself up completely to the pleasure of
Jaxon's lips and hands on her body.

Meaning what, exactly?

She couldn't actually have come to *care* for Jaxon
over these past few days alone with him, could she?

And by care, did she mean—?

No!

She wasn't going there!

Not now.

Not ever!

Jaxon was an accomplished and experienced lover—a
man used to making a conquest of any woman he went to
bed with. Those were the reasons—the only reasons!—
for her own loss of control just now.

Her chin rose proudly. 'Fine, then I guess we won't
talk later,' she said dismissively.

Jaxon looked down at Stazy from between narrowed lids, wishing he knew what thoughts had been going through her head during those few minutes of silence, but as usual her closed expression revealed none of her inner emotions to him.

He probably shouldn't have been so annoyed with her just now. No—he *definitely* shouldn't have been annoyed with her just now! His only excuse was that it had been irritating, galling, to be made to feel like a guilty indiscretion as far as Stazy was concerned—especially when he could still feel the silkiness of her skin against his hands and taste her on his lips and tongue. When he was aware that he was starting to care for her in a way he had never imagined when they had met six weeks ago...

'I really think you should go now, Jaxon.' Stazy backed away from the hand he had raised with the intention of reaching out and caressing her cheek.

Jaxon's hand dropped back to his side and he looked down at her searchingly for several long seconds before nodding abruptly. 'But we will talk about this again before I leave here,' he promised softly, his gaze intent, before he turned on his heel and crossed to the door, letting himself quietly out of the room.

Stazy felt awash with regret as she watched Jaxon close the bedroom door behind him as he left, having to bite down painfully on her bottom lip to stop herself from calling out to prevent him from going.

What would be the point of stopping him? Their love-making, her pleasure, might have been life-altering for her, but as far as Jaxon was concerned she had merely been another sexual interlude in his life...

CHAPTER TEN

'AND THAT, I'M afraid, is my reason for not telling you both yesterday evening that I was actually in hospital, having stitches put in my arm, when I spoke to you on the telephone.' Geoffrey concluded his explanation ruefully as he turned from where Jaxon stood in front of one of the bay windows in the drawing room to look concernedly at his still and silent granddaughter as she sat in the armchair opposite near the unlit fireplace.

It was an explanation Jaxon thought worthy of one of the dozens of film scripts presented to him every year!

Death threats from an unknown assassin. Gunshots in the night. The apprehension and arrest of a gunman by the security men who had been guarding Geoffrey in London. A gunman, it transpired, who held an old and personal grudge against Geoffrey, but had been unaware of exactly how and where to find him until he had seen and read that appalling biography on Anastasia published the previous year.

'You were shot at…?' Stazy was the one to break the silence, deathly white as she sat unmoving in the armchair.

Her grandfather looked down at the sling on his right arm. 'It's only a flesh wound.'

Stazy stood up abruptly. 'Someone actually shot you and you chose not to tell me about it?' She still found it unbelievable her grandfather could have done such a thing. Or, in this case, *not* done such a thing!

Absolutely unbelievable!

'Well…yes.' Geoffrey gave a regretful wince. 'I didn't want to alarm you—'

'You didn't want to alarm me…!' Stazy breathed hard as she looked down at her grandfather incredulously. 'I don't believe you, Gramps!' she finally snapped exasperatedly. 'Some unknown man has been stalking you—only you!—for days now, he finally succeeded in managing to shoot you, and you decided not to tell me about it because you didn't want to *alarm* me!'

The same night she had spent in Jaxon's arms…

'I did tell you of a threat—'

'But not to you personally.'

'No, but—'

'Admit it, Gramps, you lied to me!' she accused emotionally, her cheeks burning.

'Stazy—'

'Don't even attempt to offer excuses for his behaviour, Jaxon,' she warned hotly when he would have interceded. 'There are no excuses. I was worried to death about you, Gramps.' She rounded back on her grandfather.

'Telling you I had been shot would only have worried you even more—'

'I'm not sure that was even possible!' She gave an exasperated shake of her head. 'I'm sorry, but if I stay here any longer then I'm going to say something I'll really regret. If you will both excuse me?' She didn't wait for either man to answer before rushing from the room.

'Well, that didn't go too well, did it?' Geoffrey murmured ruefully as the door slammed behind Stazy with barely controlled violence.

'Not too well, no,' Jaxon confirmed dryly as he turned back from admiring how beautiful Stazy had looked as she left the room. That red-gold hair had seemed to crackle with electricity, her eyes had glittered like emeralds, her creamy cheeks had been flushed. The cream silk blouse and close-fitting denims she was wearing today weren't too hard on the eye either!

'Why doesn't she understand that I was only trying to protect her by not telling her the truth until the whole thing was over and done with?' the older man asked in obvious frustration.

Jaxon grimaced as he stepped further into the room, having deemed it safer to stand a little removed while granddaughter and grandfather confronted each other. 'I may be wrong, but I believe Stazy considers herself to be a little old to still be in need of that sort of protection from you or anyone else.'

'And what do you think I could have done differently in the circumstances?' Geoffrey frowned up at him.

Jaxon gave a rueful smile. 'I'm the last person you should be asking about how best to deal with Stazy.'

'Indeed?' Geoffrey's gaze sharpened speculatively.

'Oh, yes!' he said with feeling.

'Does that mean the two of you are still at loggerheads?' the older man frowned again.

Jaxon wasn't sure how his relationship with Stazy stood at this precise moment. Last night she had allowed him to comfort her. This morning they had almost made love to each other. Before having the most god-awful row when Geoffrey had arrived so unexpectedly!

No, Jaxon had no idea how Stazy felt towards him now.

Any more than he knew what to make of his feelings for her...

It had been both heaven and hell to hold Stazy in his arms all night long, and sheer unadulterated pleasure to be with her this morning.

Knowing how Stazy liked to keep her life compartmentalised and Jaxon didn't, the argument that had followed had perhaps been predictable—but that didn't stop it from being frustrating as hell as far as Jaxon was concerned.

Where the two of them went from here—if they went anywhere—Jaxon had absolutely no idea.

'More or less, yes,' he answered the older man abruptly.

'Do I want to know how much more or how much less...?' Geoffrey prompted softly.

Jaxon gave the question some thought. 'Probably not,' he finally answered carefully.

The other man looked at him searchingly for several long seconds before giving a slow nod of his head. 'Okay. So, do you think Stazy will ever forgive me...?'

Probably a lot more quickly than she was going to forgive Jaxon—if she ever did forgive him! 'I think it might be a good idea if you give her some time to—well, to calm down before attempting to talk to her again,' he advised ruefully.

'And in the meantime...?'

'I have absolutely no idea *what* you do in the meantime.' Jaxon grimaced. 'But now that security here has been lifted I intend to change into my leathers and go out for a ride on the Harley,' he said decisively.

'I'd ask to join you, but I think that might push Stazy

into disowning me completely!' Geoffrey chuckled wryly.

'There's no "might" about it!' Jaxon assured him.

The older man nodded slowly. 'Let's hope she decides to forgive me very soon.'

It was a hope Jaxon echoed…

Stazy stood with her forehead pressed against the coolness of her bedroom window, looking outside as the Harley roared off down the gravel driveway with a leather-clad Jaxon seated on the back of it, the black helmet once again covering his almost shoulder-length hair and the smoky visor lowered over his face. Although it wasn't too difficult for her to imagine the grimness of his expression!

Was Jaxon leaving for good? Or had he just gone out for a drive now that there was no longer a reason for them to be confined to Bromley House?

Not that Stazy could altogether blame Jaxon if he *had* decided to leave. A part of her knew she would have to leave too. And soon. She longed for the peace and solitude of her apartment in London, desperately needed to be alone for a while—if only so that she could lick her wounds in private. At the same time she knew she couldn't leave here until things were less strained between herself and her grandfather.

How could he have lied to her in that way? Oh, she could appreciate the reason her grandfather had thought he should skirt around the truth, but that didn't mean Stazy had to be in the least understanding about his having so blatantly lied to her at the end.

Especially when those lies had resulted in her spending the night with Jaxon…

Damn it, spending the night with Jaxon hadn't been the problem—it had been waking up in his arms this morning and the things that had followed that made her cringe with embarrassment every time she so much as thought about it! Which had been often during the half an hour or so she had spent in her bedroom.

Thankfully the maid had been up to Stazy's bedroom during her absence downstairs, so the bed had been neatly remade and the room tidied by the time she returned from talking with her grandfather. Unfortunately, as Stazy had crossed the bedroom to take her suitcase out of the wardrobe and place it on top of the bed, that neatness had done very little to stop her from remembering each and every detail of what had happened here between herself and Jaxon...

The joy of kissing and caressing him. The pleasure of being kissed and caressed *by* him. The unimagined ecstasy of the mind-blowing orgasm he had so easily taken her to...

Even now Stazy could feel the ultra-sensitivity between her legs in the aftermath of her orgasm. Her first ever orgasm...

And her last if it resulted in her not only feeling physically vulnerable but emotionally too!

Although Jaxon's abrupt departure—without that promised talk between the two of them—would seem to imply that he had no interest in furthering a relationship between the two of them, so—

'May I come in...?'

Stazy looked up sharply at the sound of her grandfather's cajoling voice. 'That depends on whether or not you're going to lie to me again.' She raised censorious brows.

He gave a self-conscious wince as he stood in the open doorway. 'I have explained the reason for that, darling.'

She nodded abruptly. 'And it was a completely unacceptable explanation. I'm no longer a child you need to protect from the truth, Gramps!'

'So Jaxon has already pointed out to me,' Geoffrey acknowledged heavily.

Stazy stiffened defensively just at hearing Jaxon's name, let alone wondering in what context he might have made that remark. 'Was that before or after he left on his Harley?'

'Obviously before.' Her grandfather grimaced before glancing at the open suitcase sitting on top of her bed. 'What's going on, Stazy…?'

She drew in a deep breath even as she gave a dismissive shrug. 'I thought I might leave too, later this afternoon.'

His gaze sharpened. 'Leave? But—'

'You've said yourself that the danger is over now and your wound isn't serious,' Stazy interrupted firmly. 'And now that Jaxon has left there seems little point in my not joining the dig in Iraq as originally planned.'

The fact that she had taken out her suitcase before she even saw Jaxon leave wasn't something her grandfather needed to know! Even if Jaxon hadn't decided to leave, how could she possibly stay on at Bromley House after the events of earlier this morning? There was no way she could continue calmly working on the details for the screenplay with Jaxon as if nothing had happened between them.

Stazy was extremely reluctant to delve too deeply into her own emotions and find out exactly what that 'something' meant to her…

'Jaxon hasn't left completely, darling. He's just gone for a ride on his motorbike after being confined here for the past few days,' her grandfather told her gently.

'Oh.' Stazy felt the colour drain from her cheeks.

Geoffrey gave her a searching glance. 'Is there something you want to tell me, darling…?'

The very last thing Stazy wanted to do was to confide in her grandfather about making love with Jaxon this morning! There was no way she could tell another man of the intimacies she and Jaxon had shared, and there wasn't the remotest possibility of her ever talking to anyone about how those intimacies had resulted in her first ever earth-shattering orgasm!

Although she might not have any choice if, as her grandfather said, Jaxon had only gone for a ride on his motorbike and intended returning to Bromley House later this morning…

'No, nothing,' she answered her grandfather abruptly as she carefully avoided meeting his piercing blue gaze. 'As Jaxon isn't here at the moment I think I might follow his example and go out—go for a run along the beach,' she added lightly. 'We can discuss later whether or not there's any point in our bothering to continue with the research.'

Her grandfather looked puzzled. 'What do you mean?'

Stazy shrugged. 'You said the unauthorised biography on Granny was the reason this man from the past was able to track you down, so just think how much more exposed you will be if Jaxon goes ahead with the making of his film.'

'There is even more reason now for Jaxon to make his film, darling,' Geoffrey insisted firmly. 'Don't you see. It's the only way to dispel the myth and show Anastasia for the true heroine that she was,' he added when she still looked unconvinced.

Yes, Stazy did see the logic of that. Unfortunately. She had just been clinging to the hope—the slim hope, admittedly—that this recent scare might result in her grandfather rethinking his decision.

She gave an impatient shake of her head. 'As I said, we can all talk about this later—when Jaxon has returned from his ride and I've been for my run.'

Geoffrey nodded slowly. 'That would seem to be the best idea.' He turned to leave before turning back again. 'Are you and Jaxon still able to continue working together...?' he prompted shrewdly.

Stazy felt the colour warm her cheeks. Surely Jaxon hadn't—? No, of course he wouldn't. 'I can't see any reason why not, can you?' she dismissed lightly.

Her grandfather shrugged. 'You both seem more than a little edgy this morning...'

'Is that surprising when we've been cooped up here together for two days?'

And nights... Let's not forget the nights!

As if Stazy ever could...

'Geoffrey has gone to his bedroom to rest for a while.'

Stazy looked up from where she sat in the library, reading one of her grandmother's diaries. Well... 'reading' was something of a misnomer; even she knew she had only been giving the appearance of doing so. Because inwardly her thoughts and emotions were so churned up Stazy couldn't have concentrated on absorbing any of her grandmother's entries if her life had depended upon it!

Sitting down to eat lunch with her grandfather and

Jaxon earlier had been something of an ordeal—so much so that Stazy had finally excused herself after eating none of the first course and proceeding only to pick at the main course for ten minutes or so, leaving the two men at the table to continue talking as she hurried from the room with the intention of escaping to the library.

She and Jaxon hadn't so much as exchanged a word during the whole of that excruciatingly awkward meal. That wasn't to say Stazy hadn't been completely aware of him as the three of them had sat at the small round table where she and Jaxon had eaten dinner together alone the past two evenings.

In the same room where Stazy had wrapped her legs around Jaxon's waist as he had pressed her up against the china cabinet and kissed her...

Her expression was guarded now as she looked across the room at him. 'Rest is probably the best thing for him.'

And what, Jaxon wondered as he came into the room and quietly closed the door behind him, did Stazy consider was the best thing for the two of *them*?

Logic said they should talk about what had happened between them this morning. Emotion told him that Stazy's feelings were so strung out at the moment that even to broach that conversation would only result in another meltdown—something she definitely wouldn't thank him for.

Because the two of them had spent the night in the same bed? Because of the intimacies they had shared with each other this morning? Stazy bitterly regretting the lapse?

Jaxon would like to think that wasn't the reason, but he still smarted at the way she had tried to push him out of the bedroom before anyone discovered him there. Admittedly, her grandfather had just flown in by helicopter, but even so…

Jaxon had had plenty of time to think things over during his long ride earlier. He had come to know Stazy much better these past three days, and knew without being told that with hindsight she would view her uninhibited response to him this morning as a weakness. A weakness she had no intention of repeating…

His mouth thinned and his lids narrowed as she seemed to recoil against the back of her chair when he crossed the room in long, silent strides. He looked down at her frustratedly. 'Do you want me to make my excuses to Geoffrey and tell him that I have to leave unexpectedly?'

Her face was expressionless as she returned his gaze. 'Why on earth would I want to you to do that?'

'Maybe because you obviously can't stand even being in the same room with me any longer?' he reasoned heavily.

'Don't be ridiculous, Jaxon,' Stazy dismissed scathingly, inwardly knowing he was being nothing of the kind; she *did* find being in the same room with him totally overwhelming. The intimacies the two of them had shared this morning made it difficult for her even to look at him without remembering exactly where and how his lips and tongue had pleasured her this morning…

'I don't understand you, Stazy,' he bit out bleakly. 'We're two consenting adults who chose to—'

'I know exactly what we did, Jaxon!' She stood up so suddenly that her chair tipped over backwards and crashed against one of the bookcases. 'Damn. Damn, damn, *damn*!' she muttered impatiently as she bent to set the chair back onto its four legs before glaring up at him. 'I don't want to talk about this now, Jaxon—'

'Will you ever want to talk about it?'

She gave a self-conscious shiver. 'Preferably not!'

Jaxon breathed hard. 'You're behaving like some outraged innocent that I robbed of her virginity!'

Maybe. Because in every way that mattered that was exactly how Stazy felt...

She had been completely in control of the situation when she had chosen her previous two lovers so carefully. And she had been physically in control too. The loss of her virginity to her university lecturer had been perfunctory at best, the second experience four years ago even more so.

The rawness, the sheer carnality of Jaxon's lovemaking this morning, hadn't allowed her to keep any of those barriers in place. He had stripped her down, emotionally as well as physically, and in doing so had sent all her barriers crashing to the floor, leaving her feeling vulnerable and exposed.

Oh, she didn't believe Jaxon had deliberately set out to do that to her. In fact she was sure that he had no idea of exactly what he had done. But, whether Jaxon knew it or not, that was exactly what had happened. And Stazy needed space and time in order to rebuild those emotional barriers.

She forced herself to relax, and her expression was coolly dismissive as she looked up at him. 'Is it being an actor that makes you so melodramatic, Jaxon?' she drawled derisively.

'It isn't a question of melodrama—'

'Of course it is,' she said easily. 'You're reading things into this situation that simply aren't there. Yes, our behaviour this morning makes it a little awkward for us to continue working together, but—as I assured my grandfather earlier—I'm more than willing to do my part so that we finish the research as quickly as possible. After which time we can both get back to our own totally different lives.' She looked up at him challengingly.

At this moment the only thing Jaxon felt more than willing to do was carry out his threat to put Stazy over his knee and spank some sense into her! Or at least spank her until there was a return of the warm and sensual Stazy he had been with this morning!

Not going to happen any time soon, he acknowledged as he recognised the same cool detachment in her expression that had been there when they'd first met just over six weeks ago.

'Shall we get on…?' She pulled her chair out and resumed her seat at the table before looking up at him expectantly.

Jaxon looked down at her exasperatedly. He felt the return of all his earlier frustrations with this situation, appreciating how it had all seemed so much simpler when he'd been riding the country roads on the back of the Harley.

Obviously, he had reasoned, Stazy had been understandably dismayed by the unexpected arrival of her grandfather. But once she got over her surprise Jaxon was sure the two of them would be able to sit down and talk about the situation like the two rational human beings that they were.

Somewhere in all that thinking Jaxon had forgotten to take into account that Stazy as a rational human being could also be extremely annoying!

To the point where he now felt more like wringing

her delicate little neck than attempting to talk with her rationally!

Had he ever met a more frustrating woman?

Or a more sensually satisfying one…?

Jaxon had made love with dozens of women during the past fifteen years, but he knew that none of them had aroused him to the fever pitch that Stazy had this morning. To the point where he had been teetering dangerously on the edge just from the touch of her lips and fingers—

That way lies madness, old chum, he told himself as he felt himself hardening again, just at thinking about having Stazy's lips and tongue on him there. *Total insanity*!

'Fine, if you're sure that's the way you want it,' he bit out tersely, and he moved to sit in the chair opposite hers.

It wasn't the way Stazy wanted it at all. It was the way she knew it had to be. For both their sakes…

CHAPTER ELEVEN

'So. The work's done, and we can both leave here later this morning...' Stazy kept her tone deliberately light as she looked across the breakfast table from beneath lowered lashes as Jaxon relaxed back in his chair, enjoying his second cup of coffee after eating what could only be described as a hearty breakfast. Unlike Stazy, who had only managed to pull a croissant apart as she drank her own cup of morning coffee.

No, that probably wasn't the best way to describe Jaxon this morning—after all, it was the condemned man who ate a hearty breakfast, and on the morning of his departure from Bromley House Jaxon appeared anything but that!

It had been a long and stressful week as far as Stazy was concerned, with the long hours she had spent alone with Jaxon in the library by far the biggest strain. But only for Stazy, it seemed. Jaxon, when he hadn't been secluded in the study with her grandfather, had been brisk and businesslike in her company, with not even a hint of a mention of the night they had spent together, let alone that conversation he had seemed so intent on the two of them having five days ago.

Her grandfather's return to London late yesterday

evening hadn't brought about any change in Jaxon's distant manner either.

Had she wanted it to make a difference?

Stazy had no idea what she wanted, except she knew she found this strained politeness extremely unsettling!

Jaxon shrugged the broadness of his shoulders in the dark grey tee shirt he wore with faded blue denims. The heavy biker boots were already on his feet in preparation for his departure. 'It's over for you, certainly, but the real work for me—the writing of the screenplay—is only just beginning.' He smiled ruefully.

Stazy's heart did a little lurch in her chest just at the sight of that smile after days of strained politeness. 'Can you do that while working on the pirate movie?'

He raised a dark brow. 'I appreciate it's a common belief amongst ladies that men can only concentrate on one thing at a time, but I assure you it's just a myth!'

Stazy felt warmth in her cheeks at the rebuke. 'I meant timewise, not mentally.'

'I'll cope,' Jaxon drawled as he studied her from between narrowed lids.

Was it his imagination, or did the fine delicacy of Stazy's features appear sharper than a week ago? Her cheekbones and the curve of her chin more defined, with dark shadows beneath those mesmerising green eyes?

Or was he just hoping that was the case? Hoping that Stazy had found the time the two of them had spent alone together these last five days as much of a strain as he had?

If he was, then he was surely only deluding himself— because there had certainly seemed to be no sign of that in her cool and impersonal manner towards him these past few days as the two of them had continued to work together on Anastasia's papers and diaries. *Frosty* had best described Stazy's attitude towards him. In fact this was the first even remotely personal conversation they'd had in days. At five days, to be exact...

'When do you expect to have finished writing the screenplay?'

'Why do you want to know?' Jaxon gave a derisive smile. 'So that you can make sure you're nowhere near if I should need to discuss it with Geoffrey?'

A frown appeared on her creamy brow. 'I was merely attempting to make polite conversation, Jaxon...'

Jaxon had had it up to here with Stazy's politeness! He stood up abruptly to move across the room and stare out of the window, the tightness of his jaw and the clenching of his hands evidence of his inner frustration. 'As we're both leaving here this morning, don't you think you should start saying what you really mean?' he ground out harshly.

Stazy watched him warily, sensing that the time for politeness between them was over. 'I thought, for my grandfather's sake at least, that the two of us should at least try to part as friends—'

'Friends!' Jaxon turned to look at her incredulously. 'You can't be so naive as to believe the two of us can ever be *friends*!' he bit out scornfully.

She knew that, of course. But nevertheless it was painful to actually hear Jaxon state it so dismissively.

'Friends are at ease in each other's company,' he continued remorselessly. 'They actually enjoy being together. And that certainly doesn't describe the two of us, now, does it?'

Stazy clasped her hands together beneath the table so

that Jaxon wouldn't see how much they were trembling. 'I'm sorry you feel that way—'

'No, you're not,' he contradicted scathingly. 'You've wanted me to feel this way. Damn it, you've done everything in your power to push me away!'

She shook her head in denial. 'It was what you wanted too—'

'You have absolutely no idea what I want!' he rasped, grey eyes glacial.

'You're right. I don't.' She swallowed hard, her expression pained. 'Nor is there any point in the two of us discussing any of this when we will both be leaving in a few hours' time.'

'I'm not waiting a couple of hours, Stazy.' He gave a disgusted shake of his head. 'My bag is already packed, and I have every intention of leaving as soon as we've finished this conversation,' he assured her hardly.

He spoke as if he couldn't tolerate being in her company another moment longer than he had to, Stazy realised. It was a realisation that hurt her more than she would ever have believed possible…

Her chin rose proudly. 'Then consider it over.'

Jaxon stared at Stazy in frustration, knowing he wanted to shake her at the same time as he wanted to pull her up into his arms and kiss her senseless.

Where the hell was the vulnerable woman he had held in his arms all night long because she had been so worried about her grandfather? The same warm and sensuous woman who had responded so heatedly to his lovemaking the following morning?

Did that woman even exist or was she just a figment of his imagination…?

Jaxon had found himself wondering that same thing

often when, time and time again, day after day, he had been presented with that brick wall Stazy had built so sturdily about her emotions.

And now, the morning of his departure, when he might never see Stazy again, really wasn't the time for him to try to breach those walls one last time…

He nodded abruptly. 'In that case…I hope you enjoy your trip to Iraq.'

Stazy no longer had any real interest in going on the dig she had once looked forward to with such professional excitement. No longer had any real interest in doing *anything* with the rest of her summer break now that the time had come to say goodbye to Jaxon… Which was ridiculous. He had no place in her life—had made it perfectly clear during these last few minutes that he didn't *want* a place in her life! So why should just the thought of Jaxon leaving, the possibility of never seeing him again, have opened up a void inside her she had no idea how to fill?

It shouldn't. Unless—

No…!

Stazy stopped breathing even as she felt the colour draining from her cheeks. She couldn't possibly have fallen in love with Jaxon this past week?

Could she…?

The threatening tears and the deep well of emptiness inside her just at the thought of never seeing him again after today told her that was exactly what she had done…

Had she ever done anything this stupid in her life before? Could there *be* anything more stupid than Dr Stazy Bromley, lecturer in Archaeology, falling in love with Jaxon Wilder, A-list Hollywood actor and director? If there was then Stazy couldn't think of what that something could possibly be!

The best Jaxon could think of her was that she had been a temporary and no doubt annoying distraction while he'd been stuck in the depths of Hampshire for a week doing research. She didn't even want to dwell on the worst Jaxon could think of her…!

She swallowed before speaking. 'I wish you an uneventful flight back to America.'

He gave a rueful shake of his head. 'It seems we've managed to achieve politeness this morning, after all!'

And if that politeness didn't soon cease Stazy very much feared she might make a complete fool of herself by giving in to the tears stinging the backs of her eyes. She stood up abruptly. 'If you'll excuse me? I have to go upstairs and finish packing.'

No, Jaxon *didn't* excuse her—either from the room, or from instigating the strained tension that had existed between the two of them these past five days. If it hadn't been for the buffer of Geoffrey's presence then Jaxon knew, research or not, he would have had no choice but to leave days ago.

Damn it, what did it take to get through—and stay through!—that wall of reserve Stazy kept about her emotions? Whatever it was, he obviously didn't have it…

He breathed his frustration. 'Will you attend the English premiere with your grandfather when the time comes?'

She blinked. 'Isn't it a little early to be discussing the premiere of a film that hasn't even been written, yet let alone made…?'

Probably—when the earliest it was likely to happen was the end of next year, more likely much later than that. Jaxon had arranged his work schedule so that he could begin filming *Butterfly* in the spring of next year, and after that there would be weeks of editing. No, the premiere wouldn't be for another eighteen months or so.

And there was no guarantee that Stazy would attend…

Did it really matter whether or not she went to the premiere? At best the two of them would meet as polite strangers, if only for her grandfather's sake. At worst they wouldn't acknowledge each other at all other than perhaps a terse nod of the head.

And that wasn't good enough, damn it!

'Stazy, I don't have to go back to the States for several more days yet if…'

'Yes?' she prompted sharply.

He shrugged. 'We could always go away somewhere together for a couple of days.'

Stazy eyed him warily. 'For what purpose?'

'For the purpose of just spending time alone together, perhaps?' he bit out impatiently. 'Something that's been impossible to do since your grandfather arrived back so unexpectedly.'

'Oh, I believe we've spent more than enough time alone together already, Jaxon!' she assured him ruefully.

He scowled darkly at her coolness. 'What have you done with that night we spent together, Stazy? Filed it away in the back of your mind under "miscellaneous", or just decided to forget it altogether?'

Stazy flinched at the scorn underlying Jaxon's tone. As if she could *ever* forget that night in Jaxon's arms! Or what had happened the following morning.

Or the fact that she had fallen in love with him…

A love Jaxon didn't return and never could. A love she wasn't sure she could hide if, as Jaxon suggested,

they were to spend several more days—and nights!—
alone together.

Even if she did feel tempted by the suggestion. More
than tempted!

To spend time alone with Jaxon away from here, to
make love with him again, would be—

Both heaven and hell when she knew full well that
at the end of those few days he would return to his life
and she to hers!

Stazy feigned irritation. 'Why do you persist in referring back to that night, Jaxon, when you've no doubt
filed it away it your own head under "satisfactory, but
could do better"?'

His eyes narrowed to glittering slits of silver. 'Are you
talking about my performance or your own?'

Oh, her own—definitely. Twenty-nine years old, with
two—no—three lovers now to her name. Two of which
had definitely been less than satisfactory, and the third—
Jaxon himself—who had shown her a sensuality within
herself she had never dreamt existed. A sensuality that
she knew she would drown in if she spent any time alone
in Jaxon's company.

'Oh, don't worry, Jaxon. If anyone ever asks I'll assure
them you performed beautifully!' she told him scornfully.

His nostrils flared. 'Stop twisting my words, damn
it—'

'What do you want from me, Jaxon?' She gazed across
at him exasperatedly. 'Yes, we spent a single night together, but we certainly don't have to compound the
mistake by repeating it.'

He became very still. 'That's how you think of it—
as a mistake?'

Her brows rose. 'Don't you?'

'I have no idea what the hell that night—and that morning!—was all about,' he rasped impatiently. 'But no doubt you do…?' he prompted hardly.

Stazy shrugged. 'The result of a healthy man and woman having shared the same bed for the night. I'm sure I'm not the first woman you've spent the night with, Jaxon, nor will I be the last!'

He gave a humourless laugh. 'You really don't have a very high opinion of me, do you?'

She very much doubted that Jaxon wanted to know what she really thought of him. That he was not only the most heartbreakingly gorgeous man she had ever met—as well as the sexiest!—but also one of the kindest and gentlest. It had been that kindness and gentleness that had prompted him to spend the night in her bed so that she wouldn't be alone with her fears for her grandfather. The same kindness and gentleness that she now had every reason to believe would ensure he wrote Anastasia's story with the sensitivity with which it should be written.

'It's probably best if you don't answer that, if it's taking you this long to think of something polite to say,' Jaxon bit out impatiently, and he crossed forcefully to the door.

'Jaxon—!'

'Yes?' He was frowning darkly as he turned.

Stazy stared at him, not knowing what to say. Not knowing why she had called out to him—except she couldn't bear the thought of the two of them parting in this strained way. Couldn't bear the thought of the two of them parting at all! 'I never thanked you,' she finally murmured inadequately.

'For what?'

'For—for being there for me when I—when I needed you to be.' She gave a pained frown.

Jaxon stared across at her, having no idea what he should do or say next. Or if he should do or say anything when Stazy had made it so absolutely clear she wanted nothing more to do with him on a personal level.

He had thought of her, of the night the two of them spent together, far too often these past five days. And of what had happened between them the following morning. The woman Stazy had been that morning, the warm and sensual woman who had set fire to his self-control, had been nowhere in evidence in the days since. But Jaxon knew she was still in there somewhere. She had to be. That was why he had suggested the two of them go away together for a couple of days—away from Bromley House and the restraints her grandfather's presence had put on them. A suggestion Stazy had not only turned down, but in such a way she had succeeded in insulting him again into the bargain.

He straightened. 'Forget about it. I would have done the same for anyone.'

'Yes, you would.' She gave a tight, acknowledging smile.

Jaxon nodded abruptly. 'Your grandfather has my mobile and home telephone numbers if you should need to contact me.'

She frowned. 'Why would I ever need to do that...?'

No reason that Jaxon could think of! Nevertheless, it would have been nice to think there was the possibility of unexpectedly hearing the sound of Stazy's voice one day on the other end of the telephone...

This had to be the longest goodbye on record!

Probably because he wasn't ready to say goodbye to Stazy yet—still felt as if there was unfinished business between the two of them. A feeling she obviously didn't share…

Jaxon forced himself to relax the tension from his shoulders. 'No reason whatsoever,' he answered self-derisively. 'I'll go up and get my things now, and leave you to go and pack.'

'Yes.' The painful squeezing of Stazy's heart was threatening to overwhelm her. Not yet. Please, God, don't let her break down yet!

'I'll look forward to reading the screenplay.'

He raised mocking brows. 'Will you?'

'Yes,' she confirmed huskily.

He nodded briskly. ''Bye.'

Stazy had to literally drag the breath into her lungs in order to be able to answer him. ''Bye.'

Jaxon gave her one last, lingering glance before opening the door and letting himself out of the room, closing the door quietly behind him.

Stazy listened to the sound of his heavy boots crossing the hallway and going up the stairs before allowing the hot tears to cascade unchecked down her cheeks as she began to sob as if her heart was breaking.

Which it was…

CHAPTER TWELVE

Three months later.

'I HAD LUNCH with Jaxon today.'

Stazy was so startled by her grandfather's sudden announcement at a table in his favourite restaurant in London that the knife she had been using to eat the grilled sole she had ordered for her main course slipped unnoticed from her numbed fingers and fell noisily onto the tiled floor. Even then Stazy was only barely aware of a waiter rushing over to present her with a clean knife before he picked up the used one and left again.

Not only was Jaxon in London, but her grandfather had seen him earlier today...

After three months of thinking about Jaxon constantly—often dreaming about him too—it was incredible to learn that he was actually in London...

She moistened suddenly dry lips. 'I had no idea he was even in England...'

'He arrived yesterday,' her grandfather replied. He was now fully recovered from the gunshot wound and back to his normal robust self.

That was more than could be said for Stazy!

Oh, it had been a positive three months as far as her

work was concerned. The dig in Iraq had been very successful. And when she'd returned to the university campus last month she had officially been offered the job as Head of Department when the present head retired next year. She hadn't given her answer yet but, having worked towards this very thing for the past eleven years, there seemed little doubt that she would accept the position.

No, on a professional level things couldn't have been better. It was on a personal level that Stazy knew she wasn't doing so well...

A part of her had hoped that time and distance would help to lessen the intensity of the feelings—the love—she felt for Jaxon, but instead the opposite had happened. Not a day, an hour went by, it seemed, when she didn't think of him at least once, wondering how he was, what he was doing. Which beautiful actress he was involved with now...

Since returning from Iraq she had even found herself buying and avidly looking through those glossy magazines that featured gossip about the rich and the famous.

If she had hoped to see any photographs of Jaxon then she might as well have saved herself the money—and the heartache!—because she hadn't succeeded in finding a single picture of him during the whole of that time. With a woman or otherwise.

The last thing she had been expecting, when her grandfather had invited her out to dinner with him this evening, was for him to calmly announce that Jaxon was in England at this very minute. Or at least Stazy presumed he was still here...

'Does he intend staying long?' she prompted lightly, aware that her hand was shaking slightly as she lifted her glass and took a much-needed sip of her white wine.

'He didn't say,' Geoffrey answered dismissively.

'Oh.' There were so many things Stazy wanted to ask—such as, how did Jaxon look? What had the two men talked about? Had Jaxon asked about her…? And yet she felt so tied up in knots inside just at the thought of Jaxon being in London at all that she couldn't ask any of them.

Although quite what her grandfather would have made of that interest if she had, after her previous attitude to Jaxon, was anybody's guess!

'He's finished writing the screenplay.'

Stazy's gaze sharpened. 'And…?'

Her grandfather smiled ruefully. 'And I recommend that you read it for yourself.'

She slowly licked the wine from her lips as she carefully placed her glass back down on the table. 'He gave you a copy…?'

'He gave me two copies. One for me and one for you.' Geoffrey reached down and lifted the briefcase he had carried into the restaurant with him earlier.

That second copy, meant for her, told Stazy more than anything else could have done that Jaxon had no intention of seeking her out while he was in England. And after the way the two of them had parted how could she have expected anything else!

Her grandfather opened the two locks on his briefcase before taking out the thickly bound bundle of the screenplay and handing it across the table to her. 'Read the front cover first, Stazy,' he advised huskily as she continued to stare at it, as if it were a bomb about to go off in his hand, rather than taking it from him.

Her throat moved convulsively as she swallowed hard. 'Have you had a chance to read it yet?'

Geoffrey smiled. 'Oh, yes.'

'And?'

'As I said, you need to read it for yourself.'

'If you liked it then I'm sure I will too,' she insisted firmly.

'Exactly how long do you intend to go on like this, Stazy?' her grandfather prompted impatiently as he placed the bound screenplay down on the tabletop, so that he could lock his briefcase before placing it back on the floor beside him.

Her hair moved silkily over her shoulders as she gave a shake of her head. 'I don't know what you mean…'

His steely-blue gaze became shrewdly piercing. 'Don't you?'

'No.'

'You have shadows under your eyes from not sleeping properly, you've lost weight you couldn't afford to lose—?'

'I think I picked up a bug in Iraq—'

'And I think you caught the bug before you even went to Iraq—and its name is Jaxon!'

Stazy's breath caught sharply in her throat at the baldness of her grandfather's statement, the colour draining from her cheeks. 'You're mistaken—'

'No, Stazy, you're the one that's making a mistake—by attempting to lie to someone who's had to lie as often as I have over the years,' he assured her impatiently.

She ran the tip of her tongue over her lips. There was a pained frown between her eyes. She knew from her grandfather's determined expression that he wasn't about to let her continue prevaricating. 'Is how I feel about Jaxon that obvious?'

'Only to me, darling.' He placed a hand gently over

one of hers. 'And that's only because I know you so well and love you so much.'

She gave a shaky smile. 'It's probably as well that someone does!'

'Maybe Jaxon—'

'Let's not even go there,' she cut in firmly, her back tensing.

'I have no idea how long he'll be in England, but he did say he would be in London for several more days yet, so perhaps—'

'Gramps, I'm the last person Jaxon would want to see while he's here,' she assured him dully.

'You can't possibly know that—'

'Oh, but I can.' Stazy gave a self-derisive shake of her head. 'If you thought I was rude to him at our initial meeting then you should have seen me during those first few days we were alone together at Bromley House!' She sighed heavily. 'Believe me, Gramps, we parted in such a way as to ensure that Jaxon will never want to see me again!' Stiltedly. Distantly. Like strangers.

'Are you absolutely sure about that…?'

'Yes, of course I'm sure.' Her voice sharpened at her grandfather's persistence. Wasn't it enough for her to suffer the torment of knowing Jaxon was in England at all without having to explain all the reasons why he wouldn't want to see her while he was here? 'Feeling the way I do, I'm not sure it would be a good idea for me to see him again, either,' she said emotionally.

Her grandfather sat back in his chair. 'That's a pity…'

Her eyes had misted over with unshed tears. 'I don't see why.'

'Because when I saw him earlier today I invited him to join us this evening for dessert and coffee.' Geoffrey glanced across the restaurant. 'And it would appear he has arrived just in time to take up my invitation…'

Jaxon was totally unaware of the attention of the other diners in the restaurant as they recognised him. He walked slowly towards the table near the window where he could see Stazy sitting having dinner with her grandfather.

Even with her back towards him, Jaxon had spotted her the moment he had entered the crowded room; that gorgeous red-gold hair was like a vivid flame against the black dress she wore as it flowed loosely over her shoulders and down the slenderness of her back!

'Stazy,' he greeted her huskily as she looked up at him warily from beneath lowered lashes.

Her throat moved convulsively as she swallowed before answering him abruptly. 'Jaxon.'

Close to her like this, Jaxon could see that her face was even thinner than it had been three months ago—as if she had lost more weight. The looseness of the cream dress about her breasts and waist seemed to confirm that impression. 'I appreciate it's the done thing, when you meet up with someone again after a long absence, to say how well the other person is looking—but in your case, Stazy, I would be lying!' He almost growled in his disapproval of the fragility of her appearance. 'And I know how much you hate lies…'

Her cheeks were aflame. 'And what makes you think you're looking so perfect yourself?' she came back crisply.

'That's much better,' Jaxon murmured approvingly, before glancing across the table at the avidly attentive Geoffrey Bromley. 'When I asked about you earlier today your grandfather was at pains to tell me how happy and well you've been this past three months…' He raised mocking brows at the older man.

'Yes. Well. Family loyalty and all that.' Geoffrey had the grace to look slightly embarrassed at the deception. 'I did invite you to join us for dessert and coffee so that you could see Stazy for yourself. Speaking of which… No, there's no need to bring another chair,' he told the waiter as the man arrived to stand enquiringly beside their table. 'I have another appointment to get to, so Mr Wilder can have my seat.' He bent to pick up the brief-case from beside his chair before standing up in readiness to leave.

'Gramps—'

'I believe you told me yourself weeks ago that you're a big girl now and no longer in need of my protection…?' he reminded her firmly, before bending to kiss her lightly on the cheek. 'If you'll both excuse me…?' He didn't wait for either of them to reply before turning and walking briskly across the restaurant.

Yes, Stazy *had* told her grandfather that—but it had been in a totally different situation and context from this one!

That her grandfather had invited Jaxon to join them this evening with the deliberate intention of leaving her alone with him she had no doubt. Quite why he should have decided to do so was far less clear to her…

Especially so when the first thing Jaxon had done was insult her. And she had then insulted him back. Some things never changed, it seemed…

Her own insulting remark had been knee-jerk rather than truthful—Jaxon had never looked more wonderful to her than he did this evening. His silky dark hair was still shoulder-length, brushed back from the chiselled perfection of his face, and the black evening suit and snowy white shirt were tailored to the muscled width of his shoulders and tapered waist.

He looked every inch the suave and sophisticated actor Jaxon Wilder. Something Stazy had already noted the other female diners in the restaurant seemed to appreciate!

'So…' Jaxon had made himself comfortable in her grandfather's recently vacated chair while Stazy had been lost in her own jumbled thoughts.

'So,' Stazy echoed, her heart beating so loudly that she felt sure Jaxon must be able to hear it even over the low hum of the conversation of the other diners. 'You've obviously finished writing the screenplay.' She glanced down at the bound copy on the tabletop.

His gaze sharpened. 'Have you read it…?'

'My grandfather only just gave it to me, so no—' She broke off as she finally read the front page of the screenplay. 'Why is my name next to yours beneath the title…?' she asked slowly.

He shrugged those broad shoulders. 'You helped gather the research. You deserve to share in the credit for the writing of the screenplay.'

This explained why her grandfather had advised her to read the front cover when he gave it to her. 'I'm sure my less than helpful attitude was more of a hindrance than a help—'

'On the contrary—it kept me focused on what's important.' Jaxon sat forward, his expression intense. 'Look, do you really want dessert and coffee? Or can we get out of here and go somewhere we can talk privately…?' He absently waved away the waiter, who had been coming over to take their order.

Stazy raised startled lids to look across at Jaxon uncertainly, not in the least encouraged by the harshness of his expression. 'And why would we want to do that...?'

Jaxon cursed under his breath as he saw the look of uncertainty on Stazy's face. 'I've missed you this past three months, Stazy,' he told her gruffly. 'More than you can possibly know.'

She grimaced. 'Couldn't you find anyone else to argue with?'

He smiled ruefully. 'There's that too!'

She shook her head. 'I'm sure you've been far too busy to even give me a first thought, let alone a second one!'

'Try telling my female co-star that—we've had to do so many retakes because of my inattentiveness that I finally decided to give everyone the week off!' he muttered self-disgustedly.

Stazy blinked. 'The pirate movie isn't going well...?'

'Totally my own fault.' Jaxon sighed heavily. 'I haven't been feeling in a particularly swash or buckling mood.' He picked up one of her hands as it rested on the tabletop and lightly linked his fingers with hers. 'I *have* missed you, Stazy.'

She gave a puzzled shake of her head. 'How can you miss someone you didn't even want to be friends with the last time we were together?'

'Because friendship isn't what I want from you, damn it!' Jaxon scowled darkly. 'The fact that I asked you to go away with me for a few days should have told you that much!'

'You seemed to feel we had unfinished business—'

'I wanted to spend some time alone with you—'

'People are staring, Jaxon,' she warned softly, having glanced up and seen several of the other diners taking an interest in their obviously heated exchange.

'If we don't get out of here soon I'm going to give them something much more interesting than this to stare at!' he came back fiercely.

Stazy looked at him searchingly—at the angry glitter in his eyes, the tautness of his cheek, his tightly clenched jaw and mouth. 'Such as…?' she prompted breathlessly.

'This, for a start!' He stood up abruptly, his hand tightening about hers as he pulled her to her feet seconds before he took her into his arms and his head swooped low as his mouth captured hers.

Stazy had always been reserved, never one for drawing attention to herself, but the absolute bliss of having Jaxon kiss her again—even in the middle of a crowded restaurant, with all the other diners looking on!—was far too wonderful for her to care where they were or who was watching.

She rose up on tiptoe to move her hands to his chest and up over his shoulders, her fingers becoming entangled in that gloriously overlong dark hair as she eagerly returned the heat of his kiss.

'God, I needed that…!' Jaxon breathed huskily long seconds later, as his mouth finally lifted from hers. He rested his forehead against hers. 'You have no idea—' He stopped speaking as the restaurant was suddenly filled with the sound of spontaneous applause from the other diners.

'Oh, dear Lord…!' Stazy groaned as she buried the heat of her face against his chest.

'Show's over, folks!' Jaxon chuckled huskily as he

picked up the screenplay before putting his arm firmly about Stazy's waist to hold her anchored tightly against his side. The two of them crossed the restaurant.

'Sir Geoffrey has already taken care of the bill, Mr Wilder,' the *maître d'* assured him as they neared the front desk. He handed Stazy her black jacket. 'And may I wish the two of you every happiness together?' The man beamed across at them.

'Thank you,' Jaxon accepted lightly, and he continued to cut a swathe through the arriving diners until just the two of them were standing outside in the cool of the autumn evening.

Stazy had never felt so embarrassed in her life before—at the same time she had never felt so euphorically happy. Jaxon had kissed her. In front of dozens of other people. Not only that, but he hadn't denied the *maître d'*'s good wishes. Of course he had probably only done that as a means of lessening the embarrassment to them all, but even so...

Jaxon had kissed her! And she had kissed him right back.

'Do you think you could stop thinking at least until after we've reached that "somewhere more private"?' he prompted persuasively.

Stazy looked up at him uncertainly. 'Where do you want to go?'

He shook his head. 'Your apartment. My apartment. I don't give a damn where we go as long as it's somewhere we don't have an audience!'

Stazy gave a pained frown and looked up at Jaxon in the subdued light given off by the streetlamp overhead. 'I'm not sure I understand...' She was still too afraid to hope, to allow her imagination even to guess as to the reason why he had done something so outrageously wonderful…

'It's simple enough, Stazy. Your place or mine?' Jaxon pressured as the taxi he had hailed drew to a halt next to the pavement.

'I—yours,' she decided quickly; at least she would be able to walk out of Jaxon's apartment whenever this— whatever 'this' was!—was over. With the added bonus that when Jaxon had gone she wouldn't have to be sur- rounded by memories of his having been in her own apartment.

Jaxon opened the taxi door and saw Stazy safely seated inside, giving the driver his address as he climbed in to sit beside her. 'Come here—you're cold.' He drew her into the circle of his arms after he saw her give an involuntary shiver in the lightweight jacket she wore over the cream dress. 'Do you have to be anywhere in the morning?'

Her face was buried in the warmth of his chest. 'It's Saturday…'

'That doesn't answer my question,' he rebuked lightly.

Probably because Stazy didn't understand the ques- tion! Why did it matter to Jaxon whether or not she—? 'Oh!' she gasped breathlessly. She could think of only one reason why he might possibly want to know such a thing.

'Yes—*oh*,' he teased huskily. 'And before your imag- ination runs riot I have every intention of keeping you locked inside my apartment until you've listened to everything—and I do mean everything—that I should have said to you three months ago. That could take a few minutes or could take all night, depending on how receptive you are to what I have to say,' he acknowledged self-derisively.

Stazy moistened her lips with the tip of her tongue. 'Will there be any swashing or buckling involved in this…this locking me away in your apartment?' she prompted shyly.

Jaxon arms tightened about her as he gave an appreciative chuckle. 'I think there might be a lot of both those things, if it's agreeable to you, yes.'

Stazy thought she might be very agreeable…

CHAPTER THIRTEEN

'So.' STAZY STOOD uncomfortably in the middle of the spacious sitting room of what had turned out to be the penthouse apartment of a twenty-storey building set right in the middle of the most exclusive part of London. The views of the brightly lit city were absolutely amazing from the numerous windows in this room alone, and there appeared to be at least a dozen furnished rooms equally as beautiful in the apartment Jaxon had told her he only used on the rare occasions when he was in London.

'Let's not start that again, hmm?' Jaxon prompted huskily.

'No.' She smiled awkwardly. 'This is a very nice apartment. Does it have—?'

'Hush, Stazy.' Jaxon trod lightly across the cream carpet until he stood only inches in front of her. 'Tomorrow, if you really are interested, I'll give you the blurb that I received on this place before I bought it. But for now I believe we have other, more important things to talk about…'

'Do we?' She looked up at him searchingly. 'I have no real idea of what I'm even doing here!' She wrung agitated hands together. 'You had lunch with my grandfather today. Came to the restaurant this evening supposedly to join us for coffee and dessert—and then didn't even attempt to order either one of them. You then kissed me in front of dozens of other people after my grandfather left—'

Jaxon put an end to her obvious and rapidly increasing agitation by taking her in his arms and kissing her again.

More intensely. More thoroughly. More demandingly...

'You know,' he murmured several minutes later, as he ended the kiss and once again rested his forehead on hers, 'if I have to keep doing this in order to get a word in edgeways this is definitely going to take all night!'

Stazy gave a choked laugh. 'I don't mind if you don't...'

'Oh, I'm only too happy to go on kissing you all night long, my darling Stazy,' he assured her gruffly. 'Just not yet. First we need to talk. *I* need to talk,' he added ruefully. 'To make it completely, absolutely clear how I feel.'

She caught her bottom lip between pearly white teeth. 'How you feel about what...?'

'You, of course!' Jaxon lifted his head to look down at her exasperatedly. 'Stazy, you have to be the most difficult woman in the world for a man to tell how much he loves her!' he added irritably.

Stazy stilled, her eyes very wide as she stared up at him. 'Are you saying you love me...?'

'I've loved you for months, you impossible woman!'

'You've—loved—me—for—months...?' she repeated in slow disbelief.

'See? Totally impossible!' Jaxon snorted his impatience as he released her to step away and run a hand through the darkness of his hair. 'There are millions upon millions of women in the world, and I have to fall in love with the one woman who doesn't even believe I love her when I've just told her that I do!'

It was entirely inappropriate—had to be because she was verging on hysteria—but at that moment in time all Stazy could manage in response was a choked laugh.

Jaxon raised his eyes heavenwards. 'And now she's laughing at me…!'

Stazy continued laughing. In fact she laughed for so long that her sides actually ached and there were tears falling down her cheeks.

'Care to share the joke?' Jaxon finally prompted ruefully.

She leant weakly against the wall, her hands wrapped about her aching sides. 'No joke, Jaxon. At least not on you.'

'Who, then?'

'Me!' She smiled across at him tearfully. 'The joke's on *me*, Jaxon! I'm so inexperienced at these things that I— Jaxon, I fell in love with you when we were at Bromley House together. I didn't want to,' she added soberly. 'It just…happened.'

Jaxon began walking towards her like a man in a dream. 'You're in love with me…?'

'Oh, Jaxon…!' she groaned indulgently. 'There are millions and millions of men in the world, and I have to fall in love with the one man who doesn't even believe I love him when I've just told him that I do,' she misquoted back at him huskily.

His arms felt like steel bands about her waist as he pulled her effortlessly towards him, his gaze piercing as he looked down at her fiercely. 'Do you love me enough to marry me…?'

She gasped. 'You can't want to marry a doctor of archaeology?'

He nodded. 'I most certainly can! That is if you don't mind marrying an actor and film director?'

'Excuse me,' she chided huskily, 'but that would be a multi-award-winning Hollywood A-list actor and director!'

'Whatever,' Jaxon dismissed gruffly. 'Will you marry me, Stazy, and save me from the misery of merely existing without you?'

She swallowed. 'Being alone in a crowd...?'

'The hell of being alone in a crowd, yes,' he confirmed huskily.

Stazy knew exactly what that felt like. It was how she had felt for the past three months since she'd last seen Jaxon...

Tears welled up in her eyes. 'I've been so lonely without you, Jaxon. Since my parents died I've never wanted to need or love anyone, apart from my grandparents, and yet you've managed to capture my heart...' She gave a shake of her head. 'I love you so much, Jaxon, that these past three months of not seeing you, being with you, has been hell.'

'Hence the weight loss and lack of sleep?' He ran a caressing fingertip across the dark shadows under her eyes.

'Yes.' She nodded miserably.

'When you said a few minutes ago you were inexperienced in things, you meant falling in love, didn't you...?'

She gave a self-derisive laugh. 'I've never been in love. I've had two lovers, spent one night with each of them, and they were both utter disasters!' She grimaced.

'Forget about them.' Jaxon reached up and cradled each side of her face, his love for her shining out of his liquid grey eyes. 'We're going to make love, Stazy. Real love. And it's going to be truly beautiful.'

'Yes, please…' she breathed softly.

'You haven't agreed to make an honest man of me yet,' he reminded her huskily.

'Is that a condition of the beautiful lovemaking?' she teased.

'I do have my reputation to think of, after all…'

Stazy laughed huskily at the dig as she threw herself into his waiting arms. 'In that case—yes, I'll marry you, Jaxon!'

'And have my babies?'

Babies. Not only Jaxon to love, but his babies to love and cherish… 'Oh, God, yes…!' she accepted emotionally.

'Then you may now take me to bed, Dr Bromley.'

She chuckled at his prim tone. 'If you think I'm going to sweep you up in my arms and carry you off to the bedroom before ravishing you then I'm afraid you're going to be disappointed!'

'I'll do the sweeping.' Jaxon did exactly that. 'You can do the ravishing.'

'With pleasure, Mr Wilder,' Stazy murmured throatily. 'With the greatest of pleasure.'

And it was.

Just over two years later…

'I'm truly impressed,' Jaxon murmured teasingly in her ear as the two of them stepped down off the stage to the rapturous applause of his peers, after going up together to receive yet another award for Best Screenplay for

Butterfly Wings. 'I think you thanked everyone but the girl who made the coffee!'

'Very funny,' Stazy muttered as she continued to smile brightly for the watching audience as the two of them made their way back to their seats.

Jaxon chuckled. 'And after you were once so scathing about the length of the speeches made at these awards, too!'

'Just for that, you can be the one to get up to Anastasia Rose if she wakes in the night!' Stazy dropped thankfully back into her seat, her smile completely genuine now as she thought of their beautiful six-month-old daughter waiting for them at home. Geoffrey had opted to stay with his beloved great-granddaughter rather than accompany them to another award ceremony that he had declared would be 'far too exhausting at my age!'

'I'll have you know that Anastasia Rose and I have come to an arrangement—I don't wake her up if she doesn't wake me up!' Jaxon grinned smugly.

'Really?' Stazy turned in her seat to look at him. 'Does that mean we can have our own very private celebration later…?'

Jaxon chuckled. 'Insatiable woman!'

She arched teasing brows. 'Are you complaining…?'

'Certainly not!' He kissed her warmly—something he had done often during their two-year marriage, whenever and wherever they happened to be.

They both knew and happily appreciated that life, and love, didn't come any better than this…

* * * * *

Available December 17, 2013

#3201 THE DIMITRAKOS PROPOSITION
Lynne Graham

Tabby Glover desperately needs Greek billionaire
Acheron Dimitrakos to support her adoption claim over his
cousin's child. His price? Marriage. But as the thin veil between
truth and lies is lifted, will this relationship become more than in
name only?

#3202 A MAN WITHOUT MERCY
Miranda Lee

Dumped by her fiancé *via text,* Vivienne Swan wants to nurse her
shattered heart privately...until an intriguing offer from Jack Stone
tempts her from her shell. He is a man used to taking what he
wants, and Vivienne is now at his mercy!

#3203 FORGED IN THE DESERT HEAT
Maisey Yates

Newly crowned Sheikh Zafar Nejem's first act is to rescue heiress
Analise Christensen from her desert kidnappers and return her
to her fiancé...or risk war. But the forbidden attraction burning
between them rivals the heat of the sun, threatening everything....

#3204 THE FLAW IN HIS DIAMOND
Susan Stephens

When no-nonsense Eva Skavanga arrives on Count Roman
Quisvada's Mediterranean Island with a business arrangement,
Roman's more interested in the pleasure she might bring him.
Perhaps Roman could help her with more than just securing her
family's diamond mine...?

#3205 THE TYCOON'S DELICIOUS DISTRACTION
Maggie Cox

Forced to rely on physio Kit after a skiing accident confines him to a wheelchair, Hal Treverne has no escape from her intoxicating presence. But unleashing the simmering desire beneath her ever-so-professional facade is a challenge this tycoon will relish!

#3206 HIS TEMPORARY MISTRESS
Cathy Williams

Damian Carver wants revenge on the woman who stole from him, and her sister Violet won't change his mind...until he needs a temporary mistress, and Violet's perfect! But sweet-natured Violet soon turns the tables on his sensuous brand of blackmail....

#3207 THE MOST EXPENSIVE LIE OF ALL
Michelle Conder

Champion horse breeder Aspen has never forgotten Cruz Rodriguez, so when he reappears with a multimillion-dollar investment offer, Aspen's torn. She may crave his touch, but his glittering black eyes hide a deception that could prove more costly than ever before!

#3208 A DEAL WITH BENEFITS
One Night with Consequences
Susanna Carr

Sebastian Cruz has no intention of giving Ashley Jones's family's island back, but he does want her. He'll agree to her deal, but with a few clauses of his own—a month at his beck and call... and in his bed!

YOU CAN FIND MORE INFORMATION ON UPCOMING HARLEQUIN® TITLES, FREE EXCERPTS AND MORE AT WWW.HARLEQUIN.COM.

HPCNM1213RB

REQUEST YOUR
FREE BOOKS!

HARLEQUIN *Presents*

PASSION GUARANTEED SEDUCTION

2 FREE NOVELS PLUS
2 FREE GIFTS!

YES! Please send me 2 FREE Harlequin Presents® novels and my 2 FREE gifts (gifts are worth about $10). After receiving them, if I don't wish to receive any more books, I can return the shipping statement marked "cancel." If I don't cancel, I will receive 6 brand-new novels every month and be billed just $4.30 per book in the U.S. or $4.99 per book in Canada. That's a saving of at least 14% off the cover price! It's quite a bargain! Shipping and handling is just 50¢ per book in the U.S. and 75¢ per book in Canada.* I understand that accepting the 2 free books and gifts places me under no obligation to buy anything. I can always return a shipment and cancel at any time. Even if I never buy another book, the two free books and gifts are mine to keep forever.

106/306 HDN FVRK

Name	(PLEASE PRINT)	
Address		Apt. #
City	State/Prov.	Zip/Postal Code

Signature (if under 18, a parent or guardian must sign)

Mail to the **Harlequin® Reader Service:**
IN U.S.A.: P.O. Box 1867, Buffalo, NY 14240-1867
IN CANADA: P.O. Box 609, Fort Erie, Ontario L2A 5X3

**Are you a current subscriber to Harlequin Presents books
and want to receive the larger-print edition?
Call 1-800-873-8635 or visit www.ReaderService.com.**

* Terms and prices subject to change without notice. Prices do not include applicable taxes. Sales tax applicable in N.Y. Canadian residents will be charged applicable taxes. Offer not valid in Quebec. This offer is limited to one order per household. Not valid for current subscribers to Harlequin Presents books. All orders subject to credit approval. Credit or debit balances in a customer's account(s) may be offset by any other outstanding balance owed by or to the customer. Please allow 4 to 6 weeks for delivery. Offer available while quantities last.

Your Privacy—The Harlequin® Reader Service is committed to protecting your privacy. Our Privacy Policy is available online at www.ReaderService.com or upon request from the Harlequin Reader Service.

We make a portion of our mailing list available to reputable third parties that offer products we believe may interest you. If you prefer that we not exchange your name with third parties, or if you wish to clarify or modify your communication preferences, please visit us at www.ReaderService.com/consumerchoice or write to us at Harlequin Reader Service Preference Service, P.O. Box 9062, Buffalo, NY 14269. Include your complete name and address.

HP13

SPECIAL EXCERPT FROM

H HARLEQUIN®
™

Presents

Maisey Yates brings you her latest story,
FORGED IN THE DESERT HEAT! As the sun rises over
the sand dunes, a forbidden passion blazes,
threatening everything…

* * *

"ONE , two, three," she continued, but he could hardly hear. His eyes were focused on her lips, on the movement they made when she said the words. Numbers, something that shouldn't make a man feel anything, much less a fire in his blood that might reduce him to ash on the spot.

Blazing, hotter than the desert sun. He'd thought he'd withstood the most destructive heat in existence. In the wilderness. In his nightmares.

But this was a different kind of heat altogether. One that burned but didn't consume. Just when he thought the peak had been reached, it only went up higher.

Hotter.

What magic did this woman possess?

"Tell me something bland," he whispered, trying to ignore the burn beneath his skin. Trying to ignore the rush of blood to his groin. The ache that was building there.

"I'm counting, isn't that bland?"

He looked at her pale pink lips.

"It is your mouth," he said. "I find it distracting."

"That isn't my intent."

"Intent doesn't matter. It's the result. When I look at your lips, all I can think of is how it felt for them to touch mine."

"I'm engaged," she said, her tone firm. "Engaged and in love and…"

He pressed his lips against hers and the dancing stopped. She froze beneath his mouth, her body rigid for a second, and then it softened. Her fingers went to the lapels of his suit jacket, curling in tightly as she rose up on her tiptoes, deepening the kiss.

Her tongue slid against his and he was pulled into the darkness. There was nothing else, nothing but the slick friction, nothing but her soft, perfect lips.

He wrapped his arms more tightly around her and pulled her flush against his body, as he'd fantasized about doing for… Had there ever been a time when he hadn't? Had there truly been a moment when he hadn't wanted her?

When he'd seen her as nothing more than a pale, fragile creature diminishing beneath the Al Sabahan sun? How had he ever seen her that way? In this woman lay the power to bring kingdoms crashing down. To bring a sheikh to his knees.

* * *

On sale January 2014!